Praise for THE WALK-IN C

"Absorbing entertainment. I walked into Nazemian's walk-in closet and didn't want to walk out." —**Kelly Oxford**, author of *Everything is Perfect When You're a Liar*

"An absolutely engrossing read from page one—Abdi Nazemian has painted a world so vivid and real that even if you know nothing of 'Tehrangeles', by the end you feel as if you are a part it. I simply COULD NOT put this book down!" —**Busy Philipps**

"At once wickedly funny and devastatingly moving, *The Walk-In Closet* is a thrilling ride from start to finish. Nazemian surprises with every turn he takes, telling a story that vividly illustrates the price of living in a closet." —**Chaz Bono**, author of *Family Outing, The End of Innocence* and *Transition*

"I relished every moment of this warm, funny, brutally engaging novel. Abdi Nazemian's Los Angeles is both uncannily familiar and entirely foreign. Put this in the canon of LA literature: Nazemian has written a side of Los Angeles prevalent in real life but rarely seen in fiction." —**Katherine Taylor**, author of *Rules for Saying Goodbye*

"Ladies: If you like Shahs of Sunset you'll love *The Walk-In Closet*. Abdi Nazemian shines a white hot, entertaining spotlight on the ins and outs of Tehrangeles. Abdi will get your inner Persian princess purring. Curl up and enjoy this fabulous debut!" —**Jessica Bendinger**, author of *The Seven Rays,* screenwriter of *Bring it On* and *Sex and the City*

"*The Walk-In Closet* is a contemporary fable of love, loss and redemption, set between cultures and between the sexes. Written at a spanking pace, with humor, suspense and a heart, it captures the voice of a generation and paves the way to a new genre of literary fiction."
  —**Lila Azam Zanganeh**, author of *The Enchanter: Nabokov and Happiness*

"Do you know about Tehrangeles? I didn't. But thanks to Abdi Nazemian's *The Walk-In Closet*. I now feel right at home among its brave, foolish, proud, unsinkable expatriates. If one of the tasks of fiction is to bring to light a world that for whatever reasons we haven't bothered to see for ourselves—and to make us see that it is our world, too—then Nazemian's book is a success. That he then adds his unique way of seeing–in which he marries his sharp satirist's eye to a profound empathy—makes this hilarious, heartbreaking first novel a triumph." —**Richard Kramer,** author of *These Things Happen,* screenwriter of *Tales of the City, thirtysomething,* and *My So-Called Life*

The
WALK-IN
CLOSET

a novel by Abdi Nazemian

This book is for my parents

The breezes at dawn have secrets to tell you.
Don't go back to sleep.
You must ask for what you really want.
Don't go back to sleep.
People are going back and forth
Across the doorsill where the two worlds touch.
The door is round and open.
Don't go back to sleep.
— Rumi

1

"I HAVE THE PERFECT shoes for you," Leila said with a smile. "They are just a little tight on me, so they should fit you perfectly." We were in her enormous walk-in closet, really more like a wing of the Ebadi house. It had once been an exercise room, but Leila got rid of the Soloflex and converted the gym into an immaculately organized, white-lacquered dressing room. The clothes were arranged by color. Sharp white suits on one end, slinky black dresses on the other, with yellow tanks, red skirts, and navy blazers between.

Leila popped open a white-lacquered panel, revealing rows and rows of shoes. Pumps. Stilettos. Boots. Hermès sneakers in every color. "You know you're like a daughter to me," she said. Music to my ears. Now, I loved my mother Harry. She had her endearing qualities, like the fact that she never cheated at online Scrabble, and that she made me matzo ball soup when I was sick even though we're not Jewish. But who wouldn't have traded in Harry for a mother who conducted spring cleaning by giving last season's couture to you? I'm not sure Harry even knew what couture was. Born and bred in Thousand Oaks, Harry lived in a world (not coincidentally, the world in which I was raised) of strip malls and outlet stores.

"Has Babak played you the new Omara Portuondo CD?" Leila asked.

"I don't think so," I responded.

"It's incredible, the music that comes out of Cuba. Repression always makes for such moving art." Leila pondered her statement and then added, "Of course, when we were in Havana a few years ago, the people didn't seem repressed at all. They actually appeared quite joyful. Ah, here they are." Leila handed me a pair of green Prada flats adorned with lavender gemstones. "Aren't they pretty? Try them on."

"Leila, I can't."

"Just one week until *Nowruz*," she said. "You know it's customary to conduct an extensive spring cleaning before the New Year and replenish the closet."

"I just feel like you're spoiling me."

"What am I going to do? Give these clothes to somebody who will not appreciate them? Give me your foot," she ordered. She was a difficult woman to disobey. I kicked off my ratty old Steve Maddens and lifted my right foot, worried that she would make note of my chipped pedicure. Gently, she slipped the right flat on my foot. It fit flawlessly. As stylish as a stiletto, as comfortable as a slipper.

"Who needs Prince Charming," I joked, "when I have you?"

Never one to dwell on a sentimental moment, Leila immediately noticed an imperfection. "One of the amethysts fell off. I forgot."

"I don't care. They're beautiful."

"Here." Leila dug through a drawer full of old buttons and thread until she pulled out an amethyst and placed it carefully into my hand. "Rosa Maria can re-attach it. She was a seamstress before she came to us. She's very talented."

"You're too good to me."

"Do you wear Chanel, or is it too old for you?" she asked.

"I'm turning thirty in less than a month. I think I can rock the Chanel now."

Leila flinched at my use of the word *rock*. To her, a rock was something you either kicked on the beach or put on your finger. She pulled a pink Chanel suit off the rack. Very Jackie O. "I never wear it anymore."

"I can't, Leila, you've given me enough."

"Stop with the *tarof*," she said.

Tarof was one of those untranslatable Farsi expressions I had picked up from the Ebadis and their friends. Basically: don't bother arguing when offered something, just accept graciously.

"Well, okay then. No more *tarof*. I'll take the whole closet."

"That's more like it, Kara *djoon*." I love when she speaks that beautiful endearment after my name.

I slipped the suit on in front of her, and it fit perfectly. It did make me look older, but in a sophisticated way. I assessed my reflection. My blond hair had recently been layered and highlighted at Leila's favorite salon. My skin was still glowing from the oxygen facial that Leila had treated me to the week before. And my body was looking firm from the Pilates sessions of Leila's that I'd crashed. For a single woman on the precipice of earliest middle age, I was looking pretty good. Of course, I wasn't single in Leila's eyes. I was abruptly reminded of that when "Gimme More," Britney's latest hit, rang from the cell phone in my purse.

Leila looked inside and pulled it out. "It's Babak," she said as she handed me the phone. On its screen was a photo of Bobby, reclining on the blue Astroturf of the Standard Hotel, palm trees reflected in his Aviator shades, his wavy jet-black hair almost blue in the glare of the sun.

"Getting impatient?" I answered.

"What are you two doing up there?" Bobby whispered urgently.

"Trying on clothes."

"Well, hurry up. You know I can't spend this much one-on-one time alone with my dad. He's making me watch golf."

"Where are you calling from?"

"The guest bathroom. Just hurry." Bobby hung up.

"What does he vant?" Sometimes Leila slips and her Ws come out as Vs.

"Nothing."

"I don't see why he can't do without you and just watch golf for thirty minutes while we try on a few things. His father was never so possessive, thank goodness." She ran her hands along one of the immaculate white-lacquered shelves. "When we built this house, it was the beginning of the eighties— Babak was five when we were renovating it, so it was 1982. I always knew I wanted a large closet, and I wanted the shelves to be white lacquer, because it allows the colors of the clothes to dominate the room. There was one day—it was when the house was still under construction—the closet was one of the first rooms to be almost done. Maybe that's because I knew exactly what I wanted it to be. I sold the old gym equipment that was in it and redesigned it immediately. So one day, we were walking the children in to choose their bedrooms, and Babak walked into this closet, and he shouted, 'This is mine.'"

Leila didn't smile at the memory; she merely shared it matter-of-factly. Despite Leila's fabulous existence, I had never seen her express unmoderated joy. Maybe a belly laugh was unladylike, or maybe she was simply trying to avoid the wrinkles. She was a woman who always seemed content, but never happy. "Once we moved in, he would often come in here to read or do his homework. He said he liked the light. I don't know. He just loved the place," she said, without a hint of irony.

"Maybe it's because there are no windows," I offered.

"I don't understand."

"Sometimes I feel secure when I'm in a room with no windows, no escape, no choices."

Leila shrugged. We had veered into overly psychoanalytic territory for her, and she speedily brought us home to Chanel. "I bought that ensemble and wore it once, to a cocktail party in honor of Bernard-Henri Lévy in Paris. I don't know why Babak stopped practicing his languages." And there she went again. Whenever we were alone, she couldn't resist bringing up what she perceived as Bobby's many faults. She wanted me to intervene, setting him back on the right course. "You know we taught him Farsi, French, and Italian from birth. We made sure he learned Spanish when we moved to Los Angeles. We sent him to tennis lessons. We even gave him piano lessons when he asked. And golf lessons when he turned thirteen."

"I'm sure he loved that."

"It's a shame. He throws everything away. Now he only speaks to us in English. It's his most perverse form of torture."

"I've heard him speak French," I said, always ready to defend Bobby's honor in his own home.

"Really?"

"Sure, with..." But I had to bite my tongue before I uttered the name Jacques. References to my ex had always been off limits in this household, for obvious reasons of consistency.

"Does he have French friends?" Leila persisted. "That would be nice."

Come to think of it, Bobby didn't have many friends at all other than me. I watched them slowly disappear once Bobby started meeting guys online. It was a leisurely process. In the beginning, it was harmless enough. If he was at a dinner with friends, he would leave early because he was anxious to get online and see who was out there. He would claim he was finally writing something new, his friends would congratulate him on his burst of inspiration, and Bobby would rush home and log on. Writing gave Bobby the ability to hide behind his computer anytime he wanted to, with the ever-elusive muse as his alibi. Eventually, the excuses became a gulf between him and his friends. He didn't have the patience to sit across from them at dinner, knowing there was an abundance of sex just a right-click away. And he didn't want to explain his new proclivities to anyone. Except to me. No matter how deep he disappeared into his dark world of anonymous sex, he still fed me the details. Perhaps Bobby realized that if he told no one at all, he would disappear completely, and the threat of invisibility scared him. It was sad watching him enter a solitary existence, but then it also made me feel all the more needed. And anytime I wondered whether I should make an effort to tame Bobby's sexual liberality, I reminded myself that he was sowing oats he should have had a chance to sow when he was a teenager, and that there is nothing more unhelpful than a friend judging another friend's sex life. Bobby was living his gay adolescence, and I was celibate. This was the routine we had grown accustomed to.

Leila took my hand, and we walked down the marble staircase holding three shopping bags. We entered the family room, where Hossein was watching golf as Bobby browsed the latest issue of *W*.

"Ooh, what did you get? Show me," Bobby demanded as he perused my hand-me-downs. "Chanel, Galliano, Prada," he listed. "If it's not a high-end brand, no Persian's gonna buy it. Persians are *all* about labels. My mother won't even take a generic drug."

"They don't work," Leila protested, enjoying the gentle ribbing her son was giving her.

Hossein fixed us in his peripheral vision and noted in deadpan that "Leila is the only woman who uses *Nowruz* as an excuse to buy a new wardrobe."

"Hardly. It's a tradition," Leila countered. Adept as she was at denying certain aspects of her culture, she was equally masterful at claiming the culture when it suited her.

Hossein aimed the TV remote and paused his golf game mid-swing. "Our tradition is to wear something new for *Nowruz*. New underwear, a new T-shirt. Not to empty your closet and buy up the spring season of every designer."

"Why think small?" Leila said with a wry smile for us, then kissed Hossein on the forehead, the tenderness and understanding of their relationship revealed in that one small gesture. Bobby, perhaps sensing that this is how couples are supposed to behave, smiled at me awkwardly. In moments like these, Bobby's primary concern was maintaining the façade, whereas mine was wondering when I would find someone to kiss my forehead with unforced intimacy.

"So," Leila said, "You'll both be here Wednesday for *Chaharshambe Suri* and then Friday for the New Year. Are you inviting anyone?"

"No, dude," Bobby said.

Leila smiled. Bobby had taken to calling her "dude" ever since the day Leila asked what the word meant. That was six years ago, but the word still made Leila smile, because now it amounted to an inside joke that she and her son shared. "What about the girls?" Leila asked, appropriating the collective Bobby had given my two best friends. "They're more than welcome to come to the New Year's Party. We'll have too much food, and it's always nice having a few guests who just appreciate it rather than compare it to what their grandmothers made. Besides, we need pretty young people to dance. Watching old people dance is depressing, even when they have all had liposuction."

The Ebadi house was transformed for the New Year's festivities. The Persian New Year, *Nowruz*, is celebrated at the exact moment of the Spring Equinox, synchronized precisely to the change of season, when the sun crosses directly over the equator someplace in the world. Through my years as an honorary Ebadi, I had celebrated the New Year at a variety of times: once at 8:11 in the morning during Leila's usual Pilates session; once at 4:55 in the afternoon as the sun shone brightly onto the Ebadi's yard, causing the ladies to sweat through their silk and linen; and my personal favorite, 4:21 A.M., when all of Los Angeles was dead but for the crystal meth addicts and the 24-hour security patrol protecting the homes of the rich and famous. I remember thinking that Los Angeles was a city where businesses got away with being called 24 Hour Fitness and closing at 10 P.M., but when *Nowruz* was in the middle of the night, the usual rules didn't apply, and stretches of Brentwood, Beverly Hills, and Westwood were bumping with music and celebration. In the Ebadi home on that dark night, festivities were in full swing. A DJ was playing Persian pop hits, ladies were dancing with their grandchildren, and Leila was delivering her usual toast consisting of a reading from Omar Khayyám.

This particular year, the Persian New Year fell at the civilized hour of 9:32 P.M. on March 20th, which made Leila and Hossein very happy. They didn't have to cancel Pilates or golf, respectively, and they were able to serve dinner at the proper hour. Leila rightly felt that there was something disgusting about scarfing down *sabzi polo mahi*, herbed rice and fish, for breakfast or in the middle of the night. Every year, the Ebadis took the opulence of their festivities one step further than the previous. As always, the valet boys stood outside to park the guests' Bentleys and BMWs. The entry was occupied by the *Haft Sin*, a table on which seven items starting with the letter S were displayed. Everything in the tiny subculture of Tehrangeles was a competition: children, clothes, income, travel. The denizens of this tiny universe vacationed in the same spots and dined at the same Italian restaurants, always looking for an opportunity to one-up each other as they exchanged kisses. In the weeks preceding *Nowruz*, Leila visited her friends and assessed their *Haft Sin* tables, so she could make sure her display would be more beautiful, more opulent, more impressive, just *more*.

This year, her *Haft Sin* was an especially glorious work of art. On an antique embroidery, she placed lentil sprouts, wheat-germ pudding, dried oleaster fruit, garlic, an apple, sumac berries, and vinegar. They represented rebirth, affluence, love, medicine, health, and patience, all the qualities and virtues one is meant to take into the New Year. But Leila being Leila, she couldn't settle for just seven Ss, and so she liberally added a few more items to the table. Some dried nuts (only those whose Persian names begin with S), candles, a mirror, some decorated eggs (which her friends' children and/or grandchildren decorated), goldfish. On most *Haft Sin* tables, worshippers placed a holy book, a Qur'an, a Bible, or a Torah. Leila's table always had vintage poetry instead. This year it was Hafez. Leila regarded the ancient Persian poets as gods and goddesses, emblems of a time when secularism, Sufism, and Zoroastrianism coexisted in her country. For Leila, the poets represented the true roots of *Nowruz*, before the Muslims invaded her beloved Persia, when wine flowed freely and a woman's body was celebrated. The *pièce de résistance* was an imposing gold coin, the profile of the Shah engraved into it. This *sekkeh*, representing wealth, was a gentle reminder to the guests that the Ebadis, too, had it all.

Beyond the *Haft Sin* table, the party began. Leila had transformed her garden into a paradise of revelry. She had laid down a dance floor interspersed with squares that lit up when stepped on, making everyone feel like Michael Jackson circa "Billie Jean." And she even eschewed the customary DJ for a live band that miraculously played songs in French, Spanish, and Farsi. Much as Leila trained Rosa Maria (and Elena before that) to cook a perfect *khoresht*, I could imagine Leila supervising the band, making sure they could perform perfect renditions of "Soltane Ghalb," "Paroles Paroles," and Gipsy Kings. As Bobby and I entered the party, "Bamboleo" was the band's choice, and while the lead singer's Spanish accent didn't sound as authentic as those of the parking guys outside, the beat still got the party going.

"Babak! Leila! Finally!" Leila called out as she approached us, martini glass in hand. She gave us both a kiss on each cheek. Her giddiness suggested she had already imbibed one, maybe two, drinks. When I first got to know the Ebadis, I always expected that their demons would come out with a little alcohol. But I was wrong. Leila was the textbook happy drunk. Not even tequila unleashed the nightmares of her past. She led us to the bar as I wiped her lipstick off Bobby's cheek with the palm of my hand. "You have to try the drink of the night," she said. "It's an apple-cilantro martini in honor of *Nowruz*. I invented it. I explained to him that I wanted the drinks to be made with things that began with S. *Seeb, sabzi*." Leila flashed two fingers to the bartender, who immediately poured two concoctions for Bobby and me. I took a sip, and to my surprise, apple and cilantro didn't mix so badly with vodka. I could see Bobby's eyes linger a beat too long on the bartender, whose thick, hairy forearms demanded attention. A Star of David dangled over the tufts of black hair left visible by the open buttons of his crisp blue shirt. He was no doubt one of the many Persian Jews who lived in Tehrangeles. Bobby, a descendant of Muslims but raised in complete agnosticism, always had a thing for Jews, especially Israelis. Personally, I thought his Israeli fetish was some kind of complicated dissenting-yet-self-hating Persian thing. I mean, Iran's president Mahmoud Ahmadinejad (who Bobby referred to as *Ahmagh-inejad*, even though he kept having to explain to people who corrected him that *ahmagh* means *idiot* in Farsi) hosted a convention of Holocaust deniers in Bobby's lost homeland. I loved the idea that getting down on his knees and servicing Zionists was Bobby's little rebellion against the idiot and all the Ayatollahs. Or perhaps Bobby was unaware of the irony, and his lust just had a keen and wicked sense of humor.

One by one, the hellos began. Bobby and I had to make our way around the room to kiss and make small talk with every one of Leila and Hossein's friends. We held hands as we circled the room, really not for the show as much to steel ourselves against the inevitably painful small talk.

Koorosh Ebrahimi, a real estate developer with bad implants, gripped Bobby's wrist forcefully. "So, Babak, I hear you're thinking of getting into real estate," he said to Bobby's confusion.

"I am?" Bobby asked.

"That's what a little birdie told me," Koorosh insisted, the expression awkward when filtered through his thick accent.

"I'm a writer," Bobby said.

"Of course you are. But writing is a hobby. There's no money in writing, is there? Unless you're Stephen King or Steven Spielberg. Unless your name is Steven." Koorosh laughed at his own joke, a piece of herbed rice unfortunately stuck above his right incisor.

"Spielberg directs," Bobby offered helpfully.

"Whatever they do, there's no way to make money in Hollywood unless you're a Jew, is there? You were born into the wrong family. You should've been a Jew."

I was about to launch a counterattack, but Bobby gripped my hand and led me far away. "It's no use," he said. "Half the people in this room are racist, anti-Semitic, homophobic, sexist, dwarf-haters. Have I missed any?" The band ripped into a bizarre Persian dance version of that Celine Dion *Titanic* theme song, which proved very popular with the crowd. "When I was a kid, I got in a big fight with Koorosh Ebrahimi. We were watching *Jeopardy!* at home, and a black guy won, and he said it was bullshit, that a black person could never win a game of intelligence, and that this was an example of the quotas that were killing America. I told him he was an asshole. I must've been eight. My parents gave me a talking to. Whatever my opinion, it was wrong to be disrespectful of elders."

"Even when the elders are racist dwarf-haters?" I countered.

"That's exactly what I said. But it didn't get very far with them. They're racist themselves."

"Your parents are not racist," I said, perhaps a little too eager to defend them.

"My mother and I were watching some news show about the trendiness of adoption, and she said, 'If you and Kara ever adopt, you better adopt blond babies like Sharon Stone.'"

"That's your mother's sense of humor. Give her some credit." Then it hit me that

Bobby had just mentioned us and a baby in the same sentence. The shock must have been visible.

"What?" he asked.

"Are you… do you want children?"

"I don't know. Maybe."

"With me?" I continued.

"I don't know. I haven't thought about it. Do you?"

"Of course I do," I answered.

"Of course you do… want kids? Or of course you do… with me?"

I stared at a group of adorable Persian brats who were using the colossal backyard as the grounds for a raucous game of tag. They zipped by their parents and grandparents, infusing the party with innocence and mayhem. I couldn't imagine Bobby as a father. Anonymous threesomes and diapers didn't exist in the same world for me. But maybe he would change as he got a little older. Stranger things had happened. And Bobby and I probably wouldn't get divorced the way my parents had.

Bobby cut the awkward tension with a sudden revelation. "I know why Koorosh thinks I want to get into real estate. Last week my dad told me 'a friend' is looking to expand his real estate business, and wouldn't it make sense for me to get another job on the side? I reminded him I have no inter-est in real estate. And what does he do? He goes behind my back and says I *am* interested. I'm almost thirty years old, for God's sake. This is like them sending me to boarding school. Like they couldn't wait to get rid of me. And couldn't wait to tell their friends I was going to the same school as former ambassadors and Natalie Cole."

"See, not so racist. Plus, if they hadn't sent you away, you never would've met me," I said.

As Bobby pondered the concept of looking on the bright side, Tanaz Ma-liki approached us. Tanaz's face got tighter each time I saw her, her eyes more catlike, her cheekbones more pronounced. Tanaz was the funhouse version of Leila. Whereas Leila got discrete cosmetic surgery, a refreshing nip and tuck,

Tanaz deformed her face, never beautiful to start with. Whereas Leila wore designer clothing that suited her body and her age, Tanaz picked clothes that were too colorful and too tight. It didn't matter that her outfit cost a thousand dollars; she made it look cheap. Worst of all, Tanaz was divorced, a rare and shameful thing among the Persian diaspora. The focus of Tanaz's middle age was spending her ex-husband's oil fortune and finding inventively passive-aggressive ways of making herself feel better.

"Kara *djoon*, you've lost weight," she said as she air-kissed me, careful not to smudge her caked-on makeup.

"*Shayad*," I said to her, showing off one of the bits of Farsi I'd picked up through the years. *Maybe* was a useful word for someone with commitment issues.

"Or *shayad* it's the light," she retorted, mimicking me as she pointed lazily in the direction of the orchid-shaped candles floating in the pool.

Bobby leaned in to give Tanaz the obligatory kisses. "Hello, Mrs. Maliki. How are you?" he asked stiffly.

"Babak," she said with concern. "Tina tells me you have writer's block." Tina Maliki, Tanaz's Wall Street success of a daughter, had been engaged for four months to a Persian broker "descended from the Qajars." Whenever Tanaz felt small around the Ebadis, she trotted out this fact.

"How would Tina know that?" Bobby asked. "I haven't talked to her in over a year."

"You said it on your Facebook page," I commented. "You wrote an update that said you were indulging your writer's block with a marathon of Doris Day movies."

"Doris Day?" Tanaz echoed suspiciously. "I saw her once, at an overpriced food shop when Tina and I went golfing in Carmel. She has too many dogs. It's not natural. Are you playing golf yet?" Tanaz asked Bobby.

"No, I've managed to resist the temptation," Bobby replied.

"It's a shame. It would make your parents so happy." And with that, Tanaz moved on to terrorize someone else.

"Please," Bobby said as he finished his *seeb and sabzi* martini. "Take me away from here."

"Take you away? Are you kidding? I love *Nowruz*. It's my favorite time of year."

"You've gotta be kidding. It's one family obligation after another," Bobby said.

"You family is *never* an obligation."

Bobby laughed. "If only that were true."

The truth was that *Nowruz* was a hell of a lot more pleasant than New Year's Eve, the dreaded December 31st when women all over Los Angeles put on our best cocktail dresses and trolled around from party to party searching for a kiss from a buffoon in an Ed Hardy shirt. New Year's Eve was designed to make single people feel lonely when they didn't have someone to kiss at midnight. And I had always been single on New Year's Eve. Even those three years I was with Jacques, we were apart for New Year's. He was with his family in Paris, and I was with Bobby at some party in the Hollywood Hills. Bobby, no surprise, always found someone to kiss and more by midnight. And I was left to listen to "Auld Lang Syne" and feel forlorn. But *Nowruz* didn't bring up any of those emotions for me. When the Persian New Year arrived, there was no kissing. Instead, Leila sauntered around the party giving all the children (yes, Bobby and I were still considered children) gold coins to bring us luck. "Between not being kissed at midnight and receiving gold, I'll take the gold," I uttered to Bobby.

But that's not why I really loved *Nowruz.* Sure, the gold was nice, and the spring cleaning did wonders for my closet. But it's exactly that sense of obligation Bobby despised that made me love it. Every year, I knew exactly what I would be doing for two days in March. The Wednesday before *Nowruz* was *Chahar Shambeh Suri,* when Leila invited a small group of people to jump over fire, literally, in her backyard. This year, I finally got the lyrics to the fire song down. It was something about giving your yellow to the fire and taking its red, meaning you give your sickness to the flames and take in their strength.

The fire jumping was the kind of bizarre and specific tradition I wished I grew up with. Raised by strict Catholic parents, my mother viewed Christmas and Easter as regimented obligations. My father, onetime radical hippie, took it a step further and believed fervently that all holidays were created to fuel the economy and hoodwink children. When I was six, he informed me that "Santa Claus was created by Coca-Cola to sell more soda to the clones who populate our world." I told him I loved Coke and asked what was wrong with selling soda. He didn't appreciate the backtalk. He might have blown up a police car once, but he was just as conservative as the Ebadis when it came to disrespecting one's elders—at least now that he was one. It was always a one-way conversation with my father. He was right, and the clones were wrong. I longed to be a clone, to be hoodwinked. I longed for Christmas trees, Easter egg hunts, church on Sundays, any form of tradition or routine that would save me from my formless life. But instead of gifts under the tree, I got screaming matches, extramarital affairs, and more recently, divorce. No wonder I took the liberty of applying to a boarding school on the other side of the country. Boarding school was a world of structure and tradition, the very things I requested when I prayed to the generic God I had been forced to create for myself.

I pulled Bobby onto the dance floor just as the music stopped and Hossein clinked a bar spoon against his scotch-on-the-rocks. Apparently, he wasn't sold on the *seeb* and *sabzi* martini. "Ladies and gentlemen, thank you for sharing the New Year with us. It's such a pleasure to have you all in our home." He smiled to everyone in the room, and finally to his wife.

"I'd like to share with you some words from Omar Khayyam," Leila began, "the great mathematician, astronomer, and poet."

My purse vibrated. *Can we crash?* The first text was from Fiona. *Is there still food?* This one was from Joanne, the one who eats.

"Alas, that Spring should vanish with the Rose!" Leila recited. "That youth's sweet-scented manuscript should close."

I turned to Bobby and whispered. "Can the girls crash? Joanne's hungry."

"Of course. Tell them to bring whoever they want. This party needs some new energy."

Come over, still food, I texted them both, keeping the phone low as Leila concluded with the verse, "The nightingale that in the branches sang. Whence and whither flown again. Who knows?" It was an uncharacteristically melancholy choice for her, but the theme of springtime and renewal was appropriate. Leila demurely accepted the applause she received for the reading, and then eyed the band to begin again.

Fiona and Joanne arrived just after Haji Firouz, and were shocked by his presence. "Um, who is the man in blackface?" Fiona gasped.

"That's Haji Firouz. He's like their Santa Claus." And like Santa Claus, he wore red. Unlike Santa Claus, he had his face and hands charcoaled black, and he banged a tambourine as he made his way through the garden singing and dancing. The effect was a little demonic. But since Haji represented the Sumerian god of sacrifice, who is killed at the end of each year and reborn at the beginning, there was already something dark and disturbing about his mythology.

"Except Santa Claus isn't a coon," Fiona continued. "This is more uncomfortable than Mickey Rooney in *Breakfast at Tiffany's*."

"Watch it, Miss Gorightry," Bobby joked. "I rove that movie."

"Where's the rice? Is the crispy part all gone?" Joanne interjected.

"Follow me, girls," Bobby said as he took their hands and led them toward the buffet, where Joanne was despondent to discover the *tadeek* had indeed disappeared.

"Has anyone here tried GHB?" Fiona asked, glancing furtively at Bobby as she perused the buffet for carb-free options.

"She's up for a movie," Joanne explained.

My social life could safely be split into two categories: "the girls" and Bobby. Actually, it was Bobby who began calling them "the girls." There were two of them, three when I was included in the collective, sorority sisters from USC. Back then, we had everything in common: a healthy disdain for Greek life, a love of tequila shots and the occasional night on Ecstasy, and a fascination with art history, which we all majored in. But as our twenties slowly wound down, we grew more and more different. Maybe sorority housing and keg parties had prohibited our cultivating individual personalities. In any case, we remained best friends because, when all was said and done, we still needed brunch dates.

"I've been researching GHB online," Fiona continued, "but I just can't seem to get a handle on what a person on GHB acts like. Is it like a coke high? Gnawing teeth, like E, or is it more in the way of some junkie-nod thing?" Fiona closed her eyes for a moment, feigning sleep. She opened her eyes. "Did you like that? That was my junkie. I got called back for *Requiem for a Dream* based on that. They thought I was too young."

Fiona left college two months before graduation when she booked a TV show called *Psych 101* in which she played a psychology student who discovered psychic powers and used them to solve psychotic crimes. The show had been running for nine years. It was a little like *Murder, She Wrote*. Fiona had been aging on television, and I could just see her at ninety, wrinkled like Angela Lansbury, squinting to see the face of the killer on the loose. Her character would still be in college, of course. Fiona led a charmed life. Besides her budding acting career, she scored USC's most eligible bachelor, Trojans-quarterback-turned-Abercrombie-model-turned-zealous-death-row-public-defender Casey Loman. They had been dating on and off since senior year, with generous breaks from each other during which they fucked models and movie stars. Fiona and Casey didn't have kids yet. Fiona said it was because she didn't want to have a child until her career slowed down, but I thought it was because she didn't want to gain the pounds. My theory: Fiona would adopt from a third-world country. No baby weight, lots of press, *and* the chance to win Angelina Jolie's respect.

"I'm so not down with GHB," Bobby whispered. His eyes quickly scanned the room to make sure no one could hear him. "It's basically drain opener. With some floor stripper." Not content with this condemnation, he added, "I only did it a few times. Doesn't mix well with alcohol, so...."

"Why would you snort Drano?" I asked. "Are you insane?"

"No, just bored," Bobby replied, "and you don't snort it, you drink it."

"How civilized," I cracked.

"We're all toxic anyway," Bobby said. "The smog we breathe is gonna kill us faster than a little GHB."

Joanne demanded, "One good reason to try that shit."

"It makes you lose your gag reflex. You'll be able to deep-throat the longest, thickest cock you've ever seen," Bobby said covertly, obviously enjoying the thrill of having this conversation in proximity to his parents and virtually all their friends. Bobby spent so much time repressing himself in front of his family that, when given the opportunity, he used language to shock and awe.

"Really?" Joanne's eyes widened. "Or are you just saying that?"

"It'll turn your throat into the inbound Lincoln Tunnel at morning rush hour," Bobby elaborated. "But so do poppers. And they're sold over the counter."

"Poppers," Joanne repeated, squinting as though making a mental note. "What are those?"

"Amyl Nitrate," Bobby explained, as if this arcane knowledge could at last be imparted to the heterosexual community.

"And it helps you with…" Joanne didn't finish the question. Instead, she grabbed a martini from one of the beautiful cater-waiters and made eyes at him.

"Don't waste your time, Joanne," Bobby warned. "I've seen his Manhunt profile."

"All the good ones are married or gay," Joanne uttered, repeating the excuse single women everywhere use to ease their pangs of patheticness.

Everyone has someone in their life they fear becoming. For me, that person was Joanne, a walking, talking reminder of everything I feared could be my future. We all thought it would be a blessing if Joanne were a lesbian. So, alas, did the men she dated. Joanne was the head of our sorority when Fiona and I rushed as freshmen, which meant she was three years older than us (for the record, 33). When Joanne turned thirty, the meltdown began. She had always thought that when she hit thirty, she had to be married, or at the very least, divorced. It hadn't happened for Joanne yet, most likely because she wanted it so badly. Joanne would do anything if she thought it would make her more appealing to guys. She read somewhere that in order to have a successful first date, you had to perform oral sex. Joanne had been handing out blow jobs, if that's not a contradiction, ever since. Needless to say, she didn't get many second looks, let alone follow-up calls. Joanne's bookshelves were filled with self-help on how to get a guy, how to keep a guy, how to get a guy and keep him, and seven years' back issues of *Modern Bride*. I advised her to hide all the books, because let's face it, no matter how nonexistent your gag reflex is, when a guy scans your bookshelf while you're on your knees and sees a very well-worn and dutifully dog-eared copy of *Stop Getting Dumped*, he ain't putting you on speed dial. Somehow, Joanne found time between therapy sessions and mani-pedis to be the assistant to a moderately successful interior decorator.

"Back to GHB," Fiona demanded. "I want to know what people act like on it. I walk into the casting office and I do what?"

"Basically, it makes you fuck for hours. It…" Bobby caught his parents approaching and immediately self-censored. Leila and Hossein had massive smiles on their faces as they approached Fiona. They adored Fiona, her television fame another symbol in their status-obsessed world. I could see the thrill on Leila's face as she watched her friends and their children whisper about the network TV star who had just walked into her *Nowruz* party.

"Fiona!" Leila exclaimed. "You're glowing."

"Thank you. I just did this amazing Kundalini yoga class with Gurmukh. It was in honor of the spring equinox. It just left me feeling so open and energetic. You should come do Kundalini sometime with me, Mrs. Ebadi."

"I do private," Leila explained.

"I know, but this is different. It's trance yoga. Very powerful stuff. Was there yoga in Iran?" Fiona asked. When Fiona first met the Ebadis, she asked them what it was like escaping Saddam Hussein. At least now she had the name of the country right. I had to give Fiona credit, though. She wasn't the brightest bulb in the bush, but like most actresses in L.A., she made her life a ceaseless quest for self-improvement.

"Hello, Mr. and Mrs. Ebadi," Joanne awkwardly interrupted. Leila and Hossein greeted her warmly, though clearly as an afterthought to Fiona.

"You need an apple-cilantro martini, Fiona," Leila said when she noticed Fiona was drinkless and holding a plate populated by three cornichons.

"I'd love to, but I can't. I have an early call tomorrow, and I'm working so hard on this audition for a movie."

"We'd love to see you in a movie," Hossein said.

"From your lips to God's ears. It's *such* an incredible part," Fiona continued. "My character gets GHB date raped on, like, page 2. And then from page 3 to page 60 she's searching for the guy who did it. And then she finds him and she drugs him with some GHB she buys from this gay friend of hers, and then from pages 60 to about 90 she tortures him and then she kills him even though she doesn't mean to and from page 91 to 115 she pretty much has to get rid of his body. And then in the last scene she's back in school and the perp is right there in her class and she realizes the guy has a twin brother and she probably killed the wrong guy." Fiona took a breath.

There were so many things about Fiona's incessant ramblings regarding her career that got to me. The first was her insistence on using the term "my character" for any part her agent bullied his way into getting her an audition for. I wasn't keeping score, but so far, it usually turned out to be "Anne Hathaway's character." Another was her bizarre fascination with explaining things in numerical breakdown. OK, I might have been a *little* bit jealous of Fiona. I had the acting bug in high school, but I decided I could do more behind the scenes. Unfortunately, behind the scenes turned into answering phones and booking tables for Janet Harrison, filmdom's least successful producer. Lest I appear as petty and jealous as Joanne, I could never tell Fiona I envied her success on the small screen, so I had to find indirect ways of belittling her. Such as: "How old is the character?"

"College."

"So, like eighteen?" I probed.

"I didn't say college freshman," she snapped back. "Eighteen to twenty-five, depending on casting."

"And how many times the character flunks sophomore English," Bobby joked.

"But you're thirty," I couldn't resist pointing out.

"Thanks for the vote of confidence, Kara, but I'm told I can still play high school, so I don't think college will be much of a stretch."

"What is GHB?" Hossein asked, mercifully cutting the war of words.

"It's a party drug," Joanne interjected, desperate to be acknowledged.

"Like Ecstasy?" Leila asked. "Do you know one of the salesgirls at Ferragamo told me once that if I ever needed Ecstasy, I should call her."

"No!" I exclaimed. I loved these moments when Leila surprised her audience with a knowledge and humor that seemed completely outside her world.

"Babak, have you talked to Pari Gol yet?" Leila inquired. "Her daughter is writing a screenplay. I told them you would give her advice."

"Because my career is such a massive success?"

"Holy negative thinking," Fiona commented. "You got a movie made. That's more than most of the waiters and carhops in this town can say. Where's your pride?"

"I left it in a men's room stall somewhere," Bobby said, confident his parents would miss the joke.

Fiona sighed in disbelief as Leila and Hossein led Bobby toward Pari and her teenaged daughter, who took a screenplay from within her Kate Spade bag and thrust it at Bobby. "That guy needs his chakras balanced in a major way," Fiona uttered. Then she immediately pulled out her iPhone and began scrolling through photos of her and Casey looking impossibly perfect at last year's Emmy Awards, until she reached a shot of a handsome shirtless blond playing volleyball on the beach. "So?" Fiona asked.

"So what?" I asked.

"He's thirty-two, he's never been married, he's straight…"

"I think he's v. cute," Joanne slurred as she snatched another martini from a tray.

"Oh, come on, Kara. You're a super catch." Fiona always called me a "catch." Given my lack of a career, I had to assume the status was due to my blond hair and big tits. "You have to get over he-who-must-not-be-named."

"Fiona!" Joanne bellowed. "We agreed."

"I didn't say his name," Fiona said.

"This isn't *Harry Potter*," I said. "And Jacques isn't Lord Voldemort. And banishing him from conversation isn't gonna help me forget him. You can't just expect me to forget some guy just by not talking about him."

"That's exactly what I expect," Joanne said. "When my boyfriend Brad dumped me in high school, I pretended he was dead. When people asked me what happened, I said he died in a car accident."

"That's sociopathic," I said. "Wasn't he going to your high school?"

"Whatever. You call it crazy. I call it coping," Joanne chirped. "Try convincing yourself Jacques choked on the bone of a *poulet roti* or something."

"That's a heartwarming thought, Joanne, but I don't think it's gonna work." The truth was that shutting Jacques out of my conversations only made him more invasive in my thoughts. Jacques was a laconic sunbather, and I was the pest of a mosquito constantly landing on his skin. When he shooed me away from his cheek, I found a spot on his chest. When he slapped me off his chest, I took a break by the pool and found a spot on his big toe. When he shook me off his foot, I took up residence on his knee. Thus far, none of my post-breakup emails to him had been answered. I should have taken the hint and started buzzing somewhere else. But a year and a half after our parting, he was still my sole romantic fantasy.

"Let's cut the crap," Fiona said. "You never date anyone in Los Angeles."

"I can't have this conversation again, Fiona," I said. Then I dropped my voice and added, "And certainly not in this house."

"Holy defensive. I love the Ebadis, too. Leila's fierce, and Hossein is a doll. I even have a soft spot for Bobby, despite the fact that he's a closeted, self-loathing sex addict. It's you I have an issue with."

Ava Hamidi, Maryam Kermansha, and Moh Feresht approached us from behind, and I quickly cut myself off.

"Hey, whitey, nice highlights," Ava chirped as she ran her hands though

my hair. "You're so going to Leila's stylist. I can tell, 'cause he did me."
Maryam glared at Ava. "Did my hair! *My hair*! Jesus, you're a *pervert* and he's
a *hairdresser*." I kissed the three of them on each cheek and introduced them
to Fiona and Joanne.

"I've met you before," Fiona told Maryam.

"Yeah, you came in for an audition at the casting office I work at."

"Which audition?"

"*Still Life*."

"Oh my God, of course," Fiona exclaimed. "The art heist movie. I loved
that part. The whore who forges million-dollar works of art. Why didn't I get
it? Do I have you to blame?"

"If so, I did you a favor. It's going straight to DVD."

"Hey, Moh. How was Prague?" I asked.

"Like Paris without the tourists or the painful exchange rate, but I took
some really cool pictures. I'd show you, except some of them are pornographic,
and I know women think all nudity is exploitation," Moh said with a glance
toward Maryam.

"I shot a sweeps episode of my TV show in Prague," Fiona interjected. She
was waiting for one of them to tell her how much they loved her show, but no
one took the bait. Ava, Maryam, and Moh were far too cool for that. All in
their early thirties, filthy rich, smart, cultured, and successful, they were the
kind of people I would have loved to be friends with if I had the option. There
was just one catch. Bobby didn't want us anywhere near them. As soon as one
of them found out his secret, he was convinced it would be splashed onto a
billboard on Westwood Boulevard.

"I don't think all nudity is exploitation," Maryam reported to the group.
"I've seen *Belle de Jour* twelve times. I love Helmut Newton. But when Moh
brings back contact sheet after contact sheet of pre-pubescent Czech girls posing for him, I can't help but be disturbed."

"It's art," Moh said with a sly smile.

"I'd love to see your photographs," Joanne offered. "I work for an interior
designer. We're always looking for young artists to pitch our clients."

Moh looked Joanne up and down, but he was the kind who slept with
models and broke up with them if their toenails were chipped or their roots
were coming in.

"I swear you got the last good Persian man in L.A., Kara. Hold on to him so you don't end up with someone like Moh." Oh, if only Maryam knew. At least Moh would give me an orgasm once in a while. I had heard through the Persian grapevine that Moh had slept with Ava, Maryam, and almost every other Persian girl out there. And Ava once told me that he was monstrously hung.

"Why don't you come to Cannes this year?" Ava asked. "That one summer you guys came was so fun. You're the only person in our whole group who's as bad at tennis as I am." Amazing that I was considered part of the group, since Bobby rejected almost every vacation invite we got that involved anyone but his immediate family. Somehow, he wasn't as confident in his closet around contemporaries. They were too hip and perceptive, and so they had to be kept at arm's length.

"It's up to Bobby," I responded.

"I'll work on Bobby," Ava replied. "There's no reason for him to keep avoiding us." The knowing look in Ava's eyes suddenly made me realize she *knew*. Maryam and Moh probably did, too. They knew, didn't give a damn, and would never dream of telling their parents. "We have to enjoy the south of France before it becomes as commercialized as Hollywood Boulevard," Ava quickly added. "It's like the whole world is a walking advertisement these days."

"Oh my God, it's my song!" Maryam yelled as the band started in on a Farsi translation of Gwen Stefani's "The Sweet Escape." She grabbed Ava and Moh and led them to the dance floor.

As soon as they were gone, Fiona launched right back into her attack. "Did you hear yourself? *It's up to Bobby.* What about *you*? I'm afraid you're turning into a Persian Stepford girlfriend."

I walked away and was immediately pulled onto the dance floor by Leila. The band was now playing a Persian jam I had heard a few times before, and Leila had managed to get both Hossein and Bobby onto the floor at the same time. "Come on, Kara," Leila said. "Do you remember the basics?" She counted in Farsi as she moved one hand, and then the corresponding shoulder, with great precision. *Yek, doh, seh, chahar.* Bobby, having had a few drinks himself, joined his mother, twirling his wrists and shaking his shoulders. This was the most feminine I had ever seen him around his parents, a testament to the powers of booze and parental denial.

When I first told the girls I had learned Persian dancing, Fiona assumed I meant belly dancing, which was about as Persian as tahini and falafel. In stark contrast to belly dancing, one's hips didn't move in Persian dance. Instead it was the torso, the arms, and especially the face that were left to express the emotion inside the body. It was a dance at once restrained and unabashedly sexual, at once open and closed, at once solitary and inviting. It was a dance I had not mastered. Where I came from, we just mashed our bodies into one another without thought or deliberation. We were not as adept at the balance of expression and repression.

"Where are you going?" Bobby asked as I shimmied away from the festivities.

"Bathroom."

"Did you see the cater waiter spill a glass of red wine on Tanaz Maliki's Hermès purse?"

"No!"

"Yes!" Bobby responded gleefully. "And the best part is, she can't return it because she bought it on eBay!"

"Genius," I cackled as I moved away from the dance floor and into the home. Through a rectangular glass door, I could see the whole party as if on a movie screen. On one side were the Ebadis, laughing and dancing the night away. On the other side were Fiona and Joanne, one glaring at me, the other stuffing her face with *ghormeh sabzi*. These were the two options that seemed available for my life: become a fabulous Persian wife or become one of the girls.

Inside, the house was surprisingly quiet. The party had moved entirely outdoors, its music and conversation echoing in a haze, as if the celebration were actually miles away. I walked upstairs to the room that had once been Bobby's. He had wanted the closet, but instead, he got a black-and-white bedroom. The room hadn't been redecorated since the 1980s, and it retained the feel of that decade: modern, geometric, and glossy. Like all five upstairs bedrooms, the room had a cast-iron balcony covered in bougainvillea overlooking the garden. Bobby had spent much of his childhood looking out from this balcony at his parents' parties.

When he was seven, Bobby expertly cut a hole in the back of his bathroom cabinet and hid his secrets amidst the copper pipes of the plumbing. At first he kept his diaries there. But when the teenaged Bobby read one of his old diaries and found an entry that began *Dear Diary, Hooray! George Bush was elected today,* he burned the entire book and all the others with it. He figured there was no need to keep a record of the days when he bought into his father's political views. Hidden along with the diaries was Bobby's trove of gay porn, which he started buying when he was sixteen. As soon as he got his license, he would risk being caught in the crossfire of gang warfare and drive to Reseda or Watts (anywhere he was guaranteed not to run into a Persian) and purchase magazines with titles like *Honcho* and *Inches.* And then he would spend the majority of the summer flipping the pages over and over again, reading the same erotic stories and masturbating to the same photos until the words and images became branded in his memory. Every subsequent sexual partner would have to compete with the standard set by the muscled cover boys and wild fiction of these magazines. The room had now been turned into a third guest room. All signs of Bobby had long been removed, even his hiding place.

A text came in from Joanne: *Where R U? Wanna go to a bar after I've given up on the guys here?*

On my way back to the garden, I stopped in front of a marble table filled with picture frames. This table always sidetracked me. It wasn't the photographs of Leila and Hossein with the Shah or with Ronald Reagan that got my attention, nor the photograph of Leila and the Shahbanou, Farah Diba, nor the one of me and Bobby on the beach in Cannes from that one summer vacation he was willing to take with the Persian crowd, nor the deep blue eye dangling from the table's edge to ward off evil spirits. It was the photograph of a ten-year-old boy, his hair moppy, his eyes large and curious, tightly hugging a four-year-old Bobby. I seldom managed to pass this table without staring again at that photograph. I'd never known anyone who had died.

2

"We really could have taken a cab," I said as I scoured the FM band for a decent song.

"Don't be silly," Hossein responded. "It's a waste of money. And I only had three drinks." He said this as if three drinks, especially when the drinks in question were Glenlivet on the rocks, weren't well over the legal blood-alcohol level. But I wasn't afraid to be in the passenger seat. Hossein was the kind of man who made you feel safe in his care, even with a few drinks in him.

It was almost three in the morning; the party had wound to its inevitable conclusion. As Rosa Maria wiped down the counters, and the temporary staff threw out the trash and put the leftovers in Tupperware to take home, Hossein insisted on driving me and Bobby home. We had taken a cab to the house knowing full well that huge amounts of alcohol would be consumed, but Hossein didn't have our issue with drinking and driving. Perhaps it was because he made his fortune selling cars. Maybe he felt cars were his true friends, and would never betray him.

"He's pretending to be asleep," Hossein now commented as he manipulated his rearview mirror to afford him a perfect image of Bobby splayed out in the back seat.

"How can you tell?"

"He snores," Hossein said. On cue, Bobby started snoring, playing it up for comedic effect. Hossein and I both laughed. Bobby avoided conversation with his father beyond two sentences. He claimed that the third sentence would inevitably be about his stagnant career and ways in which he might make money, a subject he had little to no interest in.

"Did you have fun?" Hossein asked.

"I always love your parties. Did *you* have fun?"

Hossein shrugged. "I prefer a party with a card game."

"Whenever you're ready to let me in on that poker night of yours..." I trailed off.

Hossein's laughter said the obvious, but he gallantly covered. "Kara, we're humble men. You'd leave us all impoverished."

The truth was there was no room for me at a poker game with a ten-thousand-dollar buy-in. There was no room for women at all at the game. I had been to the Ebadis' during a few of Hossein's card nights. The men sat at a round table in the living room, upping the ante in a haze of cigar smoke and scotch, while their wives played a side game of rummy in the dining room, for much smaller stakes. Persian women were allowed to shop their husbands' fortunes away, but gambling the fortune away was a privilege reserved for the men. Leila often just socialized and watched.

Hossein pulled up to our place. Home was a duplex on Beverly and Curson. Hardwood Floors. South-facing windows. Granite kitchens. Small yard. The Ebadis bought it eight years ago, before a mega-mall called The Grove opened nearby. The Grove had a fountain that danced to Frank Sinatra and Bette Midler, and a creepy trolley that traveled the short stretch of the pedestrian mall at all hours. It was garish and tacky and, needless to say, made real estate prices in the neighborhood skyrocket.

"You know we could sell this at triple what we bought it for," Hossein said.

"*You* could sell it," I corrected. "I didn't buy it. I'm just the lucky recipient of your generosity."

"Don't be silly," he said for the second time in a short conversation, making me wonder if that's how he viewed me. "You're family. This place is as much yours as it is Babak's. If we sell the place, we can take the money and buy you two a real home. You have to trade up in the real estate market," Hossein explained, as he had many times before. I could practically smell Bobby's annoyance, a pheromone emanating from the back seat. "You can start with something like this. A condo, a duplex, it doesn't matter. But then you don't stay forever. You sell and take the capital somewhere else."

"It's up to Bobby, I guess." I instinctively looked around to make sure Fiona hadn't snuck into the car to berate me for saying those words. "You guys bought the duplex in the first place."

When Bobby graduated from NYU and moved back to L.A., Hossein financed the duplex as an indirect investment. He rationalized that in a few years, Bobby would move on by marrying me, or by dumping me and marrying some nice Persian girl. This would allow him and Hossein to rent at some obscene monthly amount or cash out, depending on where the L.A. market was in its manic-depressive cycle.

"It's time you have a nicer place. You're turning thirty in two weeks." My birthday, hot on the heels of *Nowruz*, was always the anticlimax of the year. "You two are adults now. You need an adult residence."

"If it ain't broke," I said, "don't fix it." Bobby and I had always agreed that while we didn't need to correct any of his parents' assumptions, we wouldn't actively lie. The arrangement took root seven years ago by a few sins of omission. We'd been at an Ebadi cocktail party the first time I realized what was happening. Wax flowers cupping votives illuminated the pool. Torches lined the garden's pathways. The mix Leila had made alternated between boleros, French *chanson*, and Persian pop. Leila was gossiping in Farsi with her own version of the girls. One of them, Pari Gol, turned to me and asked how long Bobby and I had been going out. When I tried to straighten out her mistake, she threw in that I should be happy to know that Leila approves of me whole-heartedly, despite my not being Persian.

That night, I had told Bobby that his mother was telling their friends we were a couple. Bobby didn't seem fazed. "What does it matter what my parents' friends believe? Don't ask, don't tell," Bobby said. Every time the subject would come up during the next few days, Bobby honed his rationalization. "You can't control people's assumptions," he would say. Or, "We've been living together for two years already. Do you blame them for assuming?" Or, "Not denying something is different from lying." Or, "As long as we don't overtly lie, we're not doing anything wrong." From that first uncomfortable week of denial, I never referred to Bobby as my boyfriend, I never intimated the idea of marriage or children in front of the Ebadis, and I never gave anyone the impression we slept in the same room, let alone the same bed. And yet I somehow got myself enmeshed in a complicated fraud. Personally, I couldn't believe that Bobby's parents didn't ask more questions about the fact that we obviously lived in different sides of a duplex, with separate entrances, separate kitchens, separate utilities, even separate mailboxes. Maybe in Leila's mind, that was just the natural precursor to his-and-hers bathrooms, which she would occasionally point out are the key to a happy marriage. Bobby and I did share a yard and a driveway, and since I had a day job, I parked my Hyundai behind his Lexus. We could have avoided each other entirely, like most of L.A.'s married couples, but instead, we spent every waking non-sexual moment together. Bobby was really gracious and never claimed he chose the duplex so we could live together. Of course, he couldn't really claim he chose the duplex at all. Nor could the choice really have been his father's, either. Hossein, a man who was truly visionary when it came to the bottom line, would never have suggested purchasing a residential property and turning half of it over to me rent-free. The real estate investment might have been Hossein's deal, but nobody was fooled that it was his idea.

"Koorosh is in real estate, you know," Hossein continued. "He's developing a property in Westwood. It's a full-service high-rise with twenty-four-hour doormen and a pool and a gym. Marble kitchens. He said he'd give us a deal if we put cash down."

"That sounds nice," I lied. It really didn't sound nice at all. It sounded devoid of charm. The kind of place where so many of the Ebadis' circle lived, but where Leila wouldn't have been caught dead.

"We could all go see the building next week if you want. The units aren't finished, but they have one open for show."

I remembered Bobby and his mother renovating the duplex. The place was a mess when they bought it. It had been in the hands of a Russian couple for decades, and their cabbagey scent emanated from the stained carpets, the water-damaged ceilings, even the decayed garden. But mother and son went to work on the place, picking out granite for the kitchens, hardwood floors, *Tabriz* and *Abadeh* rugs. I'm sure Leila would be sad to see us relocate to one of those move-in-ready condos where her sole input would be providing a housewarming gift.

"I think Westwood is safer, too," Hossein said. "I don't know about this neighborhood. There's no security."

"We're not moving to Westwood, Daddy," Bobby exclaimed as he bolted up from his pretend sleep.

"I knew you were awake," Hossein said. "If you don't want to talk to us, you don't have to. Faking something always takes more energy."

"I'm exhausted," Bobby sighed as he opened the car door. "Happy New Year."

"What's wrong with Westwood?" Hossein asked, apparently not finished with the conversation.

"It's overrun with Persians," Bobby cracked.

"What's wrong with that?" Hossein asked.

"We're happy the way we are," Bobby said, speaking for the two of us. "We have a nice place. We each have our own space if we need it. We like the neighborhood."

"I can tell Koorosh we're not interested. Although I might buy one as layaway anyhow. I can always rent it out if you two don't want it, and it's the right size for your mother. If anything were to happen to me, I would want her living somewhere with twenty-four-hour security."

"We won't want it, and neither will she," Bobby assured him.

"Did you talk to Koorosh about working with him? It doesn't have to be full time. He's making good money. He's working on huge projects, even a casino in Las Vegas."

"I know nothing about real estate," Bobby said. "I'm a writer."

Hossein grumpily conceded defeat. "Well, Happy New Year."

Bobby kissed his father and exited the car. He watched through the car window as Hossein took my hands in his. "You need to whip that boy into shape," Hossein said. "A man should earn his life."

"You don't have to throw so much money at him, you know," I said, keenly aware that the money trickled down to me. "If he wasn't so comfortable, maybe he'd have to find a job."

"I know," Hossein said, melancholy *almost* reverberating in his strong voice. "I have to take care of him, though. He's the only son his mother and I have left." Cueing my exit, he started the car.

I woke up with a slight hangover the morning after *Nowruz* and mourned the days when my body rebounded immediately from a night of fun. I rolled out of bed, made some coffee, and carried two cups over to Bobby's side of the duplex. The sun, as filtered through his sheer curtains, infiltrated the room ever so subtly, illuminating the *Tabriz* rug that had been handed down through generations of Ebadis and the utilitarian-chic furniture selected by Leila and delivered from Italy: a chocolate-brown leather couch, a dark cherry wood coffee table, beige ottomans. The whole place was decorated in the safe, masculine colors of a safari, as if to introduce any brightness or pastel would be an admission. Bobby's bookshelves were more barren than they had been a year ago when, in a mood of self-loathing, Bobby decided he was a terrible writer and that reading the work of superior writers was butchering his self-esteem. The Kundera and Wilde got boxed and stuck in a closet back in Brentwood. Bobby kept literature he considered sub-mediocre, and had developed an obsession with '50s pulp novels. Stuff he felt sure he could have written better. His shelves were now lined with alphabetized CDs and stacks of smudged old paperbacks. Bobby had taken to existing only by comparison.

On the first morning of the year, the bottle of echinacea on the counter confirmed what I had expected. Next to it was a telltale half-mug of cold "Immune Support" tea. The message was clear. Bobby had sex when we got home. Bobby had a completely rational fear of HIV and STDs, but along with the fear came the completely irrational supposition that taking herbal cold remedies would fend off whatever contagion he exposed himself to. He must have spent at least a hundred dollars a week on things like elderberry extract, Cold-EEZE, and Emergen-C. None of it made any sense to me, but then again, neither did the fact that Bobby had the energy and compulsion to go online for sex when we got home at three in the morning.

I snuck into his room, also safari-hued, with dark beige walls to complete the look. I knew he was alone because the newspaper wasn't out front. Given his proclivities, we had to adopt a system, and ours was leaving the *Los Angeles Times* out front. I had never left it on my welcome mat, because, in all honesty, it had been a year and a half since I'd had sex. I hadn't felt any desire since Jacques. But Bobby had often put it out. The newspaper, I mean. The system worked because it avoided all embarrassment, and because the *Los Angeles Times* sucked, and neither of us read it, anyway. We only subscribed because we didn't want to see the paper disappear altogether. I did always get a twinge of sadness when I saw the paper out front, but it wasn't jealousy, because I knew Bobby would never develop any real connection with a sex partner. His approach to sex precluded emotion.

"Feel my forehead," he said, virtually as his eyes opened. "Am I feverish?" This being Bobby's equivalent to the loaded question that defined our era: *Does my butt look fat in this?*

I duly felt his forehead. He did feel a little balmy, but he was under a thick duvet in a closed room, and it was already an unseasonably hot spring. And besides the heat, we were both sweating vodka and tequila. "You're not getting sick, Bobby."

"How do you know? You're not a doctor." If I were a doctor, he would have found another reason to discredit my rationale.

I placed my hands gently along his throat. "Your lymph nodes aren't swollen. If you were seroconverting, they would be." Bobby looked at me, more than a little surprised. "I've done my research, Bobby. And you're fine. What you're suffering from is a hangover and too much anxiety." I ran my index finger along a scar on his forearm. It was one of my favorite things about Bobby, this small imperfection, inflicted on him when he fell in the playground as a child.

"I think this is it. I'm gonna cancel my Manhunt account and settle down." Bobby sighed. This was a scene he played regularly, one he could do in his sleep. "All I really want is someone to wake up with and watch TV with," Bobby continued. He was what I imagined gay men in the 1950s must have been like: tortured loners compartmentalizing their lives between heterosexual façades and covert hours spent in truck stops and restrooms. The way Bobby carried himself could hardly be pegged as gay. The victories of the gay rights movement didn't penetrate his existence. He was an "invert," as they once were called, a character in one of those pulpy novels he devoured. "Maybe I should try one of those speed-dating seminar things," he said. "Or go to a gay AA meeting. Find myself a nice, sober boyfriend."

"Wouldn't that relationship just be based on deception? Given that you're not an alcoholic? Maybe you should try a sex addicts meeting," I suggested.

Bobby looked offended. "I'm not a sex addict. Jesus, Kara. Addicts do crystal meth and go to bathhouses and have bareback sex. They have no limits. I just have a normal sex drive for a man my age, and I'm making up for lost time. The thirties are the adolescent years for most gay men, sexually speaking."

"Then you'll find a relationship in your fifties," I offered.

"I shouldn't have given him a blow job. I know you're gonna think this sounds crazy..."

"You? Crazy?"

"That *barbary* bread Rosa Maria put on the buffet table last night was so damn crispy it cut into the roof of my mouth. It pierced right in there." This was muffled by the way he was idiotically sticking an index finger into his mouth.

"And?"

"And that's exactly the entry route *HotWeHo9*'s precum needs to my bloodstream. I left myself vulnerable."

Bobby gave blow jobs even more liberally than Joanne and always went through a five-hour regret period convinced he had syphilis, gonorrhea, chlamydia, herpes, and, of course, HIV. Then he pulled himself together and went right back to doing the same thing.

"*HotWeHo9*? You refer to people you've had sex with as *HotWeho9* and it's some burnt bread grazing your gums you're worried about?"

"You're not amusing me, Kara."

"I'm sorry," I said. "Was he really nine inches?"

"Not even," he complained. "He was one of these assholes who think being uncut counts for extra. Stretching your foreskin does not add thirty useable millimeters. I'm only sleeping with the circumcised from now on. They're less likely to be sick anyway. The foreskin can trap the virus and make it more likely to infect. It's all I can think of when I see foreskin now."

"Well, don't ruin it for me, bitch," I said playfully, anxious to get a smile out of him. "*I* still want the option of enjoying uncut guys."

I lost my virginity in my last year of junior high school to Will Gage, star of the Westlake basketball team. It was at one of those awful junior high school parties. Somebody's parents were away, so a hundred idiotic teenagers raided their liquor cabinet and got completely shitfaced, many for the first time. Will's girlfriend was the exotic Lana Martinez. Their coupling was one of those inevitabilities. He was considered the hottest guy in school and she was considered the hottest girl, so of course fate would eventually bring them together. But Lana wasn't one for parties and booze. In her absence, a drunken Will Gage slurred that he wanted me. I figured there were worse ways to lose it than to the hottest guy in school, no matter how drunk he was. So we went up to the bedroom of some guy's parents and there, for four whole minutes, we fucked. In retrospect, I can't say Will was good in bed. Every time we fucked from that first time to graduation a year and a half later, he came in about four minutes. I don't think I had an orgasm once, but I didn't know any better back then. I thought Will was a god, my own personal pinup come to life. And I believed him when he said he would eventually break up with Lana for me. In truth, he lived in fear that Lana, or anybody else for that matter, would find out. That first night, he leaned into me after he came all over my shoes and said, "If you tell any of your friends about this, I'll kill you." Then he left me alone. Charming closing line.

Threatened by the idea of death, or worse, by the idea of Will's not loving me anymore, I kept my mouth shut for anyone but him. It became so clear to my friends that there was something unspoken between us that they all drifted away. I spent the last year of our time together lying to them. I escaped them, Will, and Lana when I went east for high school. But I've never been able to shake off Will's threatening whispers in my head. I've often thought that this is why I identified with gay men. I spent the first phase of my active sexuality in the closet.

Once Bobby had showered and I had eaten his one English muffin (whole wheat, stale), we were back in the car, headed toward Koreatown. He usually drove when we went out, because he had a Lexus with seat warmers and seat coolers, and that was more pleasant than what my four-year-old, two-door Hyundai had to offer. "Where are we going?" I demanded to know. "We already passed every brunch spot and movie theater."

"I can't believe you even have to ask," he scoffed.

Bobby parked outside a dilapidated building surrounded by signs in Korean. On a plaque by the buzzer was one sign in English: *Dr. Pony Bryer, PhD.* "Oh my God," I said. "The famous Dr. Bryer's not even an M.D.? What is he, a sociologist?"

"I've never read his diplomas. This is on me. It's the best hangover cure."

"A visit to the quack? For me?"

"Kara," Bobby said sternly as he buzzed the doctor. "Show some respect."

"Seriously, Bobby, this is an unnecessary expense. I can take some Advil."

"Kara, please don't bring up the money. It's a gift." Bobby never talked about money, possibly because he felt guilty about having so much of it. Or about his parents' having so much of it. Bobby still had a credit card that billed directly to his father's bank account, although he used it selectively. Groceries and phone bills got charged to Daddy. Online sex-site memberships and trips to health clinics were paid for out of pocket. So basically, Bobby's whole income became discretionary, since the price of the groceries and phone always exceeded what he shelled out for the mortgage. I sometimes almost asked why Hossein didn't just pay the mortgage, but it was all part of the circular labyrinth in which Bobby and his parents had chosen to live. As had I.

"Bobby, I know you don't charge these visits to your parents."

"I have my own income," he retorted defensively. "Give me some credit, Kara." Bobby did have an income, the residuals from a movie he wrote called *Lovers in the Backseat.* It was a romantic comedy set in the world of Formula 1 racing, which was beyond ironic, because romance and competitive sports were not among Bobby's interests. And I had never seen a Formula 1 car with a back seat, either. But the movie was his first job as a writer in Hollywood, it got made, and despite not being a massive hit, it played on TBS like every other week, which meant Bobby got paid for sitting around and doing nothing. The best part is that he wrote the script in a week. They hired seven other writers to rewrite his original, but all their contributions were even worse than his, so none of them got credit, and all the residuals came to his mailbox.

Bobby's luck hadn't been as good since then. His only other job after *Lovers in the Backseat* was a sitcom pilot about twenty-somethings trying to make it in Los Angeles. Bobby insisted on making one of the characters HIV-positive, an attribute the network didn't find very funny. I guess they couldn't imagine pill regimens and a laugh track co-existing. Bobby's agent told him to let it go, but Bobby wouldn't budge. He said it wasn't about making HIV funny, it was about showing that a character who had HIV could still have a sense of humor, meaningful ambition, and a hip, wonderful group of friends. Now I'm sure that was true, but since no one else in Los Angeles had those things, why should some winsome positive guy have all the luck? In any event, the network didn't feel it and killed the project. Bobby's agent dumped him, and Bobby was left to develop an epic case of writer's block. Ignore the fact that he was often on his laptop, cruising chat rooms for sex.

Dr. Pony Bryer was as disturbing as I expected. For one thing, he wore jeans and an oversize T-shirt emblazoned with a tourist map of Thailand. For another, his diplomas looked way too real, like he had ordered them off a site.

"Bobby," the doctor said as he gave the patient a hug. Who hugs their doctor? "What do you need today? Xanax? Vicodin?"

"Shouldn't you ask his symptoms first?" I said as Bobby glared at me.

"I'm sorry, doctor, this is my roommate, Kara."

"My dear Kara," Dr. Bryer said as he placed both his dirty hands on my shoulders, "I do not interrogate the people in my care. Who knows what is going on with Bobby's body better than he does? My philosophy is that the customer is always right."

"Which is a really scary philosophy when your customer is a hypochondriac."

"I need some B-12 immediately," Bobby said. "And give her a shot, too. Make it a painful one, please."

Dr. Bryer prepared a syringe filled with a thick, orange, syrupy substance. The color returned to Bobby's face as soon as the liquid pumped into his veins. "Your turn," the doctor said.

"I'm fine, really."

"You'll love it," Bobby pleaded. "It gives you energy and boosts your immunity and makes you feel vitamin enriched, like a fabulous shampoo."

Dr. Bryer took another syringe out of his low fridge, which looked like it belonged in a dorm room next to a Crock-Pot and a bong. Before I could protest, Doctor Creepster squeezed one triceps and shot me full of Bs. "Holy shit," I cried. And before the sound had died out, I had a little round Band-Aid on my arm.

The B-12 shot worked like a charm. Our hangovers were cured, Bobby seemed confident the vitamins would ward off whatever infections he may have been exposed to, and we decided to hit the gym. The gym was ground zero of Bobby's social life. Walking from one end of the gym to the other with Bobby was like getting a tour of gay Los Angeles. He had slept with sixty-four percent of the clientele by his estimations, and he loved to share the details with me. I knew who talked dirty, who collected action figures, who lived in a Frank Lloyd Wright, who shaved his pubic hair, and who prayed after cumming. Bobby usually nodded a hello to most of these people because he forgot their names, and a generic conversation followed. "You're looking slim," one of them would say to Bobby. Or, "Your glutes are really growing," Bobby would comment. The conversations usually stuck to this kind of safe and complimentary territory, unless one of the two parties wanted to sleep together again, in which case one would ask what the other was *up to*, which was some kind of booty-call code for "are you hard" or something.

Once Bobby and I had circled the gym to scope the scene, I got on one of the two-dozen treadmills lined up like a firing squad. The machine asked me to punch in my weight and my age. Normally I would have punched in the truth (29 years old, 129-and-a-half pounds), but Hot Tattooed Guy was running next to me, and I could see that he was checking me out via peripheral vision. Sure, almost all the guys at our gym were gay, but luckily Bobby and I did a weekly walk-through, during which he broke it down for me by preference. Having spent as much time in the steam room as he had, Bobby knew who was gay, who was not, and what was gay in steam room only. Two weeks earlier, we had come across Hot Tattooed Guy. On his left deltoid was a skull with the words *"L'amour est plus fort que la mort"* inscribed inside. I had picked up enough French in my three-year relationship with Jacques to get it. But not to believe it. Jacques said he loved me, then left me for dead.

Fiona's words now ran through my head. I was going to show her I could date someone in Los Angeles.

I wanted to find Bobby and tell him about the time Jacques and I got trashed in Montmartre and almost got each other's names tattooed on our asses, but bit my tongue and turned my attention back to HTG. Normally I would run away from anyone with a skull inked between the dermal and epidermal layers, but this skull was clearly tender and loving, and the guy it was on looked stronger than death. On his back was the Sphinx, drawn with the detail and specificity of an effigy from the Old Kingdom. The Sphinx's eyes framed the perfect groove of Hot Tattooed Guy's lower back, and its mouth creased down toward his round, hard ass. Bobby and I took the Sphinx, his olive complexion, and gleaming black mane as a sign of HTG's Egyptian pride. In fact, we had created a whole mythology for him. Born in Cairo, raised in Paris, he had spent a few years as a guitarist in a punk band, but had since grown up and established the Los Angeles operations of his father's textile empire.

I did my best to jog in a manner at once feminine and athletic. I had chosen a good outfit that day. White tank top that fit me perfectly, with light pink Juicy sweats and my favorite Pumas, which Bobby and I had Bedazzled one drunken night. My blond hair was pulled back into a ponytail, and I wore a minimal amount of gift-bag makeup donated to me by Fiona from the basket of goodies she received at last year's Emmys. Not so much to make me look like I put effort into my gym look; just a little blush and mascara. I had my iPod nano dangling from my neck, but I didn't put the headphones on for fear of missing the icebreaker. Unfortunately, five minutes into my jog, Hot Tattooed Guy got up and left. Antonio, a scruffy Cuban we'd nicknamed that because he resembled Banderas, quickly commandeered his treadmill. Bobby had slept with Antonio three years earlier. Back then, Antonio was pudgy with unfortunate skin, but like all new arrivals, it took him a year to develop a perfect body and an immaculate complexion. It's either that or get out of Los Angeles. Imperfection doesn't have a high probability of survival here.

Bobby found me as soon as he saw Hot Tattooed Guy leave. "So?" he asked.

"Nothing," I said. "I'm a terrible cruiser. He barely even looked at me."

"I don't see how that's possible. You're hot and he's straight. Men always check out the merchandise." Bobby looked up and nodded a hello to Antonio. "Hey, buddy?" Bobby asked with a slightly lower tenor to his voice than usual. "What're you up to?"

"Not much," Antonio said. "Just finishing up my workout. Gonna hit the steam then hang with some friends."

"Cool," Bobby said, as Antonio sauntered toward the locker room with a glance back in our direction. "What was his name again?"

"Antonio," I quickly spat out. "Jesus, Bobby. Do you remember any of the guys you sleep with?"

"Antonio is not his real name, Kara."

"Oh, right," I remembered. "Of course."

"You mind if I hit the steam room? It shouldn't take long."

It didn't. Fifteen minutes later, a flushed Bobby emerged and found me daydreaming. "You look super zen," he commented.

"Hardly. I was just thinking about high school. Some girl just walked in wearing bell-bottoms that looked exactly like those corduroy ones you wore."

"I did not wear bell-bottoms," Bobby protested, though I could sense his senior year fashion mistakes running through his brain: the corduroy, the bowling shorts, the platform shoes.

"Oh, please," I said, laughing, as we headed out the door. "There is only so much history one person can rewrite."

3

I'D BEEN JANET HARRISON's assistant for seven years. I worked with her from her Pacific Palisades living room, decorated in a hodgepodge of Janet's mother's Laura Ashley hand-me-downs, some art deco lamps from a flea market, and a clashing symphony of paintings, photos, pillows, and rugs stolen from movie sets. It wasn't the career I dreamed for myself as a little girl, but it was an easy paycheck. My title changed frequently: assistant, executive assistant, director of development, and finally, vice president. But the fact of the matter was, despite my card reading *vice president*, I was still an assistant. Better salary, same tasks. As my thirtieth birthday approached, I realized that my work consisted mostly of answering the phone, which rarely rang, and helping Janet prepare for childbirth. Artificial insemination, if you must know.

The Friday before my thirtieth, I arrived to find Janet on the couch in her favorite pink terry bathrobe, rubbing her belly, eating California rolls from Gelson's, and watching *The View*. She barely acknowledged me when I came in. There were workdays when all I did was read magazines and watch TV with her. I knew there were more productive things I could be doing, like looking for another job, one that entailed work perhaps, but the search itself required more effort than I was willing to give. Fiona was always on my case about this. She said I had given up all ambition to become a professional best friend. As usual, she wasn't wrong.

I sat down next to Janet. "Anything on the agenda today?" I asked.

She shook her head.

"I haven't had any luck with the book," I continued.

"Which one?" Janet was half-watching me and half-watching Barbara Walters sharing her take on Christina Aguilera's latest antics.

"The one about the Black Death."

"Oh," Janet said, extremely uninterested.

The Black Death project was my idea, inspired by Bobby's online research into the disease. I thought there could be a great epic love story in the history of the plague. You know, Nicole Kidman and Jude Law torn apart by a mysterious epidemic or something like that. I found a comprehensive non-fiction book about the subject, tracked the book rights, and masterminded a plan in which Bobby would write the movie, and I would finally get my producer credit. If Bobby could write a decent movie about subjects he knew nothing about, imagine what he could do with infectious disease as his muse. Unfortunately, the project was as cursed as the rest of our slate.

"There's no agent handling it," I explained. "So I've contacted the author directly."

"Mmm." I wasn't sure if Janet was reacting to me or to the peanut butter she was now smearing on her California rolls. "Oh, by the way, your birthday present is arriving at one. I know it's a few days early, but he presented himself to me, and I had to grab him for you."

"Him?"

"Don't worry. He's really cute, and just your type. Dark hair, stubble, a little rough. He lives in Studio City, though. I hope you're not a zip code snob."

"Janet, I'm going to Pilates with Leila at one. I go to Pilates at one with Leila every Friday. Look at me. I'm wearing tights and a tank top."

Janet stared off into space. "I'm pregnant, Kara. Do you expect me to remember my assistant's schedule?"

"I am your vice president," I asserted.

"Of course you are. I forgot. I'm pregnant, Kara. Give me a break.

He was reading Zora Neale Hurston. You love that God book. We struck up a conversation, he told me what he was looking for, and I decided he should meet you."

"You are disturbed."

"Kara, look at me. I'm a whale and I'm alone."

If she was fishing for a compliment, she didn't get one from me. "You decided to have the baby."

"My sell-by date was up," she sighed. "Don't let the same thing happen to you. It's time to get over Jacques."

"I am over Jacques. I haven't spoken to him in a year and a half. He's French history, like the guillotine."

•

I had met Jacques four and a half years earlier when Harry and I went to Paris. My mom, Harriet, or Harry as I always called her because I couldn't pronounce Ts as a child, got divorced from my dad, Pat, at that time. Because of the whole T thing, I called him Pa, which was a more appropriate name for a father than Harry was for a mother. The divorce wasn't particularly bitter. I was old enough not to be torn in half. Neither of them wanted the house, so they sold it, split the money, and moved to condos. Harry found a one-bedroom in Thousand Oaks. She was a creature of habit and couldn't stand leaving home. Pa moved to a studio in Miami. It was tiny and cramped, but right by the beach. I think he realized his greatest joy in life came from staring at young women in bikinis. In any case, after the divorce was finalized, Harry asked me if I would go to Paris with her for a week. She had some money left over from the sale of the house, and she felt like she could use both a getaway and some bonding time with her daughter.

Our very first day there, we went to the Louvre. Harry was too cheap to pay for a tour group, so we latched on to this undergraduate class from the Sorbonne that was getting a tour. The tour was in French, which neither of us understood, so I'm not sure where Harry's logic came from, but she somehow managed to convince this sparkly eighteen-year-old undergrad to translate the entire tour for us. His name was Jacques, and I spent every night that week in his tiny studio apartment in St. Germain. We would lie next to the fan, as his dog, Gainsbourg, licked our faces. Jacques would teach me how to talk dirty in French. He would melt chocolate into croissants for breakfast and feed them to me in bed. And I would always manage to sneak back into my hotel room before Harry's Valium had worn off. I don't think I slept that entire week. When Harry and I were midway through our thirteen-hour plane ride back to Los Angeles, I broke down into deep, painful sobs. I was hysterical; my body broken down, my heart open like never before, and my brain convinced I would never see Jacques again. I was reading *The Poisonwood Bible,* which Harry had just given me. She always gave me an Oprah book for my birthday. It was unofficial tradition. I told her I was crying because of the book. She didn't buy it for a second.

"You've been doing the deed with that adorable kid all week, Kara. I'm no fool." Harry insisted on discussing sex with me. She thought it made her hip. I thought it made her smothering and creepy.

"Mom, please!" I pleaded.

"Nobody cries like that over a book. You're afraid you're never going to see him again."

"Nothing happened," I lied.

"Was he a good kisser?"

"I don't want to talk to you about this."

"He's so young. He wasn't a virgin, was he?" she asked lasciviously.

"Mom, he's French. And you're grossing me out."

"I'm your mother, who else are you going to talk to about this?"

"Um, my friends. Bobby. Anyone but you," I explained.

"Fine. Then take a Valium and stop crying."

I accepted the pill, but the crying lasted seven months.

The TiVo beeped, asking Janet if she wanted to save or delete that episode of *The View*. She deleted it and moved on to the next day's episode. She had the somewhat strange habit of TiVoing every talk show and watching marathons once they were out of date. The doorbell rang. When I answered it, I was pleasantly surprised. Janet was right. He *was* cute. With the thick glasses, moppy hair, and muscular body busting through his white V-neck and cargo shorts, he looked like an East Coast collegiate who'd gotten the most out of his L.A. gym membership.

"Hey. I'm Cameron," he said.

"I'm Kara."

"I know."

"Right. So what else did Janet tell you about me?" I asked, flirting.

"You're turning thirty on Monday. You like running and international cinema. You have an obsessive attachment to your gay best friend. You had your heart broken by some French undergrad." He lit a cigarette.

I already knew this would never work. Number one, I never dated smokers. Number two, Jacques was a smoker, and I didn't want to be with someone who would just end up reminding me of him.

"So I was thinking we could grab something at Whole Foods and eat outside. It's a gorgeous day. I biked over here, so hopefully you don't mind driving. I'm just trying to lessen my carbon footprint, so I rarely use my car."

Behind him, I could see the Sasquatch-sized carbon footprint of Leila's Bentley pulling up Janet's driveway. "Listen, you seem great and all, but…" My voice must've sounded panicked. Leila's car window was rolled down, and she was blasting Rihanna, no doubt from one of the workout playlists Bobby had created for her iPod. Leila waved from within the car. I was praying she wouldn't get out of the car, but of course she did, holding a gift from Fred Segal, no less. Leila skipped over to the front door. The orthopedic shoes she wore to work out always put an extra spring in her step.

"Hello, Kara *djoon*," she said as she gave me a kiss on each cheek. She next turned her attention to Cameron, looking him up and down. She must have deduced he was a bike messenger or some other insignificant person, because she put out her hand for him to shake and said, "Hello, I'm Leila Ebadi. Lovely to meet you." Before he could make any conversation, Leila marched right over to Janet. "Janet, don't get up. The baby's comfortable. Here." Leila placed the Fred Segal gift on Janet's lap. "I was buying some toner yesterday, and I wandered into the baby section. I couldn't help it."

"Really, Leila, you have to stop buying me gifts."

"But I like buying gifts," Leila said with the innocence of a little girl. And it was true. Hossein once bet Leila that she couldn't go a week without buying herself anything. She proudly won the bet, until Hossein realized that she had spent the week shopping for others. Hossein should have known better than to bet his wife. Had the bet stipulated that she couldn't shop at all, she never would've taken it. She knew herself too well. She couldn't walk into a store without seeing something that was perfect for me or Hossein or Bobby or Rosa Maria or her Pilates instructor or her hairdresser or her gardener or Tanaz or…

Janet ripped open the gift and found baby Uggs. "They're adorable."

"I know. They really are. Babies are so much fun to shop for." Leila didn't mean this passive-aggressively, but I couldn't help taking this as a hint. "So do you have a project for my husband to finance yet?"

"Leila!" I chimed in. "You can't finance a movie for us."

"Why not? We have money that's just sitting there, and I'm good at spending it."

"Film is the worst possible investment you can make," I argued.

"We sell cars to make money. This would be to help you and Babak. He can write it, you can produce it. What's wrong with helping those you love?"

I tried to come up with an argument against this, but the truth was that the Ebadis might have become Janet's only chance to get a movie made anymore, and therefore, mine too. When I first started, Janet had a deal with Paramount based on a string of low-budget, high-grossing indies she'd made in Baltimore. The movies were never released theatrically, but they made a killing on DVD, and Hollywood loves a good bottom-line girl. The studio was buying her the film rights for bestsellers; *New Yorker* articles; life rights of Rwandan refugees. She was well on her way to becoming the next Scott Rudin. She had a real vice president at that point, as well as a director of development, and then there was me, the assistant. Janet promised that when a movie got made, I would be an associate producer. But none of them did. And after two years, the powers that be decided it wasn't worth it to keep bankrolling Janet, her lunches at the Ivy, her copy machine, and her staff. Any self-respecting person would have heard the exit music and bolted to another company, but not me. When Janet said she wanted to keep developing projects from her three-bedroom, country-style house in the Palisades and offered to keep me on as an assistant, I said yes.

Cameron looked at me curiously and asked, "Should we get going? I have to get back to work by two."

"Going where?" Leila asked. "Aren't we going to Pilates?"

I froze for a brief instant and then recovered. "I'm sorry, Leila. I forgot I had a work lunch scheduled."

"Oh," she said. "No problem. I'll have Marie all to myself."

"No," I said. "I made our Pilates date before I set the lunch meeting. Cameron, do you mind if I reschedule?"

"But Kara, work should come first," Leila said.

"It's not an important meeting," I explained, with a hard stare directed at Cameron.

Cameron, miraculously, took the hint. "I'll call you to reschedule," he said as he got on his bike. I couldn't tell if he was angry or hurt or, most likely, glad to be rid of me.

Leila, sensing the awkwardness, apologized to me for the mix-up. "It's not a problem," I said. "He's just a new assistant at some agency who wants to meet all the development execs. I was looking for a way out of the lunch anyway. You saved me from an hour of boredom."

"In that case," Leila said, accepting my rationale, "let's go get fit."

•

Leila's Brentwood Pilates studio was ground zero of her social life. Walking from one end of the studio to another with her was like leafing through Tehrangeles' society pages. The space was more than just a Pilates Studio. There was a Zen meditation room, four massage rooms, a personal training room, a yoga studio, and an herb and tonic bar. I wasn't sure why the Persian ladies chose this particular gym as their own. I always suspected Leila was the ringleader of the gang. I imagined that years ago, Leila had gone on a tour of Los Angeles and decided which establishments she approved of. Following her lead, all her friends agreed to make those the epicenters of their shared existence. In truth, it was probably a more natural evolution. The girls and I also frequented the same bars and restaurants over and over again, but I couldn't say why. Habit and consistency seem to insert themselves into life, whether you ask for them or not. By this point, I knew everyone in Leila's gym as well as she did, though I never said much more than a hello to them. I just watched as Leila expertly maneuvered herself past a slew of her Persian friends and an array of toned fitness instructors. "Bree, have you lost more weight?" she might say to one of the yoga teachers, or "Linda, I love your new highlights" to the front desk girl. The conversations usually stuck to this safe territory, unless one of the Persian ladies had news to share, which this time Tanaz Maliki did.

"Did you hear?" Tanaz screamed our way as she was being stretched on a mat.

"Hello, Tanaz *djoon*," Leila said, ignoring the urgency of her greeting.

"Did you hear?" Tanaz repeated, gasping for air as her leg was being yanked over her face with the help of her buxom trainer.

"Hear what?" Leila asked coolly.

"Hello, Mrs. Maliki," I snuck in.

"Tina and Cyrus have finally set a date. The twelfth of June. My birthday. They're going to be married on my birthday. Isn't that the best gift you can imagine?"

"That's vonderful," Leila uttered, her face frozen in an exaggerated smile.

Tanaz looked up to her trainer from between her legs. "My daughter Tina is marrying a stockbroker. He's descended from the Qajars."

"Cool." The trainer's nonchalant reaction made it clear that she either wasn't familiar with, or was unimpressed by, the Qajars.

"You know whose turn it is next?" Tanaz huffed.

I blushed. The answer was implicit. I knew how badly Leila wished she had pre-empted this news with her own, how badly she wished Bobby and I would finally let her plan the wedding of our dreams. And even then, Bobby wouldn't be marrying some princess descended from the Qajars or the Pahlavis or any royal lineage. He'd be marrying Kara Walker from Thousand Oaks, whose mother was a third-tier real estate agent and whose father was a beach bum. I wanted so badly to make Leila happy that I almost announced my engagement right then. But, of course, I just stood there.

"Tina and Cyrus want a small wedding in New York, but I said *abada*. She is my only daughter. I'm not letting her get married in New York, in some small apartment with a dozen people crammed inside. I want to do it in Greece. It's close enough to Iran that all our relatives can come. What do you think, Leila?"

"Greece in June is beautiful," Leila said. "Although we're all going to Cannes in July. Wouldn't it make more sense to do it then?"

"No. June twelfth was the only date that worked for Tina and Cyrus's work schedules. They're very busy these days. I hope Bobby isn't working that week," Tanaz added devilishly. "We want him there. And you of course, Kara *djoon*." Amazing how Tanaz took a term of endearment and made it sound like an insult.

Leila grabbed my hand and led me toward the Pilates room. "Such good news," she whispered. "Now it really is your turn, Kara. You're turning thirty. Did Hossein talk to you about selling the duplex? He said you can get three times as much as you paid for it."

"Leila," I reasoned. "I didn't pay for it."

"You know what I mean. Just don't let Hossein convince you to move into Koorosh's new development. It's horribly *parvenu*."

"It's really up to Bobby," I said, fully aware that Leila and Hossein were tag-teaming me because they supposed I had more power over Bobby than they did.

"Bobby dreads change. He has to learn that change can be a good thing. Talk to him. You're turning thirty," she reminded me again. Leila suddenly laughed at herself. "I'm sorry," she said. "I'm being an old nag. I hate pushy mothers. Don't let me become one."

"You?" I asked incredulously. "Never."

Leila looked up and saw Marie, our stunning twenty-three-year-old Pilates instructor. "Marie," she chirped. "I want your body by the end of the session."

"Tina dareh doh mah digeh aroosi mikoneh," Leila announced to Hossein over dinner. With the routine of accepting invitations to Bobby's family dinners came spending a good part of the evening listening to a language I didn't understand. They made herculean efforts to include me, but Leila and Hossein couldn't be faulted too much for the fact they couldn't go five minutes at the dinner table without reverting to Farsi. Sometimes Leila would throw in a little French, but that didn't help a lot. Just brought back Jacques, and I hardly ever understood the language when he talked, anyway.

I looked at Bobby and smiled. "I'm deducing from the presence of the name Tina that your mother just announced Tina Maliki's wedding date."

"Very good," Bobby said. "You'll be bilingual yet."

"Where is it going to be?" Hossein asked.

"Greece," I said. "June twelfth. Tanaz wanted a destination wedding that was close to Iran, so all the relatives could be there. Oh, and does everyone know that Cyrus is descended from the Qajars?"

Leila and Hossein laughed. Apparently, I was allowed to mock Tanaz, even if they weren't.

"So..." Leila said to Bobby. "Tanaz wants to know if you'll be there."

"Do I have to decide now?"

"We have to book tickets, and the good hotels will fill up. Santorini isn't that big," Leila pointed out.

"Okay, then no."

"No?" Leila echoed. "You and Tina grew up together. You were born in the same hospital in Tehran almost thirty years ago. You went to the same schools until you were fourteen years old. You're not going to go to her wedding?"

"Tell her I have to work."

"Everyone knows you don't have to work, Babak." This was Hossein, piping in on his favorite subject. "But maybe if you took that real estate position, it could give you a good excuse to skip the wedding."

"Except that everyone who works for Koorosh Ebrahimi will be at the wedding," Leila commented. "I don't see why you wouldn't want to come. It's springtime in Greece. We're paying for it. Kara wants to go. Don't you, Kara?"

"I've never been to Greece." It was as noncommittal an answer as I could give. On the one hand, the thrill of seeing a new country lured me. On the other, the thought of dealing with the magnified anxiety Bobby would be feeling on this trip made me apprehensive.

"I'll think about it," Bobby said. "I just don't enjoy weddings."

"I don't either," Hossein said. "It's the same thing every time. I gain weight eating all that food and cake and listening to silly toasts and the same music. But it makes women happy. That's why you go, Babak. Not for you."

"That's right," Leila added, "you go so that Kara can have fun."

"Yes, *mother*," Bobby said, *mother* being the inverse of *dude*, the word he uses when Leila is an enemy and not a friend. "I am well versed in the art of making sacrifices for others."

An interminable silence followed, during which the only audible sounds were the mashing of the rice and *khoresht* in our mouths and Rosa Maria humming next door in the kitchen.

"Have you been working out more, Babak?" Hossein finally asked.

"I guess."

"It's not nice to be too big. You will look like one of those football players."

"Am I too big?" Bobby wondered aloud.

"I don't know how young men these days are getting so big. Back in Iran, when we were kids, we used to play all day," Hossein continued. "Active sports. Every day. Before school, we were playing football in the streets. Not American football. Soccer."

I felt my phone vibrate in my purse. I covertly peeked. It was a text from Bobby. I looked over and noticed he had both hands under the table. The text read, "I've gotten this speech three times already. This year."

I lost a little of what Hossein said, but picked it back up at "And we were in shape, of course. But we didn't have these massive muscles. I don't know, I think there's something unhealthy. Maybe it's these powders and steroids, or maybe it's hormones in the food. In the paper, they were saying some girls are having their puberty as early as their seventh year. Something is wrong."

"I agree," I said. "We're so obsessed with being fat-free and sugar-free that we've been eating all these chemicals and taking all these pills that are screwing with our bodies."

Bobby glared at me. As an avid pill-popper, he must have thought I was ganging up on him with his dad. "Then again," Bobby argued, "Life expectancy is longer than ever, and maybe that's also due to all these pills." "We'll see," Hossein said.

"We're not all like you," Bobby continued. "You don't even take an Advil when you have a headache."

"It's bad for you," Hossein said.

"Well, I don't care if it's bad," Bobby said. "If people are in pain, why shouldn't they take a pill? If people want their muscles to look bigger, why shouldn't they take a pill?"

"Because," Hossein said, raising his voice just a touch, "what happens to people who have your mentality is that they always look for the shortcut. They don't know how to work for something. And what happens when a whole society thinks like you is that the society eventually loses all of its value."

"Now you're just being a reactionary again, Hossein," Leila interjected. "You can take some pills. I take something when I have a headache."

"And look at you," he said. "You haven't worked a day in your life. You don't do anything."

That one stopped the room cold. "That's unfair," Bobby said after a thoughtful silence. "You can argue that I don't do anything, but *this* dude does a lot." Leila smiled at him. "She keeps the house in perfect order, she serves on the boards of all kinds of charities, she raised me."

"With the help of a nanny," Leila added, desperate to lighten the mood. "Elena handled the diapers and the cooking." Then she added, with a gleam in her eye, "but I supervised masterfully."

"Fine," Hossein said with a laugh. "Your mother is off the hook."

My phone vibrated again. I turned to Bobby and saw him texting me again. I mouthed for him to stop it, but I still couldn't resist looking at the phone. "He's gonna ask me if I'm making any money next," it read.

"But you," Hossein continued. "You're a man. You should be taking care of yourself by now. Don't they pay you when your movie replays on television?"

Bobby and I giggled. We couldn't help it.

"What? What is it?" Leila asked.

"Nothing," Bobby said. "Sorry. Yes, they do pay me. They send me a residual check every quarter."

"For how much?" he asked.

"Not enough for me to give back your credit card," was all Bobby would give.

"Is the food too salty? Rosa Maria has a heavy hand with the salt." Leila was desperate for a change in conversation.

There was more silence. Rosa Maria had turned on the television in the kitchen. The sound of the news drifted into the dining room. Something about the latest polls in Iran showing a drop in Ahmadinejad's popularity.

"Idiot," Hossein suddenly blurted out. "We should have bombed them. And we still should."

"Dad!" Bobby bellowed incredulously, giving me a glimpse of what he must have sounded like as a six-year-old.

"The people of Iran are educated. Sixty percent of students are women, even with lunatics like him running the place. The country was prepared for democracy in a way Iraq is not," Hossein explained.

"Kara, I love your lipstick," Leila commented.

"All fundamentalists should be killed," Hossein continued. "Then maybe we can finally have peace."

Leila ended the conversation by handing me a gift-wrapped box.

"Leila, seriously, another gift?"

"This one is nothing. It's just something to complement Bobby's gift."

"You guys are too much," I said.

"No such thing," Bobby joked. "At least not in this family."

I opened the box and found a designer dog collar, black leather with Swarovski crystals studding it beautifully. It was a great present, because it made clear that Bobby was getting me a dog, pretty much what I had wanted for the past nine years, except I had been too much of a coward to go out and just get myself one. I had this obsession with Shiba Inus ever since I met Jacques's little Shiba, named after the French singer who drank himself to an early death. Shibas are the most amazing dogs, loyal and low-maintenance, compact without looking like they belong in Paris Hilton's purse, and they have the most incredible, reddish double coat. Jacques told me that in World War II, Shibas almost went extinct during Allied bombing raids. Yeah, it didn't make any sense to me, either. We could take out thousands of eighteen-pound canines in Japan, but Qaddafi and Bin Laden were still kicking. Still, that bit of lore in and of itself made me love the little dogs. I had quietly nurtured the obsession through the years, and every time I saw someone hiking with his or her Shiba through Runyon Canyon, I shocked that person with my immense knowledge of the breed.

"Thank you," I said, as I kissed Leila on both cheeks, Hossein on both cheeks, and gave Bobby a hug. "This is really thoughtful."

"Your present from me should have been here by now," Bobby said. "It could only be delivered today, and I didn't think it was right to keep her from you for forty-eight hours."

"And your real present from us is coming soon, too," Leila added. "We'll go shopping on your birthday after lunch, so we can select something for you to wear yourself."

"But you just gave me so many of your beautiful things."

"Kara *djoon*, that was two weeks ago, and it was *Nowruz*. Do you really think I'm going to give my future daughter-in-law secondhand clothing and a *dog* collar for her thirtieth birthday?" Leila pronounced the word *dog* as if it was the most distasteful noun in the English language. I knew from watching her distance herself from many hounds on the streets of Beverly Hills that she was not a canine lover, which only made her gift to me all the more moving.

Once dinner was over, Rosa Maria led me into her room. She had finally gotten time to sew the amethyst back onto the green Prada flat that Leila had given me for *Nowruz*. I followed Rosa Maria into the maid's quarters, a far cry from the rest of the house with its standard cream carpet and its faded blue wallpaper. There was a television, at least, but not a high-definition plasma like in the other rooms in the house. This one was an old Magnavox, no doubt top of the line when purchased. By the side of the single bed was *Cien años de soledad,* with a bookmark near the middle. Rosa Maria and I developed a bond when I was nineteen. That summer, she pulled me into her room and said she wanted to show me something secret. On her television, she played a series of home movies of the Ebadis barely post-revolution life, grainy images of a family in their first years in America. There on the screen was Hossein with a full head of black hair, Leila in flare pants, and most striking, two brothers innocently swimming, playing tennis, lunging onto their Slip 'N Slide, and doing impressions of He-Man. Rosa Maria told me that Leila had asked Elena to take the videos with her when she quit working for the Ebadis. But Elena had opted to store them in the maid's quarters, now occupied by her cousin Rosa Maria.

"It is crazy," Rosa Maria had said at the time. "They never talk about him. Never." The lady had a point. In the many years I had spent with the Ebadis, Keyvan came up a total of four times. I had counted. Once, it was because I asked if that was Keyvan in the photograph in the living room, to which Leila curtly replied, "Yes," and moved on to another topic. The second time, it was because Leila was in the process of redecorating one of the guest rooms, and she mentioned in passing that this was Keyvan's old room. And the third time was at a card night at the Ebadis, just as the second U.S.-Iraq war began. One of the Persian men told Hossein what a waste war was, that more men like Keyvan would be lost. What a shame, the man said, that Keyvan had to go visit his grandmother in Tehran. If he had stayed home, he never would have been drafted, never would have fought in the Iran-Iraq War. Hossein had grunted and poured himself a Glenlivet. The most recent, and fourth time, was Hossein's aside that Bobby was the only son he had left.

"Hey, what are you doing in here?" Bobby's head peeked into the room.

"Just picking up the shoe your mother gave me. Rosa Maria fixed it. Fierce, right?"

"Very cute," he said. "Come on, I need a cigarette." Bobby smoked once a month, when the stress of life became too much for him and he needed the release of playing Bette Davis for a few minutes.

"So what's wrong?" I asked Bobby as he sucked down one of the Marlboro Lights his mother hid in her dresser for the rare occasion when she herself smoked. We were circling the illuminated pool, and Bobby seemed ready to plunge in and drown himself. "You don't seem to be doing fabsolutely abulous."

"I feel yucking fucky."

This thing of changing around the consonants of words had started when

Bobby was researching something called the jumbled-word effect. When he wasn't working out or waiting for his next online hook-up, Bobby researched new topics online. He would just pick random subjects from Wikipedia. He thought it would lead to inspiration for a new screenplay. I thought it was another form of procrastination, but it did make him a really fascinating source of useless and dubious information. He also had a near-photographic memory, so he actually remembered all the research he'd done on snake venom, Madame de Pompadour, the Basilosaurus, and the bubonic plague. Anyway, a few years ago, he was doing research on psychology and words and found this site about the jumbled-word effect. Aoccdrnig to rscheearch at Cmabrigde Uinervtisy, it deosn't mttaer in waht oredr the ltteers in a wrod are anrrgaed, it olny mtaters taht the frist and lsat ltteer be in the rghit pclae. The rset can be a toatl mses and you can sitll raed it wouthit a porbelm. Tihs is bcuseae the huamn brian deos not raed ervey lteter by istlef, but the wrod as a wlohe. Bobby loved it because it reminded him of Farsi, which omitted vowels in written form unless they began or ended the word, forcing the reader to deduce the word based on context. Joanne once noted how Hebrew worked the same way. I sensed an important connection there, maybe one that could solve major international problems, but I never did work out what it was.

Bobby wondered if Americans could re-adjust to this form of reading. He tstd me wth a fw smple sntencs. At first, Bobby and I decided we would speak without vowels as a nod to his native tongue, but that was a disaster. Then we tried to speak in jumbled words to see if the effect could work aurally as well as visually, but that was a catastrophe, as well. Somehow, we settled for just swapping the first letters of different words. Like almost everything else about my friendship with Bobby, its real effect was making us feel special and important for a completely silly and self-generated reason.

"What's wrong?" I asked again, my tone more serious this time.

"Nothing." Bobby waited for a tense beat, then continued. "I think I might have a staph infection."

"What?"

"I went to the gym today, and the steam room was closed. Apparently staph infections are very easy to get in moist environments like steam rooms."

"So?" I asked.

"Well, the steam room was probably closed because there was an outbreak of staph."

"Bobby, they were probably just doing maintenance on it."

"There were no workers there," he said vehemently.

"Maybe the steam jets broke down, and they were waiting for the technicians."

"Or maybe I'm gonna die." He somehow said this with a straight face.

"Bobby, I can assure you that one day you will die, but I can also assure you you're not dropping dead of a staph infection this week. I'm not letting you miss my thirtieth birthday."

"I guess you have a point. The cosmos wouldn't let me overshadow your big day, would they?" he asked melodramatically.

"Do you have any symptoms?" I asked. From the window of the home, I could see Hossein settling into the golf game he had recorded, and Leila placing some fruit in front of him for dessert. Did they have any idea what their distraught son was working himself up about just a few yards away? "Staph infections are becoming untreatable," Bobby continued. "They're deadly. Now I can't go into steam rooms anymore."

No steam rooms, no uncircumcised men—Bobby's options were slimming rapidly. Of course, all limitations would be forgotten as soon as this wave of paranoia passed with the aid of homeopathy.

When Bobby first told me that men jerked each other off in the steam room of my gym, I have to confess, I was a little shocked. We women didn't have that option. I guess if we were lesbians, then we could have fingered each other after a workout, but I just didn't think it was in our nature. At least, not in my nature. I was what could have been categorized as a doomed romantic. I lived for those epic movies where two lovers just couldn't be together. Girl meets boy. Girl loses boy. Girl never recovers. *The Way We Were, The Umbrellas of Cherbourg, Gone with the Wind, Alien.* I saw *Cold Mountain* five times, not counting the DVD. Nothing was more romantic to me than two lovers being torn apart. Jerking off in a steam room couldn't compare to that, so maybe it was a good thing we ladies didn't have that choice. Straight men didn't have the option of sex in the steam room, either, but that was as it should have been, because straight men had every other possible advantage. They had to work for *something* in their lives. Gay men, when it was all said and done, had it easy when it came to sex. Gay sex was pretty damn available, like Starbucks. A gay man could reliably find sex on every corner and know what it was gonna taste like. Sex for straight girls was a little more like Mr. Chow. There might be a cluster around the world, but you usually couldn't get a table unless you were a model.

"We're getting old. We're almost thirty," Bobby continued. "What's to become of us?"

"At least you're a guy. Age is like denim. It looks better on men."

"I'm gonna age twice as fast. If the staph infection doesn't kill me, the anxiety will."

"I lied to the treadmill," I told Bobby. "Remember that day I was running next to Hot Tattooed Guy? I had to punch in my age, and I lied. To a machine."

"And you're afraid you've betrayed the trust you established with Life-Tread through all that pounding?"

"Something about a thirty-year-old woman lying about her age and her weight, to a device, to snag some model-actor-waiter... It's beyond pathetic. And then to be ignored by him anyway... God, that's really rubbing salt into the wound. I did something Joanne might do, and even she wouldn't confess to it without a few drinks."

"Relax, Kara," Bobby reasoned, his mood markedly improved by focusing on my problems rather than his. "It's not like you opened someone's mail or broke into someone's house. It's a victimless crime. Do you know how many times I've lied about my age online? Big deal. Sometimes I'll say I'm twenty-one. It turns guys on. It doesn't hurt them. Sometimes if I meet some kid who has a daddy thing, I'll say I'm forty. Age ain't nothin' but a numbah, as the deceased sage Aaliyah once said."

"You're right," I said. "It's just so desperate. I don't want to turn into Joanne."

"There is little danger of that," he assured me.

"You don't know what it's like. Having this example of someone you're desperately afraid of turning into staring you in the face every day."

Bobby dipped his hand into the pool and splashed some water on my face. "I wonder how much it costs to keep this thing heated all the time." With a sigh, he added, "How do people make money, anyway? How did my dad do it? I can't figure it out. I just know how to spend it." The doorbell rang, and Bobby immediately perked up. "It's your gift!" he exclaimed. "Come on!"

We rushed inside to greet an extremely tall Chinese woman holding a brown box.

"Kara, come meet your birthday present," he said. Finally, the love of my life had arrived. My very own Shiba Inu.

"Kara, this is Gong," Bobby announced. "Gong, this is Kara. And those are my parents, Hossein and Leila." The Ebadis had materialized by the front staircase, anxiously awaiting the arrival of the family's new addition.

I reached out to shake Gong's hand, which was stupid, since she was holding the box. She was looking down into it, too.

"I think she's still asleep. Do you want me to wake her up?"

"Gong's a breeder in San Diego."

"A breeder?" Breeder to me meant one thing. It meant evil money-grubbing people who made a profit off of innocent pets when millions of unwanted animals were killed in shelters every year. Even worse, some breeders abandoned the runts of their litters. Could you imagine someone breeding babies and abandoning the ones that couldn't sell because they had a harelip?

"I totally arranged for it to be fully returnable if you don't like it." Bobby never had a pet. He claimed he wanted one as a kid, but Leila wouldn't allow it because of her white carpets. As a result, he didn't really understand animal activism. He didn't get that the concept of returning a pet is a little offensive, kind of like deciding your baby is cross-eyed and asking for store credit.

I opened the box, excitement and trepidation filling my body. I could actually feel my heart beating fast and my palms sweating, which could just be a bout of hyperthyroidism, but more likely than not was anticipation about finally meeting my beloved Shiba. I lifted up the brown flaps of the box, and there she was, my new *Shih Tzu*.

"What? What is it?" Bobby asked. "Kara, say something."

"This isn't a Shiba Inu."

"I thought you said Shih Tzu."

"I would never say I wanted a Shih Tzu."

"What's wrong with Shih Tzus?" Gong asked with venom in her eyes. "The Shih Tzu was the favorite pet of the Chinese Imperial Court."

I didn't know what to say to that. I could have given her the whole spiel about Shibas and WWII, but I remembered that China and Japan weren't exactly allies in that conflict, so starting a dog war between the two countries hardly seemed constructive. "It's just a bit of a Paris Hilton dog," I said.

"What does that mean?" Gong was possibly a fan of Paris, but there was no question she was not a fan of mine.

"You know, it's fluffy and white and girly."

"I don't know much about dogs, but I think she's very cute," Leila piped in.

"Shih Tzus wheeze, don't they? Don't they snore? I have sleep problems."

Gong looked disgusted. She took a breath and headed out. I couldn't do it. I couldn't send an innocent dog back to a humorless breeder so it could end up wheezing and snoring in some ratty shelter. That had to be terrible karma. And the last thing I needed was shoddier karma.

"Stop," I yelled. "I want the dog."

Gong didn't want to surrender the animal anymore. She went on a rant about dog owners needing to be responsible and loving, which was a really low blow, particularly for a breeder. I took the white fluffy Shih Tzu in my arms and showed the bitch just how loving I could be.

Once Gong was gone, I held the Shih Tzu in my arms and ascended the Ebadis' marble staircase like Joan Crawford holding the infant Christina in *Mommie Dearest*, which Bobby had made me see about a hundred times. The dog was wheezing in my arms, her tail planted firmly between her legs and her ears pulled back. Her bug eyes were the final sign I needed that she was scared shitless to be in the arms of some strange woman.

"What are you going to call her?" Leila asked.

"How about Christina?" Bobby suggested, somehow reading my mind.

"Christina?" Hossein repeated. "Why?"

"I could give her one of those ridiculous Hollywood names. Like Apple or Audio Science."

"Somebody named their dog Audio Science?" Leila asked.

"No, dude," Bobby corrected. "Somebody named their *child* Audio Science."

"Can I put her down?" I figured I needed permission, white carpets and all.

"Will she go to the bathroom in the house?" Leila asked.

"Probably," Bobby answered.

Leila considered the question for a long time, and finally agreed. "Poor Rosa Maria. It's hard enough cleaning after Hossein. Now she's going to have to clean up after this little beast, as well."

I put the little beast down on the marble staircase. At first, she didn't move. She just bobbed her head from one side to another, assessing every nook and cranny of the Ebadi home. She reminded me of myself the first time I visited Bobby's house, a wide-eyed fourteen-year-old amazed at the beauty of everything. "I know," I told her. "It's pretty astounding the first time you see it. I especially like that Qajar painting over there." I directed the puppy's face to a painting hanging in the foyer: two bare-breasted women holding pomegranates to conceal their pert bosoms.

The Shih Tzu finally took a step down the stairs, and all of us instinctively gasped, wondering what she would do next. She took one baby step after another, down the steps and directly toward Leila. She sat down in front of Leila, let her tongue fall out of her mouth, and gazed at her with large, desperate eyes. Dogs are pack animals, and this dog had observed the room and cunningly intuited that Leila was the leader of this pack. "I love her," Leila suddenly decided, as if she had always loved animals. "She needs a Persian name."

"How about Tanaz?" Bobby joked. But he got glares from Leila and Hossein. Apparently, unlike me, he wasn't allowed to mock their friends, even if it was playful mockery.

"She should be named after a great poet. Hafez or Rumi or Omar Khayyam."

"But she's a girl," Hossein protested.

"So?" Leila said. "It's a dog. They're going to cut out her sex organs anyway. Who cares if she's a boy or a girl? I like Omar Khayyam." Leila bent down and picked up the dog. "Omar!" she squealed louder than I had ever heard her before. "Is that your name? Omar!" The little dog licked Leila's face. "It's like a free facial," Leila joked as Omar licked her face over and over again.

"She can taste the *gheymeh bademjoon* on your lips, dude," Bobby commented.

"That's disgusting," Leila said, before making sure the naming was final.

"So, is her name officially Omar Khayyam?"

Hossein approved of the name and retired to his golf game. Bobby nodded his endorsement. I wanted to correct Leila and tell her the dog's name should be Omar Ebadi. After all, she was clearly Leila's grandchild.

4

I HAD A DATE with Cameron on Saturday night. I couldn't believe he'd agree to see me again after the way I treated him in front of Leila. "You see," I explained to him over the phone, "I'm kind of my gay best friend's beard. He comes from a Middle Eastern family, and they just choose to believe that I'm his girlfriend." Cameron didn't give me the luxury of a response. "It's not like I'm really with him. I'm single. Available. In fact, I'm free all weekend. And Monday is my birthday, so this weekend is your last chance to date me in my twenties, because when I turn thirty, I might shrivel up or something. But if you have a problem with the fact that I have a fake gay boyfriend or the fact that I acted like a complete bitch in front of his mother, then just say so, and I will understand and have no hard feelings." When he finally, mercifully spoke, he asked if I wanted to have Sunday brunch. He didn't sound bothered at all by any of that screed.

Brunch turned out to be a picnic in Griffith Park. Cameron packed a canvas bag full of treats from Whole Foods. Soy crisps. Coconut-covered dates. Tacos. Chardonnay. He even brought two plastic glasses with stems that didn't snap in. I was impressed. "I don't know how Bobby survived college in New York. There's no good Mexican there," I said as I bit into my second taco.

We had already completed the requisite small talk about ourselves, and somehow I had veered into making small talk on behalf of Bobby and the Ebadis. Cameron was from Portland, the one in Oregon. He got a law degree from Berkeley, but decided he really wanted to be an actor, and law was just a way to appease his father. Apparently, he spent a summer during law school in Rio, learning how to play the bongos. As far as I knew, law students were absolutely required to spend their summers doing boring internships in big skyscrapers. Going to Rio for bongo lessons is pretty much as rebellious as a white kid from Portland can get, and I love a good rebel. He had only been in L.A. six months, which meant he didn't regret his decision yet. He was full of hope, such an overrated commodity. "And Bobby loves Mexican," I continued. "He always says if he could take one cuisine to a desert island with him, it would be Mexican. Mine would be Persian. The food at his house is out of this world. His mother doesn't cook, but she trains her Mexican housekeepers with such specificity, you would think they had studied Persian cuisine all their life. Their home smells so delicious. I swear if I could patent a perfume, it would be Eau de Iran. It would smell like stew. That sounds gross, but it's not."

The dream date ended on my front stoop. The *Los Angeles Times* rested comfortably on Bobby's welcome mat. I snickered when I saw it.

"What's the smile about?" Cameron wondered.

"Nothing. I'm just happy."

"You looked down at the doorstep and laughed."

"It's just that when Bobby puts the *L.A. Times* out there, it means he's having sex."

"Are you telling me there's sodomy going on behind them doors?" Cameron said, faking a Texas accent.

"Maybe. Or at the very least, some oral and water sports." He was taken aback. "I'm sorry. That crossed a line, didn't it? I spend too much time around Bobby. I have no self-censor."

Cameron leaned in to give me a sweet kiss. From the instant that his lips pressed against mine, I began to believe that I might be able to forget about Jacques after all. I was also thinking of how satisfying it would be to tell Fiona that my romantic life was being in no way inhibited by my deep, meaningful, and mutual commitment with the Ebadi household.

Why had I subjected myself to celibacy, I wondered silently, when the feel of a man against me made me safe, intimate, connected? The "Gimme More" ringtone issued from my purse. I pulled out the cell and glanced at it.

"Are you gonna answer it?" Cameron asked.

"Private number," I replied. "Telemarketers have started calling cell phones. Nobody's safe from them anymore."

Cameron took me in his arms. "I'll protect you," he whispered, and then kissed me again. As I allowed myself to fall into his embrace, Bobby's cell phone rang out through his open window. The same hook. We thought matching ringtones made us cute, but I could tell Cameron found it bizarre. Seconds later, my phone rang again. Cameron pulled away. "What if it's not a telemarketer? It could be important."

I answered the phone. "Kara, *djoon*," the voice purred. Definitely not a telemarketer. "I'm sorry to call you from another number. I know you young people like to screen your calls. But I don't have reception here, and I had to call you."

Cameron kissed my neck as Leila spoke. I shooed him away.

"Kara, are you in the middle of something?"

"Kind of. I'm reading a script Janet needs to answer on tomorrow. Can I call you back as soon as I'm done?"

"It will just take a moment, really, and I need your help now," she said. "I need a second opinion on a house, and I can't reach Hossein or Babak."

"A house?"

"Farideh Feresht has a new listing just today in Beverly Hills. It's not perfect, but it's workable. I'm already here with at least a dozen other potential buyers."

"Well, sure. I can come look at it for you. I love open houses."

"And please bring Babak, if you can find him?" I could faintly hear the sounds of a creaking bed behind Bobby's door. Leila rattled off a Roxbury address and hung up.

I kissed Cameron once more. "I have to go," I said. "Leila's looking at some house in Beverly Hills, and she wants a second opinion."

Cameron laughed. "You really are a member of their family, aren't you? You barely mentioned your own parents all day."

"Harry and Pa?" I countered. "They're not interesting."

"You have two fathers? That explains a—"

"No, my mom's named Harriet."

"Oh. Well, I bet they're interesting. They must be. They created you." After one more kiss, Cameron got on his bike and disappeared down the street.

I immediately put on a presentable outfit and went to our front walk. A bodybuilder type exited Bobby's lair wearing cargo shorts and pulling on a tank top. As he got into his Hyundai, I couldn't help but notice a familiar sign on his license frame. *I Got It At Hyundai North Hollywood.* The thought of Hossein selling Bobby's latest conquest a car made me smile.

"Your mother's been looking for you," I announced as I entered.

"She should know better than to incessantly call me mid-trick," he joked as he emerged shirtless in jeans, sucking on a cough drop and drinking some Kombucha, his latest healing discovery. "Did you see the body on that guy?" Bobby asked.

"She wants us at some house on Roxbury asap. I didn't even realize she wanted to move. They've been in that house for so long."

"Do you think he was on steroids? A lot of positive guys are on steroids to combat wasting away. It's strangely poetic," Bobby mused, "that the ill used to be emaciated and thin, and now they're the most buff of us all."

"Fascinating. Get dressed. It's a Leila order."

Bobby shrugged and threw on a shirt. "I hope they don't move to Beverly Hills. It's too manicured. And I hate that sign that says *Welcome to Beverly Hills, Sister City of Cannes*. I mean, how pretentiously horrible is that?"

Ten minutes later, Bobby's car zipped by that very sign. *Sister City of Cannes*. There was something hysterical about it, especially since so many denizens of Beverly Hills spent much of their summers in Cannes. I wondered if West Hollywood had a sister city. Perhaps Provincetown or some other gay enclave. Then again, why did sister cities have to be alike, anyway? Most siblings I knew were wildly different, each fulfilling a different role in the family structure. Harry's brother was an explorer who spent most of his time trekking through mountains. Last we had heard from him, he had sequestered himself in a tent in Peru, his nomadic ways a direct contrast to Harry's immobility. Fiona's brother was a corporate lawyer in Tempe, Arizona, a button-down personality as far removed from Fiona's passionate and artistic temperament as possible. I often wondered how I might have turned out had I had a sibling. Would I have been drastically different, shifting my persona in opposition to my genetic match?

It seemed to take three minutes to get from the gate of the Roxbury house to the front door—that's how long the paved driveway was. Outside the house was a stack of glossy color pamphlets with photos and information about the "estate property." *Le Manoir*. The photos didn't do justice to the imposing structure of the house, built in 1929, with its thick white shell and its beveled rustic roof tile. My eyes immediately fell on the asking price: "On Request." That meant three million, minimum. On the back of the pamphlet was a picture of Farideh Feresht, Moh's mother, who had entered into the world of real estate sales when her husband died of liver cancer and she had too much time on her hands. Now she was one of Los Angeles's premier agents, helped along by the fact that her social set was obsessed with shopping at all levels, especially for land. The photo had been absurdly retouched, making Farideh three skin tones lighter and a good twenty years younger.

"There they are," Farideh said when she saw us. She approached and gave us each kisses. "Come in, have some champagne. Look around." The twilight showing was more like a party than an open house. Behind the bar, a guy in a white shirt and bowtie was mixing drinks. On the massive patio, a band was playing instrumental versions of Piaf standards. A buffet of bite-size sandwiches and *patisseries* rested in the enormous kitchen that gleamed with its black granite and stainless steel. Clearly, this house was meant to appeal to the demographic that takes pride in calling Cannes their sister city.

"It's not perfect," was the first thing Leila said to us, loud enough for Farideh and all the other potential buyers to hear. Leila was an expert at bargaining, be the object a multi-million dollar home or a five-dollar trinket. I had witnessed this in Juan Les Pins that one summer we spent in the south of France, when Leila had managed to dicker every street dealer down to half his or her asking price for anklets, shawls, and dancing flowers. Yes, she bought the dancing flowers and gifted them to her former housekeeper Elena's children. "For one thing, there's no cell reception up here," Leila said, "which could change as they build more towers, but it's a serious problem for the moment." Leila led us into the guest bathroom in the foyer. "For another, the bathrooms need to be gutted, except for the master, which was tolerably redone." I didn't see why this bathroom needed to be gutted. It was clean and tasteful, with laminated pink and gold wallpaper flanking a porcelain and gold sink. But far be it from me to argue with Leila. "And of course, there's the air conditioning issue."

"The house doesn't have A/C," Farideh explained. "But the owners have contacted three companies and provided estimates. But why don't we talk about what the house *does* have? Four bedrooms, original jacaranda floors, a panoramic view, a beautifully landscaped half-acre, a stunning master suite with his-and-hers baths. And location, location, location."

An actress I recognized from one of those forensic shows on television approached Farideh, pretty husband by her side. "We'll definitely be in touch, Mrs. Feresht."

"Please, call me Farideh. And call me anytime." She was scribbling her home number on the back of her business card.

Leila looked at her no-bars cell phone to check the time. "Where is Hossein?" she whispered to herself. "I texted him an hour ago."

"Come on," Farideh ordered. "Let's see the rest of the house." One room at a time, she talked us through the place's many features. "Look at that beautiful sandstone fireplace, imported from Provence. Just smell the jasmines outside. The garden is full of them. And you can pick your own lemons, kumquats, and avocados from the trees in the upper garden. Organic is in. The curtains were all brought in from Amsterdam, and they stay. They're the same fabrics used in the Van Loon home, which is now a museum. The house is quiet, you can't hear street noise and nothing obstructs your view." Each room was more breathtaking than the last. It may have been called *Le Manoir,* but it felt more like a *palais.* Finally, Farideh led us to the master bedroom, which was indeed glorious and spacious, with beautiful blue wallpaper and sweeping city views. "I love this house," Farideh said. "I wish I could buy it for Moh, but of course Moh refuses to settle down. He seems to have a new girlfriend every week, if you can call them girlfriends." Farideh put her hand on Bobby's cheek. "I wish my son were more like you, Babak. Settled, happy."

I could almost feel the smile spreading across Leila's face. Was Farideh serious, or was complimenting Bobby a sales tactic? "Let me show you the lady's dressing room," Farideh said as she led us to a variation on Leila's own closet. The shelving layout was different, but the effect was the same. Enclosed white lacquer.

Bobby looked to Leila with a beaming smile. "This one's mine," he said. He ran his hands along a white shelf, memories clearly flooding his brain.

"Well, I don't know where Hossein is, and I don't care," Leila said. "I like the house. I think we should consider it. What do you think, Babak?"

Bobby shrugged for Farideh's benefit. "It's nice. It's pretty."

Leila turned to me. "And you, Kara?"

"It's gorgeous. But I don't see why you'd wanna move."

"I agree," Bobby added, glancing apologetically at Farideh. "It's so similar to your house, anyway, except yours is bigger and has air conditioning and cell-phone reception."

"But I guess if you want a change, or if you prefer Beverly Hills..." I trailed off, catching the confusion in Leila's face.

"Babak and Kara, Hossein and I have no interest in moving," Leila announced.

Bobby and I looked at each other, suddenly comprehending Leila's brilliant manipulation.

"Maybe we should let the couple discuss it alone," Farideh said, vocalizing a thought that would never have occurred to Leila, obviously viewing this as her decision as much as anybody's.

"Vonderful idea," Leila said. "I must have one of those éclairs, anyway."

"Wait," Bobby demanded. "Are you... are you suggesting you buy this house for us?"

"Of course I am," Leila responded. "Your father wants to move the two of you into some soulless new construction with doormen who invade everyone's privacy, some glorified hotel. It was my responsibility to find you something more charming." She turned to Farideh. "Architecture has a profound effect on a person's life."

I wanted to stop the madness and walk out of that suddenly claustrophobic white-lacquered box, but I found myself paralyzed and speechless. Leila had just raised the stakes to another level entirely. And suddenly it all became clear. Leila, with Hossein as her semi-witting accomplice, was on a mission to move us to the next step. Even the dog must have been her idea. Despite her aversion to pets, she must have suggested Bobby gift me the Shih Tzu. She probably read somewhere that dogs often prove to be harbingers of children, or that dogs bring couples closer together. Or that dogs need massive yards in Beverly Hills mansions in order to be happy.

Leila and Farideh disappeared, leaving Bobby and me in the closet. The silence between us lasted an eternity, or at least it felt like it did. We both were coming to the same realization. Leila and Hossein weren't offering us gifts. Their generosity wasn't just about designer clothes and designer dogs. What they were offering us was a lifestyle—*their* lifestyle. It was ours, whenever we were ready to accept. "Well," I finally said. "Are you still opposed to living in the manicured zip code?"

"I don't know. What do you think?" Bobby asked. He did his best to disguise the fact that the whole idea had a sudden appeal, now that he realized his mother was trying to hand him a house he'd have to write a dozen Formula-1 B-movies to afford.

I hardened my voice. "I think it's insane, Bobby. Living in separate sides of a duplex is one thing, but this is a completely different form of deception."

"In what way?"

"They'll expect us to share a bedroom, won't they?" We were whispering now.

"Who cares what they expect? There are four bedrooms in the house. You can pick whichever you want."

"And what about your hook-ups?" I asked.

"The house is huge. We won't get in your way. Just because the space is bigger and the zip code is different, doesn't mean anything has to change."

"But you hate Beverly Hills."

"I do." He laughed. "But it's a pretty fabulous house, isn't it?" He paused for a moment, and then added, "Maybe eventually, we all want to emulate our parents' lives."

"I don't." I took a breath. "I don't want to end up divorced like them. I don't want to end up single and lonely like my mother. I don't want to spend my adult years ogling younger lovers like my father. I don't want to be cheated on or lied to. I don't want to be my parents."

"And that's the beauty of what we have, Kara. You won't ever have to get divorced, because we won't be married. You won't be lonely, because I'll always be loyal to you. I'll never cheat on you, because we're not sleeping together to begin with. If you don't want to be your parents, then here's your chance. We can do things our way. Our rules."

"I guess you're right." I sighed. "It's just… it feels…" I was looking for the word. *Wrong. Deceitful.*

"We're best friends. We'll always be best friends. Oscar Wilde said something about friendship lasting longer than love. And he was right."

"The quote is 'Friendship is more *tragic* than love. It lasts longer,'" I said, impressed with myself.

"That's practically what I said. You and I will be friends forever. What's the difference where we live? Nothing is changing."

"I just… it's just…" I stammered. "I don't want your parents thinking we're going to get married next year. We can't let them push us further than we're willing to go."

Bobby took my hand in his. "Listen to me. We'll tell my parents the truth when it's right. When they're ready. And we've always agreed that if one of us meets someone, then we end things right then and there. I don't want to stand in the way of your happiness. I want to *make* you happy." The look on Bobby's face was so sincere that I couldn't help but be convinced.

We walked out of the closet and emerged down the marble staircase holding hands. Leila and Farideh awaited us anxiously. The other customers had all gone home, and the band was packing up their instruments. "Well?" Farideh asked.

"We love it," Bobby said.

I couldn't sleep that night. I tossed and turned, wondering whether accepting the house was stepping officially over the line. I wanted to call Fiona or Harry for advice, but I knew what both would say. Besides, was there any point in bearing the brunt of their judgment when escrow hadn't even closed? My apartment was bare but for Omar, and she was fast asleep. All the fun things to do were at Bobby's. The DVDs, the backgammon board. I did the only thing I knew how to do when feeling anxious. Eat. I opened the fridge, hoping for some tasty Chinese leftovers, maybe even some fruit and yogurt. The only foods in there were withered tomatoes and eggs. I could make myself a scramble. I took out the tomatoes and put them on the cutting board, but when my knife hit the mold, I knew the tomatoes were no longer an option. I could make some eggs but, like people, eggs are pretty dull when unaccompanied. I decided it was time to break into the earthquake stash of Trader Joe's enchiladas: green chile and roasted vegetables. I was a little natural-disaster-phobic, and so I'd prepared by storing bottled water, flashlights, a battery-operated radio, canned chickpeas, and the forgotten stacks of frozen enchiladas. There was a half-empty bottle of Grey Goose atop the enchiladas and one of those ice packs I use on my knees when I run too hard. I pulled out the top enchilada. There was a folded piece of white paper stuck underneath. As I tossed it toward the trash, it flew off course, landing on the Mexican tile. The winds of fate blew the fold of the paper open and revealed a handwritten note. I assumed it was Bobby making fun of earthquake preparedness, and picked it up with a smile.

"Kara. When you find this letter, I will be back in Paris. I know I have broken

*your heart and for that I apologize. I could have enjoyed our arrangement forever,
but I started to sense that you wanted more. You didn't seem able to keep what
we had fun and casual. Please don't contact me. A clean break is always best. Je
t'embrasse. Jacques."*

In stories we love irony, but in real life, it sucks. The fact that he put the
letter in a freezer had to mean something. Was it symbolic of our love freez-
ing over, or of his heart being an icebox? Who was I fooling, calling it love
when he referred to it as an *arrangement*? And why did I find the letter now?
After *a year and a half*? Why didn't I decide to nuke an enchilada the morning
I woke up and found he was gone? I had been depressed, I had been bed-rid-
den (Janet was very understanding about my need to take a week off work), I
had done nothing but eat. But no, I had to order Chinese every day; not once
did I crave a frozen green chile enchilada.

Omar decided to wake up at that very moment. Tears flowed uncontrollably from my eyes, and the dog seemed to think they were for her to drink. I
decided this was as good a time as any to become one of the crazy people who
pour their hearts out to their dogs.

"I don't understand, Omar Khayyam, did he not know me at all? Didn't
he understand that I never eat these enchiladas? Doesn't he know they're only
there for disaster purposes? And how could he ask me not to contact him?
Doesn't a letter like this just demand a reply?" The Shih Tzu wheezed a little. "Is that a yes? A no? You're one of the greatest mathematicians and poets
that ever lived. You must have more eloquent advice to offer than a snort." I
looked into Omar's eyes for a sign, and I could've sworn that in her wheezes
and grunts, she said, "Call him, Kara. It's nine hours ahead in Paris." And
that's just what I did. I pressed *67 so my number would be blocked, and then
I dialed the string of digits that were still embedded in my memory. I waited
anxiously, second-guessing my decision after every ring.

"Allo?" he said, in his beautiful sing-song.

"Who leaves a letter in a freezer? Who? Are you crazy?"

There was a brief silence on the other end of the line. I could hear street
sounds. Paris was waking up in the background. "Kara?" I almost melted
right then and there. I loved the way he said my name, with two flat As.

"Oui," I said with a laugh. Omar jumped into my arms. "You wanna hear
something funny? Bobby got me a Shih Tzu for my birthday, thinking he

was getting a Shiba. Now I have this girly little creature in my home. But I love her. Her name is Omar Khayyam."

"Named by your mother-in-law." I couldn't tell if he was being snide or just being French.

"She's not my mother-in-law," I said defensively.

"Not yet." There was a moment of silence, and then he announced that "Gainsbourg is gone."

"I'm so sorry," I said. "He was so young."

"He's not dead," Jacques said. "Unlike the Gainsbourg he was named after, he didn't drink himself to an early grave."

"So what happened?" I asked.

"He just ran away. After seven years of being my loyal companion, he decided he was done one day and snuck out through an open window. Apparently, it's very common for Shibas to leave their owners. They don't like to be tied down."

"Like father, like son," I replied with a sudden appreciation for Omar, who was nestled at my feet.

"Yes," he said. "There is symmetry to be found in life. But I *had* to run away."

"Because I couldn't keep our *arrangement* fun?"

Jacques laughed. "Is that what I said in the letter?"

"You want me to read it to you?" I offered.

"No. It's not necessary. I said what I had to say. The truth is I loved you very much."

"Oh, please," I said. "Don't humor me. You wanted something casual and meaningless, and I wanted more."

"You did want more, Kara. But you were too blind to see you couldn't have it. You were in a consuming relationship already."

"A faux relationship. I told you I would have a faux breakup with Bobby if need be. Bobby himself always offered to tell his parents our long romance was over. He's my friend. He never wants to stand in the way of my happiness."

"And neither did I. You were happier with him. I could tell. That's why I really left. No one wants the person they love to love someone else more. Call me old-fashioned." He paused. "So how does it feel to be turning thirty?" he asked.

"You remembered my birthday?" I was touched and flirtatious.

"Of course I remembered, Kara. I remember everything. I remember the Louvre and I remember the Trevi and I remember the way you smell in the morning and I remember how you hum in G flat when you kiss."

"I haven't kissed anyone in a year and a half," I suddenly announced. "You were the last. Is that pathetic?"

"It is a little sad," he said. "But you Americans are more puritanical than us. Perhaps celibacy is easier for you."

"It's not. I miss it. I miss human touch. I miss intimacy. I miss having an orgasm with someone else." Jacques laughed. "Don't laugh at me. I'm not even sure I know how to make love anymore. My body's frozen over, like that freezer you put your letter in."

"Then thaw it, Kara. Listen, I'm about to step into the Metro. I'm going to work. I'm designing wrappers for an ice cream company."

"But you're a brilliant artist. You went to the Sorbonne."

"Well, I need money. We don't all have exiled millionaires funding our lives."

"That was harsh."

"Maybe so, Kara, but I think you need to hear it. It's good to hear from you."

"You said in the letter not to make contact," I said.

"I didn't want to be hurt anymore." *Huh?* "I wanted to save myself. But now I am over you." I was so confused. All this time I felt that I was the one who was dumped, when apparently I had indirectly done the dumping. "A word of advice, okay? If you're going to continue your arrangement with Bobby, then don't be celibate. Have some fun, some meaningless sex. That's what he does. Otherwise, you really will need defrosting. Just don't expect to fall in love," he added. "Having two loves is asking too much of life, and looking for a second would probably ruin the one you have."

After we hung up, I pondered what he had said. He did know me, and he was probably right. I poured myself a hit of vodka. I raised my glass to Omar. "Here's to my year-and-a-half sabbatical from sex."

I texted Cameron and told him to come over right away. When I opened the door for him, I was holding my third glass of Grey Goose on the rocks.

"Is something wrong?" he asked.

I ran my hands along his abs. "Nothing's wrong," I said. "I just wanted to see you now. I felt horny."

"Excuse me?"

"Listen," I said, the vodka making me overconfident and a little insane. "I need to level with you. I already have a boyfriend. A fake boyfriend, but who cares? Having two loves is asking too much of life. We'll just both get hurt. But I can have a booty call."

"I think I should go now."

"Wait." I grabbed his arm and pulled him toward me. "I thought that's what men wanted. I'm offering you sex with no strings attached. You don't have to wine and dine me; you don't have to introduce me to your parents. You can just come over, have fun, and leave."

I pulled Cameron close to me and invaded his mouth like he was a Middle Eastern country with lots of oil and imaginary weapons of mass destruction.

He pushed me away gently. "I'm not that kind of guy."

I put the vodka down and ran my hands up his T-shirt. I lifted the shirt up. He had a perfect stomach, muscular, hairy, and masculine. The kind of stomach gay men pretended was theirs to score online sex.

"Kara, no means no," he said.

I laughed. "Only women are allowed to use that line."

He wrenched himself free. "Wow," he said, pretty loud, "I'm *really* glad I saw this side of you now."

I instinctively grabbed the puppy and held her close to me. I needed an ally. Cameron looked at me with that abhorrent thing in his eyes: disappointment. "I thought you were different," he said as he left. At least his nauseating last line told me it never would have worked: "I thought maybe you'd actually be a keeper."

Once the door was shut and I was officially rejected, I was left alone with a loud slam from the other half of the duplex. It wasn't the sound of Bobby coming to my rescue. It was just the sound of Bobby coming.

I did the unthinkable that night. I read the *Los Angeles Times*. It wasn't half bad. Not worth getting that dirty black ink all over your hands when *The New York Times* is free online, but informative nevertheless. There was no denying it was a historic time to be alive. My dad reminded me of that fact every time he called.

But this time I called him. I needed someone to talk to, and among all the people I knew in Eastern Daylight Time, he'd be awake earliest.

"So what do you think, Kara?" he asked me. "About this war? Not since Vietnam has the young generation been so needed to voice their opinion."

"I know, Pa. It's a tragedy."

"It's criminal," he corrected.

Where was I when the war in Iraq began? Out protesting? Nope. Shopping with Fiona at Fred Segal. A girl in the jeans department was on her Blackberry and broke the news to the shoppers. Fiona decided to buy three pairs of Levi's to support the American economy. Once the evidence of torture at Abu Ghraib came out, did I march through downtown L.A. to voice my displeasure? Nope. I was making my way through the just-released DVDs of *Dallas*. Bobby and I watched the first two seasons in one weekend, a fact we were at once proud and ashamed of.

"You know, when Uncle Jack and I were arrested..."

"I know, Pa," I interjected, having heard this speech many times before. "I know you were making a *statement*."

"It sent out a message. It opened people's eyes that authority must be questioned."

"Would you be prouder of me if I blew up a police car?" I joked.

"Don't get smart with me, Kara."

"Fine, Pa. Well, *you're* an authority figure to me, and I'm questioning you. I mean, do you really think you and Uncle Jack made a difference by blowing up some cop car? Do you really think that influenced the outcome of the war?"

"If it made one child like you learn to question the crap that the government tells them, then yes, I do," he insisted as the Miami waves echoed in the background. "I just worry that you have no emotional response to the world around you. People are dying. Injustice is played out daily all over the world. I want you to *feel* it. To be *present*. You're thirty now, Kara. I don't want you to get as old as I am and wonder why you didn't try harder to shape the world you're living in."

"Yes, Pa," I dutifully responded. I couldn't get into it with him. I couldn't explain to him that the only reason he protested is because he and his friends were being drafted (Pa and Uncle Jack lucked out with that number lottery and were never called). What reason was there for me to protest? I didn't know anyone in the war. Or anyone affected by the war. He wanted me to feel what was happening, but I didn't. It felt like reality TV, like a show that was being puppeted by the government for my entertainment. Was I revolted? Of course, I was. But I was also revolted by the lack of diversity on *The Bachelor,* and I wasn't protesting outside of ABC.

I was halfway through the business section of the *Los Angeles Times,* and my ass was getting sore from sitting on that damn stoop for so long, when Bobby's door finally opened. Bobby stood behind the door in black boxer briefs as he waved goodbye to a handsome guy in boot-cut jeans and a black blazer. He was dark, but his long brown hair had streaks of blond in it, evidence of hours in the sun.

"I will buddy list you," the guy said to Bobby in an irresistible Italian accent.

"Oh, yeah, sure. If I'm online, I'm looking," Bobby said.

"Maybe next time, we can get a drink or go to a movie."

"Yeah, definitely," Bobby responded, all chipper. "Not exactly a romantic way to meet though, is it?"

"I met my ex-boyfriend on Manhunt. We were together for eight months."

"And it obviously didn't work out." Ah, Bobby. The eternal pessimist. "Okay, I'll see you later," Bobby said and quickly closed the door.

The Italian walked down the stoop and stopped when he saw me.

"Hello," he said.

"Oh, sorry. I'm Bobby's roommate."

"Who?"

"I'm Kara," I explained. "I live with Bobby. Well, kind of..." His confusion alerted me to the fact that he hadn't gotten Bobby's name yet. "Bobby is the guy you just... you know..."

"Fucked," he offered. Then, as if I was Bobby's mother rather than friend, he added, "Don't worry, we used condoms."

"*Multiple* condoms?" I gasped, feigning shock. "I'm sure Bobby is busy filling them up with water to make sure there weren't any holes in them."

"I am Andrea," he said, ignoring the image of Bobby making condom balloons. "A pleasure to meet a beautiful woman."

I looked over and saw a dirty pick-up truck parked across the street. In the back were hunks of wood stacked on top of one another. "Is that yours?" I asked.

"Yes, I'm a contractor. Otherwise I would get better gas mileage."

"And from Italy, obviously?" I realized I was flirting with the handsome Italian, but on Bobby's behalf. I was hoping to reel this one into our lives so Bobby could finally have a relationship that lasted longer than an episode of a television drama.

"I am from Spoleto," he purred, turning on the charm. "I came here eight years ago when I turned thirty. It was my resolution for the new decade."

"I need a resolution of some kind." I thought about it, but only clichés came to mind: read more, exercise, work harder.

"Maybe you should go to Italy. Have you ever visited?"

"No. I'm more of a France girl."

"On that note, *signorina*," he purred, "I will say *arrivederci*."

As soon as he drove his pick-up away, I stormed into Bobby's side of the duplex. He was holding a bottle of Listerine and steeping some "Immune Support" tea. He had thrown on his baggy Madonna concert T-shirt, which covered his boxer briefs and looked like a dress. "Andrea was cute," I said.

"Who?" Bobby asked.

"You know... the guy who just... the Italian?"

"Yeah, he was." Bobby didn't smile. "I told myself no more uncut guys. I can't seem to stick to my boundaries anymore. I'm such a sad case, Kara. I don't know how you put up with me." He shot some more Listerine into his mouth like it was tequila.

I told him about the letter in the freezer, but I omitted the details of my conversation with Jacques. The last thing I wanted was Bobby feeling indirectly responsible for my heartbreak. He held up his finger to indicate he was going to respond as soon as his sixty-second gargle was over. Finally, he spit out the Listerine into the kitchen sink and looked up at me. "This is good," he said. "This is closure. Now you can toss out that filthy Jacques-strap."

"That's exactly what I'm doing," I said.

"I love this new attitude, Kara. Who's gonna be the lucky guy? Cameron?"

"Nope," I answered. "I already blew that one." I caught the look of surprise on Bobby's face. "Blew my *chances* with him. The problem is that most guys my age are looking to settle down. They view me as marriage material. They want romance."

"And this is a problem for you? You're a total romantic."

"I *was* a total romantic. I've had an epiphany. *You* have the right idea. Sex *sans* emotion. Pure and simple." And there it was. My Persian New Year's resolution.

"But I'm gay, Kara," Bobby said, stating the obvious.

"So? Are you saying women can't be as callous in the bedroom as you?"

"Kind of, yeah. I mean, you'd probably fall for the first guy you fucked. Take the guy who just left…"

"Andrea," I snapped back. "He has a name."

"My point exactly. The first thing you learned was his name. His identity. I bet you even found out what he does."

"He's a contractor."

"Oh, Kara. What did you have with him? Five seconds? You're like my mother. It takes you under a minute to find out what they do, where they're from…"

"Spoleto. He's a contractor from Spoleto. He's thirty-eight…"

"What?" Bobby said in shock. "Are you sure?" He quickly opened up his laptop and logged on to his Manhunt account, *LAConfidential*. In a macabre twist, his password was *Leila*. He had shared this with me one drunken night when he declared that if he ever died in a car accident, I was to cancel his Manhunt account, delete all the files from his computer, and dispose of all his pornography before his parents got to our place. Bobby also informed me that night that he had a will and had donated all his money to amfAR but bequeathed the duplex to me. This was meant to be sweet, but as with all things Bobby, it left an aftertaste of morbidity and sadness. Bobby pulled up the Italian's account, *LaDolceVita*. "Look," Bobby said. "Height: 5'10. Body type: Athletic. Looking for: Right Now! Status: Negative. Age: *35!*"

"So he hasn't updated his profile in three years," I reasoned.

"Kara, if he lied about his age, then chances are, he's capable of lying about everything else." I could feel Bobby's head spinning with anxious possibilities.

"You told me yourself you lie about your age all the time."

"But that's *me*. I'm trustworthy. How am I supposed to trust some random uncut Italian?" Bobby pressed the block button on *LaDolceVita*'s account, ensuring he could never contact Bobby again.

"Bobby, he seemed sweet. He wanted to go to a movie with you."

"You were listening?" Bobby asked incredulously. Ever since it became known that the government was listening to our cell phone calls, Bobby was convinced he was under constant surveillance. He *was* from the axis of evil, after all. For the most part, we found amusement in imagining George W. Bush and Dick Cheney listening to Bobby having phone sex.

"I was on the stoop. I was depressed. Jesus, can we focus on me for a second?" I demanded.

"I'm sorry. I'm focusing. Should we go for a walk? I'm feeling clammy," Bobby said, which was code for *I'm seroconverting.*

"I think I need a one night stand," I announced confidently. "It's time."

Bobby opened his fridge and stuck his nose in a carton of old Moo Shu. "Do you think it's gone bad?" He held the take-out under my nose.

"I'm serious, Bobby," I insisted. "You need to teach me."

"Teach you what?"

"Teach me how to have sex like a guy. Teach me how *not* to find out their names and occupations before I have some fun. Teach me how to dump instead of getting dumped. Teach me how to enjoy sex without bringing hundreds of emotions into the bedroom. Teach me how not to get so damn hurt. Teach me how to have no expectations." I took a breath and looked him in the eye with pupils crazy from vodka. "Teach me how to fuck. You're the master. You never feel anything after sex. And you're gay. You're supposed to love makeovers. Make me over! Create some slutty profile for me and get me laid."

Bobby stuffed his face with Moo Shu. "You're drunk. Talk to me in the morning when you don't sound like a character out of the porno version of *Clueless.*"

"No. Listen to me. I feel frigid," I went on. "Just like the letter in the freezer. I'm frozen over. There's no hope for me anymore. Except for you. You are my hope. Bobby, I haven't had sex in a year and a half. Imagine that. Just imagine it for a second. Physical contact is important to a person's psychological health. I'm not psychologically healthy."

Bobby tried to imagine a year and a half of celibacy. His perplexed look indicated that it must have been difficult to picture. He put down the Moo Shu and approached me. He placed his hand on my cheek and spoke slowly, with a sense of profound purpose. "Kara, you're my best friend."

"I know that."

"I love you, and I only want what's best for you. I always told you that if you fell in love, I would support your relationship."

"I know you would," I said, though I doubted that this was true. Bobby and I had been together too long not to view each other's romantic partners as suppressive persons, to borrow a term from L. Ron.

"And I think you're a monogamous person. But... I also think a person needs to get laid when they've had a dry spell."

"You mean you'll help me?"

"If it's what you want, then I'm here for you." Bobby raised his fist in the air, and in his best Scarlett O'Hara, declared, "As God is my witness, you will never go horny again!" I felt deceitful not telling Bobby what Jacques said, not telling Bobby that the real reason I was seeking out frivolous sex was because I finally realized romance was non-negotiable as long as Bobby was around. Two loves *is* too much to ask. My future suddenly became clear to me. Bobby and I would move to Roxbury Drive, live in separate bedrooms, sleep with a string of men, but always come home to each other. We would be a very modern, very progressive couple. We'd send Omar to the best private schools. Perhaps it wasn't the family life I dreamed of as a child, but it seemed better than diving into the dating pool again.

5

"Is it too early for a bottle of wine?" Leila asked, the sun hitting the Chanel logo on the side of her sunglasses. On this particular day, she was wearing, from top to bottom: the Chanel sunglasses; a white Armani blouse with gold buttons; a frayed dark-green Vivienne Westwood skirt, which should have looked absurd on a woman Leila's age, but didn't; and a pair of Hermès sneakers made of tan leather with a very subtle H stitched into the side (if only Harry could afford them, they would seem branded just for her). Somewhere between Jackie O and Puff Daddy was Leila on that Monday.

"*Una bottiglia del Chardonnay, Andrea, e il piato di antipasti,*" she ordered. "*Oggi é il compleanno della ragazza.*"

The waiter smiled at me. *Andrea.* The name of a certain contractor who had just fucked Bobby, or vice versa. I wondered if Bobby, who was sitting next to me at Il Fornaio, made the connection. Or was he so successful at compartmentalizing his life that it didn't even register?

"Happy birthday, *signorina,*" Andrea said.

"Oh, thank you," I said, smiling before Andrea disappeared, happy that I still looked like a *signorina* and not a *signora.* Leila insisted on taking me to a birthday lunch every year. The location was weather-dependent, but because global warming had settled Los Angeles into a ninety-degree April day, Leila chose the outdoor patio of Il Fornaio for my thirtieth. It had the best pizza, she claimed, and it was just a few blocks from Rodeo Drive, where we would be purchasing my *real* birthday gift. Usually, the birthday lunch was just me and Bobby and Leila, but this year, Leila suggested I invite Harry, as well. An innocent birthday gathering had been hijacked by a mothers-in-law lunch.

"It's so nice to spend some time with you, Lila," Harry said.

"Lay-la," I corrected.

"Sorry, Lay-la," Harry repeated dutifully.

"Oh, it doesn't matter," Leila said. "What did Shakespeare say about a name and a rose?"

"What's in a name?" Bobby interjected. "That which we call a rose by any other name would taste as sweet."

"*Smell* as sweet," I corrected. "You don't taste a rose."

"Well, some of us do," Leila corrected. "In Iranian cooking, we use rosewater in our ice cream and desserts."

Andrea returned with a bottle of Chardonnay and held it up to Leila for her approval. She nodded ever so subtly, and he uncorked it and poured her a sip. She held the glass by the stem, her perfectly manicured fingernails glowing Chanel's patented *Le Vernis* color, and then her hands conveyed the crystal to her Lancôme *Rouge Absolu* lips, which immediately left their imprint on the glass. "*Perfetto*, Andrea." Andrea poured us each a glass. As soon as he was gone, Leila raised her glass high. "To a wonderful year thirty-one for you, Kara *djoon*."

"Speaking of Iran," Harry said—and I knew it would go downhill from there—"what do you think of all this news? Do you think we'll invade the country?"

Something I love about Leila is that you can engage her on a million subjects. Fashion and art and travel. Books. NGOs and micro-finance. She speaks Farsi, English, Italian, and French. But there is no language in which she'll talk about Iran after 1977. She looked at me and smiled, and I could see how painful it was to have to stiff-arm my well-meaning mother. With a smile, Leila threw her hands in the air. "I have no idea. Shall we order?"

Could I really have neglected to remind Harry about Leila's no post-revolutionary-Iran-talk protocol? For me, there was something equally refreshing and disturbing in Leila's refusal to discuss the past. On the one hand, she blocked out all emotion. On the other, she had triumphed over exile, and, more impressive, over the death of her son. And here she sat before us, gorgeous in her sixties, the mayor of Rodeo Drive, a world traveler and charitable doyenne. Why should she dredge up painful memories as lunch conversation?

"It must be so hard for you," Harry said. "Watching all this happen in your homeland."

Luckily, *deus ex machina* arrived in body-hugging black Prada, tribal bands tattooed around his overdeveloped biceps.

"Leila!" a voice that Bobby would describe as butch-fey called from across the street. Leila looked up with relief and waved.

"Hello, Billy!" Leila kissed her hand and blew it toward the guy, who brought the Boystown aesthetic to Beverly Hills.

"I got off early to stand in line at Amoeba and meet Tori Amos," Billy said as he unlocked his two-seat BMW. "Come by and see me soon, though. We just received some fabulous new skirts that would look perfect on you."

As Billy drove off, Leila turned to us. "He used to work at Armani. Now he works at that new Prada. The one that Rem Koolhaas designed. Have you been?" she asked Harry.

"Can't say that I have. I don't make it to Beverly Hills very often, and Prada hasn't hit Thousand Oaks quite yet."

"Well, you'll be seeing a lot more of Beverly Hills soon," Leila said, to Harry's confusion.

"I think there's a Prada outlet store somewhere near Thousand Oaks," I blurted out a little too excitedly.

Leila, effortlessly catching on to my change of subject, turned to Harry and added, "We can go to the store after we eat. Perhaps Kara will find a present she likes there. The design of the store is breathtaking, Harriet. You will adore it. Leave it to Miuccia Prada and Walt Disney to bring innovative architecture to Los Angeles."

Leila, in addition to our meals (two soles with grilled vegetables for me and Harry, chicken salad for Leila, pasta puttanesca for Bobby), insisted on putting a pizza margherita in the middle of the table for us to share.

"Leila! Hi, you look gorgeous," yet another obviously gay passerby chirped.

We all looked up. Standing before us this time were two men, one blond, one dark, both gorgeous, holding hands. "I did the highlights," the dark one reported. "It took a lot of convincing."

"Not so much convincing," Leila disagreed.

"She wanted to go lighter, but I insisted on staying in the reds. She's too classy to go blond. And we don't want her the same exact shade as Mrs. Maliki."

"It looks great, sweetie," the blond one said. "Suits your coloring perfectly. Is that the skirt? Stand up. Alejandro has to see it." Leila stood up to model her green Vivienne Westwood. "I made her try it on, I told her she'd look like Gwen Stefani's Persian sister, and she said, 'Who is Ga-ven Stefani?'" He cackled, clearly pleased by his impersonation of Leila.

Leila sat back down and put her hand on Bobby's shoulder. "Alejandro. Shane. This is my son, Babak." Bobby smiled dutifully.

"Oh my God!" Alejandro, the dark one, screamed, "you're so lucky. Your mother is fabulous."

"Thank you," Bobby said, looking as if "fabulous" was outside his vocabulary.

"I can't even *imagine* having such an impeccable mother. And she's so generous," Shane continued.

"I didn't know you two were a couple," Leila said.

"Oh, it's been a while, yeah," Shane explained. "We met picking up salads at La Scala. They gave me his tuna, and he took my chicken. We both went back to return them at the same time and realized the mistake and ended up eating the salads on the steps of Rodeo Drive. It was such an unexpected first date. So rom-com!"

"I know," Alejandro concurred. "It was such a setup to a Meg Ryan movie."

"I was Meg Ryan," Shane said.

"Oh please. I'm so Meg Ryan."

"Fine, then I'm Sandra Bullock."

"This isn't a lesbian rom-com," Alejandro said. "You're Tom Hanks and I'm Meg Ryan."

Finally, the Shane and Alejandro show went to commercial, and Leila had the chance to introduce me and Harry. "I'm so sorry," she said, "I'm so rude. This is Kara, and her mother, Harriet. Kara and Babak have lived together for years, and today we're celebrating her birthday!"

I looked over to Harry, who rolled her eyes at me. "Wow, congratulations," Shane said.

"You've been in the salon before, haven't you?" Alejandro asked me.

"Yes," Leila answered on my behalf. "Luigi did her hair."

"It looks fabulous. Loving the layers."

I could tell that while Alejandro gushed, Shane was looking my mother up and down, masterminding all the fun ways they could make her over if only she could afford them. Hell, he was looking us both over, and probably speculating less about recreating our looks than about what Leila was doing with us. Slumming?

"Well, we'll let you enjoy your meal," Alejandro said. "See you tomorrow for a blow dry?"

"Yes, at noon," Leila confirmed. The two men walked away, Shane's hand on Alejandro's back for all of Beverly Hills to see. I eyed Bobby, wondering if the public display of gay affection bothered him. But before I could gauge his discomfort, Andrea approached our table, holding a tiramisu with a single candle inside it, and Bobby started a chorus of "Happy Birthday."

As planned, we walked to Prada after lunch. Inside, a slew of European women and stylish gays in matching navy-blue utilitarian wardrobe swarmed around Leila, each of them thanking her for some Christmas gift or another. I wondered what the store's other customers must have thought, watching the entire staff desert their posts to greet a perfectly coiffed middle-aged lady that they couldn't recognize from film or television.

"No, no," Leila said as they showed her this season's newest skirts, bags, and pumps, "we are not here to shop for me. I want you to find something beautiful for this lovely girl. Today is her birthday."

The salespeople brought out outfit after outfit. Cashmere. Silk. Rayon. Organza. I was Cinderella, they were the mice, and Leila was my Fairy Godmother. No, Prince Charming. No, Leila was Walt Disney, the master manipulator, the visionary. As I tried a yellow slip of a dress on, I wondered what a Leila theme park would be like. Music from the world would be playing all over, fresh *tadeek* on sticks for the kids, and perhaps a ride through the better years of the Persian Empire, complete with cutout figures of Cyrus and Farah Diba leaping through the darkness. When I emerged in the yellow dress, Leila exclaimed that the choice had been made.

Once the extravagant gift had been wrapped and bagged and handed to me, Leila marched upstairs to the men's department and picked out a pin-striped suit for Bobby.

"I don't really have much occasion to wear a suit, Mommy." It's always struck me as odd to hear a thirty-year-old call his mother *Mommy*. It made him seem so childlike, so subservient. I was glad I called my mother Harry. My mom, played by Clint Eastwood.

"Just try it on," Leila said as she caressed a black cashmere cardigan. "This would look good on you, too."

"I'm not sure I need a cardigan," Bobby protested.

"I'll just buy it," she said. "If you don't want it, your father can wear it."

As a salesgirl escorted Leila and Bobby to the dressing room, I turned to

Harry, who hadn't said much, clearly out of her element. "How're you doing, Harry?" I asked.

"Fine. It's a beautiful dress you got there. I'm sorry I forgot your gift. I'll give it to you next time. I've been so absent-minded lately. Work's been crazy."

"That's okay."

"Where do you think you'll wear it?" she said, back to the sexy slip of a dress I was clutching.

"On the beaches of St. Tropez, of course," I joked.

"Oh, is she... are you going to France with the Ebadis this summer?"

"No. I was kidding. Bobby can't stand those Persian mafia trips."

"What's to love about a summer in St. Tropez, I always say," Harry cracked, trying to joke her way out of her discomfort.

"It's different for him," I rationalized. "He has to play this part for like two hundred people on those trips. It's exhausting." Inside Harry's oversized purse, I spotted some wrapping paper with a bow on top. "Harry?"

"What?"

"You didn't forget my present," I pointed out. "It's there in your bag."

"Oh," she said, playing it off unconvincingly. "I'm such an idiot. Here it is. Happy birthday, sweetie."

She handed me the gift. I opened the card first. A Georgia O'Keefe flower, and inside, Harry had written *To my darling darling daughter who makes me prouder with every year. I love you more than you can understand. Harry.* Inside the package was a book: *I Know This Much Is True,* by Wally Lamb.

"It's not much," she said.

"Mom, it's more than enough."

"I bought it back when Oprah told me to, and then let it sit on my shelf for years. I just got around to reading it, and it's great." The cover image was of two newborn babies sleeping side by side, one child's fist resting just under the other's chin. "I saw a fascinating Discovery Channel piece about twins," Harry said. "They said that when twins are in the womb, one of them already begins to dominate. One of them literally will punch the other, and the other will retreat. They learn their relationship to one another that early."

Bobby emerged from the dressing room in the pinstriped suit, a light blue shirt, and a pair of brown loafers. He looked stunning, but apparently Leila wasn't pleased. She decided the shirt's collar fit Bobby's neck awkwardly and asked for another size.

"Kara," Harry said, adopting her serious tone, "I hope you're not really planning on stringing this woman along a lot longer."

"Of course not," I lied. The Ebadis had put in an offer on the Roxbury house. If that wasn't stringing Leila along, I didn't know what was. "But I don't want to hurt her, either."

"Are you in love with him?"

"Of course I love Bobby." My *of courses* indicated that I was on the defensive.

"I love him too, Kara, but we both know that's not how I phrased the question."

"What difference does it make if I'm *in* love with him? It's not like there are other men lining up for my affections."

"Perhaps they sense you're already spoken for." Harry glared at me with a look of superiority.

"It's not me, Harry," I sighed. "It's the guys."

"Fine. I agree I raised you in a city with a high ratio of vapid, self-involved men. That said, you're still enabling Bobby to lie to his family. And you're building that woman's hopes up."

"That woman's name is Leila."

"*Leila* is smart," Harry said pointedly. "She knows."

"She knows what?" I asked.

"She knows everything. That's why she's constantly trying to buy your affections. She's afraid you'll get sick of the arrangement. She's trying to purchase a grandchild."

"She's happy with a certain status quo, and she wants to keep it," I responded. "And she wants me to be happy with it, too. She wants everyone around her to be happy. And she doesn't *know*."

"Her son is gayer than all the Queer Eyes put together, Kara."

"Bite your tongue. Bobby considers himself very butch. Besides, people can make themselves believe the craziest things."

"What did she mean when she said I'd be spending more time in Beverly Hills soon?" Harry asked as she rolled her eyes at the price tag on a deconstructed jacket.

"Nothing."

Harry glared at me to indicate she was no fool, either.

"I think she wants these lunches to become a regular thing. That's all."

"The mothers-in-law need to bond," Harry cracked before changing tone and adding, "I'm just looking out for you, okay? I don't want your values to get submerged in all this."

"Now you sound like Dad. What do you guys want me to do? Out my best friend and blow up a police car?"

"That would be a start," Harry said with a smile. "Anything but become the fictional daughter-in-law to a charming but deluded socialite." I looked at her with my mouth hanging open. "That was harsh. But I've been trying to talk to you about this politely for years, and it doesn't get me anywhere."

"You don't get it, Mom. They lost their first-born son. If they found out about Bobby, it would crush them. Sometimes I feel like I'm the glue that's holding the whole family together."

"That's an awful lot of pressure for a young woman to carry on her shoulders. Even strong shoulders like yours."

"I can handle it," I asserted.

"I know you think it's your job to take care of the Ebadis, Kara. But my job is to take care of you."

Leila pushed Bobby toward us in what she deemed a perfect fit. He looked very *GQ*. "What do you think?" Leila beamed. "Don't pinstripes make him look vonderful?"

Later that night, Bobby and I got sloshed on white wine, and he took me on a cruise through the world of online sex. Since most of Bobby's favorite hook-up sites were set up for gay men, he decided I should post my ad on Craigslist. This surprised me, because as far as I knew, Craigslist was where people went to sell their old couches or comic-book collections. I'd found a mover on Craigslist once. The man with the van was Mexican and hot and put the moves on me, but I couldn't sleep with him. I just couldn't stand the thought of having to tell people I slept with someone I met on the Internet. So it was particularly poignant that two years later, I was sitting at home with Bobby, composing an ad to put on Craigslist.

"A pic collector is somebody who posts an ad only to collect naked photos of people with no intention of ever responding," Bobby explained. "UC means uncut, though in rare cases it can indicate a student from a UC school, as in 'UC Frat Boy Lubed & Ready.' DDfree means drug and disease free. NSA means no strings attached. And any posting using a dollar sign as the twenty-seventh letter of the alphabet means the person is a prostitute and/or willing to pay for sex." This, I found, would include postings such as "Let this Ma$ter dominate your lubed hole" and "Where are all them big black cock$$ at," both of which Bobby quickly pulled up on the "Men Seeking Men" section of Craigslist. "The first thing we need to do," Bobby continued, "is create a new email address for you so that people who respond to your posting won't be writing to your real-person email."

"Heaven forbid."

"Your new screen name should be slutty but fun," he explained like a dutiful schoolteacher.

"How 'bout *sluttyandfun?*" I tipsily echoed.

"*Perfetto.*" Bobby typed the screen name into my AOL account. "*Sluttyandfun* is already taken. We should add a number to the end. How about *sluttyandfun30?*"

"It's the Internet. I can be 21 again."

Bobby typed in sluttyandfun21, but that was already taken, as well, as were 22, 23, 24, 26, 27, 28, and 29. AOL had decided my fictional-person age for me. I was going to be *Sluttyandfun25.* I had myself a new screen name and a new age along with it. I could feel myself getting objectified already. "Now we need to create your posting. I always feel like the more specific the posting, the better. Say exactly what your type is. Be direct."

"I think before I actually post something, I need to peruse the straight section of this website. I don't wanna end up sounding like a gay man posing as a woman."

"FYI, half the women on Craigslist are homos posing to get hot naked pictures of the straight guys they can't sleep with."

"Yuck. Pic collectors," I said, gleeful to know this piece of terminology.

"Don't knock it 'til you've tried it." Bobby opened a folder in his hard drive titled "Gullible Straights" and started a slideshow of one naked man after another. The whole thing felt incredibly immoral, especially since I recognized a few. One of them was a trainer at the gym who I now knew was compensating for something else by building all those big muscles. Another was the cute old Indian man at the 7-Eleven who sold me cigarettes back when I smoked. Another was the slacker who always helped me find the ripe papayas at Whole Foods. Could I really embark on a life where men I buy produce from were going to send me pictures of their cocks?

To further the anthropological research, Bobby and I began perusing the profiles of every demographic, and the results were fascinating. "Look at these fucking lunatics," Bobby seethed as he pulled up more ads from gay men. "Must be raw. Lubed and ready and looking for loads. Twinkie looking for cream. Have these people forgotten the last twenty-five years? Do they want to die? This is why I don't go on Craigslist anymore. There are no search options. Just seeing all these bareback ads makes me insane." Bobby skipped to the lesbian ads. "Oh my God," Bobby exclaimed, "dykes are almost as raunchy as gays. I thought they were only interested in nesting, playing with their pets, and going to outdoor music festivals. Sexy Brown Femme Wants to Be Licked, Gurls Just Wanna Have Fun at Your Place, Fly Bi Femme Seeks NSA Fun. Who knew there was such a dirty Sapphic underground?" Bobby clicked over to the straight male section. The straight men began to veer into relationship territory in their postings, I would say fifty-fifty between headlines like "Handsome Jewish Guy Looking For My PRINCESS" and ones like "PUSSY LICKIN' GOOD! HERE, KITTIES!"

"Now are you ready for a lesson?" Bobby asked as he clicked on the "women seeking men" page. "Look at this," he said. "Every single posting references soul mates, Mr. Right, and connections. SWF seeking *connection* with older man… So many fish in the sea but none I have that special *connection* with… Retro loving surfer girl seeks surfer boy for love *connexion*." Bobby continued for a long time, each posting further substantiating his point. "How many responses do you think these girls get? How many guys do you think troll Craigslist looking to *connex*? Seriously, if a man is looking for a wife online, he orders in from Russia."

Bobby was right. The desperation of these postings saddened me. Had women become so anxious that they really believed their savior was to be found on the same website they went to when they needed Lakers tickets or a used car?

After an hour of deliberation and yet another bottle of white wine (one at lunch with Leila, and two since skipping work in the afternoon), Bobby and I came up with this: 25 Year Old Hottie Seeks Safe, Sane Gentleman for NSA Fun. *Hey Guys, 5'9, 129 pounds, in shape, blue-eyed blond. My type: Tall, dark,*

*five o'clock shadow. My ideal: Benicio Del Toro. You know who you are, guys.
Send stats, location, and face pic for reply or no response.*

"Now we have to post a photo," Bobby insisted.

"Wo Nay," I protested.

"If you don't post a photo, then the guys will think you're some gay pic collector like me. You need a photo, and it needs to be you, not some porn star."

The Chardonnay must have loitered in my bloodstream since lunch, because I allowed Bobby to upload a photo of me on Venice Beach at Fiona's annual summer volleyball competition. Fiona played high school volleyball, and could still kick everyone's ass, which was clearly her incentive for having a volleyball competition once a year. That girl didn't like to lose. Anyway, I was wearing a silver bikini in the picture, and the forgiving light of the sun made me look as close to a swimsuit model as I would ever look. Still, I wasn't completely comfortable posting the photo. What had been an innocent photo taken at the beach suddenly made me feel like a Girl Gone Wild. "What if someone sees me?" I asked nervously.

"Who do you know who would be scrolling through the Craigslist *women who seek men* section? All your friends are gay men and girls."

"I don't know. Some guy from the gym. What if Hot Tattooed Guy sees it?"

"If he likes you, he writes back, and you have sex. And if he doesn't like you, you'll never know, and you both lead rich and fulfilling lives. The Internet is a real time-saver that way."

"I guess you're right," I said.

"Besides, even if someone you knew saw you, do you think they'd admit it?"

"Is this like one of those *if a tree falls in the forest* moments?"

"I'm just saying. I've had tons of friends send me pictures of themselves with their legs up in the air. Do I tell them over brunch that I've seen their assholes? I mean, hello?!"

"Seeing a friend's asshole is the tree falling, and them not knowing you saw it is no one hearing the tree?"

"Exactly," Bobby said.

"Except in *that* proverbial forest where the tree falls, there's no one there."

"And me knowing they don't know is the forest primeval itself."

Let me say right now that Bobby might be charming and loyal and self-effacing, but sometimes he is just fucking wrong. I started getting responses within the hour. And the third email in *sluttyandfun25*'s inbox (after two rather unexciting emails from *JewishDoctorLove* and *ManofSteel*) was from *CupOfJoanne*. I immediately recognized the screen name, and my heart skipped a hundred beats. Bobby was aghast. "That girl has no shame."

"Open it and tell me what it says," I demanded.

Bobby opened Joanne's email and read in a respectable impersonation of her voice. "Kara, you MINX! Now I know what you've been doing every night. I can't believe you haven't told us you've ventured into the world of the online quickie. Twenty-five???? And on your thirtieth birthday no less!! You are devious. P.S. We're taking you to a birthday dinner on Saturday? Fiona made the rezzie. Tell Bobby."

"Wow." I fell onto Bobby's sofa and buried my face in a pillow. "Kill me now."

"I'm sorry. I feel like this is all my fault."

"She's probably already told Fiona. And Fiona's probably told my mother. And my mother's told my father, who's told..."

"Katie Couric," Bobby offered.

"It's not funny, Bobby. Jesus Christ, this was supposed to be a lark. I just wanted a simple one-night stand."

"This is just a little stumbling block. Look, you have twelve responses, and only three of them are from Joanne."

"My best friends are gonna think I'm an Internet whore," I wailed.

"And what's wrong with that?"

I bolted up. "I have to go home. Maybe Omar will cheer me up. She's so non-judgmental. She doesn't care about my sins."

"Sins?" Bobby repeated. "You were raised agnostic, Kara. You haven't even had sex with anyone yet. If you're a sinner, what am I? Lucifer?"

"You know that's not what I mean. I just don't know how to explain this to Joanne."

"How about the truth? Tell her you were horny after a year and a half on the bench, and you're ready to get back in the game."

"Said the man in the closet," I jabbed back.

"Touché." Bobby laughed. "But my parents are sixty-something-year-old Middle Easterners. You're talking about Joanne and Fiona here. One of them is a drunken mess who throws herself at everything with a Y chromosome, and the other spent her early career as a gossip fixture for fucking every teen actor in Hollywood. How can they judge you?"

"You're right. It's not that big a deal." I gave Bobby a hug. "Some thirtieth birthday, huh?"

"I don't think it was so bad. You got a fierce outfit and a whole new iden-tity."

As my alarm clock went from P.M. to A.M., I hung the new yellow Prada dress in my closet, cuddled in bed with Omar, and opened the Wally Lamb book. Reading the story made me realize there is one gift I always wanted that Harry never gave me. A sibling. It would have been nice to have a brother or sister. How much happier would I have been growing up with Bobby at my side, a loyal brother to protect me from the cruelty of youth? My eyes drifted toward sleep as I made it through the first few chapters of the novel. Harry had a point about Bobby and Leila, but every time I wanted to judge the need to maintain their elaborate façade, I came back to Keyvan, to the devastation of losing your son, or your brother, especially to some senseless war. If my part in easing the pain was playing a slightly compromised role, helping them believe that order had been restored, that was fine with me.

6

My INSTINCT WAS TO delete the Craigslist ad as soon as I woke up sober, but when I noticed my posting had forty-seven replies, I couldn't help but sift through them. Apparently, *sluttyandfun25* was a lot more popular than that boring prude, Kara Walker. Six of the messages were from Joanne. I ignored them. Twenty of the pictures were from men who just sent me jpegs of their dicks, which made me feel ill. Fifteen of the messages were correctly spelled and grammatically sound, but included pictures so unfortunate that not even the charitable side of me could entertain the thought of responding. Of the remaining ten, only one caught my eye. It was from *Lensman4U*. His original message was simple and to the point. It was a link to his own listing that read: "34. 6'1. 190. Italian. Former Swimmer. 'Sex is not the answer. Sex is the question. Yes is the answer.' Swami X." Inserted into the email was a black-and-white of a naked man. His long hair fell over his face, but a dark and hypnotizing eye could be seen from behind the mane. His body was lean and muscular, and he had a lion tattooed on his arm. He looked like a Calvin Klein ad, and who hasn't wanted to sleep with a Calvin Klein ad?

    Lensman4U and I began what would turn into a week of email flirting. I found out that he was a photographer exploiting the dependable need of actors to blame their failing careers on bad headshots. His tattoo corresponded to his astrological sign. *Lensman4U* even did my astrological chart. He told me I'm a leader because I'm an Aries. I emailed him back, saying I'd been stuck in the same dead-end job for the past seven years, so technically, I'm more of a follower. He wrote back that some leaders take longer to bloom. I shouldn't be surprised if I came of age late in life and took control of my life and career. I responded that I hoped he was clairvoyant as well as sexy. This was already too much intimacy for Bobby, who had been supervising our week of e-flirtation, and had declared it far too involved and personal. "Just go to his place and fuck him already. I'll buy you an astrology book if you're suddenly so curious about what it means to be an Aries." *Lensman4U* and I decided to meet Sunday night for sex. We established that we were both uninterested in traditional dating. We were going to be fuck buddies. Yes was the question. And my answer was sex.

But if the girls were the question, my answer was decidedly no. I avoided them all week, but I couldn't bail on my own birthday dinner on Saturday. They decided to take me to Comme Ça, West Hollywood's hippest new bistro, at which we could never get a reservation if it weren't for Fiona's publicist. Of course, this wasn't going to be just another birthday dinner. *CupOfJoanne* was sure to have shared the news with Fiona and Casey. When I arrived at brunch, the other two Angels were already sipping Pinot Noir, hair flipped, guns pointing at me. I took my seat and immediately stuffed a piece of baguette into my mouth. I tried to read my friends' faces to find out whether Joanne had spilled the beans. But Fiona was typing frantically into her iPhone, and Joanne was very involved in a conversation with Casey about what they feed inmates on death row.

"Hey, bitches," Bobby purred, with a special smile for Casey. "The guest of honor is here." The acoustics at the packed restaurant were terrible, causing every painfully hip patron to yell, furthering the problem.

Joanne looked at me with a mischievous smile. I wanted to hit her. She'd told them, that cunt. "Happy birthday, *chica*," Joanne said.

Fiona and Casey stood up together. "Happy birthday, baby," Fiona said as she scanned the room to make sure a few people recognized her.

Casey pulled me into him to give me a birthday hug, his ripped body pressing against mine completely, alas, innocently.

"Jesus, Casey, you're like a superhero," I said.

"*My* superhero," Fiona interposed. Fiona's hand on Casey's cheek revealed the humongous rock on her finger.

"Um, what is *that*?" Joanne, despite adoring Fiona, unabashedly harbored a hope that Casey would never propose.

Fiona looked down shyly. "I didn't want to bring this up today. It's Kara's day."

"My birthday was last Monday," I said. "I got my day."

At this point, Joanne was verging on a psychotic break. She practically developed a stammer. "What is that? Two... three... four carats."

"The band's white gold, and it's a three-stone setting," Casey explained in his ridiculously smooth, sexy and self-effacing voice. "The stones represent the past, present, and future."

Yeah, but how many carats, I could hear Joanne screaming inside.

"Didn't Michael Douglas give Catherine Zeta-Jones a ring like that?" Bobby asked innocently.

"Casey designed it," Fiona asserted as she poured wine for the table.

"I wanted it to be personal," Casey said.

Bobby tried to get the waiter's attention. He was resigned to silence whenever the conversation turned to heterosexual matters like weddings and sports. Every time he was my plus-one to a party with the girls and our USC friends, he resented how we self-segregated, girls on one side, boys on the other. Bobby said he always ended up between Casey and some other former all-American in a conversation about college basketball. I couldn't vouch for that because I was always on the girl side, but I tended to trust Bobby, because anyone who was as honest as he was about crabs, dick size, and anal penetration had no reason to lie about something as insignificant as athletics.

As we ordered our food, Bobby noticed three familiar figures heading our way. "Oh my God," he announced. "It's the Cheshire Cat."

"I'm sorry?" our waiter asked curiously.

"It's a friend of my mother's who always seems to pop up everywhere, like the Cheshire Cat," Bobby explained.

The waiter cleared the way to reveal none other than Tanaz Maliki approaching with her daughter Tina and her soon-to-be-son-in-law Cyrus. Tina and Cyrus looked the picture of newly engaged perfection. Cyrus was tall and strapping, with a thick beard covering his rugged face, and Tina cut an imposing figure herself in her blond highlights and little black dress. "Babak. Kara. What are the chances?" Tanaz asked.

"Hey, guys," Tina said. "I don't know if you remember Cyrus."

"Of course," Bobby and I said at the same time.

We all stood and exchanged kisses, including Fiona, Joanne, and Casey. "How did you get a table here? It's impossible," Tanaz said. "Tina had to have the CEO of her bank call from New York."

"My publicist booked it," Fiona said.

"Don't have the *coq au vin*," Tanaz warned. "it's soupy."

"She's exaggerating," Tina said. "It was actually really delicious. Hey, are you guys coming to the wedding?"

Bobby and I looked nervously at each other. We hadn't yet decided whether to RSVP. We knew our presence there would lead to the inevitable barrage of questions about when our own wedding would take place. "I'm working on a new project," I lied. "I just have to figure out the shooting schedule, and then we'll let you know."

"No pressure," Tina said.

"You two will be busy moving, won't you?" Tanaz asked me and Bobby. "That's going to be a big house to furnish, and I know Leila wants to redo the bathrooms."

"You're moving," Fiona blurted out. "Together?"

"And the best part is you'll be just a few blocks from me," Tanaz explained with a sly smile. "We'll be shopping at the same Whole Foods now."

"It's not a done deal yet," Bobby explained. "We just put in an offer."

Tanaz laughed. "Have you ever known your mother not to get what she wants, Babak?"

"Well, congratulations," Tina said sincerely.

"Yes, congratulations," Fiona echoed insincerely. "I'm sure you two will be very happy in Brentwood."

"Beverly Hills," I corrected with an angry glare toward Fiona. "Sister City of Cannes."

"Look," Tina said, giving me an odd look, "if you're busy with work and interior design, then please don't feel pressured to come to the wedding. I wish it was here, or in New York. I wanted something low-key, but my mom insisted on renting out some hotel in Santorini."

"We're thinking of having ours in Venice," Fiona exclaimed.

"You're getting married too! Congratulations!" Tanaz was looking at me and Bobby. "Everyone's getting married!" she cackled devilishly.

Joanne was eyeing a chandelier, no doubt wondering whether she could hang herself on it with the nearest tablecloth. She emptied the bottle of wine into her glass and chugged.

"We're thinking of asking Bocelli," Fiona said.

"As a guest?" I went for the easy shot. When did this conspiracy of Andreas invade my life?

"He did Rachel Heinberg's kid's *bat mitzvah* for a quarter million," Fiona added.

"Wow, she must have had to book a really big hall for that many guests," Bobby tried, but no one got it.

Now Joanne was contemplating ending her life with the nearest piece of cutlery. Even a spoon would do. "I'm going to die alone," she whispered. We ignored her.

"Let me ask you something." Fiona was facing Tina, two potential Bridez-illas bonding. "Bocelli is only available one day in September. I know it's ridiculous to plan a wedding around a blind Italian opera singer, but I really want him to perform. The first time Casey and I hooked up was in Vegas, and that Bocelli song was playing in the background. You know, at the dancing fountain. It's been our song ever since. But you have to be honest with me, bride to bride. Is it insane to pick your wedding date because of a singer's availability?"

"Not at all," Tina said. "I actually think that's really romantic."

"Okay, we should go," Tanaz interrupted. "Tina and Cyrus are only in town until tomorrow afternoon, and we still haven't found a dress. We are starting our day very early tomorrow."

Tina rolled her eyes as Tanaz led her away. I could see Bobby's eyes lingering on Cyrus's ass, which was pretty perfect. In another universe, Bobby would be able to bring a nice Persian man home and have his mother spend as much time and energy planning his wedding. But this was not that universe.

"So September twenty-nine it is," Fiona said, as much to us as to Casey. "The palazzo we're renting in Venice is small, so let me know if you guys wanna bring a guest."

"Don't invite me plus-one. That's like a jinx," Joanne said.

"Joanne, there is no such thing as a jinx," I replied.

"Oh really? Then explain to me why my grandmother died one week after I told my teacher she was dead to get out of a paper. It's karma. Remember that *Field of Dreams* movie with Kevin Costner. If you build it, he will come. Bullshit. Building it is jinxing it. If you RSVP yourself plus-one, then you'll always remain a zero."

"Being single isn't being a zero," I reasoned.

"Oh whatever, Kara," Joanne seethed. "You're practically married to Bobby. And now you're playing house to boot. Anyway, this book I'm reading says that relationships only come if you're not looking for them, so as of now I'm not actively pursuing it anymore. I've moved on. I'm taking Spanish lessons. If I can't pick up a man, I might as well pick up a new language." Joanne took a deep breath. "*Hola. ¿Donde están los servicios?*" We ignored her.

"What about you?" Fiona asked. "Is Bobby your plus-one, or should I invite him separately?"

"I guess he's my plus-one, right?" I said, looking to Bobby.

"And now you'll have the same address," Fiona commented. "No more separate mailboxes, no more separate bedrooms..."

"It's my birthday, Fiona," I snapped. "Can you lay off?"

"I'm sorry. You're right." Fiona took a breath, then added, "But I'll send you your own invite anyway, Bobby. In case one of you is dating someone by September."

"Enough wedding talk," Joanne demanded. "It's Kara's birthday dinner. This night should be about her." Joanne cut the tension by thrusting my birthday present at me. "Open it now," she demanded, so I did. It was a pink T-shirt that said *thirty and flirty*, only the age was in numerals, so the rhyme didn't show. I made a mental note to donate it to The Salvation Army.

Fiona reached into her purse and handed me a small box. Everybody knew what was inside. A gift certificate for a massage at Burke Williams. Fiona always gave us the same thing, mostly because she knew how much we appreciated the gift.

"So," Fiona said. "This new guy is working at Casey's law firm. He's obviously not an actor. He's very cute."

"Sounds hot," Joanne said.

"It's Kara's birthday dinner," Fiona retorted mischievously. "This night should be about her. There's only one catch, though. He's twenty-five. Is that too young for you, Kara?"

"Kara could definitely pass for twenty-five," Joanne said venomously. "*Vente y cinco.*"

"*Venticinco*," Fiona corrected.

"*Venticinco*," Joanne echoed.

"*Venticinco*," Fiona repeated.

Okay, I got it. I got it loud and clear. The bitches were baiting me and torturing me. I didn't blame them. If I found out one of them was looking for sex online with a fictitious age, I would find a creative way to torture, as well. But chorusing my made-up age en Español was truly evil. *Venticinco. Venticinco. Venticinco.*

"Okay, guys," I finally yelled, "you can stop now. Yes, I am the mystery woman behind the screen name *Sluttyandfun25*. Venticinco. Very funny. That's me. Yes, I put up an ad on Craigslist looking for sex."

Fiona, and especially Casey, looked at me in complete shock. "Why would you do something like that?" Fiona asked.

"I could set you up with a hundred of my friends," Casey added. "They all think you're hot."

Joanne sulked in her chair. Casey had never offered to set her up with a single one of his friends.

"Did you guys really not know?" I asked Fiona and Casey, who shook their heads in response. I turned to Joanne. I guess the bitch actually knows how to keep a secret.

"I would've told them if it was fun gossip, but this is just too depressing, you know. I thought you'd wanna keep it *privado*."

"It's not depressing," I insisted. "I'm going to have sex like a man. Like a gay man. It's gonna be fun." They didn't look convinced. "It's like an anthropological experiment." Still unconvinced. "Look at Bobby. He has his friends, his family, his work, and his sex life, all carefully compartmentalized like a fucking Joseph Cornell box. It works for him. I don't see why women believe sex and friendship are a matching ensemble."

Fiona looked to Bobby. "I guess that's true," she whispered feebly.

"It's not like I've even done anything yet," I added. "I just thought it would be a simpler way to get laid than going on a dozen dates and making small talk. I'm supposed to meet some photographer tomorrow night. He seems really cool. He's into astrology, he knows how to spell. I don't see the problem."

"Nor do I," Bobby piped in.

Fiona couldn't take it anymore. "I have to go to the bathroom," she said, eyeing me. I knew I was meant to follow her, and I did. As did Joanne, leaving Bobby alone to discuss college basketball with Casey.

"Are you insane?" Fiona screamed as soon as we were alone in the art deco bathroom of the hip brasserie. "This is the final straw. It's bad enough you pretend to be his girlfriend. Now he has you meeting guys online like him.

Don't you see it, Kara? He is turning you into another version of him so that you never leave. If you become as desperate and pathetic and self-loathing as he is, then he's guaranteed to have you forever."

"Fiona, enough. He's my friend. And he didn't push me into this. It was my decision. It's been a year and a half. I thought it would be fun and simple. I didn't think anyone would find out, and I don't even know if I'll end up sleeping with anyone."

"It's not about whether you end up fucking someone," Fiona said. "By all means, slut around. I fucked Jared Leto, Leo, and Tobey in the same month, and everyone who reads *Us Weekly* knows that. It's the secrecy of it, the sneaking around with some false screen name. It just reeks of shame and repression."

"I don't remember Jared's and Leo's publicists putting your flings into *US*. Why don't you talk to them about shame and repression?" I thought she actually might hit me.

"You guys," Joanne said. "It's Kara's birthday. Maybe we should go back and have a good time."

Fiona wasn't done yet, though. "Bobby has no choice. He's a gay man in a culture that doesn't accept them. He's acting out of repression for a reason. You're just being irrational. You are not a gay man, Kara. Do you hear me? You are not a gay man."

"And you are not my mother, so stop lecturing me."

"I'm not lecturing. I'm illuminating. Can't you see it from within your tiny little universe? He's moving you into a mansion, he's pushing you into having anonymous sex. He's ruining you, Kara. He's ruining you for other men."

"That's absurd," I said. "You yourself always say I'm eligible. You and Casey constantly try and set me up. Now can we go enjoy my birthday dinner? My *moules frites* are probably cold."

"Oh, wait," Fiona said. "This is gonna sound like an insane segue, but will you do GHB with me later tonight?"

"Excuse me?"

"Joanne's too much of a pussy to try it."

"I'm not a pussy," Joanne protested. "I have a drinks date later with a guy I met at Home Depot."

"Look, they're screen-testing me for the movie," Fiona explained. "It's me and three other girls. Do you know how huge this movie could be for me? It would change my career."

"So you have a twenty-five-percent chance?" I said. "That's great."

"The way I see it my chances are always fifty-fifty," Fiona reasoned. "Either I get it, or I don't."

"Are you sure doing GHB is gonna help you get the role?"

"I'm kind of scared to do it alone. But if we did it together, it could be perfect. I could get sense memory for my screen test, and you could get gangbanged."

"Fiona?"

"I'm just kidding. God, you'd think it was funny if Bobby said it. Where's your sense of humor, Kara?" As usual, Fiona was right. I would have laughed if Bobby had made the same joke. "Besides," she continued. "It's not like we didn't do E and coke in college. Our bodies have already been ravaged by chemicals. What's one more drug experience for old time's sake?"

"I *have* been wanting to let loose," I said.

"And if the new purpose of your life is to have sex like a gay man, then you might as well do their recreational drugs. It could be perfect for your anthropological experiment." Fiona's tone was so dripping in sarcasm that for a moment I thought her GHB plan was a joke. But when we returned to the table, Fiona announced to Casey that he was off the hook. "Kara has agreed, as part of her new life plan, to try this drug with me tonight."

"I don't know if this is a good idea," Casey said. "Do you really have to go out and try GHB? Can't you just act?"

"I want this part," Fiona insisted.

"You take care of her," Casey said to me. "She can barely handle a margarita."

I had to hand it to Fiona. She was committed to something. If only I could have committed to something as hard as she did, perhaps I would have had more to show for my life.

"Do you feel it yet?" Fiona must have asked that question thirty times in five minutes. We were sitting in her BMW convertible, blasting some Fiona Apple bootleg (Fiona was a huge fan of her namesake rock star), and waiting for the drug we'd mixed with Lemon Ice Gatorade to take effect. In the distance loomed USC's fraternity row. Fiona decided that since her potential character was a college student, she would do GHB at a college party, have me videotape her all night, and then mimic her behavior in the audition. It was, in my estimation, an insane plan. But what else did I have to do? "Do you feel it yet?"

"Honestly, Fiona, I don't think I do."

"Which frat should we hit?"

"I don't know. Sigma Nu is right here."

"But the Zeta Beta Tau guys are hotter," Fiona pointed out.

"Does it matter, Fiona? You're not gonna sleep with them, are you?"

"Um, hello. I'm engaged now."

"Exactly," I said. "So who cares if the guys are hot?"

"But what if we get date raped?" she asked morbidly.

"Fiona, we're not gonna get date raped."

"We're going to a frat party on GHB. There's a very good chance we're gonna be date raped. And if we're gonna get date raped," Fiona said with a smile, adding some humor into a potentially risky situation, "I'd rather it be by someone hot. So let's walk to Zeta Beta Tau."

I didn't realize how much I'd aged until I walked into the frat party. Somehow I always imagined that the girls and I looked the same as we did in college. But the people battling for the keg in front of me now were so... small. Either I had aged, or USC was populated by a bunch of Doogie Howsers. Fiona made a beeline for the keg as soon as we entered the party. "Are you sure that's a good idea?" I asked as I peeked into a bathroom, where two girls were snorting coke off a Fergie CD.

"This GHB is bullshit. I don't feel a thing."

"It's only been a half hour."

"I might as well get drunk." Fiona made her way to the keg line, which was a clear sign that the girl was distraught. I haven't known her to touch something as caloric as beer since freshman year of college.

"Maybe you should hold off on the beer," I suggested. "The drug might still kick in."

"Good. Then I'll be drunk *and* high." Fiona picked up a red plastic cup and held it out.

A bearded jock in a USC hoodie and cargo shorts poured the beer for Fiona. "You're the chick on TV?" he asked, though he obviously knew the answer.

"Yeah." Fiona always feigned indifference when she was recognized, but secretly she loved it. She just couldn't stand being perceived as one of those actresses who craves attention.

"You're hot," the bearded jock said. "We're doing body shots later. Maybe I can get a picture? My little sister likes your show."

"I'm not sure about a body shot, but maybe an autographed picture. You could give me your address." Fiona took her phone out of her purse.

"How about my phone number?" The line for the keg was getting longer, and a few angry teenagers were screaming at the bearded jock, whose name was apparently Mitch, to stop flirting.

"I'm engaged," Fiona responded coyly.

"Good, then we still have time before it's adultery," Mitch replied.

Fiona looked over to see if I was listening to her conversation, and was pleased to see that I was. "I have to go," she said. She pulled me aside and whispered in my ear. "Can you believe that guy? He totally hit on me."

"He's eighteen and drunk, and you're on TV. What did you expect?"

"You sound bitter."

"I'm not bitter," I replied bitterly.

"Well, you sound it, which is all that matters. Appearances are everything, Kara." Fiona took a large sip of her beer. "This shit is nasty." Was Fiona right? Was I bitter? Was I losing hope? Was I jealous that an eighteen-year-old was hitting on my friend? Had celibacy turned me into a lonely, angry bitch?

"He's kinda cute, though," Fiona continued. "I mean, in a hypothetical I'm-eighteen-and-single-again kind of way."

I looked back at Mitch, who was now filling a blond cheerleader's cup with nasty beer and apparently flirting with her as well. The truth is, I didn't find him cute at all. He struck me as one of those guys whose attractiveness lay entirely in his beard. Shave the beard, and it would expose just how below average he really was. But I couldn't say this for risk of sounding bitter again, so I just said, "Yeah, he's cute."

But by the time I responded, Fiona had moved on. Her eyes were dilated, her hands were shaky, and her mouth was opened wide with shock and elation. "Oh my God," she said. "Do you feel it?"

"I don't know."

Fiona pulled out her digital Elph. "This is the video option. Here." She pressed a button.

"Fiona, I know how to use a digital camera."

"You really don't feel it yet?" she asked a little too excitedly.

"I don't think so."

"You know what I really wanna do?" Fiona leaned into me and spoke into my ear. "I really wanna suck dick." And with that, she was off, directly toward Mitch, who couldn't believe his luck when Fiona pulled him to the dance floor by the hood of his hoodie and began to grind against him. I didn't know Fiona had the stripper skills she was displaying, but then I remembered those pole-dancing classes she had been taking.

As it turned out, Fiona didn't really need me to videotape her at all that night. Displaying the intelligence that got them into USC, many of the partygoers used their own digital cameras and cell phones to capture the TV star in all her hedonistic glory. Highlights included twelve frat guys doing body shots off Fiona's belly button; Fiona taking her bra off, dousing it in keg beer, and gagging Mitch with it; and Fiona displaying her fellatio skills on a Corona Light bottle. If what Fiona wanted was the chance to study herself on GHB for the role, she was in luck. The footage of her was on YouTube within minutes, and played on VH1 and E! around the clock all week. Luckily, the cameras couldn't pick up what Fiona whispered to me right before we left.

"I think I shat my pants," she whispered.

"What?" At this point, I was high, too, and I couldn't tell if I was hearing correctly.

"Don't make me say it any louder," she begged. "We have to go. NOW."

I started laughing uncontrollably, which is really an awful reaction to a friend having an unexpected bowel movement in her denim.

"Stop laughing."

I couldn't.

"This stuff is crazy. I didn't even realize what I was doing. I just felt something—oh, Kara, come on. Let's go." Fiona pulled me out of the party. The downtown L.A. street looked different than it had when we came to the party. The trees were a little greener. The sky was a little blacker. The music blaring from inside the party was pulsating in my head. Fiona rushed to her car and got in the driver's seat. "I need to get home." Fiona grabbed the camera out of my hands. "Why did I do this?" Suddenly, in an imperceptible instant, tears were flowing down Fiona's cheeks. "I've ruined everything."

Once again, I started laughing hysterically. I couldn't help it. Everything Fiona said and did seemed like part of some comedic farce to me. This time, Fiona didn't seem to register my laughter.

"Who am I kidding, Kara? I'm just not that good of an actress. This girl I'm up against went to Juilliard and co-starred in some play on Broadway with Laura Linney. I mean, look at me. I look dumb. I play dumb. I keep trying to improve. I work with all the right coaches. I take the right classes. But I still suck. Oh God, Kara, I'm *B-list*. I'm a B-list talentless druggie in shit-stained jeans."

I was stretched out on the gravel at this point, and I found it in me to say, "I think I can see Mars."

"And Casey hasn't fucked me in months. He says our schedules are misaligned because I've been shooting nights and he's been working days, but we always used to find time to have sex. Now it feels like we have to schedule it in. I'm engaged to the hottest guy I've met, and I never even get to make out with him. My life is a disaster. I need to go home."

"Do you think that there are people on some other planet looking at us right now?" I wondered aloud.

"Kara, I'm driving home. I want to be with my husband. Oh my God, did you hear that? I called him my husband, but we're not married yet. What do you think that means?"

"Hellloooo!" I screamed as I waved up to the sky.

"Kara, what are you doing?"

"I'm waving to the aliens," I said, as if this were obvious.

"Are you coming with me or not?" Fiona turned the ignition on. The Fiona Apple music immediately started blaring from her car. *I've been a bad, bad girl.*

"Hello!" I screamed.

Fiona slammed the door and pressed the accelerator. Her BMW took off at Indy 500 speeds into the dark Los Angeles night.

With the Fiona Apple music gone, the silence of the night engulfed me. I walked closer to the frat party. Three teenage jocks, who looked like they could have been wrestlers, were passing a joint back and forth. I walked toward them, almost by instinct. I just didn't want to be alone. I felt light-headed and tactile and emotional. I wanted someone to hold me and tell me life would be okay, that those aliens up there wouldn't come down and get me. One of the wrestlers caught my eye. His taut teenage body was evident under the oversized T-shirt and baggy jeans he was wearing. I smiled. This was it, I thought to myself. I was cruising, just like Bobby always did. A simple smile, and the next thing you know, you're on top of someone, satisfying your physical needs.

The wrestler turned his attention back to his friends. I couldn't make out their conversation. Just a few words here and there. *Physics. Dyke. Sophomore. Cheating.* I filled in the blanks. They were going to cheat on a sophomore physics test with a lesbian teacher. Or... they were discussing the physics of how lesbians have sex, because one of their sophomore girlfriends cheated with another girl. Or... The wrestler glanced up at me again. I was ready, I caught his gaze. Perfect timing, I thought to myself. Now he knew I was ready for action.

"What the fuck are you staring at?" he suddenly blurted. His two friends turned around and glared at me. I must have been a sight. A thirty-year old woman ogling freshman wrestlers at a frat party, my eyes dilated, my hair a mess.

"I'm sorry," I whispered as I rushed back into the party. Idiot, I thought to myself. Paranoia: one of the unpublicized side effects of GHB. Suddenly, I had to wonder, was everyone looking at me? Was everyone judging me? That girl over there, the one with the camel toe and the Courtney Love tank top? Is she staring at me? What about those guys playing "quarters" in the kitchen? Are they all staring at me? What about the couple with matching eyebrow piercings necking on the couch? Are they staring at me? The guys with bulging biceps arm wrestling? The guy carefully reading a vacuum-cleaner manual like it was *War and Peace*? The guy dripping hot wax from a candle onto his furry arms? And then my paranoia shifted gears. Was *nobody* looking at me? *Why* was nobody looking at me? Why wasn't anybody hitting on me? Why wasn't anybody date raping me? My God, I was an in-shape woman on GHB in a frat party, and I still wasn't getting any play. What was wrong with me? Through the corner of my eye, I caught a glimpse of Mitch and rushed over to him, out of breath despite the fact that I'd been standing still for the last ten minutes. "Hey, Mitch."

He was holding a deck of cards and a stack of poker chips. "Hey. Do I know you?"

"I'm Kara. Fiona's friend." Another blank stare from Mitch. "The actress."

"Oh right, of course, duh, cool." He smiled. "Where is she? Does she wanna play poker?"

What about me, Mitch? What about me? Am I invisible? I am flesh and blood, I am a woman who needs to be held, who needs the touch of a man at least once every eighteen months. Put down those poker chips and run your hands through my hair. Tell me I'm desirable. Thaw out the exotic and tangy frozen enchilada. Gobble me up!

"Are you okay?" he said. "You don't look so hot. You gonna barf?" I guess my eyes must have been rolling into the back of my head or something. Is that why no one was hitting on me? Did I look like Linda Blair in *The Exorcist?* Without thinking, I got into wheel pose and tried walking up the stairs backwards, hands first. My many yoga teachers would have been proud. My body was never this limber sober. *Somebody take advantage of me. My body is limber. I'm feeling loose.* Mitch looked down at me, aghast. "What are you doing?"

"I'm Linda Blair in *The Exorcist.*" I didn't even make it up the first step before I started shouting, "My mother! My sister! My mother! My sister!"

"Um, what are you talking about, lady?"

Lady? Did he reserve that term for those above thirty, or did he call all the campus girls that? I burst out laughing. "That wasn't *The Exorcist,*" I screamed. "It was *Chinatown.* Mixed movies, mixed metaphors. My mind is a mélange. A melancholy mélange. That's a good band name. The Melancholy Mélange. Do you play an instrument? I used to play the recorder. It's not hard, you just put your lips together and blow." Mitch just looked at me as I continued babbling in wheel pose, blood rushing to my beet-colored face. I guess Fiona wasn't the only one who wanted to give head on GHB. "Let's start a band," I screamed. "That's how you get play. Groupies!"

"Here." He put down the poker chips and held out his hand. I collapsed at the foot of the stairs and let him prop me up. I leaned on him as he walked me up the stairs and into his bedroom. The walls were covered in tapestries, incense was burning, and there were magazine clippings of soccer players in front of his desk. On his computer, his screensaver moved from left to right. It was a picture of his family. Mom, Dad, Mitch, Older Brother, Younger Sister. All smiles. *The perfect family.*

"This is my room. You can barf in there." He pointed to the bathroom. Formerly white towels were strewn on the floor, and I could see from afar the dark ring around the unwashed toilet. If I didn't need to barf, I sure needed to now. "You're not driving, are you?" I shook my head. "Good. I can take you home when you're ready," he offered. I must have gazed at him accusatorily, because the next thing he said was, "Don't worry, I don't drink. Only non-alcoholic beer in my cups. My mom was an alcoholic, and my brother is too. Figure I shouldn't tempt fate." *The perfect family.* "Kind of sucks for me, right? But at least I didn't gain the freshman fifteen."

He turned on some music. Dave Matthews. Yuck. "Listen, I gotta get back to my poker game. Do you want me to call Fiona?" *Yeah, go ahead. She's probably crashed her car into Pershing Square by now.* I shook my head. "Just barf in the toilet, okay?"

He walked out of the room. The first thing I did was turn Dave Matthews off. I needed to forget I was in a frat house. I went into that bathroom, kicked the toilet seat down with my foot, then reconsidered sitting on it. Wouldn't wanna catch anything. Yoga to the rescue again! This time, I squatted in chair pose to pee. Of course, there was no toilet paper. I stood and flushed with the heel of my shoe. I looked at myself in his dusty bathroom mirror. I didn't look my best, but I certainly didn't look possessed by the devil, either. It was Saturday night. It was midnight. I was high. I decided that if no one was going to hit on me, then I would have to take care of matters myself. I clicked a key on his computer, and immediately, that tortured family picture of his disappeared. I opened up Safari. I checked *sluttyandfun25*'s inbox. There was a new email from *Lensman4U* telling me not to wear panties the next night. Part of me felt I should save myself for *Lensman4U*, but I couldn't resist reading the thirteen other emails in my inbox. One by one, I deleted them: too young, too blond, terrible speller. Until, finally, I got to a photo of a swarthy, beautiful guy with darkly mysterious eyes. The photo was a close-up, just his rugged face and an ornate mirror behind him. I zoomed in on the photo, and in the reflection of the mirror, I could see a well-populated bookshelf. I couldn't make out the names of the books, but at least I could deduce that this guy was both gorgeous and literate. I moved on to reading his email. "Hey there. I liked your picture. You're very beautiful. I'm 36 years old, VGL (or so I've been told), 8 cut in case that matters to you. I'm visiting and staying at a hotel in Beverly Hills. I'm looking for NSA fun now if you are."

I emailed him, explaining that I couldn't send a picture because I wasn't at my computer. He didn't seem to mind. In his response, which came back within thirty seconds, he told me to call him. Four Seasons Hotel, he said. Room 2430. I looked at my cell phone. Not much of a signal. I picked up Mitch's phone and dialed. The concierge patched me through.

"Hello?" The voice on the other end of the line was deep and masculine and held the slight hint of an accent I couldn't place. A foreigner? Perfect. I could have my fun, and he'd be on a plane the next day. I could forget him. *Like you forgot Jacques*, I thought to myself.

"Hi," I whispered, afraid that Mitch would catch me using his room for more than barfing my way back to sobriety.

"So..." he said.

"So..."

"What are you up to tonight?" he asked.

"Oh, not a whole lot." *Just doing GHB with my friend the television star at a frat party with guys ten years younger than me.* "Just got home from a dinner party," I lied. "Had a few drinks."

"Okay."

On the computer, *sluttyandfun25*'s inbox was still open, with that email from *Lensman4U* staring me in the face. A wave of guilt suddenly swept over me. Was I cheating on *Lensman* by talking to this guy?

"So do you do this often?" I asked.

"What?"

"Meet girls online," I clarified.

"I've done it a few times," he answered. "Here and there. You?"

"Never. But..."

"Yes?"

"Well, I've been exchanging emails with a guy, and we're supposed to meet tomorrow." I paused and waited for him to say something. He said nothing. "So if you don't wanna meet, that's okay with me. I mean, I have a date tomorrow. Not a *date* date. A sex date. And maybe talking to you is cheating. Maybe I should just get off now."

"I'd like that very much," he joked. It took me a second to get it. At least he had some wit. Not an idiot, I told myself. Maybe an idiot would be better. Easier to forget.

"So you don't think it's a problem? This other guy?"

He laughed. I could tell even over the phone that his laugh was infectious. "You're afraid about being unfaithful to some guy you've only spoken to via email?"

"I don't want bad web karma," I explained.

There was that laugh again. This time it lasted even longer.

"Hey, are you laughing at me?" I asked.

"No, I'm sorry," he said between chuckles. "It's not you at all. I find it perfectly charming that you believe in Internet karma." *Perfectly charming?* Definitely European. Suddenly, he started singing. John Lennon. *"Bad web karma's gonna get you. Gonna knock you right in the head. Better get yourself together. Pretty soon you're gonna be dead."*

"Depressing."

"What?" he asked.

"Death," I explained.

"The rest of the song gets more uplifting," he insisted.

"I don't remember."

"Sure you do; everyone knows John Lennon."

My father did play John Lennon all the time. Consciousness music, he said. He even still had some Phil Ochs. The soundtrack of his angst-ridden suburban youth. Music to inspire the bombing of patrol cars. I remembered the lyrics and burst into song. *"What in the world you thinking of?"* I screamed, high in pitch and high on drugs.

"Very good," he said.

"Laughing in the face of love!" Even more off-tune.

"I'm sorry," he interrupted. "But is this Celine Dion? I haven't seen a picture of you, but that voice is unmistakable."

I laughed. He had charmed me, and at the same time reminded me that he didn't even know what I looked like. Maybe that's why flirting with him felt so safe. "I'm considerably less talented, less Canadian, and more younger than she is," I said, attempting some grammatical humor.

"Oh really, how old are you?" he asked.

I was about to answer when I looked down at the computer. I had emailed him from *sluttyandfun25*'s account. "I'm twenty-five," I lied.

"So...."

"So…" I repeated.

Ten minutes later, my taxi appeared outside the frat house.

By the time I arrived at the hotel, the drug had mellowed. I was still feeling good, just no longer seeing Martians, which was fine by me since I had a humongous bouncer to contend with at the entrance of the Four Seasons. He was holding a guest list, which was understandable at a nightclub, but really obnoxious outside the lobby of a hotel. "You're not on here," he said.

"I just got off the phone with him. He's expecting me. I promise."

"What room number again?"

"Kyle," I snapped anxiously. "Room 2430."

"I'm sorry, miss, but I don't have a Kyle in 2430."

"Just call up to the room," I pleaded.

"It's one in the morning. I can't call up to a guest's room unless I know the guest has invited the… visitor."

It suddenly hit me. I had walked right into the life of a call girl. High-end, okay, but a whore's a whore. "I appreciate your position, but he did invite me. He said his name was Kyle. He's thirty-six, he's…"

When I was about halfway through making a fool of myself, an updated guest list arrived. Too bad, since I was about to reveal "Kyle's" dick size to the increasingly distressed bouncer. I was on the update, by first name only, but apparently at the Four Seasons Beverly Hills at one in the morning, that's enough to get you in.

The picture didn't do him justice. He was six feet tall, broad, and lean without looking like the product of six hours at the gym a day. His hair was jet-black and messy, chunks of it pointing in every direction as if he had just slept with someone else. His skin was dark; he could have been Mediterranean, Middle Eastern, or South American. His eyes were the color of this raw organic honey I get at Whole Foods, a perfect hazel. He had what on most guys would be a five-day beard, but given the exposed hair of his chest, I guessed on him was a one-day beard. He didn't shave his chest or even pluck his eyebrows, which were almost one. It looked better on him than on Frida Kahlo. He was wearing dark worn jeans and a white V-neck with a gold chain around his neck. The first thing that went through my mind when I entered that room was *Damn, this guy is just Bobby's type.* Swarthy, rugged, Israeli or Israeli-looking. *Wait 'til I get to tell Bobby about this one...*

The suite's TV was tuned to CNN, some story about Google and China and censorship. In front of the bed was a table littered with shrimp tails from shrimp cocktail past and a bottle of scotch next to a bucket of ice. His breath smelled like single malt. He didn't say anything. He just cocked his stubbled chin toward the bedroom, and I followed.

"It's like some kind of hip-hop convention outside," I said. "Puff Daddy, I mean P. Diddy, or Sean Combs, or whatever you call him. You think people would get confused, what with him changing names all the time. You would think..." I trailed off, sensing his lack of interest. "You're not from here." He changed the channel of the television to one of the hotel's many music channels. The first one that came up was Latin Pop. *Amor de papel...* Click. "You know, they almost didn't let me in," I continued. He went up one channel. 1980s. *Everybody Wang Chung tonight...* Click. "Can't find a good station, huh?" I asked. Standards. *You're a Waldorf Salad....* Click. "Hey, do you speak?" I asked, irritated.

"Any requests?" It was the first thing he said.

"I don't know," I responded. "Something mellow."

Classic Rock. *Sing with me. Sing for the year...* Click. Oldies. *Tell him that you're always gonna love him...* Click.

"New Age," he said triumphantly. A forlorn Irish vocal undulated through the room.

"Nothing gets me in the mood for sex like Enya," I joked.

"Great. Since that's what you're here for."

It sounded so cheap put that way. My sudden sobriety put me in a state of panic. Instinct told me to turn away, or at the very least, to make myself feel more respectable by finding out *something* about this man. He cleared the bed of some half-browsed magazines. *The New Yorker. The Economist. The New York Times Magazine,* open to the crossword puzzle. "So what's your real name, anyway?" I asked. "Because when I was down there I asked for Kyle, and they said there was no Kyle. Is it a nickname or did you lie?"

"What I understood was we were both in the mood for *sex*," he said. "Not a battle."

"Who said anything about a battle? I just asked what your name was."

"And I told you," he replied. "Kyle."

"Fine," I said. "It's just..."

"What?" he asked impatiently.

"I know I signed up for the no-strings-attached thing by coming here, but lying about your name makes you seem shady." He didn't respond. "Are you shady?"

"Let's take a rain check," he sighed.

"You're kicking me out?"

"I didn't put it so bluntly, but this seems not to be working out...."

"I don't... I mean..." But I couldn't find the words. My hands were shaky, my head was buzzing, and my lips had tightened in response to equal parts fear, anger, and desire.

I stormed out into the Four Seasons hall. A bellboy disappeared into the elevator as I walked out, glaring at me with disapproval. A bored, elderly German couple struggled with their key card, the husband looking embarrassed, his wife judging me with her fixed gaze. I closed my eyes for a moment. I blocked out the harsh sounds of the German couple and the ding of the elevator and focused on Kyle. He was sexy and had kissable lips and a gorgeous body. Why was I blowing this chance, and not him? Why did I care if he lied about his name and had a confrontational personality? Mystery and friction can only make for better sex. It was now or never. The time had come to end my self-imposed celibacy.

When I knocked on the door, he opened it as if he knew I was returning. He looked down at me. The Enya was still on. "Yes?" he said.

I peeled my shirt off seductively, still standing in the hall. "What's in a name anyway?" I asked as I kicked the door shut behind me.

He pushed me onto the bed and threw himself on top of me. He shut me up with a kiss. "That which we call a rose by any other name would taste as sweet," I continued.

"I think it's 'smell,' isn't it?"

I licked his neck, running my tongue toward his ear. I could feel his cock get hard as the salt of his skin invaded my lips. "Taste," I repeated.

That laugh again. And then he turned up the music. Fucking Enya. *Sail away, sail away, sail away....* He reached his hand down my pants, exploring me. Instinctively, I pulled away. *Pull away, pull away, pull away.*

"What's wrong?" he asked.

"It's just, I haven't done this in a while."

"Which part of it?"

"The whole enchilada." Interesting word choice there. "Sex. Any kind of sex. I haven't had sex in… a long time."

"Good," he said.

"Good?"

"No muscle memory. People who have boring sex all the time develop muscle memory," he whispered in my ear. "They can't have sex any other way after a while. People who have no sex are open to new ideas. They have no default setting to revert back to." He ran his hands through my hair and pulled my head back. My scalp hurt from the tug, but I couldn't get out from under him. He put his lips on mine and kissed me with brute force. His mouth tasted so different from Jacques's. Jacques was a boy; everything about him was clean and fresh. I idealized his youth and his inexperience. But this was a man, thirty-six years old, or forty-one if he'd age-adjusted the same way I had, and I could taste the years in his mouth. There was sting in his kisses. He stopped kissing me and stood above me on the bed. "Take your skirt off," he ordered.

Maybe it was the residual GHB. Maybe it was that this guy was gorgeous. Maybe it was to prove to myself that I could finally sleep with someone besides Jacques. Who knows why, but I submitted. *We can reach, we can beach far beyond the yellow sea.*

"Now take everything off."

I obeyed.

"Show me how you masturbate." He unzipped his own pants as he said this. *We can sail, we can sail.* I slid my hands between my legs and started to play with myself. "Keep going," he whispered. "Forget I'm here." With his foot, he started rubbing my neck. It was the most strangely erotic thing. I turned my head to the side and licked his foot. Innocuously at first, but then more vigorously. I took his big toe in my mouth and sucked it. "That's right. Suck it," he said in a bad porn voice that was nevertheless a turn-on.

"Take your pants off," I ordered. He didn't obey. "Please," I begged. I reached up and ran my hands down his hips, pulling his pants down along the way. He grabbed my hands firmly and gripped them tight. Too tight.

"You're hurting me," I whispered.

He let go of my wrists and ran his hands through my hair. "Don't touch me, okay?" His face changed in that moment. He became a petulant child, cross and cowering.

"I'm sorry," I said.

"It's fine. I just, I'd rather be in control, if that's okay with you." "Yeah, it's fine," I said. In fact, I wanted to say, I like you in control.

Just when I thought the mood was dead, he pushed me onto the bed, spread my legs, and ate me out with abandon. The song changed. *The sound of holding on, almost a whisper.* The sensation of his tongue became too much for me to handle. "I'm gonna come," I screamed. "Don't stop." He didn't. He kept going and going until finally I climaxed with a scream that must've been heard by Diddy and Busta and Missy downstairs. He jerked himself off and came into his hand.

He disappeared into the bathroom, leaving me alone on the bed. I surveyed the room. There was a metal case in the corner, begging to be opened. On the floor next to the bed, I caught a glimpse of a boarding-pass stub on the floor. Delta. Where had he come from? All I could make out was the seat number. 2A. So, first class. Oh, but I already knew that; he was staying at the Four Seasons, for fuck's sake. There would be a name on the stub. Something I could Google. I couldn't make it out, but finally after much squinting, I made out a number on the side. DL247. Bingo. I took a peek at the half-finished *New York Times* crossword puzzle on his bed. When he came back from the bathroom, I noticed his limp. It was as if he was dragging his right leg to keep up with the rest of his body. This small deficiency, and the way he worked so hard to conceal it, made him all the more sexy.

"Are you okay?" I asked.

"Never better," he replied, with a grin that indicated he was ready for round two.

"No, I meant you looked like you were limping."

"Twisted my ankle playing tennis." He threw himself on the bed beside me.

"You should ice it," I suggested.

He ran his tongue in and out of my ear, an act I often find disgusting, but suddenly enjoyed. The heat and sound of his breath seemed to travel into my body with each exhale.

"I'm serious," I insisted. "You should be icing it every twenty minutes and taking Advil every four hours. If you don't take care of it within the first forty-eight hours, it's gonna take forever to get better."

"Are you a nurse?" he asked. "Or just bossy on some genetic level?"

"First of all, you won't tell me your name, so I don't have to tell you what I do for a living. Second, what makes you think I'm a nurse? Why can't I be chief of orthopedics at UCLA, Mr. Sexist?"

"I'm not sexist," he said with a smile. "I'm very pro-sex."

It wasn't very funny, and his question *was* sexist, even if it was rhetorical. I could really get to hate this guy. I should've left right then and there, but the lure of the unfinished crossword puzzle was too tempting. So was knowing what was inside that stealthy and spy-like metal box.

"Sopranos," I said.

"What?"

"Fifty-four down. High parts. It's 'sopranos.'" I picked up his half-completed crossword and handed it to him. He quickly filled in the answer with a black pen.

"What about this one?" he asked with a smile. "Four down. Screen Delilah."

"Hedy Lamarr." He looked at me blankly. "H-E-D-Y. Lamarr with two Rs."

"I'm terrible with actresses," he said as he penciled.

"You're doing okay with D-girls, though."

He ignored it, didn't get it, or didn't think it was funny. "Who gives a shit about stars?" he said. "There are people dying in the world. Genocide. Hunger."

"I work in Hollywood," I said.

"Well, it's very important work you do," he said without missing a beat. "Entertaining people. Making them laugh. Holding a mirror up to society. Making sure there are enough soft-drink placements to keep the global economy from collapse."

Uh-oh. I was sensing a pattern here. My father the radical hippie. Jacques the socialist. And now this guy. If I wasn't careful, I would end up falling for him. "No worries," I assured him. "I'm not in it for the Nobel."

"Just an Oscar, huh?"

Speaking of gold, I noticed the dangling pendant and chain around his neck. An insignia in Arabic, hidden beneath the tuft of black hair between his clavicles. I ran my hands through the hair until I reached the necklace and pulled it into view.

"You know who did change the world," I continued. "Hedy Lamarr. Not only was she a fabulous movie star, but she invented the technology that led to the cellular phone and Wi-Fi."

"I'm not sure I believe that."

"It's a fact," I insisted. "My roommate makes me watch a lot of old movies. He's unemployed...."

"So you support him?"

"Oh, no. He gets money from...."

He looked at me expectantly.

"It's boring. Let's talk about you." I was *not* going to make the mistake of nattering on about Bobby. "What does this necklace say? Your real name?"

"Allah."

"Your name is Allah?" I joked uncomfortably, then refocused my attention on the crossword. "I got it. The trick has something to do with the states. State of oblivion? *Unaware in Delaware.*"

He stared at the crossword for a long beat before saying, "You're amazing."

"You did all the prep work. You filled in all the little ones."

"But I never get the big picture. The main concept of the crossword always eludes me."

"There's a couple at this coffee shop I go to," I said. "They do the crossword together every morning. It's really cute."

Oh, Jesus Christ, *totally NSA* Kara, *totally NSA*. Why did I have to string the words *crossword, couple,* and *cute* into a vocalized thought?

"*Unlucky in Kentucky.* Thirty-one across," I said, back on message.

"Wait," he exclaimed. "State of dusk? *Gloaming in Wyoming.* It fits. We got it. Just one more. State of smell. What's a state with a K and a? Oklahoma. *Aroma in Oklahoma.*" He wrote it in. "We did it. We finished the whole crossword. I never finish the whole crossword in one day." He leaned over and kissed me on the lips. Tenderly. And suddenly it was clear that this couldn't be the first and last time I saw this bastard. I impulsively grabbed his cell phone from the nightstand.

"What are you doing?"

"In honor of Hedy Lamarr, I'm inputting my number into your phone book," I explained.

"And why is that?" he said.

"Because," I said as coyly as I could, "I have a feeling you're gonna need help getting through next weekend's crossword."

7

THE NEXT MORNING, I was hiding in the warm, womblike salt water of the Ebadi pool. Something melancholy and French was playing through the underwater speakers. Doing GHB had seemed like a harmless idea, but I had forgotten how lonely and difficult drug hangovers are. To the same degree that the altered state makes everything seem magical, the aftermath makes it all dubious. I surfaced and quickly took in some air, spying Bobby dousing himself with tanning oil, and then resubmerged. I could still feel Kyle's body against mine. I could smell his scotch breath and hear the New Age music playing from the hotel television. I had broken my year and a half of celibacy with sex more charged and bizarre than I'd ever had. Which left me wanting more. My head aching, I swam a lap under the surface, picturing a future of blissful domesticity with Kyle. I pushed myself out of the water for more air. The evidences of my hangover must not have departed yet, because Leila was hovering over me with a tray, on which rested a glass of watermelon juice, a Bloody Mary, and sunny-side-up eggs atop toast. Omar, smelling the food in Leila's possession, was climbing her leg to get a piece. "You need to eat something, Kara *djoon*. Eggs are the best thing for a hangover."

"I know. Dr. Oz says so. There's some enzyme in eggs that helps your body process the liquor, apparently."

"Well, we Persians figured it out long before that Turk," she said, reminding me that in the universe of the Arab world, Persians always considered themselves first and better. She tried to set the tray on a chaise longue. "Omar, sit down already. Sit!" Omar finally obeyed. "Eat up. You'll feel better in no time."

I could hardly tell Leila I was recovering from GHB, not from alcohol, and eggs might not do the trick. Even my reflection in the forgiving pool water was horrible that day. The bags under my eyes were multiplying by the second.

"It does look like you had quite a night, you two," Leila said, now turning her attention to Bobby, who was lounging in the sun reading the Wally Lamb book Harry had gifted me.

"*Quite* a night," Bobby cracked with a glance my way.

I propped myself up on the side of the pool and took a sip of my Bloody Mary, then began to eat. "Thank you, Leila. This is delicious."

"Thank Rosa Maria. I just carried it out here. She even mixed the Bloody Mary from scratch, the way Babak taught her. So, did you go dancing?"

"Nobody goes dancing anymore, dude," Bobby said. "Dancing is done."

"That's sad." Leila unwrapped her sarong, proudly revealing a turquoise one-piece. "I bought this suit in the Bahamas for five dollars." She pulled a book out of her tote bag, something in French with a risqué image of a half-naked woman on the cover. "Back when we were young, all we did was dance. We would go out every night in Tehran until the sun came up. They always brought the new European music. Aznavour, Dalida, Mina."

"You *danced* to Aznavour?" Bobby asked.

"Why not? It was a different style of dancing then. A man actually held a woman. Now people just dance alone in a mob. People do everything alone now. It's the *Me* generation. I read something about it in a magazine. You two are part of the Me generation."

"Dude, the Me-generation was the yuppies. You're still living in the Reagan era. We're barely old enough to be Gen X."

"Then the *me, me, me* generation." Leila seemed to enjoy the repetition. She picked Omar up and squeaked to her, "You, you, you!"

A brief wave of nausea overtook me. I kept the same bite of eggs in my mouth for at least twenty seconds, unable to swallow for fear of puking and unwilling to spit for fear of forever ruining Leila's hopefully pristine image of me.

"Kara *djoon*, are you sure you're okay? Maybe you need to sleep. You could take a nap in one of the guest rooms."

I forced the eggs down. "I guess I can't handle my liquor now that I'm thirty." From a distance, the sound of a tennis ball being hit back and forth was driving me bonkers. Hossein and Koorosh Ebrahimi were playing a game of singles on the court across the hedge, and from the panting and grunting that reached us, it must have been quite a head-to-head.

"Oh, by the way," Bobby announced. "We saw Tanaz, Tina, and Cyrus at Comme Ça last night."

Leila nodded. "I know. Tanaz called me first thing in the morning. She said you looked gorgeous, Kara *djoon*."

"Thank you."

"Tina wants a small wedding," Leila said. "I don't know why Tanaz can't just let her child have what she wants."

The irony of this last statement was interrupted by a primal grunt from the tennis court. "Damnit, Hossein. Finish your stroke! Make contact with the ball in front of you!" And then the crack of a racquet.

Leila got up and announced she should go keep an eye on her husband. The only time Hossein's emotions penetrated his controlled surface was during tennis or golf, and he often needed Leila to remind him that it's just a game.

As soon as Leila was gone, Bobby put Wally Lamb down. "This book is really good," he said disappointedly. "I thought it would suck."

"Oh, poor Bobby, is it making you doubt your own abilities?"

"Kara, I haven't written more than an email in years. I don't doubt my abilities anymore. I mourn them."

The hypnotic rhythm of the tennis match commenced again, which I assumed meant Hossein had been sufficiently calmed by coach Leila. "Could the day be any more gorgeous?" I asked.

"Okay, cut the crap and tell me everything," Bobby commanded. "I want the dirty details, and I want them now."

I plunged back into the pool. I had told Bobby about the frat party and my rendezvous with Kyle, but I had omitted all the good details other than those relating to Fiona's self-humiliation. Given particulars about what happened at the Four Seasons, Bobby would immediately point out that I had failed in my mission—a genuine, anonymous, NSA one-night stand—by giving Kyle my number. He would note that I had been secretly watching my cell phone all day, forcing me to deny it, even though I *had* been. And it had yet to ring.

"Well," Bobby said when I emerged from the water once more. "I can tell you about my evening, and then maybe you'll be inspired to share. After Comme Ça, I was really craving a grapefruit, so I went to Gelson's and arrived just before they closed. I grabbed a nice big fat ruby red and headed for the express line, where I happened to find myself standing behind a muscle bear buying eleven bottles of Bacardi. 'Hosting a party?' I asked. He said, 'Why, you looking to party?'"

Knowing what *party* means in the gay community, I had to ask, "You did coke?"

"No, you know I don't mess with that devil drug anymore. But they did coke."

"Who's 'they'?"

"The thirteen guys at the party. No, twelve of them did coke. I was the thirteenth. The bear took me to some other guy's dingy apartment on Kings Road, and in front of his three cats, this college student pretty much got gang-banged by all of us."

"And how much echinacea does one take to recover from a gang bang?" I said, only half-jokingly.

"Not enough echinacea in the world if you're on the receiving end. But since I wasn't, I visited Dr. Bryer this morning while you were still asleep. He gave me a B-complex shot and some Xanax for the anxiety. I feel really okay about it now. We all used condoms, and none broke."

"Sometimes you render me speechless," I said.

"Okay, I shared. Now it's your turn."

I got out of the pool, polished off the remnants of my Bloody Mary, and lay next to Bobby. "There's nothing much to say. I was high, I went online, and I met this pretty gorgeous, pretty sweet guy named Kyle. And we hooked up."

The *thwock-thwock* had stopped across the hedge.

"You're an atrocious storyteller, and my parents are gonna rejoin us any second, so I'm losing my patience."

"Okay, fine. He's totally your type. Swarthy, hairy, definitely Middle Eastern of some kind. He even had an Allah necklace around his neck."

"Hot," Bobby said.

"You are a major mental case," I said with a shake of my head. Bobby could turn anything into a fetish: a cowboy hat, a pair of dirty socks, even a necklace representing the very religion that he and his family claimed to despise.

"More detail please," he demanded.

"He had a stub of a boarding pass lying around, and of course I researched it immediately. He came from Dubai."

"Uh-oh," Bobby muttered ominously.

"What?"

"You're falling into the trap," he explained. "You're *curious* about him, when you should be moving on to the next guy."

"Bobby, I'm never gonna see the guy again. Forgive me for wondering casually what country he's from."

"Well, he's not from Dubai. No one is. It's just a transit point. Can't you just be content to narrow it down based on whether he's cut or uncut?"

"No, not really," I scoffed, wanting to add that his endless fascination with foreskin was somewhat ridiculous.

Rosa Maria peeked her head out from the kitchen window. "Babak, you want more drink?" she yelled.

"No, thanks. We're good," Bobby screamed back, before turning to me with gravitas. "Look, you asked me to teach you how to be more noncommittal, how not to have expectations. If you really wanna learn, then there is one cardinal rule. Never sleep with the same person twice."

"I didn't sleep there. But why is that the cardinal rule?"

"Because that's when *emotions* creep into the picture. If you really want to learn not to be needy, then you have to break the pattern of caring every time a guy gives you an orgasm. That is the goal here, right? Teach you how to be more aloof so you don't get hurt again and again?"

"Yes," I said with a pout. "I guess."

"Good. Now please tell me you didn't exchange numbers with this Kyle character."

"No." I hated lying, especially since Bobby would have appreciated the "in honor of Hedy Lamarr" bit. But it was only a half-lie, anyhow—Kyle hadn't given me his number, so it wasn't an exchange. And my phone had yet to vibrate, and since the chances of Kyle ever calling me were slim, I'd probably never have to confess the truth.

Bobby stood up and tested the waters of the pool with his foot, as if the temperature wasn't always exactly 78 degrees. "Isn't this fun? The two of us recounting our exploits to each other the morning after like two whores in a brothel."

"Thanks for putting it that way."

"You're the real hooch. You have another date lined up for tonight."

Of course, *Lensman4U*. I had spent the day actively trying to forget I was supposed to meet him that night. The last thing I wanted after a night of GHB and sex with Kyle was more sex. "I think I'm gonna bail on the photographer," I said. "I feel way too hung over."

"Wo nay," Bobby protested. "I can already sense this Kyle character creeping into your consciousness. The best way to forget him is to sleep with someone else. I will personally drive you to *Lensman*'s place."

I barely had any more time to protest before Leila and Hossein approached with a sweaty and defeated Koorosh by their side. Omar immediately bolted toward Koorosh, barking her little heart out at him. "I'm so sorry, Mr. Ebrahimi," I said. "She tends to bark at people she doesn't know."

"I never understood the idea of animals and humans living together," Koorosh said. "You know, in Iran, that never happens. Dogs are unclean, and the black ones are considered evil." Omar, whose English was limited to a few words, but who picked up energies easily, recognized an enemy and increased the volume of her bark.

Leila picked up the dog. "Oh, Omar, my beautiful baby," she said. "If Babak had ever made as much noise as you're making now when he was a child, I would have locked him in a room until he was quiet."

"How lovely," Bobby said. "The dog gets better treatment than the son and heir. No wonder I'm so well-adjusted."

"I think Omar's a little more tense than usual because she's constipated," I explained. "She hasn't gone number two in days."

Leila immediately found a new subject. "Babak, Kara, we have an announcement to make. I wanted to wait until we were all together to tell you." Leila looked to Hossein, granting him permission to break the obvious news.

"Our offer on the Roxbury house has been accepted," Hossein reported proudly.

"Congratulations," Koorosh said. "I still think you'd be happier in a full-service condo on Wilshire, but if a big, old, endless-maintenance place is what you two want, then that is what you should have."

"I'm so happy," Bobby said, though the conflict on his face was easy to read. "I can't believe we're really moving. It's amazing. Isn't it amazing, Kara?"

"It is. It is amazing," I said, suddenly excited by the prospect of my future in *Le Manoir*. I asked Koorosh and Hossein about their tennis game.

"He wins every time," Koorosh sighed. "I don't understand it. I'm always ahead, and then he beats me in the end."

"I don't want to crush you too early," Hossein joked. "That would be no fun."

"Crush me? We went to five sets." Koorosh looked to Bobby. "Your father is a sneaky and fierce competitor."

"I know. That's why I stopped playing tennis when I was fourteen," Bobby cracked. "He was just too good for me."

Hossein didn't seem to appreciate the remark. He had tried through the years to find father-son bonding activities. Unfortunately, these activities were usually athletic, and Bobby, who saved his endorphins for the gym, never wanted any part of them. The first year I met Bobby in boarding school, he failed to get a spot on the tennis team. Rather than face his father's disappointment, he lied and said he never tried out. He then decided he would never pick up a racquet again, a pledge he remained loyal to, despite his parents' insistent desire to see him back on the court.

"Koorosh and Hossein are going to see a movie at the Pavilion. I told Rosa Maria to make some *karafs* for dinner. Do you two want to stay?" Leila asked. *Khoreshteh karafs*, a stew made primarily of celery and a coterie of delicious herbs, was one of my favorite dishes, and appeared rarely on the Rosa Maria rotation menu. "We could go through my old issues of *Architectural Digest* and pick out some themes and colors for the new house."

Between sex with some random guy and a night of stew and interior design, the choice was clear. Sadly, my reaction time was slowed by the hangover, and Bobby beat me to the punch. "We're busy tonight," he said.

"It must be nice to be young," Leila uttered. "Two nights out in a row."

"Oh please, you have a more active social life than we do, Leila," I said. "Wait, what are we doing tonight again?" I asked Bobby with a hard stare.

"That hangover is really affecting your memory, Kara. We're meeting your old friend from junior high. *The photographer.* Remember?"

Bobby parked three addresses up from *Lensman4U*'s Silverlake house. Silverlake was the kind of neighborhood where ten-million-dollar rehabbed silent-screen-star mansions hulked within sight of the ninety-nine-cent stores, and where digital-effects workers took great pride in restoring humbler houses designed by '40s architects who did eight hundred aircraft hangers but only one residential project. Taking Sunset from Brentwood to Silverlake was like crossing three international borders. On the West Side, Sunset was immaculately paved, tree-lined, and quiet. West Hollywood announced itself loudly with blaring music, valet-blocked traffic outside ultra-hip hotels, and naked models on billboards advertising invisible clothing. After West Hollywood came Hollywood proper, which had been taken over by the Scientologists. I mean, L. Ron Hubbard even got a street named after him. About the only other people I knew with streets named after them in the city were George Burns, Gracie Allen, and General Thaddeus Kosciusko, a Pole who served in George Washington's army. I guess that put L. Ron in some fairly B-list company. After Hollywood, Sunset took you through Los Feliz, hipster central, where zoot suits and Mary Janes were still in style. Then Silverlake, which was kind of like Tijuana, except that the strip malls had trendy bistros. The hills of Silverlake were full of beautiful old houses, the kind of houses that people with an appreciation for architecture and history might have liked. Personally, I preferred central air to a vintage window, but there was something sexy about a man with a thing for architecture.

"You gonna be okay? Should I wait outside?" Bobby asked, looking down the block toward the photographer's dark windows.

"Aren't you gonna get bored?"

"I have Wally Lamb to keep me company. Or I could call a phone sex line. Maybe I'll do some Donald Rumsfeld roleplay in case the government is listening." Bobby looked down at his cell phone. No bars. "Fucking hills. If he turns out to be a mass murderer and you need to call 911, you won't have any reception."

"Thank you for that thought. Seriously, can we turn around and go to your parents' for dinner? I'm still hung over, and all I want is rice and stew. My stomach is homesick for Persia."

"Kara, you emailed this guy for a week. You were excited about meeting him."

"Don't you mean fucking him?" I corrected. "Whatever, it's past-tense."

"Because of Kyle?" Bobby asked.

"No, because of the good work Kyle did," I retorted. "I'm sexed out."

He was looking at me skeptically.

"I know the concept of a person being sexually satisfied has never penetrated your consciousness, but that's just one of your many shortcomings."

"Please, Kara, I know you. You have to go inside, if only so you don't wind up thinking about Kyle tomorrow."

"I haven't been thinking about him today."

"No, you've been very deliberately *not thinking* about him. That's just one level down from obsession."

"So I should *not think* about *Lensman4U* tomorrow?"

"Think about either one. About what a great dick he has, or about how he wears too much Brut. Just not anything emotional. Keep it on the surface."

"Now you sound like your mother," I cracked.

"Vat's wrong with sounding like my mother?" Bobby asked in a pitch-perfect imitation. "She is a very smart voman. And let's say this Kyle character is *the one*, if such a myth really exists. Then what you don't want to do is push him away. And by obsessing over him, you'll push him away. By sleeping with someone else, you'll forget about him, appear detached, and he'll come jonesing for more."

I pouted. "But I don't wanna go inside. I'm tired."

"You asked me to teach you," he said. "I'll gladly stop."

Just for good measure, I pulled out my cell phone to make sure I hadn't missed the vibration. Only one missed call since we left the Ebadis. It was Fiona, no doubt calling to ask how she looked in her mug shot. "No, I'll follow your guidance. Just tell me what to do."

"It's not complicated," he said. "No emotions. No attachments. No fucking the same person twice. Now go, go, go!" And for some reason, I did. I didn't want to disappoint Bobby. Like any good Persian Stepford girlfriend, I was eager to please my man.

I rang *Lensman4U*'s doorbell and awaited my dark and rugged demigod. His appearance at the door was like getting a Shih Tzu when you were expecting a Shiba. His hair was thinning, his skin was pockmarked, his eyes were puffy, and he was oozing sweat from every visible pore. He smiled, revealing teeth yellow like jaundice. "Hey, I'm Ben."

"Um, Peggy," I replied quickly, realizing this was the right time to make up an identity.

"You used your own picture," he said, surprised.

"Yeah, I thought that was the reason jpeg was invented."

"I know. It's just I'm an actor, so I can't send around pictures of myself to strangers. You could sell them to the tabloids." I recognized him, but had no clue as to his name. "But I found a pic that looked similar to me." I pulled up his photo from my brain's hard drive. The man in that photo was perfectly built and gloriously tan. Was this guy delusional? I was mute, completely unable to respond, but like all actors, he had no problem having a one-way conversation. "You don't recognize me? I've been in hundreds of movies and TV shows. Maybe I should do the face. Hold on. Girls love the face." He scrunched his features into a look of creased anger and smiled an evil, snaggle-toothed smile, and that's when I recognized him. His many roles came flooding back to me. Yes, indeed, he was a character actor extraordinaire, one of those faces you see in every other movie at the multiplex and forget before you find your car in the ten-story garage. His specialty is evil. He's the guy who blows the buildings up in big action movies, and the mean father who stands in the way of his daughter's happiness in romantic comedies. And then it hit me fully. He was Fiona's dad. Not her real dad; her *TV* dad. He'd started guest starring in season two when her character, Mona, locates her biological father. After an entire season of growing close to him, she begins to have visions at the end of the season. Season three was devoted to her realization that her father is a sex offender. Suddenly, all I could think about was a scene in which the creep standing next to me fondled a young girl picking daisies. Cliché, sure, but so disturbing.

"This is a beautiful mid-century." Under the circumstances, it was all I could think of to say upon entering.

"It's actually a post-and-beam."

"What?"

"It's not a mid-century," he asserted. "It's a post-and-beam. See those?" He pointed to large wood posts that supported the roof. "Those are typical of the style. As are the ridge beams. It's completely different than mid-century, which is really a period rather than a style or a school."

I take it back. There's nothing sexy about a man with a thing for architecture. "Well, it's nice."

"Can I get you something to drink?" he offered. "I'm in AA, so all I have is a little wine from when I fell off the wagon last week."

"I think I'm okay."

He smiled that disgusting snaggle-toothed smile that had bought him a post-and-beam, and put his hand on my thigh. I pulled away from him instinctively. I imagined Bobby peacefully reading his Lexus owner's manual, something he hadn't done since leasing the car two years ago.

"Listen, you're already all the way over here, and we're both horny, so we might as well make the most of it." As I mulled the faulty logic of his statement, he grabbed my hand and led it to his crotch. He was hard and his dick was wet. He was wearing drawstring sweatpants, and he liberated his dick from the fabric with one tug of the elastic. He smiled again.

"I'm sorry, can I use the bathroom?" I asked, as I bolted away in revulsion.

"It's just to your left," he screamed. I found my way into the aubergine bathroom, turned on a light, and locked the door. Once inside, I cursed myself for not bolting the other way, right out the front door. I could sit in this bathroom all night, I thought to myself. I could read... *Us Weekly, In Touch,* or *People* Magazine, all sitting atop his toilet. I opened *In Touch.* SCARY THIN, the cover read in bold letters over bikini shots of Kate Bosworth, Nicole Richie, and the emaciated half of the Olsens. I tried to turn to the corresponding page, but the pages were stuck together. This guy got off on anorexia. How much more Hollywood can you get?

When I opened the door, I broke the bad news to *Lensman4U.* "I think I have some kind of stomach bug," I said. "I should really go home."

He looked at me suspiciously. "You're a bad actress," he said.

"Seriously," I said, "I ordered bouillabaisse at dinner. There must have been some bad fish in it."

"If you don't like me, you can just say so. There's no need to pretend you have violent diarrhea or something." He placed his hand on my breast. "Come on," he said. "I'm a great lay." How can a person touch another person's breast after saying the words *violent diarrhea?* He leaned in and kissed me, smearing my lipstick across my face with his chapped lips.

I pushed him away from me aggressively. "You should really send people your own picture," I said.

"None of the other girls mind." Wow, this guy said the sweetest things.

"I don't see how they wouldn't mind. It's a lie, it's a... a... misrepresentation."

"Sure it is, *sluttyandfun25*," he snapped. "You're not slutty, you sure aren't fun, and I bet you're well into your thirties."

Well into? That was it. "I'm gonna go now."

"This sucks. Now I have to get back on the net and look for someone else." He headed toward the kitchen and uncorked a half-empty bottle of wine. He took a slug. "It's sour," he said, slurping as he drank.

"I'm sorry it didn't work out," I offered as a parting statement.

"Fuck off."

"Excuse me?"

"Just fuck off," he repeated, before adding, "you cocktease slut."

"That's an oxymoron."

"Excuse me?"

"How can a cocktease be a slut? It just doesn't make sense."

"Fine. Then fuck off, you fucking bitch," he bellowed.

"No, you fuck off. You... You... *character actor.*"

He looked genuinely hurt by my jab. He took a breath, and whispered, "*All* actors are character actors."

I was out of breath from the showdown with *Lensman4U* when I got to Bobby's car. He was listening to an NPR report about underground fashion shows in Iran. He turned the volume down and looked over at me. "That was a quickie," he said.

"Yeah," I replied, desperate to get the coach off my back.

"So, was he hot?"

"Gorgeous."

"Wow," Bobby said. "And are you gonna see him again?"

I looked up and saw *Lensman4U* peering out one of his windows with that bottle of wine still in hand. He gave me the finger. "Not my type, really."

Bobby revved up the engine and turned the car westward. "I have to say that I am very impressed with your attitude. You met a sexy guy, you fucked him, and you're walking away with your gun back in its holster. You are embracing the philosophy. Don't you feel great? Liberated?"

"Yeah, I feel a profound sense of freedom," I lied. "I've seen the light." And indeed, I had. In one take, I understood that online sex is like salted nuts or MTV. You kept telling yourself the next smokehouse cashew was your last, the next video would be the good one, but the nuts got staler, and videos peaked in the '80s. As Bobby drove home, I understood better than ever the trap he was in. The trap that told him he had to fuck and run—not because the next guy would be all that much better, but because the next guy may not have been as bad.

I woke up Monday morning feeling used and dirty. I could still smell the essence of last night's botched tryst with *Lensman4U* on my body. No fancy Fred Segal *savon* or hotel-stolen scrub could seem to wash him off me. I had taken a hot bath immediately upon returning home, exfoliated in the tub, washed my hair, and moisturized. In the morning, when I could still catch hints of his noxious sweat amidst the clash of coconut, grapefruit, and avocado from my skin and hair care, I repeated the routine. But somehow, the memory of the scent was enough to keep recreating it on my body.

The last thing I wanted was for Hossein to smell an old pervert's perspiration on my skin. Monday was the day of my Hyundai's check-up. As a valued customer of Hossein's flagship dealership, I didn't pay for my service appointments.

Hossein's original Hyundai dealership, on a desolate stretch of road in the 818, was the last place one would expect a man who lived in a big Brentwood house to work. There were far more glamorous Hyundai dealerships in Los Angeles, and Hossein ran them all. But North Hollywood was where Hossein made his start, back when he was just an émigré with an education. And something about the stale, diminutive, nondescript office he had kept for almost three decades must have reminded him of those early days of ambition, before he had been numbed into complacent silence by a demanding wife, a dead elder son, and a distant younger son. I stood outside Hossein's office, engulfed amidst the many varieties of vehicles Hossein was selling, and watched him at work. He had unbuttoned his blue shirt and rolled up its sleeves. The valley heat had created puddles under his armpits. I recognized the shirt as a Leila purchase. Whereas Leila chose the hip designers (Prada, Gucci, Versace) for her son, she went classic for her husband, decking him in Ferragamo, Pierre Cardin, and Zegna. She wanted him to look like an Italian playboy, but in that moment, sweating in a strip mall car dealership, he looked every inch the Middle Eastern immigrant.

Hossein looked up and saw me. He nodded and pointed to the headset, which dangled from his ear. I could hear him through the glass of his closed door. Hossein was of the generation of men who didn't trust technology, and believed you had to compensate for the natural faults of the telephone by screaming into it. At the moment I entered, he was explaining to a customer that she could either take a car in red or drive to Encino to pick up the black. Hossein's demeanor with this obviously annoying customer was patient, affable, and firm, a far cry from the quick intolerance he displayed for Bobby when Bobby demanded something other than financial assistance from him. Bobby always said that when he took a trip with his family, his father would talk for hours with the person sitting next to him on the plane, but then not say a word to Bobby for the entire trip other than "How's the food?" and "Do you need any money?"

Bobby had discovered some of the great stories of his family's past by slyly eavesdropping on his father in such moments. From the back of a cab in the south of France, Bobby listened as his father told a cab driver of the rough neighborhood where he grew up, the Tehran street fights he got into, and the time he broke an arm defending an insult against his mother. From the deck of a boat in Mexico, Bobby listened to Hossein tell their tour guide the tale of his first job as a mechanic in Iran. It was then that Hossein had fallen in love with cars. Iran was a land of the rich then, and Rolls Royces and Jaguars were brought in for them to play in. Hossein recalled fondly to the Mexican tour guide the joy he would feel upon lifting the hood of one of these foreign vehicles, and laughed when he recalled the time he was caught by his father taking a customer's irresistible Mercedes convertible for a joy ride to impress girls. These stories, as rehearsed as they sounded to Bobby's ears, had never been rehearsed on him. Perhaps Hossein felt that Bobby, with his blasé urbanity, didn't care to hear stories of the old world. I preferred to think that Hossein knew Bobby was always in earshot of his yarns and told them with a keen understanding that he was having a removed degree of bonding with his son. Perhaps that was wishful thinking. Or perhaps Hossein felt that fathers were meant to be imperturbable, steady forces in the chaotic lives of their wives and children, their exultation expressed only outside the gaze of those they provided for.

A no-nonsense Korean in a skirt suit asked if she could help me. I told her who I was and pointed to Hossein, who smiled and waved to the both of us. His conversation about the red car had somehow turned into a friendly discourse about the future of women's golf. "You're Kara," the Korean said. "Leila's mentioned you." After I got over the ever-hilarious image of Leila stepping her Chanel pumps into the valley, I nodded. "I can't imagine asking for a better father-in-law than Ebadi. He's so goddamn funny. I swear to God, it's not even like coming to work. He makes being a car salesman the best job in the world. I was offered a job at Saab in Santa Monica, which is so much closer to where I live, but I couldn't leave Ebadi." I loved the way she referred to him by his last name, as if they were in a secret society in college rather than a dealership. "Anyway," she continued, "if I can get you anything, just let me know. We have tea and coffee and bottled water." She walked away toward another lost-looking customer peeking into the window of a boxy sedan.

Finally, Hossein emerged from his office, wiping his brow then rolling his sleeves up some more, further wrinkling the crisp-design perfection Leila had draped him in. He shook my hand with fatherly vigor, a far more relaxed man away from the fancy trappings of his home. As he leaned in for the customary kiss on each cheek, I hoped and prayed he couldn't smell *Lensman4U* on me. I felt, perhaps for the first time in my life, shame. Had it been Harry, I could have told her the truth, and we could have laughed about it. But Hossein would never have understood what a single young woman, and one who was about to move in with his son, no less, would be doing going to a stranger's house for a rendezvous.

Hossein led me outside, where the sun's reflection on one shiny Hyundai after another seemed to increase the already oppressive valley heat. Hossein started sweating even more, periodically wiping his brow with a handkerchief. It seemed to me that Leila never perspired; if anything, she glowed. And I've never seen Bobby sweat outside the gym. Bobby must have inherited the dry gene from his mother.

Every car salesman in the lot waved to Hossein with a small bow, as if he were royalty walking through his kingdom. "There is something important I would like to discuss with you," Hossein said in a pointed whisper. I couldn't remember Hossein ever having something to discuss with me, or with Bobby, for that matter. Hossein wasn't a discusser; he was a doer. I braced myself for what was coming next. He didn't say anything for a very long time, he just led me across the lot in silence, a leisurely, excruciating, interminable silence.

Finally, Hossein stopped and tilted his head ever so lightly toward me. "So," he asked with a smirk rising up the right side of his face. "What do you think?" I must have looked fearful, or at the very least perplexed, and he smirked again. I had never seen this side smirk out of Hossein. He was like a child in this environment, that teenage kid who was still allowed to play with cars. Hossein ran his hands along the scalding, silver hood of a Hyundai Sonata, a four-door family sedan. The confusion increased. "I was thinking about your birthday presents, and I felt terrible. Usually, I let Leila buy the gifts from both of us, but sometimes it just seems so impersonal. Obviously, I didn't have any part in purchasing you a dog collar or a dress."

I had to interrupt Hossein and tell him he had given me more than enough through the years. "Not to mention you're buying us a house."

"The house is an investment. You will just happen to live in the investment. I need to give you something that's yours. Besides, you can't live on one of the nicest streets in Beverly Hills and drive a tiny, beat-up old Hyundai Accent. You'll stand out. You won't fit in."

"Well, that's not always a bad thing," I insisted.

Hossein shot me a disapproving look. "Please, no *tarof* with me. I'm not offering you a Ferrari, just a small upgrade from what you have. Your car is a dinosaur. We'll take that one back at no charge and recycle it for you. This one has GPS, it has one of those plugs for your iPod device, and it's one of the safest cars around today, which is very important." Hossein paused for a beat, and then, probably against his better judgment, he added, "especially if you want to have children."

I almost gasped. It might have been difficult before, but now it was plain impossible to deny that Leila, with Hossein as her willing accomplice, was on a mission to supply herself with a grandson. Or perhaps, given her history with boys, Leila would prefer a granddaughter. Regardless, a family car and a mansion needed children to populate them. I told Hossein I had to think about it. I told him I didn't feel worthy of his generosity. The truth was that I wasn't prepared to hold up my end of the bargain.

As I took the Sonata for a test drive, Hossein was comfortably seated next to me, playing around with the satellite radio to show me its many options. He listed them off one by one, tediously and adorably, as if hearing that four different smooth jazz channels, a Broadway station, and numerous talk radio options would clinch the deal. Amazing how some old men ended up sexually harassing younger women, while others, like Hossein, became classy and generous elders. Hossein and the character actor weren't far from each other in age. I wondered whether Hossein ever cheated on Leila. Did he hire high-class call girls when Leila attended her charity benefits? Did he have trysts with beach babes in the south of France? And if so, did Leila mind?

The repugnance I felt at the whole escapade with the character actor made me feel like there were worse lives than having kids with Bobby. If we eventually become our parents, then Bobby would become either Leila or Hossein: exceedingly generous, frustratingly secretive, intellectually curious, unbearably stylish, and always dependable. I could imagine worse husbands or fathers. Through my rearview mirror, I glanced at the back seat, and against my will blurted out, "It's so roomy. You could fit three kids and a dog back there." The smile lit Hossein's face. Not a smirk this time, a full-fledged smile. I felt horrible. Those simple words uttered in vulnerability had been my most blatant act of collusion yet. Until now, I had allowed them to weave the fantasy on their own and allowed my silence to speak for itself. Had something in me changed? Was I suddenly ready to accept my inevitable mantle as the next Mrs. Ebadi?

8

"WHAT DO YOU MEAN she hasn't taken a shit in three days?" Fiona was sitting on my couch. It was Wednesday evening, she was waiting to hear whether she got the movie, and she couldn't stand the anticipation, so she had reached out. We had spent a good hour and a half discussing the three actresses she was up against, and the pros and cons, from a box-office perspective, of hiring each of the four, and now the conversation had moved mercifully on to the subject of Omar's bowel movements.

"I have a shitless Shih Tzu," I cracked.

"Kara, are you high? You need to take the dog to the vet."

"She'll be fine," I said. "I sometimes don't go for days."

"You're not a dog, Kara. You're a girl. All girls are constipated." Fiona paused. "What's wrong? You seem, I don't know, preoccupied."

I shrugged. Kyle never called. He never would. I felt silly for giving him my number, and even sillier for believing I could have anonymous sex and not feel anything.

"Kara!" Fiona crackled. "There's a living thing that's relying on you."

"Maybe she's depressed," I reasoned. "Like her owner."

"Why are you so depressed?" she asked.

I shrugged again. Melancholy had gotten the best of me. I was supposed to be learning how to fuck and run, but instead, I was pining. Again. Hadn't I just done that for a year and a half?

"Does this have something to do with your Internet whoring? Because we told you that was a bad idea." I buried my head under a cashmere blanket that Leila had gifted me many *Nowruz*es ago. "Don't be such a drama queen. First the anonymous sex, now the drama. You really are turning into Bobby. And if dogs take after their owners, then Omar will soon be as fucked-up as you are. Tell me, how would you feel if Omar gave up her own life to become the beard for some King Charles Spaniel and his fabulous parents? And then decided to put an ad on Craigslist looking for someone to mount her?"

"Hey," I yelled from within the safety of the cashmere, "you're the one who went out and did GHB and shat your pants and got arrested. I'm not the only fuck-up here."

"I did all of that for my career, Kara. I had a goal in mind. What's your goal?" I didn't answer. My goal had been to learn how to be noncommittal. But it seemed too silly to vocalize. "And by the way, my publicist, agent, and manager agree that all the press from that night on GHB made me a serious contender for the part. Every time the director turns on the television, he's gonna see me doing a perfect rendition of what he wants me to play. So that night was not a fuck-up. It was a success. A massive success."

"I'm happy to hear that," I said, finally coming out from under the blanket.

"Can we go get a Pinkberry or something?" she asked. "I haven't eaten since breakfast."

"I can't. I have dinner at the Ebadis tonight."

"Tonight and every night," she snapped.

"You know what, Fiona. I love you, and I know you want the best for me, but enough. Is there a single aspect of my existence you don't disapprove of? You hate my friendship with Bobby, you hate my relationship with the Ebadis, you think I'm a failure at work, a bad mother to my dog—am I missing anything?"

Fiona took my hand in hers. "Listen, I'm a decent actress on film, but a terrible one in real life. Funny how that works. I guess I just can't help being honest with you. So... how is the Internet stuff? Have you met anyone?"

I couldn't stand any more judgment or advice from her. "No," I said. "I dropped the whole thing. It's not for me."

"Well then, there you go. There's something you did that I approve of wholeheartedly. Now if you'd just give up this idea of moving to a house in Beverly Hills with Bobby," Fiona suggested as she texted into her iPhone. "I know you've rationalized the decision, but you're stepping into a prison. Like Goldilocks or Mariah Carey or Hedy Lamarr."

"Hedy Lamarr?" I asked with a smile.

"Yeah, her first husband kept her locked up in this Austrian mansion, and she had to drug her maid and pretend to be her to escape."

"I know the story. I was there when Bobby told it to you."

"And all about the movie he was going to write about her. Did he ever write anything?" I shook my head. "This life you two lead lulls you into inaction." She finally stopped texting. "I'm referring you to Pedro. He's a licensed vet and the most respected dog trainer in Los Angeles. He trained Reese's dogs, and they're dolls. Plus they're definitely not constipated."

"Fiona, I don't have the money for an end table, let alone a dog trainer."

"I'll pay for it."

"Wow, I'm a charity," I murmured. I had always felt inadequate and envious of Fiona's level of success, but this took it to a whole new level.

"You don't have any trouble accepting gifts from the Ebadis," she shot back quickly.

I was speechless because, as usual, she was right. In Fiona's eyes, I was on the Ebadi payroll, just like Rosa Maria and their gardener. Yet somehow, it still felt more desperate and pathetic to accept help from one of my girlfriends, with whom I was supposed to be on the same level.

"Anyway, I'm not doing this for you," she went on. "I'm doing this for Omar. She obviously needs help. You haven't fully committed to being her provider yet."

"I have too," I pleaded unconvincingly.

"You're still bitter she's not some Japanese thing like the one Jacques had."

"I'm not. I love Omar."

"You have to commit to something to love it," she said, once again quoting one of her yoga gurus or acting coaches. "And you're textbook noncommittal."

"I wish. If I was noncommittal, then I'd be over Jacques by now."

"That's not commitment. That's falling for unattainable men. You have a kooky, hippie father who you could never please, and so you keep finding men that you can't possibly please either, Bobby being the obvious example."

"Jesus," I said. "Easy on the analysis. One interview on *Loveline* doesn't make you Dr. Phil." Fiona had been on *Loveline* earlier that year. No surprise, she proved to be an incredibly perceptive advice-giver.

"It's a fact, Kara. Deal with it or end up alone. And how do you expect to commit to a man if you can't commit to a dog?" Fiona's cell emitted two chirps. "Perfect. Pedro is on his way."

"What? Now?"

"Do you think your dog should wait for medical attention?" Fiona demanded to know.

"Bobby and I have to be at dinner at his parents' in an hour."

"Persian food reheats well." Fiona took a breath and looked in the mirror. "I can still play college, can't I? I had an oxygen facial right before the screen test. My skin looked better than this."

By the time Pedro arrived half an hour later, Fiona had left. She'd roped her manager into going to dinner and convincing her that she could absolutely play college, and that she would most definitely get the part. Pedro's license plate read DogLuvR, which was ridiculously cheesy, but became instantly adorable once Pedro got out of the car and revealed himself to be a brutally hot Colombian with thick moppy hair, five o'clock shadow, and a perfect body. All that, and a vet's license too. I lifted the Shih Tzu into my arms and carried her to the door with me to greet the matinee idol dog trainer. "Hi, I'm Kara. And this is Omar."

"I am Pedro." He held out his callused hand, and I shook it eagerly. His black T-shirt and jeans were covered in fur, clearly from different dogs. There was some long white fur, some short brown fur, and some fluffy gray fur. It only made him sexier. Was this Fiona's sneaky way of setting me up, since I always rejected her efforts? If so, she was brilliant. "So Fiona tells me your dog doesn't go potty."

"That's right. No potty for Omar." I handed her over to Pedro. "But she seems very happy despite that."

Pedro placed Omar on the couch. I had no idea what he was doing, but he appeared to be touching her inappropriately. "Your dog is constipated," he said. "We're going to start with some simple techniques to regulate her."

"Metamucil?"

"You will feed her cottage cheese once a day, and you will put a match in her rectum once a night to stimulate her bowels."

As this wildly disgusting piece of news was being shared, Bobby entered the apartment. "You almost ready? I promised we'd be on time and…" He stopped upon seeing Pedro. "Oh, sorry. I didn't realize you had company. I'll, um, come back later."

"Bobby, this is Pedro. Omar's new trainer."

"Oh." Bobby laughed. "Okay. I thought maybe… you know…"

"Fiona referred him to me. Pedro, this is Bobby, my roommate."

Bobby's eyes were fixed on Pedro. "So where are you from, Pedro?"

"Colombia, originally. But I have been living in Los Angeles for six years."

"I'd love to visit Colombia," Bobby said. This coming from a man too scared to drive through East L.A.

"It's not a very safe country."

"Safety is overrated, don't you think?" Bobby smiled. To my surprise, Pedro smiled back. Bobby reached over to pet Omar, and on his way he gently rubbed up against Pedro's crotch, one of Bobby's patented moves. Pedro gave Bobby one of those I'm-gonna-fuck-you smiles. How did he make these things happen so damn *fast*? "Pedro, do you speak Spanish?" Bobby asked.

"Of course. Why?"

"I'm a screenwriter, and there's this article on a Spanish website about female matadors that I'm researching, and it would be really helpful to have someone translate it." Wow, he was good. Bobby was taught Spanish early in life by Elena, who was under strict Leila orders never to speak English with the children. I always thought this spoke to Leila's generosity of spirit. A selfish mother would never allow her children's nanny to converse with her children in a language she herself didn't understand. She would be too paranoid that it would distance her children from her, that soon her children would be talking about her behind her back with their nanny.

"No problem." Pedro turned to me. "Do you have any matches lying around?" As it turned out, I used to collect box matches, subconsciously waiting for the day I could stick them up a dog's ass.

"Wooden OK?"

He nodded. "Take Omar out and gently place an unlit match inside her. Wiggle it around until you feel her bowels moving. Then quickly pull out and let her potty."

I suddenly wished I lived by the Southern Pacific tracks, so I could choose between what Pedro prescribed and lying down in front of a locomotive. "Don't you think you should help me out? I've never stimulated a dog's bowels before."

"I'll be right inside."

Inside is right.

"You have to learn to be comfortable around your pet," Pedro said.

"I am comfortable around my pet," I replied. "Just not sticking blunt objects up my pet's rectum."

"Well, Kara"—Bobby leaned over and gave me a kiss on the cheek—"some of us do that with our pets all the time. It's good for them." He picked up his cell phone, hit a speed-dial number, and spoke rapidly in Farsi. I heard my name sprinkled throughout the conversation. Blah blah blah Kara blah blah Kara blah blah blah blah blah Kara. Finally, Bobby hung up.

"What did you say?" I asked.

"I told them you're stuck at work."

"Great," I sighed. "Lay it on me."

"It's a perfect excuse. It's not like I can say I'm stuck at work. I told them your boss was producing a commercial and that you were on set. Just to get the story straight, I said you had no idea when the shoot would end, so we would call them when we could make it. They're gonna start dinner without us." Bobby eyed Pedro, who was waiting for him by the doorway. "I'll knock on your door when we've got this translated."

Omar was staring up at me desperately when she heard the door close behind Bobby and Pedro. Did she realize what an injustice had just been done to me, or was she just desperate to take a shit?

I took Omar out with a box of matches from Buddha Bar in Paris. Jacques had taken me to the uber-hip lounge. We had sipped Buddhatinis, listened to lounge music, and made out under the shadow of the enormous Siddhartha. I snagged the matches on our way out so I could always remember that night. Now I aimed one toward Omar's butt. I gently brushed some of her white and gray fur aside to make sure I pushed the match into the right spot. "I'm sorry, Omar, but just know this hurts me more than it hurts you." Omar wiggled away from me. I held her in place and rammed the match in. She barked like a madwoman, yelping and shivering. I tried to remember the first time I put a tampon in, the odd sensation of being invaded by a foreign object. "It's okay, Omar. It's okay, baby. It's all gonna be over soon." I could faintly hear Bobby moaning from inside when suddenly I felt Omar's body pulsating. I quickly pulled the match out of her ass and she unleashed a hefty and healthy-looking turd, stored in her body for far too long. My face formed into a smile, then I laughed, joyously and uncontrollably. I held Omar up above my face and kissed her. Her excited tongue ran up and down my nose.

"Good girl, Omar. Good girl." I took out a doggie treat and fed it to her. She chewed it up appreciatively. I was filled with pride and joy as I scooped up the crap with a plastic bag from Whole Foods and threw it in a trash bin on the corner. "Come on, Omar," I said. "Let's go for a long walk while Uncle Bobby does his business." Omar followed behind me. I could sense she trusted me now, that she had faith in me as her provider. It was a long time since I'd felt trusted, and even longer since I'd felt needed. Omar and I walked farther and farther away from the sound of Bobby's creaking bed.

"Well," Leila said as she escorted us toward the living room. "Better late than never. Rosa Maria kept the food warm in the kitchen."

"I'm sorry. I had no idea the shoot would go so late."

"It's alright. It's nice to know you work hard," Leila said, more for Bobby's benefit. "And I can't believe Janet is still working. Amazing how active pregnant women are these days." When we reached the living room, we found Hossein asleep, his reading glasses on, the latest biography of Nixon perched on his belly. Nixon's mug moved up and down rhythmically with the flow of Hossein's breathing. "Hossein, the kids are here," Leila said. Hossein grunted then went even deeper into a trance, beginning to snore. "Hossein!" Leila grabbed an embroidered pillow and threw it at him. Hossein leapt up, Nixon fell with a thud to the floor, and Bobby laughed at his parents' little performance. "Hossein, *pasho*," Leila demanded. "The kids are here."

"What time is it?" Hossein mumbled.

"It's nine-thirty. Come, have some more dessert while they eat."

"It's nice to see you work hard," Hossein said, more for Bobby's benefit.

A few moments later, the kitchen was filled with the smell of fresh mint. Leila had prepared two plates of rice and *khoreshteh kadoo* for me and Bobby, and two glasses of hot water with mint for herself and Hossein, along with fanned slices of mango and papaya for dessert, a wedge of lime complementing their colors beautifully.

"So?" Leila said. "Tell us all about this commercial you were working on. Is it something we'll see on TV?"

"Fortunately not," I said, a masterful liar at this point. "It's Kim Basinger doing a hair product, only to air in Japan. Per her contract."

"As if she couldn't use *any* kind of exposure," Bobby helped out.

"Then I can see it on YouTube," Leila said.

"You go on YouTube?" I asked, amazed.

"I do it for Hossein," Leila explained. "He loves old Persian music and movies, and any footage of anybody anywhere shaking hands with the Shah. I find the most amazing things on YouTube. Videos of Googoosh and Hayedeh. Scenes from movies we watched at the Azadi when we were young."

"Really. I'd love to see them," I said.

"You'd be bored," Hossein said. "It's all in Farsi."

"No, really. You've all included me in so much of your family life, and I don't know anything about what Iran was like back then. At least not first-hand." It was a risky gambit. Normally, this would have Leila veer off kamikaze-style for LACMA, an upcoming sale, or a spa she'd just read about.

"Tehran was like Paris back then," Leila began. "We had Sinatra come and play; Europeans would vacation in Iran; we had the best skiing and the best nightclubs."

"So it wasn't religious?" I asked.

"It was. But the Shah was modernizing," Leila stated proudly. "And at the same time, he was taking us back to our roots, before the Islamic invasion. This is why we call ourselves Persian and not Iranian. We are from the empire, not from the country."

"But he tried to modernize too fast," Hossein added. "And then the revolution..."

"Okay, enough," Leila said, lurching out of her reverie. "We can all read about the revolution in history books. Or on Wikipedia." Leila winked at me. "You see, I even know about Wikipedia. Your mother-in-law is a modern woman." She took my hand and led me toward the study. "Come, I'll show you how fabulous Iran *used* to be." She turned to Hossein and Bobby. "Come on," she ordered them.

In the study, Leila navigated to YouTube and typed in a few keywords. The first clip she showed me was Googoosh, whom Bobby voice-overed as "the Cher of Iran." I guess he wasn't worried about outing himself with such statements. In the grainy color video, Googoosh was standing in a fake garden, her hand dramatically clutching fake branches and flowers, her lips painted red, her hair dyed auburn and styled in a Farrah flip. Fawcett, not

Diba. A purple gown clung to her body as she belted out what sounded like a torch song. For all I knew, it was the national anthem.

"What're the lyrics?" I asked.

"The song is called 'Two Windows'," Hossein said. "She's saying that there is a wall with two windows in it, but they can't reach each other. One is you and one is me. She's wishing the wall breaks so the two windows can hold each other in a world without pain."

I guess metaphor is weirdly literal in barely post-medieval societies. "Sounds uplifting."

"You wanna hear uplifting?" Bobby asked. "Googoosh stayed after the revolution, and she wasn't allowed to sing until she escaped to Toronto seven years ago."

"She didn't escape," Hossein said. "They granted her a visa."

"They silenced her for twenty years. Imagine the government not letting Cher, or Lisa Loeb for that matter, sing publicly ever again."

"If they outlaw The Pussycat Dolls, it's fine by me," I joked. "But women aren't allowed to perform publicly at all, right?"

"Enough," Leila said. "Why can't we have a conversation about Iran without immediately going to all the horrible things our long-suffering country has become? For once, let's just enjoy the memory." Leila loaded another clip, this one of a hefty redhead they identified as Hayedeh, singing an apparent homage to the Pahlavi regime. Over a melancholy ballad, black and white images of the Shah and Shahbanou. The images were at times intimate, the rapidly aging monarch and his beautiful wife cooing over their newborn child, and at times disturbing, crowds of apparent supporters being held at bay as the Shah walked through a dusty village. In every clip, the Shah and his wife were the height of glamour, draped in gold and dripping diamonds.

"The Shah was a great man," Leila said, as an image of him vacationing at the beach played. The queen wore a headband around her blondish hair. This appeared to be a thing among Iranian women, from Googoosh and the Queen to Leila herself. They all lightened their hair to strawberry, or in Tanaz Maliki's case, platinum. Maybe they thought the color shift made them appear more Persian than Iranian.

As Leila searched for her next clip, my cell phone beeped three times, indicating three new text messages had arrived. I ignored the first two, assuming it was Bobby texting me covertly. But by the third beep, I apologized to Leila and peeked at my phone.

"I wanna C U tonight," the first one read.

"Kyle here BTW," went the second one.

"Cum over now. I'll be waiting in bed," went the third one.

Had I been anyplace else, I would have texted back, "With your pants on?" Instead, I just closed the phone, making sure Bobby didn't see it.

Leila had pulled up another clip. "This is Vigen," she said, as a man in a tuxedo sang what sounded like a Persian rumba. There was a classic handsomeness to him. Not Omar Sharif, but the same thing Omar Sharif had. Same thick black hair, same strong, straight nose, same thin upper lip and strong chin. Bobby was riveted by the hysterical mariachi band backing Vigen, but I could see Leila was watching the singer. Was he the Jon Bon Jovi of her dreamy teens?

I opened the phone and texted Kyle back. "On my way," was all I said, before I stood up.

"I'm so sorry," I announced. "Major emergency. The director of the commercial lost a reel of film. We have to go to the set tonight before they break it down, so we can do a reshoot."

"What a shame," Leila said. "Hossein and I were really enjoying showing you these old clips." Leila looked over to Hossein, who had fallen asleep in his chair, a small string of drool dangling ominously over the green alligator of his Lacoste shirt. "Well, you know how Hossein expresses his happiness."

"Rain check?" I asked. "I really want to see more."

Bobby's eyes were fixed perversely on me. "So the director lost a reel?"

"Yeah. Brilliant, but a drunk."

"Where's this director from?" Bobby asked.

"He's... Czech. Maybe Hungarian. One of those."

"And the whole crew is going back now. Is that legal with the unions?"

"Overtime," I replied quickly.

"I'll give you a ride," Bobby said.

"No, they'll pay for a cab," I said. "Stay here and watch clips with your mom."

"No, I insist on giving you a ride. Can't have those Teamsters see you pulling up alone this late at night." Bobby turned to Leila. "You're cool, right, dude?"

"Of course. You should drive Kara. A taxi would take half an hour to get here, and they can never figure out which is the right house. I'll just clean up downstairs and go to bed." Leila glanced at Hossein. The drool had now landed squarely on the alligator. "Should I let your father sleep here?" Leila chuckled at the idea, then stood and gave us both kisses on the cheek.

At the front door, she said, "But call me tomorrow so we can schedule the inspection of the house."

"Spill it," Bobby demanded as soon as we were back in his car.

"Was the third degree really necessary in there?" I asked.

"Oh, no, of course not. Who doesn't love being lied to?"

"It's your lie," I snapped back. "You invented the fictional commercial shoot I'm working on. I just appropriated it."

"Well, it's not the lie that matters, it's who you lie to." Classic Bobby logic.

"Lying to your parents is okay? Is that what you're saying?"

"It's different. They don't *know* they're being lied to. I do. So where am I really taking you?" I couldn't tell Bobby to take me to the Four Seasons. He would know I was going back to Kyle, and he would scold me for breaking his absurd rule of not having sex with the same guy twice. "Come on, Kara, what's this emergency booty call you got?"

"Don't bitch at me, Bobby. This is the ethos I learned from you."

"I'm not bitching. I just wanna know who he is. And don't think I'm gonna let you get away with words like 'ethos,' missy."

"It's some guy I chatted with online while you were doing your imitation of a roast turkey for the dog whisperer. Now can you just drop me off at Sunset and Larrabee?" A cross street where cabs would be abundant.

Bobby stopped on that corner. "Which building?" he asked.

"He's in an apartment up Larrabee. I can walk from 7-Eleven. I need some gum. Gotta get that Persian food flavor out of my mouth."

Bobby looked me directly in the eyes. "What are you keeping from me?" he asked.

"Jesus, Bobby, stop it. I appreciate your guidance, but I don't want to share every detail of my sex life with you. Girls are different that way. They like to keep a few things for themselves."

"Fine," he said with a laugh. "Play the girl card. I can't argue with that."

I entered the 7-Eleven and waited until Bobby's car was far out of view, and then I walked toward the Mondrian Hotel. As I made my way to the line-up of cabs waiting outside, I pulled out my cell phone and texted Kyle to say I was on my way. And it hit me. His very long international cell number had appeared with the texts on my phone. Now I could find out where the mystery man was from.

I dialed 411 as I entered a cab. "Four Seasons Hotel," I told the driver before the operator answered. "Hello," I said, "can I have the international operator?" When the operator came on the line, I said, "I'm just trying to figure out where a calling number originates. It's a cell phone." I opened Kyle's first text from the inbox in my phone. "It's 00989122066322." That was a lot of numbers; Jacques' phone number wasn't that epic.

I could hear the operator punching the digits into her console. "That would be Eye-ran."

"Ee-rahn," I instinctively corrected.

"Excuse me?" she said.

"That's how you pronounce it."

"Do you have another number you want to request?" she asked.

"No."

"Then thank you for using AT&T." She hung up, and I deserved it. The cab turned down Doheny, past a group of blondes waving their bras out the sunroof of a stretch Hummer. What was my life coming to?

But hold on. *Iran?*

Of course, it was too perfect. My life was being colonized by the Empire.

When the door opened, the other shoe dropped: Kyle. Vigen. They didn't look alike, but they had the same look. I should have realized that Kyle, whose name could obviously be anything *but* Kyle, was probably Persian. Or Iranian, depending on his own complex relationship to Islam, the Shah, and Googoosh's greatest hits.

He had the TV on, as before. This time it was porn. OK. More aggression. I'll put the gloves on. Of course, I didn't want to launch into these thoughts as I walked into the hotel room, so I just let the porn play and ignored it.

On screen, a fat, hairy man with a decidedly large dick was playing the part of therapist to two busty and blond identical twins, who were fighting too much at home. One of the twins hogged all the bathroom time. The other twin snored. The therapist's sophisticated clinical analysis was that there was only one way to solve their sisterly issues and eradicate the animosity between them. The boom-chicka-boom music came on, and the two sisters started sixty-nining, flicking tongues into pussies as the fat, evil therapist jerked his misogynist dick.

I reached the bed and sat. Kyle was under the covers. I pulled the covers back to look at him. He was shirtless this time, but the fucking pants were still in place. His chest was so beautiful, built with just the right amount of black hair covering his pecs. His dick was already hard. He reached his hand up my skirt, and before I could say hello, he began fingering me. He threw me down on the bed and tied my arms together with a striped Ralph Lauren necktie. I moaned, not a moan of disapproval. I wasn't sure whether being tied up by him was what I wanted, but I was certainly willing to find out. With another necktie, he blindfolded me, which was fine by me, since I wanted to avoid staring at those poor abused twins on screen anyway. I heard him put his hands in the ice bucket next to his bottle of Glenlivet. His lips found mine. He had a piece of ice in his mouth and he kissed me deeply, passing the ice back and forth between our mouths. He took the ice back and chomped it, undressing me with his hands as he used his mouth to scratch every part of my body with the ice's surprisingly sharp edges. Water was dripping down my body, his tongue licking up every drop. Finally, he went down on me until the ice melted, which was when I did, as well.

As he took off my blindfold, I heard the porn click to the BBC news. Kyle was still wearing his pants, and putting his shirt back on. I realized that other than a few dirty orders here and there, we hadn't spoken to each other yet. "Hey," I said.

"Hey," he countered.

"So, did you have a good week?" He leaned back on the bed and zoned out to the news. "Did you go out of town or something?" On the news was something about Pakistan selling nuclear secrets to Iran. "You mind if I clean up?" I asked as I walked to the majestic bathroom.

I remembered what Bobby had taught me about bathrooms and booty calls. Always peek into the medicine cabinet for evidence of illness. I didn't have as much reason as Bobby to be paranoid about STDs, and I was a big believer in karma, so I had never resorted to the bathroom snoop. Bobby had actually gotten himself into trouble many times by rifling through people's medicine cabinets. Once he had casually tried to ask someone about a drug he had never heard of. Assuming it was a new HIV drug, he might as well have just accused the trick of lying to him online. Turned out it was a diabetes medication. And that also turned out to be the end of the hook-up. Bobby went home with blue balls and a short-lived feeling of guilt. After that botched sleuthing experience, he had learned his lesson, and had since just stayed in bathrooms another minute to Google whatever medication he found via the browser in his cell.

The water pressure of the Four Seasons shower was just what I needed. I wrapped myself in a fresh and fluffy bathrobe and walked back out into the dark room. I lay back on the bed next to Kyle, who was still zoned out in front of the television. He had finished a glass of whiskey and had a vacant look in his eyes. He seemed more distant this time than the first, like he had been stewing in this room since Saturday.

We lay there for a good ten minutes.

He blinked first. "So you're not going to launch into another interrogation?"

"No." I'd decided that playing it cool was the best method of interrogation.

"Great. We get to keep our trivial secrets."

"I don't think you're in a lot of danger of losing your mystery."

"There's nothing mysterious about me," he said flatly, as if he almost believed it.

"There's plenty that's mysterious. Not that I'm curious."

"Like what?"

"Sex with your pants on. That ominous metal box." I pointed to the metal case that still begged my attention from the corner of the room. "Whatever. My fantasy's probably better anyway."

"What's your fantasy?" he asked, having fun now.

"Now who's giving who the third degree?"

"I am. So, what's the fantasy?"

I had to think fast. "That you're a Colombian drug trafficker."

"You want me to be Colombian?" He sounded like an eager young actor in one of those expensive workshops along Santa Monica Boulevard.

"More like I enjoy imagining you as a criminal."

"You think I look like a criminal? Or I look Colombian?"

"A little. Or Israeli. I don't know." Yes, I do know. I wanted to scream. You're from Iran. Eye-ra-an! I know because you let your number slip. I know because I defied orders, made the mistake of sleeping with you twice.

I shrugged. "You look like you could be from a lot of places. You probably just want people to think you've got something to hide. For fuck's sake, you keep a locked metal case in the corner of your hotel room. Don't pretend you don't want people to wonder."

He smiled at me indulgently. "Go on, then. Open the box." That should have been my victory, but it was his. This was a cool customer.

"Sure you're ready for that step, tough guy?"

"Yeah. I feel we've established a, like, *incredibly* high level of trust."

I suppressed a laugh.

"Just fucking open it," he ordered. I walked over to the metal box. "The combination is oh-four-one-three."

I worked the numbers and lifted the lid. I was awed by what I found. Money. Stacks and stacks of money. But it wasn't money-laundering money or *Medellín* Cartel money. It wasn't the kind of money you worried was marked. In fact, there wasn't even a U.S. bill to be found. Instead, there was money from every country I'd ever heard of. And some I hadn't. A fifty-*dinar* bill from Algeria, its colors of the desert; a sheik and his camels were depicted on the back, and two bulls squared off to fight on the front. A five-hundred-*peso* bill from Uruguay displaying a green rendering of a hydroelectric dam. One *taka* from Bangladesh: a woman preparing grain on the front of the bill, a hand firmly holding a rice stalk on the back. One thousand *riels* from Cambodia, its front illustrated with a classroom scene with smiling schoolchildren taking diligent notes. Fifty thousand *mantas* from Azerbaijan, the bill showing a clean-lined elevation of someone's mausoleum; the blues, greens, reds, and oranges of the bill were so vibrant, it could have been a tapestry. Two thousand *rials* from Iran, an image of the Ayatollah Khomeini on the front. Every bill had its own scent, its own size, its own texture, and its own history.

"Have you been to all these places?" I asked.

"Yeah, I think," he said.

I looked at him as if to say, How could you not know?

"At the beginning, I put in money I got in airports—just passing through a country to connect to another flight. But I decided that didn't count. I'm not sure I pulled all that stuff out."

"Wow. There are bills here from almost every single country I know about."

"I've traveled a lot," he explained nonchalantly, as if visiting every country on Earth is routine.

"Why money?"

"What do you mean?" he asked.

"Why collect money? Why not stamps or, I don't know, dirty postcards?"

"Because money is the most powerful force in the world," he explained.

"After sex," I joked.

"No, it's a lot more potent than sex. Especially to women." He saw I was looking at him curiously. "Women are a lot more apt to trade sex for money than the other way around." Suddenly he was very serious. "All the major issues are fundamentally economic. Human history has been a matter of learning how to co-exist economically, usually failing. Oppression is almost always economic. Race and gender and religion have all been created to justify economic gain and oppression." He looked at me as though making sure I was paying attention. "The history of the world is summed up in money."

"What are you favorites?" I asked. I couldn't believe the stupid stuff I was asking, when what I really wanted to ask him about, now more than before, was the fact that he was from Iran, the same country as Bobby.

"The ones that no longer exist," he answered. "Something is always more beautiful when it's gone."

"You mean the currencies that no longer exist? Or the countries that no longer exist? Like…Rhodesia, or South Vietnam, or, ummm, Zaire?"

He looked at me for an extended moment. His facial expression had softened. Somehow it was saying, *Maybe you're not the brainless Jetta-driving D-girl I took you for.*

I felt his arm graze mine as he reached into the box. "Maybe I mean both. But I only thought about the currencies until now. Europe, for example. We've all been a part of history watching them adopt the euro."

I hadn't given the single currency much thought. When Harry and I had gone to Paris, we spent scads of them. I remember that much. I also remember Jacques having some very strong opinions about France selling out to the devil of consumer capitalism.

"This is one of my old favorites right here. Five *francs*, with an engraving of Victor Hugo. I love the former French money because of the figures they chose to honor. With few exceptions, they shunned political and religious leaders in favor of great writers, artists, and thinkers. Debusssy, Voltaire, Racine, Cezanne. They acknowledged on their currency that art was more important than politics. Now they have the euro. Italy was the same. Look at this 100,000-*lira* bill."

"Caravaggio," I said. He looked at me inquisitively. "I was an art history major." He held up a 50,000-lira bill. "Bernini," I said. A 10,000-*lira* bill. "Michelangelo."

I wondered if he knew that he bore a striking resemblance to the young Vigen, who would no doubt have wound up on the money if Leila had stayed to assume the mantle of empire once the Shah fled to Panama.

"Every denomination of the *lira* was a symbol of national pride. Now they're stuck with the euro, too. When a kid's parents give him pocket money, he won't be handed Michelangelo or Victor Hugo or Goethe. He'll be handed some nondescript map of Europe and an architectural landmark that doesn't even exist."

I meticulously stacked the bills and placed them back into the metal box. At the bottom of the box, I found a ratty letter. Before I could read the name on the envelope or inspect the postmark, Kyle shut the box and announced, "That's enough tutorial for one night."

I sat back down on the bed. "See, you don't really mind answering questions. The answers are pretty stimulating."

"When you ask stimulating questions," he said.

Just spoiling for a fight, this one.

"So are you a nomad? A journalist? A global door-to-door wholesale carpet salesman?"

"The second one," he said. "But cute, the rug joke. Real original."

So now I had to act like I didn't get that. "A journalist." There was a glint in my eye, and that evidently annoyed him. Score one for me at least. "TV or print?"

"Listen, I'm not up for getting to know anyone," he said, turning away.

"I'm not hyper about it myself," I said unconvincingly. "I came for anonymous sex." I paused for a beat, turned him toward me, and looked into his eyes. "But for me, cheap sex is better when you can look in a person's eyes and know a little of what's behind them. A little bit about the way that anonymous person thinks. Maybe that's a female thing. Men like it better when they can treat the girl like a blow-up doll."

"You think anyone eats out a blow-up doll as ravenously as I do?" he asked. "Plastic tastes nasty." He tried to sound jokey, but I could see the disappointment. He'd met yet another typical woman, demanding communication when she vowed she could stick to sex.

"I'm sorry I'm curious about you. Aren't you curious about me?" He mulled this for too long. "A little curious?" God, I was practically begging. This was going in the wrong direction.

"Fine," he said, "go ahead. More questions."

So what did I have to lose? "What are you doing here? Are you staying for a while? Do you have a girlfriend? A wife? A pet? When are you leaving, and where are you going back to?" I was laughing by the third one.

So was he.

"Why won't you ever take your pants off?" It just came out.

"That one we'll answer next time," he said as he stood up. "It's getting late, and I need to sleep."

"I get it," I said. "There won't be a next time."

"That's not what I said."

"You force me to read between the lines."

He kissed me once on each cheek. "I don't force you to do anything," he said. "You do it all by choice."

9

AFTER GOOGLING EVERY VARIATION of *Kyle, Iran,* and *journalist* and coming up with nothing, I decided to use Fiona's birthday gift and booked myself a massage. "A massage," Bobby said later that night, "is basically an opportunity for sex." We were sprawled on his couch, indulging in a DVD marathon of *Dynasty,* which I commented could easily be recast with the Persian diaspora in the leading roles. Clearly, Hossein and Leila would have to play Blake and Krystle. Tanaz Maliki would have to be Alexis, even though she was nowhere near as fabulous as Joan Collins. Bobby would be Steven, the gay son. And I would be Sammy Jo, the white-trash intruder who worked her way into the moneyed world of Denver, much as I had somehow ended up a supporting character in the cast of Tehrangeles.

"What are you talking about?" I said. "I have been getting massages for years, and there's nothing sexual about it."

"That's because you're not doing it right."

"Doing what right?" I asked. "I lie there comatose. What am I supposed to be doing?"

"You don't know how to send and receive the signals," Bobby explained.

"There are signals?"

"Of course there are. Massage therapists are an easy fallback for getting off when all else fails. By mastering the ability to get a full-release massage, you guarantee that as long as the spa industry is flourishing, you will never be left hanging. And this way, if you're dating a guy and he's not returning your calls, or if you're pining over someone like Jacques, you know you can always create your own happy ending."

"Why not just hire a prostitute?" I asked.

Bobby glared at me as if it were the silliest question I had ever posed. "Come on, Kara, do you really think you and I are going to pay for sex? You should try Antwon, by the way. He's super hot."

"Straight?" I asked.

"I think so."

"French?" This question was hopeful.

"It's spelled with a W."

"Black?"

"Nope. They use pseudonyms," Bobby clarified. "Just like hustlers do. Probably afraid of getting stalked or something."

"Aliases are all the rage," I said, thinking of the ever-mysterious Kyle.

"Do you want me to show you how to make it happen?" Bobby asked.

"Make what happen?" I asked with trepidation.

"Get a full release."

"Bobby," I protested as Joan Collins bitch-slapped Linda Evans on screen. "I am going to a spa with your mother. I do not want a full release."

"My mother's going with you?"

"Sure. We love doing spa dates together."

Bobby seemed briefly perturbed, and I wondered if it was because *he* wanted to go on Pilates and spa dates with his mother. His parents had tried to turn him into Hossein, when the parent he really aspired to be was Leila. "Come on," he pleaded, back on message. "You said you wanted me to teach you how to be a hooch."

"I had my one-night stand," I declared. "I'm done."

"By my count, you've had three one-night stands. Kyle, Lensman, and the mystery guy on Larrabee."

"Well, that's enough sex for one year." I shrugged. "I can go back to celibacy now."

"First of all," Bobby explained, ignoring my wishes, "the more a massage therapist knows about what you do and where you're from, the less sexual energy there will be in the room." Another key was the moan. Bobby lay down on his stomach and made me massage his back. He began to moan softly, inconspicuously. "The key to the moan," Bobby said, "is to make it seem like you're moaning because the massage is hitting the right spot, but to give it just enough sexual edge to turn them on." I continued massaging Bobby's back. He told me to move lower, and I did. Bobby gently lifted his ass up. This was another one of his tricks: the gentle ass-lift. Bobby said this should work "just as well for women as it does for men. The gentle ass-lift is a subtle signal to the therapist that you're open for business. And finally," Bobby continued as he opened his palm and placed it on his side, "there is what I call 'optimum palm positioning'. You move your palm toward your massage therapist's crotch. Eventually, he will find a way to brush his crotch up against your hand." My crotch pressed up against Bobby's hand. "At this point, you feel around to see if you have wood. If you do, game on. If you don't, leave your hand there until you get wood." There was something dirty and inappropriate about Bobby on his stomach with his ass in the air and his hand on my crotch, but this was the benefit of having a friend who's like a brother. "The beauty of being a man in this situation," Bobby said, "is that when they ask you to turn around, you have a hard-on, which they just can't ignore." Bobby turned onto his back. Luckily and unsurprisingly, he wasn't hard. But he was utterly sincere in this little lesson he was doling out.

I arrived at Burke Williams half an hour early so I could take advantage of the steam room, sauna, Jacuzzi, and cucumber-infused water. As far as I'm concerned, heaven is a Jacuzzi jet on my lower back and a glass of cold infused water in my hand. Leila and I usually gabbed in the spa's lounge after our massages, so I hoped to have half an hour of solitude and relaxation. When I arrived at the spa, I saw that a customer named Kyle had checked in two hours earlier for a deep-tissue massage. I stared at the name. I stared at the words "deep tissue." It couldn't be, could it? It wasn't even his real name. But maybe it was an official nickname. Just as I was building an elaborate fantasy of reuniting with Kyle in our matching spa bathrobes, a teenaged Beverly Hills brat pushed me aside. "Hey, babe," he said to the woman now manning the front desk. "Kyle Kaplan checking out. The tip is on the gift certificate, right?"

The attendant, Cheryl, clearly an aspiring actress who either couldn't afford a good dye job or who thought letting your roots show was *in* again, showed me to my locker. I opened the locker and slipped into my fluffy robe. I made a beeline for the Jacuzzi, which was empty. I hate sharing the Jacuzzi with someone. Something about nudity and small talk strikes me as unnecessary. I got in and positioned myself perfectly. One jet hitting my back, another hitting my raised thigh. It was heaven.

I was almost drifting off when I heard Leila's voice over the gurgle of the jets.

"Well, hello. We both had the same idea," she said. "It's nice to loosen up your body before a massage, isn't it?"

She peeled off her bathrobe and hung it on a hook to her right. My eyes came back to focus on her perfectly manicured foot, dipping to check the temperature. She had visible tan lines and a shower cap over her hair, and her makeup was surprisingly intact. She refilled my cup with cucumber-infused water, handed it to me, and then poured a cup for herself. "Here's to a girl's night," she uttered as she pressed her plastic cup to mine. The memory of Bobby lifting his ass and teaching me how to solicit sex from my massage therapist floated into my brain.

"What's Hossein doing tonight?" I asked, trying to force the image of the moaning Bobby as far away as possible.

"He's sleeping. What does he ever do? He sells cars and sleeps. Every time I leave him alone at night, he sleeps. He's become one of those men who can fall asleep sitting up. In the middle of conversation, he can sleep. In front of a nail-biting golf tournament, he can sleep. I thought old people were supposed to sleep less and less. It's certainly true for me." She paused and took a sip of the infused water. "Perhaps he doesn't have as much keeping him awake."

"Maybe," I said. "I hope I'm like you."

"Please, don't be silly." She raised her hand to her head and realized she had left the shower cap on. She slipped it off and ran her fingers through her hair, making sure its highlights were all falling in the right place.

"Why is that silly?" I asked.

"Hossein likes to say that we are all dealt a hand of cards. You know he likes to speak in references to cards or sports. It helps him make sense of life." Leila snickered, but it wasn't a snicker of judgment. Instead, it conveyed how deeply she cared for Hossein, how much his thinking amused and charmed her, even after all these years. "Some of us are handed a pair of threes, some of us a full house, and the lucky few a royal flush."

"I'm not sure I follow. I just meant I hope that when I'm older, I sleep less rather than sleep more."

"Oh," Leila laughed. "I thought you meant you actually wanted to *end up* like me."

"What would be wrong with that?" I questioned. "I admire you a lot."

"You heard my husband, Kara. I don't *do* anything. I'm so useless even Babak defends me."

"Useless? You're on the board of a million charities, you speak four languages, you raised two children, you support the arts…"

"I did the best I could with the hand I was dealt. That much is true. I could have played it far worse. But you were dealt a much stronger hand, Kara. You were born in a freer country, into a more liberated generation. You have opportunities. It would be a shame if you didn't take advantage of them."

"You made your marriage work," I argued. "That's a real achievement, and not a very common one in my free, liberated generation."

"You'll make your marriage work, as well. But you won't have to sacrifice your dreams to do it. You and Babak understand each other in a way people of Hossein's and my generation never could."

The intimacy of the moment was discomfiting. I always assumed Leila was prepping me to be the next her. But the truth was more complicated. She was prepping me to be the next *version* of her. Leila 2.0. She wanted me to improve on the original. Take all the good qualities and add to them. Like all successful immigrants, Leila believed in progress. And then it hit me. I *believed* in her vision. I longed to be Leila 2.0. I ached to have her poise, her grace, her worldliness, and yes, her wardrobe.

"For example," she continued. "In your marriage, you will be the bread-winner, and Babak will be the housewife. Hossein has illusions, but I have given up any hope of Babak having a career. He isn't like other men, and he's very lucky to be with a woman who understands that." She looked away. "Whatever his shortcomings, and we all have them, Babak will be a good father," Leila said. "Responsibility always brings out the best in people."

"Responsibility..." I echoed. "He doesn't really have any responsibilities, does he?"

"That's because your generation resists growing up. You're thirty years old, and you act like children. Hossein said the other night that childhood to your generation is like Iran was to our generation. A place you want to stay in forever, but are forced to leave." Leila shrugged. "But the irony is, I always wanted to leave Iran. And I always wanted to grow up."

"What were your dreams, Leila?" I asked, realizing I had never heard her mention any aspirations of her own.

"Excuse me?"

"You said I could make my marriage work without sacrificing my dreams. What were yours?"

"They're not important." She shrugged.

"I'm curious. Did you want to be a lawyer, a painter, a writer?"

Cheryl approached the Jacuzzi. "Mrs. Ebadi, your manicurist is ready now."

Leila stood and wrapped herself in her bathrobe. "I forgot I booked myself a manicure before the massage," she announced. She looked down at me as she tied the strap around her waist. "I've forgotten my dreams, Kara. That's how long it's been."

"Are there any particular spots you want me to focus on?" I was on my stomach, staring at Antwon's legs. He was wearing shorts and Birkenstocks, and his blond hair layered his tan skin beautifully. His toenails looked bitten. Either he was a secret toenail biter, or he engaged in kinky foot play with some surfer girl. He began oiling me up in eucalyptus as soothing spa music drifted from the speakers.

"I store most of my tension in my lower back," I said.

"We can work on that. Are you familiar with Reiki?"

"Kind of. Moving energy. Chakra work. Right?"

"I want you to take two deep breaths in and one quick breath out. Two in. One out. Two in. One out. Every time you breathe out, " he explained, "I want you to release negativity. Release your bad day, release your fears, release anyone who causes you pain, any memory that causes you pain. In order to relax the body, you have to master relaxing the mind. Two in. One out. Two in. One out," he repeated over and over again until I fell into a trance-like state.

Kyle drifted into my mind. That thick, dark head of hair. That grim laugh. I knew I needed to release him, too. He was probably back to work, collecting currency in Algeria or Albania. He'd no doubt forgotten me altogether. I took a breath in, ready to release Kyle, when Antwon lifted the towel that was covering my ass and pressed into my crotch. "Your tension isn't in your back. It's in your root chakra. The root chakra is located here in the perineum. Breathe into the root chakra. Two in. One out."

I didn't know what breathing into a chakra meant, but I did my best to satisfy.

"The root chakra represents your ability to be present in your life. To allow yourself to be taken care of. It can be indicative of a need to re-examine your relationship with your mother."

"I'm on good terms with my mother."

"I'm referring to your spiritual mother. Mother Earth." And with that, Antwon pressed one hand into my lower back and one into my perineum. I couldn't help but moan, and my reflexes made my ass rise up. Without trying, I was following Bobby's ass-in-the-air tactic. "Try and relax," he said as he continued pressing into me. "Just keep breathing." My breath got heavier as he continued to speak in his silky voice, a fascinating mixture of surfer and guru. I started to become entranced. "Feel free to express joy, grief, laughter, pain; it's all part of the process of releasing energy. Let energy flow through you. Stop trying to control it." He was standing on my left side. I couldn't see his legs under me anymore. Just the rust-colored carpet. "Energy is stronger than you are. If you try and fight it, it will destroy your body," he whispered into my left ear.

His crotch brushed against my palm, just as Bobby had wanted. I felt something hard and stiff. Instinctively, I pulled away. Bobby would be so disappointed. But Antwon moved over two steps, until his hard-on fell into the palm of my hand once again. I was going to pull away again, but the song on the spa mix suddenly changed to something familiar. Enya. *We can reach, we can beach far beyond the yellow sea.* I closed my eyes and imagined Kyle, the scent of Glenlivet coming back to me, the feel of his oversized hands on my body, the sensation of his tongue inside me. *Sail away, sail away...*

"Sex is a pure expression of energy," Antwon said. "Don't repress it. Let sexual energy flow through you."

Suddenly, his finger found its way inside me.

"Are you comfortable?" he asked as he expertly fingered me. All I could respond with was a moan. Suddenly, two more fingers entered me. I was so taken aback that I yelped.

"Shh," he whispered.

But it was too late. I heard a sharp knock and the creak of the door opening. I raised my head up from its cradle and saw the perky smile of dark-rooted Cheryl. Antwon's fingers were still inside me. "Antwon, I gather we have a problem."

I kept my head down as Cheryl escorted me through the hallways. I was desperate to not be seen by Leila. Cheryl hovered next to me in the locker room as I dressed. A lady in the Jacuzzi watched me intently from afar, trying to catch the echoes of our conversation. Before leaving, I had to ask Cheryl. "Is Mrs. Ebadi still in her manicure?"

"I can't divulge information about our clients," she shot back curtly.

"Look, Cheryl. Woman to woman, if Mrs. Ebadi asks, you cannot tell her what happened in there." Cheryl gazed at me icily. I couldn't believe what I was about to do as I reached into my wallet and fished out all the cash I could find. I handed Cheryl eighty-eight dollars. "Tell her my massage therapist called in sick, and my massage was canceled."

"Blood money," Cheryl whispered. "Are we in the Persian mafia?" She relished the power position I had placed her in. As she pocketed the money, she finally cracked a smile. "*Is* there a Persian mafia?" she asked, her tone lighter.

"The Ebadis have never woken up with a horse head in their bed, if that's what you're asking," I said.

"You're dating her son, aren't you?" Cheryl asked, and before I could stumble through a response, she added, "Mrs. Ebadi mentioned it on her way in. It's too bad, 'cause Antwon is a pussy-eating ninja."

To my surprise, Antwon was waiting for me outside the spa after I had done my walk of shame out of the establishment. He had changed into board shorts and a white tank top. "Hey, I'm Michael," he said. "I'm really sorry about that."

"Yeah, same here. Did you lose your job?"

Antwon/Michael nodded.

"Jesus, I'm so sorry. I can go tell them it's all my fault if it would help," I offered.

"Don't bother. I hate it there. They rob their therapists even worse than their customers. Hey, you wanna go to my place and have some fun? My roommate's surfing up in Baja this weekend."

I hesitated. Tempting, but after Kyle, how much interest could I have in a guy who thought of Baja as *up* in relation to L.A.? "I'm kind of seeing someone," I responded.

"Kind of?"

"It's complicated," was all I could think to say.

"Cool." He turned.

"I'm sure I'll regret it," I said, almost to myself. He turned around to face me once more. "You're sexy," I continued. "And Cheryl called you a pussy-eating ninja." He smiled, pleased with the characterization. "But this guy that I told you I'm seeing. Well, I've only seen him twice. And I'm kind of obsessing over him right now. And I don't wanna get him out of my system. I already regret that, too. I wish I *did* want to get him out of my system. I wish I did want to fuck your brains out and forget about him. But apparently, I'm just a boring serial monogamist. I find one guy I like, and all my energy just disappears into him. And in my case, it only takes if the guy is emotionally and geographically unattainable."

He stared at me for a second, as if to be sure I was finished, then reached into his backpack. He pulled out a flyer. A breathing circle in Venice. There was a picture of him in the lotus position, with a dove resting atop his head. "Here's some information about my healing meditation group. You *really* need to chill," he said, and then followed a perky blonde into an open elevator.

10

JANET WAS ON THE couch, watching the previous week's *Ellen* episodes, when I arrived Monday morning. "Your friend is on the cover of *Variety*."

"Who?"

"Fiona whatsername. The TV actress. She just booked some huge Warner Brothers movie. Something about date rape." Janet reached into a jar of chocolate-covered ginger and popped a piece into her mouth. I picked up *Variety*, and there was Fiona. The caption read, "Thesp set to get DATE RAPED." It was a tacky headline, but the name of the movie was *Date Rape*, so the tackiness originated elsewhere. The article was short and factual, reporting only that Fiona's deal was rumored to be in the low six figures and that she would be directed by Eamon Flanagan, an up-and-coming Irish "music video auteur." Fiona was right. Her flagrant behavior and night in jail gave her just the image makeover and free publicity she needed to book the movie. That's the amazing thing about Fiona. Even when she fucks up, she ends up on top of the world. I wondered whether that was just luck, or whether she had some secret power I was sorely lacking.

"This is incredible. I have to call and congratulate her."

I hit speaker and checked the voicemail before calling Fiona. There were two new messages.

"This message is for Kara Walker. My name is Stan Lindberg. You've been calling me about my book, *Black Death*. I'm sorry I haven't returned any of your calls. My mother has been ill. She had lung cancer and well, I'm sorry, you don't care about her, or maybe you do, or maybe this is the wrong number. I don't know much about movies, but I think you wanted to make a film out of my seven-hundred-page non-fiction book, which I have to tell you is a terrible idea, but I don't know anything about movies, like I said. So strangely enough, I'm in the Los Angeles area because my aunt lives in Inglewood and"—but the answering machine cut him off. I moved on to the next message. "So sorry, this is Stan again. I ramble. My editor says it's why my books are so long. So I'm flying out of the Los Angeles airport at ten, but if you're serious about the book, maybe we can have dinner at the airport, at around eight o'clock. Okay, thank you, call me if you're interested, okay, this is Stan Lindberg. Bye."

I hung up and looked hopefully to Janet. "What do you think?"

"I don't know. I didn't read the book."

"Janet, you've been sitting on that couch for four months. I can't believe you haven't read the book."

"I'm bloated, I'm in pain, I'm tired. Do you really expect me to read a three-thousand-page book about dying?" she asked.

"It's seven hundred and forty pages," I corrected.

"Sorry, but I fell asleep during the prologue."

"Janet. I have a vision for this. There's never been a movie about the Black Death. It's a great backdrop. It's tragic. It's romantic. Let me offer him some money for an option."

"Kara, I need money for the baby."

"No, Janet. You need to work for the baby. You're gonna go broke if you don't make another movie."

"I still get residuals from those awful Baltimore movies," she said. "They play on IFC all the time."

I was surrounded by people content to live off past scores, to ask nothing of the future. "Well, I'm going to meet him, Janet, and I'll offer him money if he needs it. I'll use one of my credit cards."

"Kara, I don't wanna burst your bubble, but who is going to see a movie about two lovers torn apart by a plague? Let me rephrase that, who is going to *make* a movie about two lovers torn apart by plague? Hollywood wants super-heroes, goblins, and weddings. Hollywood does not want the *Black fucking Death*."

"I told you about this project. You said it sounded interesting."

"I feigned a polite interest because I thought nothing would come of it."

"That's the rudest thing I've ever heard," I said.

"Excuse me?" Janet said in a displeased tone.

"You heard me, Janet. That was a nasty thing to do to me. This is the only project I've been passionate about in years."

"Then maybe you should refocus your energies."

"Look at me, Janet," I said, grabbing my bag. "This *is* me refocusing my energies."

"Kara, you can't leave me. We're sisters. We belong together, and don't make me sing that Mariah Carey song to prove it," she said. Janet was a master of using her nails-on-a-chalkboard singing voice as a threat.

"You are beyond hormonal right now," I offered.

"Cameron called me," she said. "He said you're an alcoholic nympho."

"What? What an asshole."

"It made me like you more. Knowing you threw yourself at him." She looked at me with a discomfiting maternal gaze.

"I didn't, there was this letter in my freezer, it's a long story..." I stammered.

She stopped me. "Kara," she said in a tone that implied a loaded conversation was about to begin, "there's something I need to tell you." She took a long breath. "I didn't do artificial insemination."

"But I went to the sperm bank with you. We spent a week in casting, evaluating all the potential fathers." The faces of all the prospective donors flashed through my memory, along with their sperm counts, their levels of education, and their family histories of mental illness and alcoholism.

"I know. I was already pregnant," she clarified.

"I don't think I understand."

"I went through a phase."

"What kind of phase?" I asked.

"A one-night-stand phase. A *nympho* phase," she said. "I went to therapy, and it turned out, well, I was... I am... a sex addict."

"How long did the phase last?" I asked, suddenly realizing that the reason my producer boss hadn't *produced* anything is because she was too busy fucking the men in Los Angeles who wouldn't fuck Bobby.

"I don't know. Two, three... decades... I was always careful, but I guess not careful enough."

"Why are you telling me this now?"

"I don't know. Because given what Cameron told me, I thought you wouldn't judge me." She smiled a heartbreaking smile that reminded me of a guilty toddler. "Because I have no friends. I acted out of loneliness. And I'm still lonely."

"But you'll have a baby soon," I offered. "You won't have the option of being lonely anymore."

"I hate that I'm lying about this baby. But you have to understand, Kara. There is nothing worse for a woman in this world"—her voice dropped conspiratorially—"and in this industry, than being perceived as a slut." Janet took a breath. "So say you'll stay."

"What is this? Are you opening up to me or just guilting me into keeping a dead-end job?"

"You think I'm a dead end?"

"We're all dealt a deck of cards, Janet," I began. "Some of us…"

"Kara, skip the metaphor. There is no game where you're dealt the whole deck."

"Well, I'm not making the most of my hand by staying here and watching reruns with you and letting my time slip away. I need to play my hand more aggressively if I plan on making something of my life."

"Kara, please stop. I'll give you a raise. I'll make you president of the company. Don't quit when I need you the most. And when we've just gotten so close. You're the *only person* who knows how my child was conceived."

"Janet, come on, don't blackmail me. Isn't it obvious? You need to hire a nanny, not promote your VP to president of a production company that doesn't make anything."

"But I want you with me, Kara. I really do," she pleaded.

And suddenly it hit me that both Janet and Bobby were sex addicts who wanted me to fill the void of companionship in their lives. What were the chances? I laughed to myself, then explained to Janet, "I feel like Rita Hayworth in *Gilda* when she says 'you wouldn't think one woman could marry two insane men in one lifetime.'"

"Bobby has turned you into such a gay man," she seethed. And if I wasn't careful, Janet was liable to turn me into her longtime companion.

"I want to be a movie producer," I said as I threw the few items I owned in that house – a Filofax, a half-eaten bag of Taro chips, a DVD of *Reds* – into my bag. "I'll be here for you, Janet," I said as I opened the door. "We're friends. We'll have brunches and dinners and go to movies."

"We'll get you new business cards. Please, Kara. I don't want to spend the last two months of my pregnancy alone. I'm groveling!"

She was actually trying to maneuver her unwieldy form to a supplicant posture. I pulled her up to her feet, holding both her hands. "Pick yourself up, Janet. You'll be a mother soon. You've got to learn how to appear strong, even when you feel weak."

The moment had been years in the making. Janet followed me to the door, but she was smiling through her tears. It was like one of those *The Best of Lifetime* DVDs that she'd had me order. The air tasted sweet when I walked out, like the world was a giant scoop of rosewater ice cream, waiting to be licked. I knew what I wanted. To make this movie. And I wanted Kyle. Before starting my car, I grabbed my cell phone and pulled up Kyle's cell number. Quickly, before I could convince myself it was the wrong move, I texted him. "It's Kara," I wrote. "Have meeting at 8. Want company at 10? That is my only question… for now." Triumphantly, I drove home for my first day as an unemployed independent producer.

Stan Lindberg and I were on our first drink when Bobby arrived. We were at Encounter, a space-age restaurant overlooking the Los Angeles Airport, or at least its clogged roadways. The restaurant was built in the 1960s as some kind of representation of what the future would look like, but as it turns out, the future didn't end up having many restaurants floating under 135-foot-high parabolic arches.

Nearly one drink in, and Stan and I hadn't said word one about the book. Perfect, I thought. Friendly small talk is the key to a good meeting. We discussed his deceased mother at length, which led to discussing my mother at length, which led me to wonder whether Stan and my mother might be a match. Stan was slightly overweight, wore thick glasses, and had mild body odor, but in the plus column, he was Harry's age, had a charming smile, and a huge intellect. I thought that with a stop at L'Occitane, he would make a perfectly charming stepfather.

"Sorry I'm late," Bobby said as he sat down. "It was too late to cancel my dinner meeting, but I rushed it to make it here relatively on time."

"Well, thank you for that," Stan said flatly.

"Stan Lindberg, Babak Ebadi." The man who fast-forwarded through a booty call to meet you, I was dying to add.

"Pleasure to meet you," Stan said. "I've seen your movie on TV several times."

"I'm so sorry."

"I think it's quite good, but then again, they always seem to play it very late at night when I'm too drunk to be critical."

Bobby eyed the waiter, who was wearing tight black pants that perfectly cupped his ass. If it was just the two of us, Bobby would have made some lewd comment about the buns, but this was a meeting.

"I'll have a martini, please, and should we get some calamari for the table?" Bobby asked. Stan and I both nodded.

Outside the plate glass, two planes were taking off.

"It's amazing the way life brings people together, isn't it?" Stan said. "I'm an old Southerner, you're a California girl, and you're from Iran. And yet here we are in a restaurant that looks like a spaceship, awaiting a plate of fried squid."

"How did you know I was from Iran?" Bobby asked.

"I spent three years in the Middle East researching a book about Alexander the Great."

"Most people think I'm Colombian," Bobby said.

"You really get Israeli more than anything," I added. And it was true. He got more Israeli than anyone I knew.

"I get everything except Scandinavian," Bobby said with a half-smile.

"So tell me before my plane starts boarding, why do you want to base a movie on my extremely un-cinematic book?"

I had thought this one out and was prepared to launch in. "I think the plague has relevance for our times," I said. "But obviously, that's not the movie we wanna make. We don't want to preach to the audience or make them feel like they're watching an episode of *Frontline*. We wanna show them the nature of tragedy, take them on a ride, which is why I suggest using all the brilliant detail of your book as the backdrop for a doomed love story. There's nothing more romantic than not being able to be with the one you love. Think of that last scene in *Casablanca*. You want them to be together so bad, and yet if they did end up together, the story would have flatlined. Or the last scene of *Moulin Rouge*, Nicole Kidman dying of consumption in Ewan McGregor's arms. The final scene of *The Way We Were*, Barbra Streisand and Robert Redford, torn apart by politics, realizing they're strangers. Or *Brokeback Mountain*."

Stan looked lost, so Bobby saved me. "Kara likes old-fashioned tear-jerkers."

Stan still didn't get it.

"Even straight guys could get behind the cowboy romance," Bobby elaborated, "because one of the lovers dies a brutal death."

"You're suggesting that no one likes a happy ending?" Stan wondered aloud.

"We're suggesting making the most romantic kind of love story: one that ends in tragedy. Set against the backdrop of the Black Death. One lover is healthy. One is sick—and at the end, dies in the other's arms. Classic and timeless. And we can use all the brilliant research that went into your book to create the characters and the world."

Stan watched me with interest as I vamped. I was waiting for him to say something, to give me something to react to.

I put a hand on Bobby's shoulder. "Bobby is a brilliant writer. *Lovers in the Backseat* was only the tip of the iceberg that is his talent. And he's done tons of research on the Black Death. I think he has a real grasp of the fear and the paranoia at hand here. Which is why I trust him to bring this world to life cinematically."

"So you've done your own research?" Stan asked Bobby.

"I'm kind of obsessed with epidemics," Bobby said. "For personal reasons. I guess plague history was a natural extension."

This, Stan got completely. "The similarities between the Black Death and the AIDS epidemic *are* eerie. But history does tend to repeat itself, unless society chooses to break its cycles, which, let's face it, happens rarely. After all, the Medieval scapegoating of the Jews for the plague is like Castro's quarantining the HIV-positive. Or like Reagan barring people with AIDS from entering the country."

"Don't even get me started on that fucking Jesse Helms amendment," Bobby added, heated up.

From within my purse, I heard the beep of a text. I peeked at the screen: "10, rite?" I beamed, assuming it was Kyle, but it was Joanne, with whom I had completely forgotten I had made plans. Her boss recently got the break of designing Lindsay Lohan's new house. Now, courtesy of La Lohan, Joanne had been put on the list for a secret Prince performance that night at Teddy's. Fiona was having drinks with her Irish auteur to discuss her character, which had left me Joanne's plus one, a position I wasn't very comfortable with. The truth is, I'd never been all that fond of going out alone with Joanne. I always needed the buffer of Bobby or Fiona to handle her. One time, we went out alone, and I met a really hot archeologist who was speaking at LACMA. Joanne refused to leave our side. It was insanely awkward. She stared at us flirting for about an hour until the archaeologist became so uncomfortable that he excused himself and never came back. Another time, we went to the birthday party of some frat guy we'd gone to college with. At the end of the night, when it became clear I was planning on going home with him, Joanne pulled me into the bathroom and began to cry. She confessed that she had been in love with the frat guy since college, and that it would really hurt our friendship if I were to sleep with him. I tried to reason with her. I told her she had never mentioned his name to me in our years of friendship. She said she'd never mentioned him because she was too embarrassed, because it hurt too much. I was drunk on margaritas, so I fought back. I explained to Joanne that she was, in Bobby's words, a cockblocker. She hated to see me get a guy if she didn't have one, too, and since she never did, she made sure to sabotage my every opportunity. I told her somewhat dramatically that who I slept with was none of her business, and that if she ever really loved someone, I would be able to sense it as a friend, even if she didn't talk about it. Joanne just cried more, and I argued more, and by the time we were done and left the bathroom, the party was severely over and my guy was gone. Once again, Joanne had successfully cockblocked me.

I was about to text Joanne back and tell her we were indeed on when another text came in. "Sure," was all it said. This one *was* from Kyle.

It took a few seconds to return my attention to Stan and Bobby, but they didn't seem to miss me.

"I want to show the horror of it," Stan said, "the acral necrosis."

"Of course," Bobby chimed in. "This movie can't gloss over the terror. I want to write in close-ups of those subdermal hemorrhages turning our hero's skin black."

"It occurred mostly around the extremities."

"The disease manifests itself on the skin. Exactly like Kaposi's sarcoma," Bobby added.

"What fascinates me about plague," Stan continued in a tone that indicated he had rehearsed this particular bit on a book tour, "is how it's a somatic manifestation of the decrepitude of a society. We might try and run away, but every hundred years, nature, or perhaps humanity, finds a new way to literalize, making our flesh putresce with lesions."

The calamari had arrived, and Stan popped a ring into his mouth. Yeah, that part was definitely rehearsed.

Bobby picked up for me. "So what are you working on next?" Bobby asked.

"I've been researching cannibalism. It began with my interest in the Great Famine of the fourteenth century. Evidence suggests that there were widespread incidents of cannibalism in Livonia and Estonia, even Ireland. Then I started nosing around for other evidence of cannibalism, and it seems there's just loads. Even recipes. It's all very hush-hush, of course. No society wants to admit to eating each other, be it the Ukrainians during the famine of the 1930s or the North Korean refugees of this very day. But human beings, when put to the test, devour each other for the sake of survival."

"Some human beings even want to be eaten," Bobby added. This was clearly yet another mind-meld for these two morbid freaks. "A few years ago in Rotenberg, in Germany, these two guys met online. One wanted to eat a young boy; the other wanted to be eaten. They consented to it, all negotiated online. And they went ahead with the deal. The older guy cut the other's body parts off and cooked them up, and they feasted together until the younger guy died."

I forced a piece of calamari down my throat. "That is disgusting," I said as I covertly replied *C U Then* to Kyle. "I hope the guy is in jail."

"He is," Bobby said. "Life imprisonment. But there was a whole paper trail proving it was consensual."

"Consensual murder?" I asked.

"Isn't that what euthanasia is?" Stan continued. "If you ask me, and granted, I have a trace of the Southern Gothic in me, but if you ask me, everything can be consensual. Human beings have a far greater capacity for the taboo than we give ourselves credit for. We should embrace our darker natures. In the next century, consent will be the most important word in our language. As we lift the taboos, the question will no longer be 'are you allowed to kill someone' or 'are you allowed to infect someone' or 'are you allowed to drug someone,' the question will be whether you can find someone eager to consent to your apocalyptic desires. Those guys in Germany entered into a compact that they really have every right to make."

Well, speaking of business….

"So, Stan, I don't have a studio behind me, and this project is a labor of love. So I can't offer you the world." An exec I once went out to dinner with had told me to always bring up money terms when they've got food in their mouths. It puts them at a disadvantage. I didn't want to let Stan get on the plane without some verbal agreement. I was, after all, a producer now. Kara 2.0.

"How much can you offer?" he asked after swallowing a bite of calamari.

I visualized my credit card bills. I owed a few thousand to Visa, a few hundred to AmEx, and had maxed out MasterCard. I figured I could give him a thousand and start running up the AmEx. In a dire situation, I could put some of those hand-me-downs that belonged at the Costume Institute on eBay. Perhaps Tanaz Maliki would bid on them. Wouldn't that be poetic, Tanaz purchasing her best friend's sloppy seconds? The thought distracted me briefly, but then I came back to the bidding. We'd have to bargain up to a thousand, so my first offer to him was five hundred for one year.

"Three thousand," he said.

"Seven fifty," I countered.

"Two thousand," he snapped back.

"One thousand. Final offer."

Bobby's head was moving back and forth, as if he was watching a heated tennis rally. Finally, Stan shook his head. "Nah. I just can't do it."

I tried not to look crestfallen.

Stan started to get up, reaching for his wallet.

"It's on me," I said as coolly as I could manage.

We went through the pantomime: Stan insisting, me insisting back. Finally he relented.

As he thanked us and started away, Bobby spoke.

"Fifteen hundred."

Stan turned. "Deal," he said with a smile.

I swallowed hard as I shook his hand. "I'll have an agreement to you tomorrow. It'll be a very simple option. The purchase will be two-and-a-half percent of the budget. Not less than two hundred and capped at five."

"I love it when you talk like that!" Stan said.

They were both looking at me like they were impressed. I couldn't hide my shock and excitement as I squeezed Bobby's leg under the table.

Stan ran off to catch his plane, and Bobby and I ordered a split of champagne to celebrate. "You were brilliant," Bobby said. "I especially loved the part where you pretended to text people. That made you seem very important and powerful."

I smiled. "Oh, I wasn't pretending to text," I said. "It was Joanne. We're supposed to go see Prince at Teddy's tonight, but Harry is freaking and really wants me to spend some time with her. I think the divorce is finally hitting her." I could have told him I had yet another online booty call. It would certainly have been a cleaner excuse as far as Bobby was concerned, but I wanted my sexual education over and done with. After the *Lensman* fiasco and the Burke Williams disaster, which I was too embarrassed to tell Bobby about, what I really wanted was an end to my lessons. "Bobby, maybe you can go out with Joanne. Do you have plans yet?"

"I don't get it. Something is off. You're skipping a private Prince concert to go spend time with your mom?" Bobby asked. "Why don't you just go see her after the show?"

"Bobby, my mother called me crying when I was on my way here. Do you know what that's like?"

"Well, no," he said. "My mother doesn't cry."

"I have to call Joanne and bail. It would help get me off the hook if I offered you up as a consolation prize. She always accuses me of not wanting to spend time alone with her."

"And what's wrong with an accusation if it's blatantly true?"

"Don't pretend you don't want to go," I said. "You love Prince."

"I love Prince Alberts," Bobby joked. I knew for a fact piercings weren't his thing, and he knew for a fact I wasn't going to my mother's.

"Come on, Bobby, just do it for me," I pleaded. "After all, you owe me five hundred dollars."

"I do?"

"You trumped my final offer to Stan!"

"Oh, Kara, my parents will pay the option for us."

"No," I said firmly. "This is my deal. I want to do it myself." Bobby looked confused. "It'll put more fire in me to know real money is on the line."

"My parents' money is real, Kara," Bobby protested.

"Of course it is," I said. "It's just that sometimes it feels like Monopoly money, doesn't it?" I wanted to add that it felt like a game of Monopoly in which the player could constantly dip into the bank for more.

Joanne sounded disappointed when I called her. "We never go out together," she said. "You're my only single girlfriend. We need to be each other's wingwomen."

"Joanne, it's not my fault. Harry is distraught." It felt semi-awful to be pimping out my mother's semi-fictitious misery to get laid. "You know who you should go with? Bobby. He's right here, and he loves Prince." I handed the phone over to Bobby.

"Yo, Jo," he chirped.

"Bobby!" Joanne yelled into the phone. I could hear her from the speaker. "So you wanna come out tonight?"

"Sure," he said. "Is Lindsay gonna introduce me to Jared Leto?"

"Oh, Bobby," I could hear Joanne yelp, "homeboy is straight as an arrow. But you can have your pick of Lance Bass, Neil Patrick Harris, or T.R. Knight."

"None my type," Bobby said.

"Colin Farrell is on the guest list."

"How soon can we get there?" Bobby joked.

"I'll swing by your place at ten in a cab so we can both get fucking shit-faced and dance all night. I've been learning to salsa as part of the Spanish lessons. It comes with the package."

"Are you mild, medium, or picante?" Bobby asked.

"Like you even have to ask," Joanne said.

Bobby snorted loudly. "Listen, I have to go, but I'll see you at ten," he said before hanging up and handing me back the phone.

The mood was different as we headed to the parking garage. We should have been going out to talk about our new project. We should have been dishing whomever it was Bobby had rushed out of his place so he could get to LAX by eight o'clock. We should have been talking about the reason I was really ditching Joanne. But we weren't. We were silent as we headed to our separate cars, which were parked right next to each other in the dungeon of a lot. We both pressed our unlock buttons at the same time, and the ring of beeps echoed in the cavernous space.

"Well," I said. "Congratulations. You and I are going to make a movie. I can feel it."

"You're not gonna go Hollywood on me and decide halfway through to cut all the sex and all the sickness and all the dark, depressing truth from the thing."

"Never. I'm your friend first and your producer second."

"You know what they say... friends shouldn't get into business together."

"We'll prove them wrong," I said with a smile. "Well, I should go. Harry's waiting."

"Send her my love," Bobby said as he clicked his keychain and his lights flashed.

His tone left no doubt that he didn't believe I was seeing her.

"Sure." I turned to him, but he was already climbing into the driver's seat.

11

There I was, just lying there, when what I really wanted to do was forbidden. "Wow," Kyle sighed as he crept up from between my legs and lay next to me. "That was amazing. You taste like…"

"Don't do it," I said.

"Don't do what?"

"No woman wants to know she tastes like a bonbon or like your favorite tropical fruit, or like anything, for that matter."

"So women like to think they're bland?" he said.

"Exactly."

"Very good, then. You taste like a rice cake."

"Better be a crisp one." I grabbed a pillow and hit him over the head with it. He held back, considering how to fend off the playful gesture, then pulled me in close and kissed me. "I wish I knew what you tasted like," I said.

"I probably taste like the calamari I had for dinner."

"Not your mouth," I coyly uttered as I moved my hand to his crotch, where his cock was still hard. "You didn't even come."

"I don't need to. I'm satisfied."

"I have a theory, you know."

"There's a surprise," he said as he reclined, his arms behind his head, exposing the perfect shape of his armpits.

"You have a wife back in…" I caught myself. "Wherever you live. And you've convinced yourself that as long as someone doesn't blow you or get fucked by you, then you're not really cheating. So you travel to all these different countries for work, you eat the local girls out, tell them they taste like rice cakes, and you go home with a clear conscience."

He laughed. "You're not even close."

"Okay, how about this? You have a whole harem, but the theory still holds." He glared at me angrily. "What? I'm sorry, did I say something?"

"Is this how you think of Muslim people? As philandering polygamists?"

"Actually, I hardly think of Muslims at all." That wasn't what I meant to say. "I don't know any. So I shouldn't have said anything. No, hold on. I didn't say anything about Muslim people. I said 'harem,' and you assume that's a slur. It's as much a slur on Muslims as a joke involving a Fiat is a slur on Italians." He'd been ignoring me since the first pause.

"How about this one?" he offered. "I don't take my pants off because I have bombs strapped to my legs. I'm part of a covert mission to blow up the Four Seasons Beverly Hills."

"Okay, that's not even funny. Let's just stop."

"No," he said, suddenly passionate. "Let's keep going. I like the theories, because believe me, almost anything you can cook up is better than the truth."

"Just forget I mentioned it," I huffed.

"How can I forget it? You mention it every fifteen minutes."

"I haven't even been here fifteen minutes!" I said. "Don't turn me into some nagging wife you can ridicule."

"So don't act like one. Don't act like a wife at all, nagging or non-nagging."

"Yeah, I bet there's a line out the door waiting to marry a prize like you." I turned half away.

"I just mean, can't you relax? So we *can* get to know each other a little?"

I heard the echo of Antwon/Michael's parting words. Apparently, I was in dire need of mellowing out. And Kyle's tone had changed. I took a breath. "I'm sorry. It's just hard for me, as I think it would be for anyone, to understand why you never take your pants off."

"I do take them off," he insisted.

"Just not when we're having sex?"

"Kara. This is the third time I've seen you. Have you revealed everything of yourself?"

"No, but only because you haven't asked!" Now I was playing the nagging *and* neglected wife.

"That's why you're forcing me to push you back."

And with that, he unzipped his pants and dropped trou, revealing beautifully built thighs. Then, as he let the pants slide lower, below his right knee, the leg turned prosthetic. "Still want to know more?"

My heart raced with fear and excitement, and it struck me that this fake leg made him somehow so much more real. "Of course I want to know more. What's it made of?"

"Granite and titanium," he explained.

"Sounds heavy. I understand now. I'm so sorry."

"It's not your fault."

"No, I'm sorry I badgered you. Can I ask what happened?"

"You just did," he said, laughing, and then shifted tone. "I was riding in a van on Route Irish, and we got blasted by an IED."

"A what?"

"Improvised explosive device. Do you not watch the news?"

"I'm sorry. What's Route Irish?"

"It's the road from the Baghdad Airport into the city," he said. "It's littered with bombs, mines, and booby traps."

I ran my hands along the smooth stone and metal. The touch was surreal and yet somehow exciting. The whiff of death made me feel more alive than I had in years. My heart pounded like a stereo with the bass tuned way too high. Maybe this is why Bobby convinced himself he was always on the verge of illness. So he could feel the heart-thumping, pulse-throbbing emotion of life at full bass. "Why were you driving there?" I asked.

"It's part of my job. It's the only way in from the airport."

He poured two glasses of Glenlivet on the rocks to indicate he was done with this segment of the conversation, but I couldn't let it go. "What does it feel like, putting yourself in the line of fire like that?"

"You mean you don't feel like you're in the line of fire? You don't live every day in fear that insurgents are gonna bomb your stucco apartment building?"

"I don't live in stucco, thank you very much. And no, I think terrorists have better people to bomb than me and better places to bomb than Los Angeles."

He smiled. "I've noticed that almost every American I've met since 9/11 feels like they personally are Al-Qaeda's ultimate target. I'm glad you're not one of them."

Harry had called me at dawn on September 11. "Stay at home, Kara. The planes are on their way to Los Angeles. I heard it from it from a very good source. This is serious." It turned out Harry's very good source was a barista at her Starbucks.

In the moments of uncertainty when none of us knew how many planes had been hijacked, the people of Los Angeles showed more than ever how self-centered they really were. Within moments, gossip spread that we were next. Fiona called at six in the morning. "They're going to attack Paramount. Or Disneyland!"

Joanne called three minutes later. "There are still three planes not accounted for, and they're all headed toward Los Angeles." If this was true, then they were all headed toward Phoenix, too, by that point. Were low-desert retirees going gaga with this kind of excitement?

I watched the Twin Towers fall from the comfort of Bobby's bed, with him by my side. Tearful and horrified as we were, we were fascinated by our city's strange reaction. Was it our imagination, or did Angelenos *long* to be attacked? Did we feel our status diminished that morning? If we were as important as New York and Washington, then what about *us*? *Where was* our *apocalypse?*

In the weeks that followed, terrorism-envy only increased. We convinced ourselves that the villains were saving their major attack on Los Angeles for a more portentous date. Joanne summed it up over a brunch. "Los Angeles is too spread out for terrorism. There are no easy targets. There is no *one* epicenter of power that would make a statement the way destroying the World Trade Center or the Pentagon would. That's why they're waiting until the Oscars."

"That makes total sense," Fiona said. "I mean, they've hit government and finance, two major U.S. industries. What's left? Movies."

"Entertainment is America's biggest cultural export," Joanne added. "Imagine if in one day they could cripple the entire film industry. Take down all the stars and the studio executives and the directors."

"There are so many options," Fiona continued. "Emmys, MTV Music Awards, People's Choice Awards, Blockbuster Awards, ShoWest Awards, MTV Movie Awards, SAG Awards, Golden Globes."

"I hate to say it," I joked, "but the world wouldn't be so bad without one of those awards shows. Although if Osama bin Laden *was* thinking about the People's Choice Awards, my respect for him would really be diminished."

"America is its *icons*," Fiona ranted. "The World Trade Center and the Pentagon were icons just like superstars are."

"We've identified our point of vulnerability," I deadpanned. "Cher."

"Careful," Joanne warned. "Someone could hear you."

"Come on, Joanne," I said, "do you really think they're gonna throw three white girls into prison for discussing the possibility of annihilating the Grammys?"

"People are looking at us funny," Joanne said.

"That's 'cause of your padding," I responded. This was the era during which Joanne was convinced that bigger breasts meant better men, and would dramatically enhance her cup size.

"Seriously," Fiona said. "I don't know if I'm even gonna go to the awards shows this year. It's too freaky. This could be the end of awards shows as we know them. People might be too scared to show up."

"Yeah, right," I said, "like anything would scare an actor away from the red carpet."

"You laugh now, but when all our worst fears come true, I'll remember this conversation."

"I guess I'm just not that worried," I said, shrugging. "I don't believe in paranoia."

"Paranoia can protect you," Joanne interrupted. "If you use it correctly."

"Do you really think Al Qaeda cares that much about Hollywood?" I asked. "I mean, I understand their animosity toward the government or toward economic inequalities, but I'm not sure Nicole Kidman is high on the *jihad* target list."

"You're so wrong," Fiona corrected. "Taking down Nicole Kidman would be hugely symbolic."

"Symbolic of what?" I asked. "She's Australian."

"Yeah," Fiona answered. "But she is the American Dream."

I suppose there was some truth to what the girls were saying. A terrorist attack could hit Los Angeles any time. But with every day that passed *sans* attack, I could feel Angelenos become more and more resentful. Didn't the world care at all about us anymore? Al Qaeda had done the unthinkable. They had made the world capital of attention-whores feel ignored.

"You're not here on business, are you?" I asked Kyle. "Why would somebody who covers wars come to a place as mundane as Los Angeles?"

"Now you're fishing again. My family is here."

The ice in my glass was clinking and clanging, and I was working on the math. He must be about thirty-six. Thirty-six minus twenty-nine equals seven. Kyle had come to the United States at age seven, in 1979 or '80. When they all came, flooding Los Angeles like a tsunami. I swirled the ice in the glass to cover my practically audible thinking.

"The only reason I came," he went on, "is to see my family. I haven't seen them in a long time, but now that I'm here, I don't know that I want to."

"They live right in L.A.?"

"Unless they moved. No, they would never move. My mother is way too involved in her superficial little version of high society. Anyway, that's the whole story. I came to make peace with my family. But I think I've decided against it. I had these visions of some Hallmark family reunion, kisses and hugs and apologies. It was a stupid idea. I'm going back to Iraq on Saturday."

"Is Baghdad where you live?"

"No, just where I work. To cover the war."

"Isn't losing one leg enough?" I cracked.

He smiled and placed his hand on my thigh. He was getting hard again. But I couldn't linger for another round. I now had a vital piece of information about this man. He was not just a journalist from Iran, but a journalist maimed on Route Irish. I was dying to curl up with Google and find out who he was. Maybe, I thought, I could even be the agent of his reunion with his family. There was almost no way his family didn't know the Ebadis, or at least have some connection to them. Tehrangeles is like *Cheers*, where everybody knows your name. The Ebadis could connect me to Kyle's family through the non-electronic Persian Orkut that seems to permeate 310 and the higher elevations of 818. My plan was in motion. With my newfound producorial chutzpah, I would *package* his reunion with his family. He would stay in Los Angeles. I would finally have the unattainable by my side and eating out of my hand.

"I have to go," I suddenly said.

"Oh." He ran his hand down my face, tickling my neck, finding his way to my breasts. "You're not gonna deflate on me, are you? I was winding up for round two."

"Well, I can't."

"So sex isn't always so great when you, how did you put it, know what's behind someone's eyes?"

"That's not it," I protested. "Talking about your family reminded me I said I'd go stay with my mom. She lives in Ventura County. I should get going before I'm too tired to drive."

"So is this it?" he asked.

"Why so dramatic?" I wondered. He looked at me with a twinge of sadness and said he was leaving Saturday. "Don't worry," I assured him. "You're not rid of me. I guarantee it."

I made it to Thousand Oaks in record time and parked outside Harry's. She had given me the key to her new one-bedroom, mostly for emergency purposes. I hadn't used it yet, but I figured this was a definite emergency, and the last thing I needed was Bobby hovering over me, asking questions as I tried to fill in the missing sections of Kyle's biography.

As I tiptoed into the living room and began pulling out the sofa bed, a flashlight illuminated my exhausted face, and the barrel of a gun pointed at me. "Put your hands up." The voice was far too deep to be my mother's.

I squealed and shielded my eyes.

"Kara?" It was Harry. I couldn't see well with the flashlight still pointed at me, but I could have sworn she was wearing black lace lingerie. "It's okay, Luis. It's my daughter."

The mysterious Luis dropped the flashlight. As it moved down, it illuminated parts of the living room I would rather not have seen. Two wine glasses and an empty bottle of Pinot Noir on the coffee table. A bag of marijuana and rolling papers on top of a Marvin Gaye CD. My mother's shoes and favorite jeans, thrown onto the kitchen floor. Luis finally turned the flashlight off. Either the light of dawn was playing tricks on me, or Luis was a good two decades younger than Harry. And he was standing in front of me in a pair of boxers that clung in a way that Bobby would have noted approvingly. No way someone older than thirty-five had the twelve-pack this man did. Unless, of course, he had just gotten out of prison, but I was giving my mother's judgment the benefit of the doubt. His hair was buzz-cut, his lips were full, and he had a tattoo of the Virgin of Guadalupe on his arm and a map of Mexico on his ankle. And he was wearing nothing but plaid boxer shorts. The same kind Harry used to buy for my dad.

Luis walked over and gave me a hug. His armpits pressed against my cheeks, and I could smell his odor. More disturbing, I could also smell my mother's perfume on him. Angel by Thierry Mugler. She'd been wearing it since the divorce. "It's so nice to meet you, Kara," Luis said. "I have heard a lot about you."

I looked at Harry incredulously. She had picked her jeans off the kitchen floor, put them back on, and thrown a blanket around her shoulders. She had also found time during my three-second hug with Luis to hide the pot and rolling papers. "Kara, this is Luis," she said, in a tone that implied I should know everything about him. "The one I told you about," she continued. "From my office." She could see I wasn't going to give an inch. "Luis and I went to Palm Springs last month, remember?"

I was exhausted and irritated, but I knew I hadn't heard about any trip to Palm Springs. I had never heard of a Luis with perfect abs and religious skin art. In fact, every time I had made the time to call Harry in the past few months, she had told me her life was a completely boring routine of work and television. "Ever since the divorce," she had told me just the previous week, "I have to work twice as hard to make ends meet. I'm so tired at the end of each day that all I can do is fall asleep in front of the living-room TV. Thank God I got that sofa bed."

"Of course. It's nice to meet you, Luis," I said with a smile. "I've heard nothing but lovely things about you. My mom's been talking about that Palm Springs weekend ever since."

Harry gave me an approving smile. "Is everything okay, sweetie?"

"Yeah," I said. "I just..." I hadn't even prepared an excuse as to why I was here. "There was some construction across the street from us, and I couldn't sleep. Some rich people building a house. Wait a minute. This guy carries a gun?" I asked.

"Your father gave it to me after the divorce. To protect myself."

"Dad gave you a gun as a divorce present? That's so... uncharacteristic. He's totally anti-NRA." And somehow so like him. He no doubt wanted her to protest corporate greed by firing .22 slugs into the air at Disneyland. Something symbolic. Something to show she really cared.

"I'm going to get dressed and go to work," Luis said.

He smiled and disappeared into the bedroom. "I'm sorry," Harry whispered to me. "I'll explain when he's gone."

"What? Did you meet him online?"

She gave me a look of horrified shock. And then she followed Luis and closed the bedroom door. From inside I could hear their chatter and some giggling.

I sat down on the sofa and took a breath. In the corner of the room were two brown boxes labeled with my name in black Sharpie. I moved toward them. They were filled with all the stuff from my room in the old house, no doubt inhabited now by some other insecure teenage girl. The first box held a strange mishmash. Programs to high school musicals Bobby and I were in together. I played Sheila in *A Chorus Line*, and Bobby was Paul. None of the Latinos at Northfield did musical theater, so Bobby was the closest thing. On the cover of the program was a picture of me, Bobby, and a group of our classmates in white polyester suits and white-and-gold top hats. We were one singular sensation back then, a group of tap-dancing teenagers ready to take over the world. A few of us did. More of us didn't.

I dug deeper into the box and found a strip of photos from a photo booth. Bobby and I were sixteen when they were taken. In each photo, we were making fish faces. This was the brief phase when we'd decided we were going to start a band called *The Drowning Fishes*. We wore matching pins with a laminated dead fish on our mandatory collared shirts, and spent our study hours in the language lab writing songs called "Tuna Tataki Rumba," "Black Eel Down," and "The Assassination of Señor Salmon." On a scrawled Spanish syllabus, I found Bobby's absurd lyrics to the latter: *Pink skies and cherry pies. The crowds have gathered, the sun is high. Swimming steamboat into Arctic Square. The procession begins, every fish is there. Draw the gun, mercury is rising. Prepare the poison, the president's coming. President. President. President Salmon. Will be overthrown this Monday morning.*

I laughed at the memory. There was a time when my friendship with Bobby was innocent, consisting of making fish jokes, mocking classmates, and bitching about homework. Sex and deception had yet to enter the picture. I dug out our old sophomore *Facebook*, depicting every student in miniscule images taken on the first day of the new school year. Bobby and I had rated each guy and girl in the school, giving ourselves (and no one else) 10.0 despite the acne on my face and the goofy cowlick atop Bobby's head. I found a crumpled black-and-white photograph Bobby had taken of me for his photography class. The assignment had been to emulate the style of one photographer. Bobby chose George Hurrell. He'd filled our black-box theater with smoke and posed me within the shadows and light like a teenage Bacall or Harlow. He even got permission for us to use cigarettes in the photos, severely bending the school's rules. The result, in retrospect, was stunning. I looked like a *noir* Lolita, ready to devour any pubescent Sam Spade who came my way.

Deeper in the box, I found odds and ends from junior high. Notes I wrote to my girlfriends. Sketches I made in art class. At the bottom of the box was a long black braid. I'd always been obsessed with my friend Lashan's hair, so one day, she pulled out one of her braids and gave it to me. I hadn't spoken to Lashan in years. She was one of the many friends I'd sacrificed to my closeted relationship with Will Gage.

"Kara, Luis is leaving," Harry announced awkwardly.

I looked up and waved goodbye. "See you later, Luis." Luis gave Harry a clumsy kiss on the lips and left.

Harry was in a more sensible outfit now. She had put on an oversize T-shirt with the Eiffel Tower bedazzled onto it that we'd bought in Paris. She sat down next to me. "You want me to hold on to those boxes, or you want to take them with you?"

"Harry, can we please talk about what just happened here? Who is he?"

"He's the janitor who cleans for the agency. And thanks for covering for me, sweetie. It would have broken his heart to think I hadn't told you all about him."

"What about my heart?" I inquired.

"You're stronger than he is," she said with a smile. "You're a woman." Harry ran her hands through my hair. "You want some breakfast?"

What I really wanted was my mother to go to sleep so I could use her computer. "How long have you been with him?" I asked.

"I'm not *with* him. Four months." She thought for a moment, then corrected herself. "Six months. Give or take."

"I don't get it. You're always butting into my business, asking about my sex life. How could you keep this a secret?"

"I really don't want your father to know."

"You think I'd tell Pa?"

"I trust you," she said. "But if he asked you and you lied, he would still know. Parents can read their children too well."

"Who is this guy?" I probed.

"I just told you. And don't say it like that. He's very nice."

"But are you thinking this through? I just don't want you to get hurt."

"Yes, sweetie, I am thinking it through. Actually, I take that back. I'm not thinking it through, but that's the beauty of it. When you fall for someone, you throw logic and rationality out the door. I feel more alive than I have in years."

"But... but you're going to have your heart broken. I mean, what's your future with this guy?"

"Stop calling him 'this guy.' His name's Luis. With an accent on the *i*."

"Fine. What's your future with *Luís*?"

"Because he's a Mexican janitor?"

"No. No, that's not what I meant."

"Well, there's one major bonus to dating a Latin man." Harry's face opened into one of her devilish smiles. I knew where this was going, and I did not want to hear it. "He's huge, Kara. Meaty. Girthy. Like an eggplant."

"Stop!" I stuck my fingers in my ears. Everyone had been worried that I was turning into Bobby, when all the time my mother was.

"And he's the first uncircumcised man I've ever been with," she continued, to my dismay. I started humming tunelessly and loudly. "Much bigger than your father. Your father swaggered around like he was packing heat, but he was... average. It's like going from a gherkin to a hothouse cucumber."

I pulled my fingers out of my ears. "Really, Harry. How many vegetables are you going to compare this man's penis to?"

"What? You can't take a little off-color humor?" She cackled.

"Do you really think I want to hear about my father's penis?"

"I just said that to check if you were listening. But it is true." What was with these Southern California parents? Was there no middle ground between Leila's sweep-it-under-the-Persian-rug tactics and Harry's tell-all post-hippy openness? If only Bobby and I could have switched mothers. I could see the reality show playing in my head. *Mom Swap*! It seemed like the perfect solution. Bobby would've had no trouble coming out to Harry, and I would never have had to suffer through Leila on comparative penis girth. "I love torturing you. Promise you'll do your best not to tell your father. I know he's probably hired thirty prostitutes by now, but I just don't want to get into this discussion with him."

"Believe me, I won't tell him."

"Thanks, sweetie. Your father's not dating anyone serious, is he?"

"Really, Harry, you want me to give up his secrets, but protect yours."

"A child's allegiance should always be to the mother." Harry put her hand on my knee and tickled me the way she'd done when I was a child. "So," she said with a gleam in her eye, "He's cute, isn't he?"

"Sure," I said with a shrug.

"You'll love him when you get to know him. He's very smart. Not book smart the way your father is, thank God. It's so refreshing not to be with someone who's constantly lecturing me. Luis has knowledge of the heart."

I giggled. "What exactly is knowledge of the heart?"

"It's when somebody intuits what you feel. When someone says and does exactly what you want without your asking for it. If you allowed yourself to fall in love, you might know this." Harry had silenced me. "There is something very special about feeling loved in that way. Friendships are great. So are parents and children and cousins and teachers. But to have someone in the world who thinks you're beautiful, and who treats your body like a temple, well… it's something I wish my daughter could have."

I wanted to tell her all about Kyle, and all about the house the Ebadis were buying, and all about the secrets I was suddenly keeping from Bobby. But I couldn't. And so, instead, I just told her it was late, and I needed some sleep. She hugged me hard, sensing that I needed to be comforted. "I'm happy for you, Harry," I managed to say. "You deserve to be loved." She didn't need to vocalize her response. Her eyes told me that I deserved the same.

As soon as Harry went to bed, I booted up her computer and went straight to Google. *Journalist Iran Route Irish*, I typed in, which gave me 258,000 links. I tried Google Image, but there were 16,300 hits, and most were pictures of tanks on Route Irish. *Highway to Hell*, they called it. *The most dangerous road in the world, and the only way in and out of Baghdad.* One picture, though, immediately caught my eye. It was of an Iranian man ablaze in the streets of Paris. He looked to be about Hossein's age, but much thinner and darker. He and two women had set themselves on fire to protest the raiding of the offices of an Iranian opposition group in Paris. The image was distressing. Blowing up an empty cop car was one thing, but actually setting yourself on fire seemed too extreme a form of protest, and in the most beautiful city in the world, no less. Finally, I decided the images were too distracting and went back to the web pages. I must have read thousands of news articles about the war, about Iran, even a few about the Irish Republican Army, until finally I came upon a story about an Iranian journalist named Ali Sefeed. The blurb simply reported that "international journalist Ali Sefeed was injured while embedded with U.S. troops on Route Irish. Sefeed had no comment."

I'd even heard that name before, Sefeed. No way the Ebadis didn't know them.

I quickly Google-Imaged Ali Sefeed, but nothing. And then I remembered Leila saying she could find anything on YouTube, and I figured it was worth a try. So I typed the name into the YouTube search engine and got one video, apparently from BBC News. In it, a newscaster discussed recent fatalities as a cause of the war. At the end of the broadcast, he added that a frequent contributor to their program, field producer Ali Sefeed, was injured on Route Irish. Sefeed was expected to make a full recovery and be back at work soon. And there he was. *Kyle.* It was a grainy picture of him in a helmet in the desert, but it was definitely *him*. I looked at my watch. How early was too early to barge in on the Ebadis? I decided that eight o'clock was an appropriately inappropriate time. I could ask Leila all about the Sefeeds of Los Angeles. By the time I was done, Kyle would be reunited with his family, and he would have me to thank for it.

12

"KARA, DARLING? VAT ARE you doing here?" Leila was wearing no makeup. I had never seen her face without the benefits of cosmetics. I analyzed her skin, searching for wrinkles, for a sign of age, for a sign of pain, for a sign of anxiety, but there were none. Her skin was smooth and wrinkle-free.

"I'm here for Pilates," I lied.

"Kara, it is Tuesday. Pilates is Friday, and this week is canceled because Marie is out of town." The only sign of age I could find were a few sun spots on her chest, revealed by the white robe she was wearing.

"Oh, right. I don't know why I thought… I woke up and rushed over here thinking I was late."

"You are not even dressed for it."

"I was running late, and I figured I could just buy an outfit there. I don't know what I was thinking."

"Are you okay?"

"I'm fine," I said. "I guess I must have slept badly."

"So, come in," Leila offered, ever the hostess. "I was having tea."

"That would be lovely, thank you."

"Excuse the mess," Leila said as she took my hand in hers. "Rosa Maria spent the night at her cousin's, and she's not back yet."

From within the family room, I could hear the sound of a tennis game on television. Leila led me toward the room, where Hossein was eating a banana and enjoying the match. From the sweat on his T-shirt and the towel around his neck, I gathered he had just finished a workout.

"Hossein, look who's here," Leila said.

Hossein immediately stood and gave me a kiss on each cheek. He was always proper, always gallant. "What is the occasion?" he asked.

"Just my stupidity," I responded.

"Sit down, Kara," Leila insisted. "I'll go bring you some tea."

Alone with Hossein, I realized he was the person to ask about the Sefeeds. Leila would bump into Ali's mother or aunt or godmother, if Iranians have those, at the Design Center, mention my inquiry, and it would take about an hour for word to come back to her that some slut with my name had been shagging the elusive one-legged journalist. I was safer with Hossein, who was too stoic to gossip.

"Hossein, can I ask you something?"

"Of course," he said, his attention squarely on Federer and Robredo.

"Well, I was wondering if you knew the…"

The phone rang, loudly cutting into the tension of the room. Hossein reached over and picked it up. "Allo," he said too loudly. "Allo. Allo." He slammed the phone down on the receiver. "Another fucking hang-up." Hearing Hossein swear left me a little shaken.

"I had those several times yesterday," Leila said as she arrived with my tea. *Damn, Leila was back. Opportunity missed.* I would have to ask Hossein about the Sefeeds later.

"It might just be kids," I explained. "When we were young, my friends and I would call people and do the whole heavy breathing thing. It was awful, but then again, it was before caller ID."

Hossein picked up the phone again and pressed the caller ID button. "Blocked number," he announced.

"It's kind of reassuring. To think kids still harass strangers for fun," I said.

Hossein laughed and turned up the volume on the television, our signal that he was ready to return to viewing in peace.

"Let's go into the kitchen," Leila suggested, "so Hossein doesn't have to work so hard to ignore us."

"Is it okay if I watch for a bit?"

"You're a tennis fan?" Hossein asked, his interest suddenly aroused.

"Totally. Bobby's never told you?"

"Babak doesn't tell me anything," Hossein practically grunted, exasperated by his lack of closeness with his son.

"Well, I am going to get dressed. I will leave you two here," Leila announced. "Kara *djoon*, if you are gone when I come down, I'll see you Friday night."

"What's Friday night?" Hossein asked.

"You're not invited," Leila responded playfully. "It's a cultural event, and you'd be bored."

"Well," I stammered. "You *could* be invited. If you wanted to be. Fiona is on the host committee of some art opening benefiting the House of Ruth."

"You would hate it. It's said to be very avant-garde." She then explained to me, "I don't want to have him dragging me out after five minutes." She gave me a kiss on each cheek and disappeared.

"So who are your favorites?" Hossein asked.

"Artists?"

"Tennis players."

"Federer," I said. His name was staring at me from the screen, so it was a safe choice.

"Best player the game has ever seen. There's never been better."

"He's a thrill to watch. Hossein?" I spoke his name with urgency, hoping to change the tone.

"Yes?"

"You know most of the Iranian families in L.A., right?"

"Many of them." He turned the volume up again. He really didn't want to talk about anything but tennis.

"Have you ever heard of the Sefeeds?" I asked.

"Of course I have," he said, and then surprised me by adding, "and so have you."

"Really?" I searched my mental Rolodex for every Persian face and name I had been introduced to, but couldn't seem to remember a Sefeed amongst the handsome men, the beautiful women, or their embalmed parents.

"The Sefeeds are Leila's father's family. I'm sure you've heard the name. There's a cousin or an uncle in Chicago. But I don't think any of the Sefeeds came to L.A."

It took me a moment to work through the implications.

"Excuse me," I announced. "I'm gonna use the bathroom." Hossein was already refocused on the screen.

I walked through the kitchen, where a few dirty plates and cups were left on the counter, awaiting Rosa Maria's arrival. So this tiny imperfection is what Leila was referring to when she told me not to mind the mess. I went straight back to Rosa Maria's room and made a beeline for those home movies I had seen over a decade ago, convinced they were the only piece of Keyvan left in this house.

I opened the closet and found the carefully organized videos underneath the sweaters. I immediately gravitated to the most recent one. I needed to see if Keyvan Ebadi bore any resemblance to Kyle. I needed for there to be no resemblance. The side of the video, in Elena's careful handwriting, read *Keyvan and Babak. January 1984.* I wondered why there were no videos taken after that date.

A few moments later, I was transported to Disneyland. The camera was trying to focus on two brothers inside the teacups ride. The ride was spinning and spinning, and it was impossible to make out a face. Children were screaming, their arms in the air. Elena's voice resonated from behind the camera. "Señor Keyvan. Babak. Look this way. Over here." But it was no use. The ride was moving too fast for Elena to catch a glimpse of her two... what were they to her? They weren't her bosses. They weren't her sons. Someone should have invented a word for nannies to call the children they care for and love. As I pondered this, I heard a voice behind me.

"Kara."

I turned around and saw Hossein standing there, a plastic bag of almonds in his hands. "You startled me. I..." Instinctively, I turned the video off. "I'm sorry, I was just putting my teacup in the dishwasher, and I... I stumbled on these videos and I couldn't resist watching them, you know. It's fascinating to see Bobby as a kid."

Hossein chuckled. "Most of the time it seems Babak still is a kid."

I was so confused. Wasn't Hossein angry with me? Wasn't he going to scold me for being a devious snoop?

"Let's get out of here," he said. "I don't think Leila would be very happy if she knew those videos were still here. Elena was supposed to take them with her."

"You mean these videos have been here for all these years, and neither of you even knew?" I asked incredulously.

"We don't go into Rosa Maria's room," he said curtly. Hossein led me to the kitchen. "Can I offer you something else?"

"No." I stopped for a moment. Hossein popped an almond into his mouth, and the sound of the crunching was suddenly deafening.

"Can I ask you something?"

"Of course," he said, looking at the last couple of fragmented almonds in his hand.

"Were you religious? Back in Iran?"

"My family wasn't religious at all. But Leila's mother, Homa, is devout. She prays five times a day, believes deeply in the revolution, even still. Why?"

"I don't know. I'm curious, I guess. Sometimes Bobby says something about Iran, and I realize I hardly know anything about it."

"Ali Sefeed, Leila's father, was a very religious man. A farmer. He died when Leila was very young."

My mind was reeling again. "Leila's dad was a farmer?"

"Yes. You sound surprised."

I had always figured that Leila came from a long line of money. Caravans of cash stretching back from Brentwood to Tehran, from the twenty-first century to Xerxes.

"Bobby told me once you were friends with the Shah."

"Babak prefers the stories he gets from his mother. They are a lot alike. We *met* the Shah. Once. In a receiving line. Like several million other people. I graduated from the imperial college of engineering; His Majesty always attended the ceremony. Leila and I had just started going out, but I was already crazy about her. He shook our hands, and he told Leila she was very beautiful. I wasn't in awe of the Pahlavis, but at that moment I almost exploded with pride. I think I would have done anything for that curious little man that day. He had given the woman I love such a feeling of self-possession. Leila always had very fair skin, and back then she would read all the European magazines and copy the fashions."

"She'd sew them?"

He laughed. "Leila? With a needle and thread? No, her mother would reproduce the gowns and skirts and jackets. Homa was always very good with practical things. Pomegranate syrup from her own trees. Sewing. She disapproved of the styles, of course, on religious grounds, but this was the time of Googoosh, like you saw."

I looked out to the yard. A paved path led from the pool to the tennis court. Bright flowers grew from every corner at what must have been an astronomical expense. I had always imagined all this was done partly with Leila's wealth. It never occurred to me that Hossein had brought all this about by starting a car dealership. The house that Hyundai built.

Leila met us back in front of the TV. She was her normal self again: Chanel flats, Armani skirt, silk top, makeup flawlessly in place. "I'm off to the hairdresser," she said.

I stood and picked up the plate that held Hossein's banana peel.

"Kara *djoon*, please don't clean. Rosa Maria will be back soon."

"It's no problem. Where is she anyway?"

"At her cousin's," Leila explained, in a tone that indicated she hated repeating information.

"I'm going back to watch tennis," Hossein announced as he disappeared. "Feel free to stay, Kara."

I turned back to Leila, trying to seem as nonchalant as possible in my questioning. "Where does her cousin live?"

"Elena? She lives in a cute little house in Valley Village." She pulled her car keys from her purse. "Oh, wait, we need to schedule the inspection. Hossein!" Hossein reappeared on command. "They can do it Sunday at noon or four, or anytime next Monday. What's best for you and Babak?" he asked me.

I could've said "it's up to Bobby," but for the first time, I didn't. I couldn't move into a new stage of life with Bobby until I figured out what was going on. "Is there any way to stall them?" I asked.

"Stall them?" Leila looked up. "But why?"

"I don't know," I explained. "It's just... it's such a big step."

"Oh, second thoughts. That's normal," Leila said. "It is a big step. We should still move forward, though."

"No!" I yelled a little too forcefully. Leila and Hossein were taken aback, as was I. This was the first time I had ever said no to the Ebadis, and the word hung in the air like thick smog. "I'm sorry, it's just... I need time. You can buy the house for Bobby if you want to, but if you're doing it for *us*, then I need time."

Back in my car, I quickly called 411 for the phone and address of Elena Sanchez in Valley Village. Luckily, there were only two, and one had an apartment number, so I knew I was on the right track as I headed over Coldwater.

My mind raced as I weaved up and then down the canyon. I did my best to convince myself that Kyle wasn't Keyvan. That it was just a coincidence that he had Leila's father's name. Maybe Ali Sefeed was the most common name in Iran, the John Smith of Iran. "He's dead," I repeated to myself over and over again. And he didn't look that similar to Bobby. Kyle's forehead was wider, and he had a widow's peak. His hair was thinning a little bit. Baldness is hereditary from the mother's side. There you go, I told myself. Crisis averted. Bobby had a full head of hair, and Kyle didn't. Genetically, they just couldn't be brothers. Right?

And then I remembered Bobby complaining how Leila had him using Propecia preventatively since he was sixteen. Damn. I searched for other differences. Kyle's eyes were negligibly darker. His body was certainly different. He was taller and beefier and hairier. That had to mean something. Then again, they both had those long eyelashes that women work so hard to achieve with mascara. Both of them with those thick, dark, curled lashes. Their lips, though, were completely different. Bobby's lower lip was round and dominant, while Kyle's lips were thin and pursed. I wanted so badly for Elena to tell me all my thoughts were those of a paranoid lunatic, that Keyvan Ebadi had never eaten me out.

Elena's house was deep in the 818. The first thing I noticed was the Hyundai Azera parked outside. Slate gray. Latest model. Fully loaded. The front yard was distinguished by a lemon tree and some children's toys (the Slip 'N Slide that I immediately recognized from the home movies of the young Keyvan and Babak rested on the front lawn, next to a volleyball net), and toward the side of the house, a makeshift vegetable garden. I rapped on the door frantically, and a middle-aged woman answered. Her curly hair was tied in a ponytail, and she wore a silk top over Gucci jeans with Chanel flats. Apparently, she was also on the list for Leila's hand-me-downs.

"Yes?" she asked. "What is it?"

"Is this Elena Sanchez?"

"Yes. Who are you?" she snapped in the defensive voice one saves for telemarketers.

"My name is Kara. I'm Bobby Ebadi's roommate."

"Some people say his girlfriend?" she asked suspiciously. This woman meant business.

"So you've heard about me?"

"Of course I have, but I'm not as gullible as Leila and Hossein."

"Oh, so you... I mean, you *know?*" It was so Persian of me to ask the question without saying the word.

"Kara, my cousin and my children are waiting for breakfast inside. Is something wrong?"

"I have an odd question for you."

"Yes?" She was clearly irritated with me.

"It's about Keyvan. Is he..."

"Look, Kara, whatever you're about to ask, don't."

"You don't even know what I was going to say," I said.

"Kara, listen to me. Don't go digging into this. The family has made up their minds. Leave it alone. I have to go."

Theories about Keyvan Ebadi swirled in my head as I entered my apartment. Bobby and Joanne were drunkenly splayed on my kitchen floor. Omar was nudged into the crevice of Joanne's armpit, drooling all over my favorite pajamas, which Joanne had obviously decided to borrow. There were four empty packages of frozen enchiladas on my kitchen counter and two empty bottles of red wine next to them. I didn't particularly want to wake them up and face them. But Omar gave me no choice. She began barking like a maniac when I arrived. In fact, she practically began attacking me, as if I was the intruder and they were her owners. The yappy little Shih Tzu was ripping through my pants when Bobby finally got up and stopped her. He pulled her off me and into his arms.

"My own dog doesn't even recognize me," I said somewhat melodramatically. Clearly, I was looking for sympathy. I began to unpack the boxes I had brought back from Harry's. I had taken them partly because my place had nothing in it, and partly because I knew Bobby would accuse me of doing something covert and illicit with my time, and this was proof that I was spending an innocent night with my mother.

"You have to take better care of her, Kara," Bobby said. "She remembers when you desert her."

"I stuck a match up her ass while you were fucking her shrink, so don't talk to me about taking care of her." My tone was obviously laced with more anger and bitterness than the situation called for. "I'm sorry, Bobby," I said. "I'm not myself right now. I couldn't sleep all night. I felt ill."

"You want some immune-boosting tea or something?" he asked.

By this point, Joanne was awake. I hadn't seen her first thing in the morning in a long time. Without the effort she usually puts into her hair and makeup, Joanne is actually a very plain girl. And yet the crust in her eyes and the drool on her mouth somehow made her more appealing, more relaxed. For the first time in years, she didn't look like she had something to prove. "Bobby and I thought maybe you were having a hot, hot love affair," she said as she sat up and took a slug of Smart Water.

"I told you. I had a stomachache."

"So where were you all night?" Joanne asked. "You got Advil around here?"

"I was at my mother's." I opened one of the boxes and pulled out our old high school *Facebook* with one hand and Lashan's braid with another. "See. I even have proof if you're gonna give me the third degree."

"You see any hot lights here," Joanne barked. "Since when is asking a friend what she's been up to the equivalent of Avu Grabe or whatever it's called? I just want to live vicariously through you if you're having hot sex. Even if you're having unhot sex."

To my disgust, Bobby was amused by her. "We got no action last night," he added helpfully. "What is that?" He pointed to the braid.

"It's nothing. It's my friend Lashan's weave. From junior high."

"That's kind of gross," Bobby said.

"Sorry we trashed your apartment." Joanne was up and throwing out the enchilada containers now. "It was like four in the morning and we were starving and you know there's like nothing good open at that time and we remembered you had all the enchiladas..."

"From the letter-in-the-freezer story..." Bobby continued.

"We were kind of wondering what kind of person decides to leave a letter in a freezer," Joanne added.

"Do you think he meant for you to find it at some moment of calamity and upheaval?" Bobby wondered. "If he knew you at all, he would be able to divine that you would never eat those things, except in crisis."

"What if you hadn't found it, and we'd found it last night?" Joanne said. "That would have been insane. I don't even know if I would have shown it to you. You're better off leaving he-who-must-not-be-named in the past."

"He is in the past," I told Joanne. "And this time I mean it. Okay guys, I need to shower and get some rest. I feel awful."

Joanne looked to Bobby. "Is she kicking us out, Bobby?"

"I think so."

"I'm not kicking you out," I said. "I just need to get some rest. I'm sorry. How was your night, anyway?"

Once again, Joanne looked to Bobby, addressing everything to him. "Rue McClanahan," she said, and instantaneously Bobby started howling with laughter. What in the world was happening? I ditched my life for one night, and already Bobby and Joanne had inside jokes. This wasn't how it was supposed to work. Joanne was supposed to pass out and go home. Bobby was supposed to blow some stranger, and then freak out on me in the morning as he freebased elderberry extract. The comfort of my routine was shattered.

Bobby clearly realized I was annoyed by their private hilarity and tried to explain their joke to me. "Joanne said after she's learned Spanish, she wants to learn French…"

"I studied it in high school for three years…" she added. Whether intentional or not, they were starting to sound like those old couples in *When Harry Met Sally.*

"Anyway," Bobby continued, "I said that if we moved to Paris, we'd have to buy a little street and call it Rue McClanahan." Once again, Bobby and Joanne entered a zone of frightening cackles.

"Don't you get it?" Joanne asked. "*Rue* means street in French."

"I get it," I snapped.

"By the way," Joanne said, "We totally translated 'Like a Virgin' into Spanish."

"Oh my God," Bobby added. "Did we sing it in front of La Lohan?"

"I think we did."

"I am mortified."

"She loved it." Joanne decided I would love it too and started singing. Bobby joined in. "*Como un virgen. Hey. Tocada por la primera vez. Como una vi-i-i-i-ir-gen…*"

"We are such dorks," Bobby said.

"When we join Lindsay's Scrabble-*en-español* club, then we'll really be dorks."

"Next week. We told her we're in." Since when was Bobby a Scrabble player? Backgammon was his game. *Our* game.

"There won't be a game next week," Joanne assured him. "I'm gonna get Lindsay's housekeeper to explain to her there's no N with that little squiggle on it in her Scrabble box. That should put it off for a while." Joanne stood up and took my pajamas off. "Oh, Kara, I hope it's okay I borrowed these. I couldn't sleep in vintage Halston, could I?"

"It's fine," I said. And under any circumstances, it would have been fine. We borrowed clothes from each other all the time. In fact, Fiona's Dolce & Gabbana wrap-around dress and her Catherine Malandrino top, as well as Joanne's pink cashmere sweater, were all in my closet at that moment. But something about Joanne in my pajamas, eating my enchiladas, with my best friend, was just too much for me to handle.

Joanne went to my hall closet, where she had hung a silver-sequined dress. She changed back into it, then hung my pajamas onto the hanger.

"It's fine, Joanne. You don't have to hang the pajamas."

"It's no big deal. I'm just gonna put them back where I found them. It's the least I can…"

"It's *fine*, Joanne," I snapped. "I'm just gonna throw them in the wash anyway."

Joanne looked at me defiantly, then threw the pajamas onto the floor. Omar, thinking she was meant to fetch, bit into them and carried them back to Joanne, who ignored her. "No girl brunch this week, FYI," Joanne said. "Fiona's having another one of her *meetings* with Casey. You didn't hear it here first, but it sounds like Casey wants to change the date of the wedding. And I don't mean to earlier." Joanne smiled. Why did other people's misery always make her so chipper? She turned to Bobby. "Why don't we have brunch today? You and Kara are unemployed, and I make my own schedule. Let's make the most of a Tuesday morning."

"That sounds perfect," Bobby said. "I must wash away the taste of those enchiladas."

Joanne turned to me. "Brunch?"

"Sure," I said. "Why not?"

"I'm just gonna run home and wash my face and change, and I'll pick you up in fifteen. Be ready."

Joanne walked out, the sequins of her dress jingle-jangling. I could smell the booze and the cigarettes emanating from her as she walked by, evidence of the fun I'd given up. For what? For a night of confused, sleepless neuroses.

I couldn't remember the last time Bobby and I were alone together and felt this uncomfortable. Usually at this time of morning, I would sneak into his side of the duplex, jump into bed with him, and hear his stories about the fantastically seedy activities of his evening. I suddenly realized I was the one who'd had crazy sex the night before. And unlike Bobby, who was always so honest with his escapades, I was lying to him about mine. I had to cut the awkward silence. "I figured you would've found some hot trick last night," I said.

"I was too drunk. Benicio was there. I tried to slip him your number."

"Thanks," I said softly.

"So I have an idea. Let's continue your sexual education today. We can teach you how to cruise. Maybe hit some sports bars."

"I don't know..." I trailed off, before finding the courage to complete the sentence. "I don't know if I want to continue my sex education."

"Because..." Bobby said, annoyed.

"Because I don't think getting gang-banged by some football team in the bathroom of a sports bar is going to make me happy." Once again, my tone was harsh, and I knew it.

"Well, golly. It's my dream date," Bobby said, in his best Gidget impersonation.

"I'm sorry, Bobby. There is something I need to tell you." This was it. Here it came. The truth, plain and simple. "Remember that guy Kyle?" I said.

"Yes?" He leaned in, awaiting a revelation.

Just say it, Kara. Tell him what you suspect. He's your best friend. He deserves to know that his brother might be alive. "I saw him again."

"Okay..."

"Last night. Before I went to my mom's. He texted me and I went to his hotel and we had sex." *On the other hand, he might already know his brother didn't die.*

"I'm confused," Bobby said.

"About what?"

"Why is this such a big deal?" Obviously, Bobby wanted a better story. "Why didn't you just tell me in the first place?"

He had a point. Why *didn't* I just tell him in the first place, before I suspected Kyle's true identity? Oh, of course: I was afraid of proving Bobby right. I didn't want to admit I was falling for the first guy I slept with. I didn't want to give Bobby the satisfaction of having me pegged. All that seemed minor and stupid now.

"Kara," Bobby continued. "I know I told you not to see the same guy twice, but that's only because I don't want you to get hurt. I want you to have fun, but not subject us to *Jacques 2: Despair Over Dubai.* I don't think I could stand another year and a half of seeing you like that." Bobby pulled out his cell phone from the pocket of his cargo pants. "My mother has been calling incessantly this morning," he said as he checked his messages. Through the speaker of his phone, I could hear Leila speaking in Farsi. The only words I understood where *Kara* and *Roxbury*. Bobby hung up, clearly upset.

"Bobby, let me explain."

"You told her to stall the house. Is that true?" he demanded to know.

"I'm not ready," I said.

"Because of Kyle? Because you're fantasizing about playing house with him?"

"It's not just that. It's..." I trailed off, unable to find the right story to fabricate.

"Look at me, Kara. You met him online for sex. That's not how girls like you meet their future husbands."

"Why not?" I asked.

"Because the kind of person who goes on those sites isn't husband material."

"*You're* on those sites."

"And I am not husband material," he shot back, without a trace of irony.

"Well, then some people might wonder whether *you're* ready to settle down."

"Oh, no. Don't try it," he barked. "If you had doubts about us really living together, you ought to have talked to me. Not to my mother."

"Okay. I'm not ready, Bobby. I'm not ready to spend a year decorating with your mother. I'm not ready to throw a housewarming party for the diaspora to attend. I'm not ready to decide which room should be the nursery. I'm not ready."

"So why didn't you discuss any of this with me?"

"I should've. I'm sorry. But your parents suddenly asked me to schedule an inspection. I was on the spot. I told them they're welcome to buy you the house if they want to. You should have the house, if it's what you really want."

"That is so absurd. Do you really think I'd want to live there all by myself?" He caught his breath. "What were you doing at my parents' house this morning at eight forty-five, anyway?"

Now I was stumped. I might have just confessed the whole thing right then, but Bobby huffed out, punctuating his exit with a slam of the door. I followed him to his side of the duplex and pleaded for forgiveness while he changed, even though I wasn't sure I had done anything wrong. "I'm not trying to hurt you, Bobby. I just don't know if I'm ready for this move. I don't feel it's right."

"You said that. I get it," he screamed from his bedroom. "It would have been a good idea to say it earlier. I'm not upset that you don't want to move in to some mansion in Beverly Hills. I'm upset that you would tell my parents before you told me. I'm upset that you hid your relationship with Kyle from me."

His home phone rang. He rushed out in khaki cords and a gray hoodie to pick it up. "Hello? Hello?" Bobby hung up angrily. "Some fucking freak has been calling from a blocked number all week. This is why I should set up a separate line for tricks." Bobby slammed the phone down hard on the receiver a few times. "Asshole!" he screamed at the blameless telephone.

I heard the honk of Joanne's car from outside. She was honking to the tune of "Like a Virgin." "Are you still coming to brunch?" Bobby snapped. "Or do you have a secret date with Kyle?"

"Do you want me to come to brunch?" I wondered aloud.

"I want you to be happy, Kara. I've always wanted you to be happy. Come to brunch, don't come to brunch. Move to Roxbury, don't move to Roxbury. Move to fucking Dubai with Kyle if that's what you want. Just do what you want to do and be honest about it."

"I don't think I'm gonna join," I said with a shrug.

"Maybe get a little sleep," he grunted as he fled out the door. "Take care of that stomachache."

I was about to head back to my side of the duplex when Bobby's home phone rang again. The machine picked up. The greeting played—my voice, sounding kind of wispy: "Once upon a time there was a little boy named Bobby, who believed in messages."

Silence on the other end. Silence—and the faint sound of a British news segment. "A new U.S. poll suggests little support for military action against Iran for their nuclear program..." A hang-up, then a busy signal, then more silence.

I immediately called Kyle's phone from my own. From the other end of the line, that same faint British voice seemed to be attacking me in surround sound. "The United States, however, remain firm in their mission to block a nuclear Iran and are calling on European allies..."

I breathed heavily. Here it was. Unignorable evidence that Keyvan Ebadi, the journalist Ali Sefeed, and my online fuck buddy Kyle were all the same person. I had gone on a search for anonymous sex and found sex with a person who couldn't be less anonymous to me. I laughed at myself. Of course, out of all the responses sent to me, I would pick Keyvan. I just can't get away from the vortex of the Ebadis.

"Kara?" he said. "Are you there?"

"Yes."

Questions swirled in my brain. Did Bobby and his parents really believe his brother was dead? Elena said the family had *made up their minds*. That sure implied knowledge of some kind.

"Listen," I said. "Wanna hang out tomorrow night?"

"Sure. What time do you wanna come over?"

"How about dinner around eight?"

"Cool. They have not-bad room service here."

"No. I mean *dinner*," I said sharply. "Isn't it time we learned a little bit more about each other?"

He laughed. "Fair enough. If dinner will help you ease into the sex... Sure. I'll see you tomorrow night. I'll even book a table someplace decent."

In the background, the news was still on. "In December, France joined the United States in calling for sanctions against Iran…"

Keyvan hung up. I needed to find out what exactly had happened in the Ebadi family. I needed to know what it was that made Hossein and Leila send their son back to Iran. I needed to know why Keyvan couldn't actually say something when he called his brother or his parents. I needed to go back to Elena and make her tell me the truth. She was my shot. I called, but there was no answer. I went to Bobby's bedroom. I knew he kept a little phone book there. I searched around, but I couldn't quite remember which cupboard. Finally, after finding too many pairs of Calvin Klein underwear, different brands of lube, and a few meditation CDs, I found Bobby's phone book, and located Elena's cell number. I took a breath and dialed.

"Hello," her gravelly voice answered.

"Elena, this is Kara, Bobby's…"

"I remember you just fine, Kara."

"And I know Keyvan is alive."

There was a long silence on the other end of the line.

"I want to know what happened," I said.

"Is it your business?"

"I think it is. Bobby's my best friend, and I'm sleeping with Keyvan."

"Then you should talk to them, not to me."

"I need to come see you."

"I'm out of town. I brought the kids to San Diego to see the zoo." Another pause. "I'll call you when I'm back."

"Elena, can you just tell me now?" I pleaded. "Tell me what happened."

"I am with my children. I will call you when I'm back."

"When is that? When will you be back?"

"Friday."

13

KEYVAN MADE THE RESERVATION at La Scala. Its Hollywood mafia décor, complete with red vinyl booths and sketches of famous clients on the wall, was stately without seeming pretentious, and made it a Leila kind of place. She hated prix fixe, foodie restaurants, and held a particular disdain for those that charged seventy-five dollars for a miniscule piece of cod garnished with ginger, soaked in some exotic reduction, and surrounded by some fruity coulis splattered to look like a Jackson Pollock. She liked her food simple, and La Scala's chopped salad was her favorite in the city.

"Allow me to recommend the veal scaloppine," Keyvan intoned archly. "I grew up on it." He ordered a Pinot Noir. When the wine arrived, though, he insisted that I be the one to taste it. I self-consciously did what I thought I was supposed to: hold the glass at the stem, spin the wine around in the glass, smell it first, take a small sip, and then nod to the waiter in silent approval. I watched Keyvan as the waiter poured his wine. He looked different out in the real world, away from the claustrophobic haze of his scotch-soaked hotel room. He cleaned up pretty nicely. His hair was still wet from either a shower or from one of those wet-look grooming products. Hair from his receding widow's peak fell toward his eyebrows in sexy chunks. He had shaved, which made him look much younger, almost like a child. And to my surprise, he wore a charcoal pinstripe suit, paired with a pale pink shirt and loafers. As for me, I wasn't fucking around, either. I figured dinner at a fancy Beverly Hills restaurant was the perfect occasion to wear my new yellow Prada dress. Turns out we were both in outfits Leila would approve of. She'd only picked out mine, though, most likely.

"So," he said. "You are a girl after all."

I looked down at my breasts in the dress. "Is that the polite way of telling me I'm dressed like a hooch?"

"No," he laughed. "You're beautiful in that dress. It's a good color for your skin."

"Thank you." I blushed at the compliment. I'd dragged him to dinner to get him to come clean with me, but even still, I wanted him to like me, to approve on a level deeper than sex.

"I wasn't talking about your breasts, though. I meant this. *Dinner.* A proper date. Most women demand it right up front. I was shocked that we had our three rides around the block before you either bailed out or demanded something just like this."

"I'm not one for gender stereotypes."

"Some of them," he said with a smile, "are true."

"For example?"

"For example, men are able to separate sex and love more easily than women."

I laughed. "You might be right about that one." I paused briefly before asking, "Have you ever been in love?" He looked at me curiously and then said no. "Never?" I insisted. "Not even just a little bit?"

"What does it mean to be a little bit in love?" he asked. "There's no such thing. What about you?"

"Once," I said. "Although the more time passes, the less sure I am whether it was love or infatuation."

"You're very hung up on definitions, aren't you? Love, infatuation, obsession… Who cares? If you enjoyed it, and it made you happy, then it was what it was. So was he as good in bed as I am?"

"No," I said. It was the honest answer, and the one he wanted to hear. "But he was more…"

"Dull?"

"Tender. He was more tender. And a hell of a lot more romantic."

"Sounds dull," Keyvan said between sips of wine.

"It wasn't. He was French."

"And what is he now?"

"Smartass," I said, kicking Keyvan under the table.

"I'm sorry. So what made the Frenchman so romantic, other than the accent?"

I took a sip of the wine. "One night, after too much *grappa* in Trastevere, we were walking past the Forum. I said I would give anything to be able to walk through the ruins without other gawkers, without the flash of digital cameras. Jacques asked me if I was adventurous. Then he took my hand and led me to a large fence on the side of the Forum. Jacques went first. He climbed the fence without a problem and jumped down on the other side. Then he held my hand and told me not to be scared. He guided me to the top and told me to jump. I did my best, but the fence was too high and too sharp. I didn't know what to do. Jacques kept screaming for me to jump. I gripped my hand onto one of the fence's sharp edges. As I let go, my pinky finger scraped against the edge. Look," I said as I gave my hand to Keyvan. "Can you see the scar right there?"

"It's barely visible," Keyvan noted.

"Well, it was bleeding pretty bad that night. Jacques took off his T-shirt and wrapped it around my finger tightly."

"And you've kept the bloody T-shirt ever since," Keyvan mocked.

"Hey. You collect money. Don't blame me for keeping mementos of my own past."

"Go on. So the romantic Frenchman literally gave you the shirt off his back. Now he's shirtless, like the cover of a romance novel."

"He led me into the Forum. It was dark and eerie and quiet. Had I not just left the land of Fiats and Vespas and Gucci, I would never have known the modern world existed. Jacques sat down in the middle of the Forum. And then we, well you know, we..."

"Fucked? Tenderly?"

"And when we finished, I rolled over onto the ground next to him and, for the very first time, he whispered that he loved me. I reached into my pocket and took out my digital camera. I knew this was a moment I needed to capture. The flash illuminated the entire Forum."

"Sounds like a powerful little camera."

"All right, a lot of the Forum. It's my favorite photo of Jacques. The shadows from the columns are on his body, and his smile is radiant. You can tell he's in love in the picture. It's a perfect image."

"It's a shame only frozen images can be perfect," Keyvan said.

"Our last night in Rome," I continued. "I led him to the Trevi Fountain. There were all these tourists and Italians gathered together in the piazza. They were strumming their guitars, singing songs, eating gelato, making out, and throwing coins into the fountain. It was like a Fellini movie."

"Without the dubbing," Keyvan cracked.

I giggled. I had seen *La Dolce Vita* with Bobby. We'd gone through an Italian film phase and devoured all of Fellini. At times, I couldn't understand the hype. More than anything, it was the dubbing that disturbed me. It reminded me of cheap kung fu movies. Bobby, on the other hand, loved the dubbing. "My roommate says the dubbing is Fellini's way of illustrating that all human beings worked on two levels," I said to Keyvan. "What they expressed to the world and what they were truly thinking."

"Your roommate is giving Fellini too much credit. The thing about Fellini is he cared more about creating a beautiful or surreal image than about the overall substance of the work."

"Well, anyway, I love that moment in *La Dolce Vita* ..."

"When Anita Ekberg swims in the Trevi?" Keyvan asked.

"Exactly. So I led Jacques to the edge of the fountain and sat with him. I told him that I wanted to swim inside. Jacques was opposed. He said they filled the water with toxic amounts of bleach to keep the fountain clean. And he pointed out the entire area was filled with *carabinieri*, who would arrest us and throw us into an Italian jail. But I didn't care. Bleach wouldn't kill us, and Italian jail doesn't scare me. So I kissed Jacques hard on the lips, and without even thinking, I tipped us both over into the water. When we brought our heads up and out of the water, we realized everybody was looking at us, like we were part of the art or something, frozen in time."

"Another perfect image," Keyvan commented.

I could smell the strong, pungent bleach as I continued the story. "When we came back up again, we noticed that the majority of the crowd was *carabinieri*, guns in hand. Jacques and I exited the side of the fountain, and without consultation, we both started running as fast as we could. The men with guns were in hot pursuit behind us. Jacques had an idea. He led us right back to the forum. This time, I climbed the fence like a master. By the time the *carabinieri* reached us, we were safe inside the ruins."

"It's a beautiful story," he said.

"I made that last part up. We weren't really chased by men with guns."

He stared at me a second and then laughed.

"Aren't journalists supposed to be able to tell when someone's making something up?"

"Some are better liars than others."

"You know what makes the story even more beautiful? I'm finally over him. I held onto the idea of him for so long. I thought we could reunite some-day. But now I'm truly over him. He's just a memory now, a very nice mem-ory." I took a breath. "And you?" I asked again. "I find it hard to believe you don't have a romantic story to go with every country you've visited."

"I have a few," he said. "Nothing as good as yours, true or not."

"Like?"

"A torrid twenty-four hours with a Saudi Arabian princess."

"Ooh," I sighed. "The journalist and the princess. It's like *Roman Holiday*."

"Hardly. She was no Audrey Hepburn. We had sex in the bathroom of an airport and never saw each other again."

"Sex in a bathroom for twenty-four hours?" I joked.

"That's how we started. Then there was the French anarchist."

"Do anarchists still exist?"

"In theory," he said. "Rebellion against her bourgeois parents made her very passionate. She had the key to their house in Neuilly, and would only make love in their bed."

"That's disturbing."

"Or titillating," he countered. "Depending on your perspective."

Maybe the brothers weren't so different after all.

"Would you like me to go on?"

I nodded apprehensively.

"Dancer from Morocco. Belly dancer. Need I say more? And a few flings with journalists and field producers and photographers, but those are all the same, rushed and dirty."

"Did you ever want more from any of these girls? Did any of them connect with you?" I probed.

"Why do you want to know?"

"I'm just curious. I want to know what your life has been like. I want to know who Keyvan really is."

He froze with the wine glass halfway to his lips. It took me a second to realize what I had said.

•

Earlier that evening, Fiona had called and asked if I was free. I told her I didn't have much time, but she insisted.

"Do you know how much Joanne tips Elba?" Fiona asked after I rushed into her place.

Fiona was on her imported Italian couch in her decadent Benedict Canyon living room. She had bought the house the moment she had the feeling that Casey was going to propose to her. She decided that if she was going to move in with a man, she would want her name on the mortgage papers. She bought the house from Ursula Andress and had hired Joanne to decorate it. It remained Joanne's biggest solo gig. When the papers were signed, Ursula insisted that Fiona meet Elba. Elba was a forty-something Guatemalan, or Guatemalteco, as they call themselves. She had escaped the country after losing the majority of her family to a volcanic eruption, an earthquake, a chickenpox epidemic, and thirty years of civil war, in no particular order. Elba had decided her two children weren't going to be raised in a place with such a high infant mortality rate, so she snuck them across the Mexican, and then the U.S., borders. She had met Ursula Andress when Ursula was volunteering with Jessica Lange and Tyne Daly at a charity organized to educate immigrant women. Ursula, impressed by how quickly Elba learned English, hired her as her maid. Ursula referred Elba to Fiona, who referred Elba to Joanne. I was pressured to hire Elba but didn't, only because I couldn't afford her.

"I give her three hundred dollars for Christmas every year," Fiona said. "And I give her all my old clothes." Fiona looked up at Elba, who had turned on the vacuum. Fiona leaned in closer so I could hear. "I just can't bear the thought of looking cheap."

"Is this why you asked me to come here? Is this why you *needed* me?" For fuck's sake, I had been a basket case ever since confirming Keyvan's identity. My date with him was in a few hours, I had no idea how I should handle the situation, and Fiona wanted to compare housekeeper tipping numbers with me.

Elba turned off the vacuum and began dusting. "Did you know Miss Joanne is speaking Spanish now? She speaks with me yesterday. She is very good."

"I took four years of high-school French," Fiona said. "I watched all of *Day for Night* without subtitles just last week."

"And she is decorating Lindsay Lohan's house," Elba continued.

"Her boss is decorating the house. Joanne's just helping." Fiona smiled indulgently, then added, "Sigourney Weaver's gonna play my mother in the movie!"

"Really?" Elba beamed. "Oh, I love her in *Ghostbusters*."

Fiona looked satisfied with Elba's reaction to her seeing Lohan and raising with Weaver. No wonder she wanted an invite to Hossein's poker parties. She grabbed my hand and led me downstairs toward the basement that Casey had converted into his office. Fiona swung the door of the office open. Casey was sitting at his desk. He was shirtless and wearing nothing but gym shorts. He had clearly just been for a run, because his skin was glowing with sweat. Casey's desk was covered with stacks of files. "I brought Kara here," Fiona announced curtly. Now I knew why Fiona needed me. When a couple needs a mediator, they are on the verge of collapse.

"Good. Can I at least have a few moments of peace to present my argument?" Casey begged.

"Of course you can," Fiona said. "But put a shirt on and stop trying to distract the mediator. Kara, please take into account that he's a lawyer, so his argument will seem more polished than mine."

"What did I do that's so wrong? Did I cheat on you? Did I lie to you? Did I beat you?"

"This is a courtroom tactic. List all the things that are worse than what the defendant actually did to make him appear innocent, when in fact, he's a selfish prick."

Casey stood and faced me. "I got this case handed to me. Mexican guy working minimum wage. Accused of killing his wife. He's being railroaded onto death row."

"Tell her the court date."

"It was pushed to September."

"Tell her the exact date," Fiona yelled.

"The date got *pushed*. I didn't know it would conflict with the wedding when I took the case. But if I drop it, I let this guy fry."

"Oh, please, it's lethal injection. And someone else will take the case," Fiona argued. "You have a team of lawyers."

"We have two lawyers who deal with death-row cases, and Linda is completely overloaded right now. She has no familiarity with this case."

"Are you hearing this, Kara?" Fiona shrieked. "He wants to postpone his wedding so that he can save a fucking wife-killer."

"There's reasonable doubt," Casey said.

"Oh, please, Casey. Face it. Your entire life is about saving murderers. Out of all the people you've gotten out of the chair, how many of them could actually have been innocent? One percent?"

"That's not the point," Casey said. "We discussed this a long time ago. I thought you were against the death penalty."

"Right now I don't even object to lynching, Casey. What's at stake here is me and you and our future, not some soapbox you're standing on."

"Kara," Casey said, suddenly calm again, "I have proposed not taking a single new capital case after this one until next year. We could postpone the wedding by two months and be completely safe."

"We are never completely safe. We just aren't. Something could always happen. Something could always go wrong."

I wondered if the two of them were aware I hadn't said a word since I had been brought into this absurd verbal scrimmage.

"I want to get married, Fiona. I just don't want to feel like somebody died unjustly because my wife didn't want to lose her deposit."

"Don't make this about the deposit," Fiona hissed.

"Isn't that what it's about?" Casey directed his words back to me again. "She put down fifty thousand for the palazzo. And a hundred to reserve Bocelli."

"I make enough money to pay for five weddings," Fiona said. "That's not the point. The point is, if your job is more important to you than our wedding, then I don't think I should spend my life with you. I just don't want to be second on someone's list of priorities. I'm sorry. I need to know that I will always come first."

"And I need you to stop putting yourself in competition with my work, which you insist on calling a job. I would never do that to you."

"I would never postpone my wedding for *work*," Fiona asserted. "Not if Scorsese asked me to be in his next movie."

"Oh, please. We have always lived on your schedule. Always. How many basketball games have I canceled to attend stupid premieres with you? How many nights with the guys have I bailed on to hang out with your girlfriends? No offense, Kara."

"Are you saying you're unhappy with this relationship?"

"I'm saying that we need to be individuals. You need to respect what I do and my friends, and I need to respect yours. We haven't even sent out invitations yet. I don't see why postponing is such a big deal."

Fiona, apparently having had enough back-and-forth, turned to me. "Kara, what's your verdict?"

"Back me up here, Kara," Casey pleaded. "I know you're a rational person."

Fiona and Casey had always been my romantic role models, my great hope for urban love. Every time I became jaded and thought that no couple could survive anymore, every time I thought that a man and a woman couldn't both have successful careers, every time I thought that all men cheat, I would think of Fiona and Casey, and I would remind myself that it's just a matter of finding the right person.

I opened my mouth to speak, but my voice cracked, and suddenly I erupted into loud, violent, primal sobbing.

"Kara?" Fiona asked. "Are you okay?"

No, I wasn't okay. I was going insane. The secrets inside me were gnawing at my core. I wanted to tell Fiona what was happening, but I knew she would tell Joanne, who would tell Bobby. A good secret, after all, is like a good maid. It just has to be passed on. I held Fiona's hand tightly, and in my best impression of sanity, I said, "I think you should call Joanne for advice. She's in a much better place than I am right now."

"Where did you pick up that name?" Keyvan asked from across the table.

"Why don't you use it anymore?"

"I haven't used it in ten years. I've never used it for work. You would have to be some kind of stalker to find out my old name."

"Isn't it your *real* name?" I prodded.

"It's the name I was born with. Does that make it real?"

"Keyvan," I repeated, aware of the American inflection in my voice. "It's pretty."

"That which we call a rose...."

"Don't you get confused with three names? Kyle the anonymous sex machine, Ali the worldly journalist, and Keyvan... Who is Keyvan?"

He laughed. "Why do I have the feeling that you think you can tell me? Where *did* you learn it, anyway?"

"I have a lot of Persian friends."

"Iranian, please," he corrected. "Your friends are no more Persians than they're Ottoman Turks. Nationalities cease to exist."

"Like money," I said. "Okay. I have a lot of friends from *Iran*."

"You live in Tehrangeles. Not unexpected. Who are your friends? A few women whose faces are frozen by their many years of surgeries and Botox. Men whose cologne you can pass out from while they're driving by."

"When did Iranians become the last minority people are allowed to say bigoted things about?" I asked.

"You're forgetting gay people, fat people, disabled people, little people. Besides, I'm not making fun of Iranians. Only of *Persians*. Only those who need to think themselves part of some dead empire as they lighten their hair, shave down their noses, and vote Republican."

"Not all Persians are as awful as you make them out. Some of them are class acts. Cultured, generous, caring, intelligent. I know at least three with those qualities."

"I stand corrected. You still haven't explained where you tracked down the name."

"I Googled you, found out your stage name, and asked a few of my tacky Persian friends. You're kind of a celeb."

"Yeah?" He circled his finger around the rim of his wine glass, the echoing sound reverberating around the restaurant. An elderly couple seated in an adjacent booth glared at him, but he didn't seem to notice.

"I think you should reconnect with your family," I said.

"I don't need you to think about my family."

"I'm trying to help," I responded defensively.

"Trying to *help*?" He cackled too loudly. "You Americans think you can just fix everything, don't you? *A tyrant we set up in the Middle East has quit playing things our way. Let's invade. Iran is about to nationalize its own oil. Let's arrange a coup and overthrow the elected government. Russia is gaining ground in Afghanistan. Let's arm the Taliban.*"

"Keyvan, calm down."

"*There's an Iranian family with some problems. Let's presume we understand their problems better than they do. Then we can impose a solution! Let's bring democracy to this fucked-up family. Let's export our self-help bullshit to their sad, uprooted lives. Which only got that way because we imposed our culture onto their country in the first place.*"

I wanted to ask him, as nicely as I could, to stop. But I had no counter for what he was saying. The attention of the restaurant was firmly on us as Keyvan pushed back his chair and walked calmly out. I followed him out to the street, forced to play the final part of the scene in front of the parking crew.

"I'm sorry," I said.

"I adopted my grandfather's name because it seemed like the appropriate way to tell my parents to fuck off. My mother hated him because he had approached life as something serious, and she thinks of it as a buffet table."

"She might have grown up some. I bet you have. Keyvan, she could be..."

"Will you just call me Kyle, please?" he bellowed.

"You want me to call you by some name you made up for online sexcapades?"

"Fine, call me Ali."

"I like Keyvan," I insisted.

"What is wrong with you? I just rudely told you off. Why are you still talking to me?"

"I don't know... I just want you to... I want..." Coming at me from all directions were memories of days in Beverly Hills with Leila. Shopping trips. Lunches. Then late nights with Bobby. My test-drive with Hossein. "I want you to have a future."

"I'm an award-winning field producer," he said. "I have a future."

"I mean I want Keyvan to have a future. He doesn't even exist. You've made yourself disappear."

"That wasn't my decision. My family took care of that."

"Then go to them and show them why they were wrong. Families are meant to work through their issues, no matter how hard. My parents are divorced, and they still speak. They have to. They share a daughter. They share a history."

"It's moving how you take an interest in my well-being, but I made up my mind when I was sent into exile for the second time, when I was seventeen. I like my life the way it is."

"What happened when you were seventeen?" I inquired.

"Why do you care so much?"

"I just do. It's a girl thing. We become emotionally attached to the men we sleep with. We want to be of use to them."

"How very Iranian of you," he teased pointedly.

"I'm an honorary Iranian. I've earned that distinction."

Keyvan's face froze when he saw the valet pull my Hyundai Sonata behind his rental car. His eyes were trained directly on the dealer frame around the temporary plate. He stepped into his car, handed a few bills to the valet, and looked at me one last time before driving away. "Well, if you're really an honorary Iranian," he said, "You know the really essential Iranian behavior is avoiding anything unpleasant, even when it's staring you in the face. And in families it goes double. But second on the list of what's really Iranian? Respecting other people's privacy."

14

I SPENT ALL OF Thursday convincing myself that Elena was right. *The family has made up their minds.* Who was I to invade their fucked-up existence? I had more important things to deal with, like restoring my friendship with Bobby and getting a career together after wasting my twenties. I decided that since nobody had seen me wear the yellow Prada, I could wear it again to the art opening Fiona was co-hosting with a slew of other celebrities. Bobby and I had planned to attend together since we got the invite jointly, so it surprised me to hear a car honking to the tune of "Like a Virgin" outside. Jesus Christ, how did *she* end up crashing our date? I took a look out the door. I was in my dress, but was halfway through putting my makeup on. Joanne rolled her window down. "Are you guys ready?" she screamed.

Bobby emerged from his side of the duplex looking dapper and handsome. "*Hola, chica,*" he said to Joanne. "Park the car. I'm driving."

"*Por qué?*" Joanne asked.

"*Por qué* you can't handle your booze," Bobby responded. Coming from me, this would have angered Joanne. But coming from Bobby, this caused her to laugh it off, and she parked her car as told.

"Do you wanna come with us or take your own car?" Bobby asked as he unlocked the doors to his Lexus.

"I'll come with you," I said. "I just need a few more minutes."

"*No problemo,*" Joanne said. "We're gonna see how well we can translate the Spanish radio station."

I went back inside and tried to put Joanne and Bobby's new-best-friend-ship out of my mind. I had no ownership of him, I told myself. Their sudden rapport wasn't a threat to me. And yet that's what it felt like: an encroachment on my territory.

I was putting the finishing touches on my eye shadow (I was going for a hazy effect around the eyes) when my cell rang. Assuming it was Bobby and

Joanne rushing me from the car, I answered it with a "Hold up, guys. I'll be out in three seconds."

"It's Elena."

"Elena?" I parroted.

"Don't act surprised, Kara. I told you I would be back Friday. Come over if you want to talk. We're about to have dinner."

My call waiting chirped, and a picture popped up. Bobby and the Astro-turf.

"I'll be there. Thank you. I'll be right there."

My call waiting went off again. This time a picture of Joanne came up. I had taken the picture one night when Joanne passed out at Bar Marmont. It was mean but irresistible to photograph her in that state. Fiona did it, too. Every time Joanne called us, we saw that sloshed image of her.

"I hope you eat carbs and meat. We are having spaghetti Bolognese," Elena said.

"Yes, I'll eat anything," I responded hurriedly as Bobby's face now flashed on my phone. "I'll be right over."

After I hung up, my phone was ringing, and there was pounding on my door. I rushed to the door and there was Bobby, holding his phone in one hand and banging on the door with the other. From Bobby's car, I could hear salsa music. "What the fuck, Kara?" Bobby screamed. "We're gonna be late."

My makeup was obviously half done. "I'm not ready."

"Are you gonna be ready this year?" he sneered.

"Sorry. You guys go. It was Janet on the phone. Something's happening with the baby. She wants me to take her to the hospital."

"What's happening with the baby?" he asked, deadpan. "Did her water break? Is the baby gonna be born tonight?"

"No, she's just..." I fumbled around my words. "She's having pain. She's not feeling..."

"You're a terrible liar," he interrupted. "You don't even work for the woman anymore."

"Well, she's still my friend. She still counts on me in times of need."

Bobby looked at me like a puppy that had just been kicked. "We never even used to have secrets. Now half what you say is lies."

"Bobby, please. I'm not lying." I felt terrible for saying that, and quickly added, "Besides, you trust me, right? So if I am lying, I'm doing it for your own good."

"That's the most absurd thing I've ever heard."

"Of course it is. I'm quoting you." I hoped that would put an end to the increasingly tense conversation.

"Well, it's rude to throw someone's words back at them. And it's rude to ditch an event that you RSVPed 'yes' to weeks ago."

"I'm not ditching. I'll be there late," I explained.

"Oh, right," he said. "After a brief stop at the emergency room."

Joanne honked loudly from Bobby's passenger seat. She didn't bother doing a cutesy Madonna song for us this time. Bobby disappeared into his car without a goodbye. I could just hear the two of them in the car gossiping about me. Their imaginary dialogue echoed through my head as I finished my makeup. *What is wrong with her these days she's acting crazy she's fucking some new guy he's making her insane she's lying to us she's lost her mind she's a terrible friend she's so self-involved she's a bitch total bitch uber-bitch kick her out and I'll move in she hasn't even decorated the place and I'm so much more fun.*

I felt a little over-dressed for Valley Village in my Prada dress and smoky eye makeup. When I knocked on the door, a young girl answered. She wore overalls and a tank top and thick glasses.

"Hello," she said. "You're Keyvan's friend."

"Yes. I'm Kara."

"You're gonna spill spaghetti on your dress," she announced. "Everyone always spills when they eat spaghetti. That's why I'm wearing my overalls. You should change."

"Well, I didn't bring my overalls," I laughed. "What's your name?"

"Leila. I'm twelve."

Little Leila ushered me into the clutter of the house. There were children's books everywhere. Math textbooks, English dictionaries, an in-progress game of Monopoly on the living room rug, an in-progress scarf attached to two knitting needles. Everything in the house was unfinished. Nothing was neatly tucked away. I became mesmerized by an odd-looking creature in a fish tank. It was white with beady little eyes and three fins on each side, but it walked along the bottom of the tank instead of swimming. It looked like a fish as rendered by Japanimation.

"It's an axolotl," Leila announced.

"A what?"

"It's a Mexican salamander. It's a walking fish. I've had him for seven years. My dad gave him to me when he left."

"Where did he go?"

"Back to Mexico to be with his girlfriend."

I gave her my most supportive look.

"It's okay. I prefer a good fish to a shitty dad. He's an endangered species now. That's what they say. His name is Jake Gyllenhaal."

"Your fish?"

"Yeah. Duh. I named him after my boyfriend." I couldn't help but smile. Something about the girl's no-nonsense energy put me at ease. "Wanna feed him?"

"Sure," I said.

Leila rushed for the kitchen, her muddy sneakers clomping onto the tile floors, and then rushed back to the living room and handed me a jar. I opened it, and without looking, stuck my hand inside. I could feel the moving slime right away. I looked down and saw my recently manicured nails sunk within a mass of worms. I quickly pulled out and gave Little Leila an angry glare.

"Hello? They're carnivores! What's the big deal?" She seized the jar from me and nonchalantly grabbed a few worms. She threw them down to Jake Gyllenhaal, who devoured them gratefully. "Are you mad?"

"No, not at all. But I wouldn't mind washing my hands."

"I thought if you were a friend of Keyvan's, you wouldn't be so afraid of a few worms. He's an adventurer. Have you seen his pictures of Iraq and of Africa? He's amazing. Keyvan's not afraid of anything."

As if I didn't have enough problems, my main rival for Keyvan Ebadi's attentions was a twelve-year-old.

"Well, I don't know about that," I said. It was weird, to say the least, that this girl had such intimate knowledge of a person who was supposed to be dead.

The sound of Elena's voice came down from upstairs. "I'm coming. I'm sorry. I'm sorry." She emerged holding a boy who looked around eight years old, Marco, who was pressing a packet of ice on his nose. "Volleyball accident. His nose was bleeding, but he's okay now. Right, Marco?" Marco nodded feebly. "Did she get you to touch the worms? That's her new trick. Come on, you can help me make the salad. Leila, take your brother outside, and make sure he keeps that ice on his nose. Do not play volleyball with him." Elena put Marco down and looked firmly into his eyes. "No volleyball until tomorrow, okay?"

Leila and her brother rushed outside, and Elena led me into her kitchen. A pot of Bolognese sauce steamed into the room, filling the cluttered space with its rich scent. Elena handed me some cucumbers. "Can you cut these?"

"Sure." I grabbed the cucumbers and placed them on an available cutting board.

"Good. I'll make some dressing," she said as she poured oil and vinegar into a teacup. "So?" she said. "You are quite the nosy little roommate, huh? Will you pass me the salt?" I did. Elena put a spoonful of mustard into the teacup and then a drizzle of honey. "Marco likes everything to have honey in it. He will put honey on his spaghetti Bolognese. Mark my words. I call him Winnie the Pooh. He eats it out of the jar. I tell him it's not meant to be eaten that way. Leila went through a phase like that with mayonnaise, but thank God she grew out of it."

"How did you know I'm his roommate and not his girlfriend?" I asked. "Did Bobby come out to you?"

Elena laughed. "It is such a ridiculous American expression, this coming out. I was with Babak every single day for the first eighteen years of his life. Well, I take that back. I missed the first year when he was still in Iran. So every day for seventeen years of that child's growth. Do you think he needs to come out to me? You think I am blind?"

"But Leila and Hossein, they seem to have no idea." I was done with the cucumbers. Elena handed me some tomatoes, which I swiftly began chopping.

"Aha," she said. "But Leila and Hossein *are* blind. Not blind in all things, of course. They are both very brilliant people. But they've blinded themselves to a lot about their kids. It's how parents survive without going insane."

"Is that why you named your daughter after Leila? Because she's brilliant?"

"Why wouldn't I name her after Mrs. Ebadi?" she announced proudly. "Most people name their children after their grandmother or grandfather. But my parents didn't do anything of honor. My father was a drunk pig, and my mother was just a drunk."

"I'm sorry."

"I don't care anymore. If there's one thing Leila taught me, it is that you can get over your past. Most women are such victims. I'm so bored with victims. Why wouldn't I consider Leila Ebadi a very good role model? She is an incredibly strong person."

"She is," I agreed. "And apparently, you still see Keyvan? Did he visit you this past week?"

"That depends on what he told you," she said slyly.

"Your daughter mentioned seeing his photos."

"Oh. Well, she has a crush on him. Apparently, he is *dope*." She laughed at her use of the expression.

"Why would Leila and Hossein say that Keyvan is dead?"

Elena finished setting the table, and she threw the spaghetti into boiling water. "There are certain things they don't reveal, or talk about, and I respect their right to privacy. As should you."

"But what if it's too late? What if they spend their whole lives never knowing their sons?"

Elena sat down now. "Kara. Billions of people become parents in this world, and most never know their children very well."

"You seem to know yours pretty well," I offered.

"You seem to arrive at judgments pretty quickly." She smiled as she stirred the sauce. "Leila and Hossein aren't us. It's not for us to force something on them. Come sit. The salad is ready. There's nothing left to do but wait for the spaghetti to cook." From the front yard, the kids' screaming could be heard. "They're playing volleyball again. I can tell." She smiled. "You used a condom, yes?" she asked.

The question took me aback. "Excuse me?"

"With Keyvan? You were safe?"

"Well, we actually didn't have intercourse," I said, somewhat awkwardly.

"What did you do?" she demanded to know.

"Is this really relevant?"

"Yes. Second base, third base?"

"Oral sex. Him handling the oral part." I shifted uncomfortably, wondering how much more detail she needed. Perhaps this line of questioning was her way of paying me back for *my* difficult questions. "Anything else you want to know?"

Elena shook her head. "I have to feed the children," she said. "But we will talk after dinner. You're staying, yes?"

"If it's not a problem."

"Not at all," she said, softening. "We are in-laws."

Dinner was delicious. The Bolognese was perfect, and the salad was excellent. I noticed that Elena's dressing tasted exactly like the dressing I always loved at the Ebadis'. "Sometimes," Elena said as she served the spaghetti, "I make them *khoresht*. They love it."

Once the kids sat down, Little Leila dominated the dinner table conversation. She was ranting about environmentalism and the depletion of the ozone layer. "The way I see it, Mom, it's irresponsible of you to bring children into this world and then drive a car that's pumping dangerous emissions into the air."

"Oh really?" Elena said, obviously proud of her informed daughter.

"Yes, really. There's a girl at my school"—Leila addressed this part to me—"whose uncle just moved to a green house. Not like a house full of plants or a house painted green. It's like solar and stuff. They barely use any energy. Plus, they have a Prius, and they bring their own bags to the grocery store. If everyone was like them..."

"By that, she means rich," Elena joked. "Leila, first of all, will you please stop slurping the spaghetti?" I looked down at Leila's overalls. They were daubed with tomato sauce and even a few meat chunks. What would her namesake think of this very uncouth way of eating? As for Marco, he had indeed poured honey onto his spaghetti. "Second of all," Elena continued. "I would love to move to a green house if I could afford it, but as it is, we can barely pay the mortgage."

"I'll call Uncle Hossein and tell him we'll return the car and get a hybrid. I checked online. Hyundai's gonna start selling them by the end of the year."

"Okay, Leila," Elena laughed. "You head that up."

Satisfied, Leila moved on to how Gwen Stefani was a sell-out. "She used to be all punk, and now she wears these clothes that you need three million dollars to buy. It's so stupid. I liked her better when she was real."

Marco stayed quiet for most of the dinner. He didn't spill anything on his clothes, and he ate two full plates of spaghetti. When dinner was over, Leila stood and asked if she "could please finally watch *Grey's Anatomy,* please."

"Have you finished your history paper?" Elena asked.

"Mom, it's the weekend. I have two whole days to work on the paper. I've been waiting twenty-four hours to watch this episode."

"She's not doing well in history," Elena told me loudly.

"I hate history!" Leila screamed. "My teacher is a bitch."

"Leila, watch your mouth." Elena took a breath. "History is important. How can you expect to figure out where you're going if you don't know where you come from?"

"It's not Mexican history, Mom."

Elena smiled at me. "She has a mouth on her, doesn't she?"

"Please let me watch *Grey's.* Please! I'll do the homework tomorrow morning."

Elena shrugged her approval. Leila picked up Marco and carried him upstairs, talking a mile a minute about McDreamy and McSteamy. Once the TV was on, Elena snuck a pack of cigarettes from behind her stereo. "Come on," she said. "I won't make you clean."

Elena led me out to the front yard. There were no chairs, so I sat on the Slip 'N Slide, passed down from Casa Ebadi to Casa Sanchez. I didn't want any grass stains on my Prada. Elena offered me a Parliament, which I refused. She put one in her mouth and lit it with a smile. "I don't want the kids to know I smoke," she said. "Isn't that silly? I always tell them to be honest about everything, but if ever one of them starts smoking, I want to have the authority to kick the shit out of them." She laughed. "I didn't mean that literally, of course."

"Elena, will you tell me what happened?" I begged. "Why did you stop taking videos of the kids in 1984?"

After a long pause, she finally answered. "Because nobody would want to document what was happening."

"What was happening?"

"Keyvan always had a harder time than Bobby. Adjusting. When I first came to work for the Ebadis, Keyvan was seven, and Bobby was one. Keyvan spoke a little English, but with a thick accent. When he went to school, all those rich children of entertainment lawyers mocked him. They called him Ayatollah, and then during the hostage crisis... He wasn't exactly well-liked." Elena used the butt of her cigarette to light another one. "Bobby was so young during all this. I don't think he remembers any of it. The revolution, the hostage crisis, the difficulty of settling in. The Ebadis didn't have much money when they came. Enough for an apartment in Brentwood, but not a house."

"But they had enough money to pay you."

"They did. That's true. In the beginning, I wasn't a live-in. I was just a babysitter. As the money started coming in, they relied more and more on me. Leila wasn't born to clean house or cook. I used to joke that she should have been born a queen, and then she always said that even if she had been, she would be living in exile anyway, banished from her palace, with a dead husband. When Keyvan was young, he remembered Iran well. He would tell me stories about his grandmother. He especially loved her. Homa. You know her name, I suppose."

"Have you met her?" I asked.

"Just once. She came from Iran and visited. I think it was 1982. Hossein was still with Toyota. But Maman Homa is very religious, and she wasn't impressed with her daughter's new life. After that, Leila and her mother didn't speak very often. And Bobby was so young that he barely remembers his grandmother. But Keyvan missed her, spoke to her often. He remembered so many things. Sometimes when we were alone, he would tell me about escaping from Iran. About his mother crying and screaming. About walking into their house in Tehran and finding it ransacked, all their belongings stolen. Keyvan carried all of that with him into this new country, where people only saw him as a terrorist."

"So what happened?"

"When Keyvan turned thirteen, he met a couple of young actors. You probably know who they are now. Back then, they were just kids who had roles on a few television shows and too much money at their disposal. Keyvan had too much new money at his disposal, as well. Hossein was a huge success. He did very well at Toyota, but once he opened the first Hyundai dealership in the United States, he started making more money than any of them knew what to do with. And so he shared it with all of us. They are very generous to my cousin and me, the Ebadis. Maybe to a fault. Maybe Keyvan would've done better if he suddenly wasn't given a credit card that went to his father's account."

"He got a credit card when he was thirteen?"

"Hossein said he wanted to have his kids build a line of credit early so they could purchase their own homes." Elena put her second cigarette out. She took out a third one, then reconsidered and placed it back in the pack. "Keyvan was suddenly rich and hanging out with these teen celebrities, and every night they were going to parties and clubs and they started drinking and smoking. In the beginning, he would tell me about it, and I told him to be careful, but I didn't stop him. Nobody did. We were all so happy that he had friends, we were so happy that he was having fun, that he was socializing. It seems stupid in retrospect. Any parent would stop their thirteen-year-old from engaging in this kind of behavior, but the circumstances were not normal.

"Of course, we didn't realize exactly what he was doing. We thought they were kids, just having fun. We thought it was harmless. But it became very clear very fast that for Keyvan, it wasn't harmless. He started acting crazy. He would have violent tantrums. His eyes started twitching, and he would fall asleep at the dinner table. He became very violent toward Babak. He hated Babak. He hated how composed Babak always was. Babak was an exceptionally polite and well-behaved child. He never did anything or said anything to upset anyone. He was always clean and always got perfect grades, and he fit in at school from the moment they put him in. I always thought it was because he didn't have any culture shock, but perhaps it's just their personalities. Anyway, Keyvan started hitting Babak. It was harmless at first, but then it became bad. Then he cut Babak with a knife. He said he didn't mean to do it, that he was only trying to scare him. Babak wanted to go to the hospital. I think Babak was only nine when this happened. Keyvan said he had to keep quiet; he said if he went to the hospital, then they would get in trouble, and so he tried to repair the cut with Krazy Glue. I'm the one who found them. I came back from the grocery store and took them to the emergency room. Leila and Hossein were at a party. They left and came right to the hospital. Babak was all right. I think he still has a scar on his arm where it happened. But it was Keyvan that was the real problem. The doctor at the hospital insisted on speaking with him, and when he was through, he told us that Keyvan had tested positive for heroin." Elena took a breath and looked at me. "Are you bored? I could give you the shorter version."

"No. Please. I want to hear every detail you're up to remembering."

"I won't share every detail. They are so dark. Keyvan's behavior became worse and worse. Mostly toward Babak, but also toward Leila and Hossein. He ripped up all of Leila's clothes once. Cut them up and left them on the floor of her closet. He said she was superficial and only cared about money. And when Hossein got him a car for his sixteenth birthday, Keyvan crashed it into the garage on purpose."

"He gave a car to his son the junkie?"

"They liked to throw money at the problem. The more Keyvan acted out, the more they spent on him. And the more they spent on him, the more he acted out. I told them they should just throw him out on the street, but they couldn't do that. They thought he would kill himself if they forced him out. So they kept giving him more and more. They would send him to the most expensive rehabs, and he would sneak out and steal their cars and sell them for more drug money. It was just an endless cycle. It was horrible. I can't tell you how sad it is to watch a child wasting away like that. Every day, every hour, he seemed to look worse. He became thinner, his eyes became crazier. He was always sick from the drugs, but that still didn't prepare us."

"Prepare you for what?"

"When Keyvan was seventeen, he got sick." Her voice trembled as the memories flooded back.

"From withdrawal?" I asked, hoping the story stopped there, wishing for a happy ending.

"We didn't know. He had disappeared for a month. We didn't know where he was. He would sometimes come home to ask for money or steal food or steal a car. It sounds so ridiculous. We should have thrown him in jail. I wish we had, but then again, the same thing could've happened in jail, if you believe the statistics."

"What could've happened?"

"He came home after that month, and he begged for help. I remember that night very clearly. Babak had invited one of his friends over. A girl, of course." Elena eyed me knowingly. "Even then, all his friends were girls.

They were at the table. The four of them. Leila and Hossein and Bobby and his friend, whatever her name was. They were having a nice conversation about the girl's father, who had just produced some movie that won an Oscar. It was a big deal, and she was his date to the Oscars. Babak was eleven at the time. So the girl is talking about what it feels like to be at the Oscars and have your dad win the big award when Keyvan comes in looking like a ghost. His arms were bruised from all the needles. He was skin and bones. He was so pale. He looked like he was dying. God, I can remember the look on Babak's face so well. He was so embarrassed to tell his new friend that this was his brother. Leila and Hossein told Keyvan to go upstairs and clean up. I could tell how devastated they were, but they never showed it. With them, it was always, 'go clean yourself up, go wash your hands, sit at the table.' I didn't say a word. I was speechless. Keyvan showered and came back down, but he didn't look any better. The girl kept asking what was wrong with him. Keyvan said he was sick. The girl said her Dad had a friend who was also sick recently. She said the friend had died. That's when Hossein snapped at the girl. I've never seen him like that. He said Keyvan wasn't dying. Why would she say such a thing? He raised his voice to this young girl, who had no idea what was happening. When the girl's mother picked her up, the little girl didn't even say goodbye to Babak. She just ran out of the house and held her mother. She was afraid, with reason. Babak was just angry that he had lost a friend he liked, and he rushed upstairs and locked himself in his room. He spent a lot of his childhood alone in that room, watching old movies or reading. He never bothered anybody, just kept everything to himself. Keyvan sat with his parents and said he'd never felt worse and he said this time he would change. He promised he would change. He said he was done. I made him tea. When I went to hug him, I was shocked by how thin he was. He hardly filled my arms, and he was such a strong kid before."

I reached into her pack of Parliaments and lit a cigarette for myself. Elena followed my lead. We looked at each other for a long beat. She must have sensed that I was afraid of what would come next.

"Keyvan did stop the drugs for a few weeks, but he wasn't getting any better. He had already damaged his health. They had him on methadone, but that wasn't helping. No doctors were helping." Elena stopped for a moment. Her voice choked, and a single tear fell into her mouth. She simply inhaled the tear into her mouth with the cigarette. "Neither of them ever really grew up, did they? No matter how hard I tried."

"How hard did you try?" I said with bitterness in my voice. "Bobby spends his whole life living in fear. He's a sex addict who doesn't even *enjoy* sex. And Keyvan doesn't have the strength to pick up the phone and speak to his own family. Why don't you *make* them talk to each other? Why don't you *force* them to make peace?"

"I don't see *you* forcing them, Kara."

"Why do they think he's dead? Did Keyvan make up the story to disappear, or did someone else…"

"Listen, please. I have known the Ebadis almost their whole life in this country. Please trust me when I say their resentment is deep."

"But they know he's alive," I said in disbelief. "How can they shut him out?"

"You know," she said, "it's Keyvan who quit speaking to them. When he got sick, Leila and Hossein decided to send him to Iran. It was a strange decision, but they thought it would be best if he went to live with Maman Homa. She was a caretaker, they said. And they didn't want Keyvan around any temptation, around any drugs. And they didn't want him around Bobby. It was a cruel decision in many ways. Still, in the end, it achieved what was needed. It saved his life. But three years later, he still wouldn't take their calls. He said he never wanted to speak to them again, would never come home again. Leila's lie was all she could think of to cope with the fact that her son was gone forever, and trust me, that was not what she wanted. She wanted him back."

"So Leila lied? She killed her son. She only wanted him if he was perfect."

"Don't underestimate her love for him. She made the right decision to send him away. He wouldn't have survived another month in Los Angeles. He wasn't ready for this city. Not the way Babak was. Babak always knew how to handle temptation."

I laughed.

"Babak doesn't have a death wish. He never did. He was always too proud. Keyvan was the self-destructive one. He didn't care about anybody. Isn't that how you know if someone really wants to die? When they stop caring about even their family?"

"Does Bobby even know his brother is alive? Or did they keep that from him too?"

"He knows," Elena uttered. "But he didn't find out from them."

I hated hearing that Bobby had lied to me. "When did Bobby find out?"

"At first, he believed the story about the war. When he was in his teens, Keyvan started to send him letters. I was home all day, and I was told to intercept them. Once Bobby turned sixteen, I decided I had to let one through."

"Is that why you left the job?" I wondered aloud.

She blinked, but said nothing.

"So what happened? Did Bobby write back to Keyvan? Are they in touch?"

"Bobby looked at the envelope and handed it back to me. He didn't even open it. Just asked me to send it back. No one in that family is short of pride."

"Why did you leave the videos at their house?"

"Babak should have some good memories of his dead brother, shouldn't he?" Elena put out her cigarette and stood up.

As she walked me to my car, I asked her, "Did Keyvan actually join the Iranian army, during the war with Iraq?"

"Oh, yes," she confirmed. "He enlisted and started training, but when they found out his medical history, they threw him out. A heroin addict is not good enough to die for Allah."

15

It was after ten when I finally walked through the doors of the gallery. I was two hours late for the opening, there was a half-rinsed-out speck of Bolognese on my yellow dress, my once-perfect eye makeup was streaked down the side of my face, and I stunk of Parliaments. The exhibit was called *Compartments.* The artist was a thirty-year-old Somali woman who had been the victim of genital mutilation. She'd gotten out of her country and gone to Amsterdam, where she learned to use art as the expression of her rage. The brochure read, "the show is a reaction to the male culture of violence. The artist is embracing the images she is supposed to be ashamed of." I looked around for a sign of Leila, Bobby, or the girls, but all I saw was a sea of celebrities. I went into the gallery's back room.

Pussy. Cunt. Vagina. Twat. Snatch. Slit. Poontang. Chocha. The words were all glowing in the dark of the cavernous black-lit space. Next to some of the words were glow-in-the-dark paintings of vaginas. Close-ups of lips, some mutilated. In the darkness, it was hard to make out the faces of the party-goers, but a few voices were unmistakable, like Fiona talking to Joanne and Bobby. "Eamon is trying this insane thing where he shoots every scene in one take. He never cuts. And we're shooting out of order, so the very first scene I had to shoot was the rape. It's literally my first day on set, I have a giant zit that hair and makeup spent like forty-five minutes covering, and I have to shoot an eleven-minute rape scene in one take."

"That sounds like a real acting challenge," Joanne said.

"I think it's interesting that all the words on the wall are in English," Bobby observed. "You think she would respond in the language of the men who oppressed her."

"I think she has different versions of the exhibit in different languages," Fiona explained. "She's already shown in Amsterdam, Paris, and New York. And the proceeds from each show go to a local women's center."

"Oh my God," Bobby said. "The glow-in-the-dark vagina show is a *franchise?*"

"So you guys, *que pasa con la Kara?*" Joanne asked. "Is she not here yet?"

I inched away from the voices and into the shadows of a corner.

"I'm a little concerned about her," Fiona said. "I asked her to come over two days ago, and she had a total meltdown."

"She *has* been acting like a bit of a freak," Joanne confirmed.

"I've called her like thirty times and invited her to come visit me on set, and she hasn't come once," Fiona complained. That wasn't entirely true. She had asked me twice, but the concept still holds, I guess.

"Maybe it's just some thirty-year-old midlife crisis," Joanne suggested. "I went through it when I turned thirty, remember?" Of course they remembered. Joanne's midlife crisis didn't have an expiration date.

"It sucks," Fiona said, "because her behavior has made me feel really distant from her."

"That's what happens when you hide something from people," Bobby lamented. "You become distant from them. It's inevitable."

"So you think she's fucking someone?" Count on Fiona for the non sequitur that cuts right to the subtext.

"I will neither confirm nor deny..." was Bobby's unsubtle diplomatic response.

"I don't know, you guys," Fiona said. "Casey and I were a little worried about her. Maybe we should all confront her together. You know, like an intervention."

"What exactly are we intervening?" Bobby asked. "It's not like she's doing drugs."

"Um, hello. GHB!" Joanne cackled gleefully.

"That was once," Fiona said. "And she wasn't even that high. I was the crazy one, as everybody who watches *Access Hollywood* is well aware of."

"She is not doing drugs," Bobby asserted.

"I don't know," Joanne responded. "Her absences can be traced precisely to the night you guys did GHB. Isn't that when she stopped returning people's calls, started mysteriously disappearing to be with her mother? What if she's a GHB addict?" There was a twinge of glee in Joanne's voice.

"Then I would be the guiltiest person on the planet," Fiona said. "I mean, I introduced her to it."

"You guys," Bobby said. "I really think it's premature for anyone to take credit for making Kara a GHB addict."

"Honestly, Bobby, you should've seen her when she came to mediate between me and Casey. She looked strung out. Even Elba asked if she was on something. I shooed the idea off then, but now it seems like Elba was clairvoyant. You know, she totally predicted I'd get the movie. And she predicted the breakup. She's a Guatemalteco Cassandra."

"What breakup?" Joanne asked hopefully.

"Didn't I mention it already?" Fiona wondered. "Casey and I broke up."

"I don't understand. Why do you seem so fine?" Joanne asked. "Shouldn't this destroy you? Shouldn't this cause you to be depressed, or at least make you drink yourself into a depression? Did you give him back the ring?"

"I'm not fine. I'm *acting* fine," Fiona explained. "Besides, Casey and I both decided that we had great times together, but that we ultimately wanted different things. It was the right decision. I'm not gonna compromise my life away for some guy who's not really in love with me anymore. Anyway, I'm too busy with the movie to really think about it. Eamon is constantly scheduling more rehearsal. You know that on most movies, actors don't even rehearse. Like you're supposed to just have an instant rapport with the person who's playing your father or your boyfriend. You know what that leads to? Selfish performances. No chemistry. No heart. That's what Eamon says. I think he's right. I mean, think about it. You wouldn't expect a football team to play without practicing together? Or a marching band? Everything is better when you get to practice with your partners."

"Except for sex," Bobby interrupted.

"Really?" Fiona said. "You don't think sex gets better with time?"

"You can't practice spontaneity," Bobby continued. "But everything else is fair game."

I rushed out into the main space before any of them could see what direction I was entering from. "What a vonderful show!" Leila exclaimed as she took my hand in hers. I was admittedly nervous about inviting her to this show, especially since it dealt with genital mutilation, a wretched condition with links to the religion from which Leila had tried so hard to disassociate herself. So I was pleasantly surprised when Leila seemed unfazed by the content of the art. "What a brave woman," she said. "Is she here?"

"That's her," I said, pointing to a striking woman being questioned passionately by a visibly moved Mandy Moore.

"Marc Jacobs didn't make that dress in eggplant," Leila commented. "He must have made it especially for Mandy. She's cute in person. Her features are a little big for her face, though." And then, without missing a beat, "Where's Babak?"

"He's around, I think."

"Well, didn't you come together?" she asked.

"No, actually. We arrived separately tonight."

She eyed me suspiciously and then said, "I'm glad galleries like this are cropping up all over Los Angeles. I'm so sick of people who mock this city as having no culture. Of course, the haters and detractors are all just insecure."

"Haters?" I repeated. "Leila, did you really just use that word?"

"My manicurist taught it to me. I need to understand the slang if I'm going to keep up. I like that word. Haters. It's very useful."

"Listen, Leila, about the house, I'm sorry if…"

Leila brushed me off before I could complete my awkward sentence. "Stop thinking about it. Farideh already accepted another offer from some Indian family. They put down cash. You were right. The house was too much for you two. We need to find you something a little more eclectic, maybe in a younger neighborhood where you would feel more at home. Farideh's ready to show us some places in Los Feliz and Venice next week."

"Sure," I somehow found myself saying, even though all I wanted to do was confront her and tell her everything I now knew.

Bobby approached us and gave his mother a kiss on each cheek. "Glad you made it, dude."

"What happened to your dress?" Leila asked, suddenly noticing the Bolognese stain.

"Looks like tomato sauce," Bobby said. "Did somebody have sloppy joes for dinner? The cafeteria at Cedars ain't what it used to be."

"You were in the hospital?" Leila asked.

It took me a moment to catch up. "Oh," I said. "Yeah, no, I took my ex-boss there. She was having painful contractions, but she's fine. And I grabbed a slice of pizza on the way here and ate it in the car."

Leila looked relieved. In the back of her mind, she had to have been wondering why Bobby and I had arrived separately. "You shouldn't eat pizza," she said. "It's the worst thing you could put in your beautiful body. You do want to live a long life, don't you?"

By ten-thirty, the opening had died down. The celebrities were gone. Leila was gone. The champagne was gone. Even Fiona had gone to bed for her seven-o'clock call. In a corner, Bobby and Joanne were scheming where to go next. "This interior designer I know is promoting a party at Fubar," Joanne said to Bobby. "He said he'd get me a free round of shots if I came."

"Sure, why not?" Bobby responded. "I wouldn't mind getting loaded tonight."

Joanne turned up and gazed at me. I was standing at an awkward distance from them, pretending to read the brochure to the show. "You wanna come with, Kara?" Joanne offered.

Bobby's gaze indicated he was still pissed at me. I thought about it for a moment. Keyvan was getting on a plane the next day. I had failed miserably in my mission to reunite him with his family. Maybe it was time to try and mend my friendship with Bobby before Joanne had taken over my role completely.

As I was debating, Joanne said, "You notice how she didn't answer when I asked whether she gave Casey back the ring, right?"

Twenty minutes later, she led us into Fubar, looking for her interior designer friend. The bar was dark and sweaty, a haze of testosterone with me and Joanne providing a dim whiff of estrogen. So much for my Prada. Adding to the Bolognese stain was now the sweat of a hundred different guys, their moisture wrinkling the gorgeous dress. I must have looked a wreck, but then no one was looking at me. In fact, the attention of the entire bar was on a mock stage area, where a drag queen in red vinyl stilettos and a stringy bikini presided over a dick-size contest. Hanging on a clothesline were numbered photographs of men's dicks. A whole row of cock shots, some thick and short, some hairless, some uncut, some hard.

"Joanne!" a voice called out.

We looked up and saw an extremely tall guy, well over six feet, waving at Joanne. "Laird!" she screamed back with a wave.

Laird grabbed the veiny arm of an overdeveloped guy and made his way toward us. Joanne took the muscle guy's hand. "And you must be Jackson. I've heard so much about you."

"Who's Jackson?" the guy asked.

Laird glared at Joanne. "Jackson is my boyfriend, but don't worry, he..." But the guy was already gone. "Nice one. Very smooth," Laird bitched to Joanne.

From the stage, the drag queen was calling for more customers to join the contest. As added incentive, the guys who went to the backroom to have a Polaroid snapped of their dicks would get a free kamikaze shot. Women would never do this, I thought to myself. Then I remembered *Girls Gone Wild*, hundreds upon hundreds of girls flashing. And for what? Did they even get a free kamikaze shot?

"This is Bobby and Kara," Joanne said as she introduced Laird. Laird had clammy hands, no doubt a function of being in such a dank and humid bar, but I knew immediately that Bobby wouldn't want to sleep with him. Clammy hands were one of his biggest pet peeves. He associated them with the flu, which he associated with HIV, and that was that.

"Gonna enter the contest, Bobby?" Laird asked.

"No, thank you," Bobby replied.

"I keep telling them to do the contest a little later, once people are trashed."

"Smart business," Joanne said. "Get 'em drunk, take their clothes off, charge a cover."

"It's a little extra income. Not all of us are decorating for La Lohan. Come on, I promised you a shot, didn't I? Maybe then Bobby will show us his monster cock."

Bobby cringed. It was one thing for him to pass dick shots back and forth in the anonymity of cyberspace. But the idea of dangling from a clothespin in public made him queasy.

Laird ended up buying us two rounds of tequila shots, which turned out to be more than enough to get us good and drunk, Joanne in particular. When The Pointer Sisters' "Automatic" came on, Joanne got up on a barstool and began writhing like the lost cast member from *Coyote Ugly*. "I loved this song when I was a kid," she screamed. Oh, Joanne, so drunk she wasn't even aware she was date-stamping herself. Bobby and I were shoved from one end of the bar to another by the moving chain of men, ninety percent of whom were now shirtless. I asked Bobby if he was going to take his shirt off, too. "Ha, ha," was all he said. Thinking back, I realized Bobby and I never went to gay bars together. In fact, Bobby never went to gay bars at all. Maybe it was because he'd actually have to talk to people before sleeping with them. Despite the abundance of Polaroid cock shots developing before our eyes, people were actually conversing. I caught bits and pieces of conversation. One guy was hailing the mid-century modern architecture of Palm Springs. Another guy was saying that spin was more addictive than crack, and said he belonged to four gyms because he needed spin-teacher diversity. Another guy said he spent two years studying Kaballah and had never even met Madonna, and now he was quitting the bullshit and going back to church on Sundays. No one approached Bobby and me. I understood why I was ignored, but I would have thought Bobby would get a little traction. Perhaps in the sea of buff West Hollywood blonds, the slim Persian was lost in the crowd.

"Should we try and meet someone?" I suggested. "There are tons of hot guys here."

"Why bother? It's so much easier to just meet someone when I go home."

"But it might be nice to meet someone outside the Internet," I said. "You know, actually get their name before you fuck."

"The end result would be the same," he said with a shrug. "It's simpler not to pretend you're interested in getting to know them."

"But getting to know them can be fun sometimes, Bobby. Don't you wanna know what it feels like to look into someone's eyes and envision a future together? To share a bottle of wine and taste that wine on someone else's lips at the end of the night? To receive flowers? To send flowers? To hold hands and walk along the Seine? To do a crossword together?"

"No, Kara. I don't. And if I did, I wouldn't need your help meeting someone. So stop your sermonizing, please."

"Bobby," I pleaded. "I don't want to fight."

"Okay," the drag queen announced. "Let the contest begin." Joanne, still atop that barstool, jumped on some shirtless guy's shoulders and cheered. "I'm going to call out the numbers, and our handy-dandy cheer-o-meter here will tell us who gets the loudest applause. Okay, number one. Hmmm, I think I recognize number one. Laird, is that you?" From below the stage, Laird blushed. The crowd went wild for the clammy-handed promoter. Joanne screamed his name.

I felt a hand on my shoulder. "Oh my God, hey!"

I looked up and saw a dark and attractive man in front of me. It took me a second, but then I remembered.

"Alejandro. Remember? I do Leila's hair." Alejandro pointed to Bobby. "Hey, remember me?" he asked Bobby.

Bobby just blinked, his face neutral.

"I'm Kara," I said. "And this is..."

"Babak!" Alejandro screamed over the sound of the competition. "How can I forget that name? I hear it every day when I'm styling her. I practically know everything about you." Alejandro stopped and squeezed Bobby's arm. "Well, almost everything."

I could feel Bobby's discomfort, his desire to get out of there as fast as possible. And yet he was a master of holding it together, of acting like nothing at all was bothering him. "Hello," was all he said.

"Shane and I were wondering if you guys were *really* together. We thought there was no way such a diva could produce a straight son?"

"Well, we *are* together," Bobby snapped.

"Cool, man. Great. I think more straight couples should go out and enjoy a big-dick contest together."

"Where is Shane?" I asked, desperate to change the subject.

"Oh, we broke up," Alejandro announced curtly. "Why else would I be cruising this dump?"

"I'm sorry," I said. "Breakups are never easy."

"Yeah, well, what are you gonna do? One of my best friends met him online for sex. Nothing happened, of course. My friend would never do that. But now I know his whore screen name and I keep tabs on him and he's in the chat rooms practically every night. I guess I'm glad I found out now. We were talking about buying a condo, but who the fuck wants to marry an online sex addict?" From atop her barstool, Joanne flashed her bra and screamed to the drag queen that it should be a cock and tits competition. "And who let in that freak of nature?" Alejandro asked.

"Actually," Bobby said, "she's one of our closest friends. Her buddy promotes this party here. That's why we came." Bobby placed his arm around my waist territorially.

"Well," Alejandro seethed, "it's nice to learn that assholes get stretched out of shape whether they're gay or not."

"I'm gonna get some air," Bobby said. As he pushed past, Alejandro backed away, as if Bobby was about to hit him.

I mouthed an apology to Alejandro, then rushed after Bobby. When I got outside, it was like I was still in a bar. A pack of men, their tank tops back on, were smoking and crowding the area outside the exit. I pushed through the smoke, searching for Bobby. Finally, I remembered where he had parked and found him inside, the lights on. He was in the driver's seat, staring out at a billboard for HIV medication that featured an especially gorgeous rock climber. I tried to open the car door, but it was locked. I knocked on the window, but Bobby ignored me. "Jesus Christ, Bobby, open up. You're acting like a baby." He unlocked the door, and I crept into the passenger seat.

"I hate these fucking billboards," he said angrily. "Like that's really what having HIV looks like. Get infected and you too can look like this gorgeous, ripped mountain climber."

"It's a commercial, Bobby. No one really thinks you soften your hands by doing the dishes, either."

"But isn't that the message of that image? *It's not so bad.* Well, it *is* bad. It sucks. Have you ever seen someone with AIDS? How much weight they lose and the lesions and the fucking dementia…"

"Things have changed, Bobby. You're talking about decades ago."

Suddenly, it all made sense. He was talking about Keyvan, when he was what, eleven? He was talking about Keyvan, who had protected me from his disease. And if Bobby could see him now… if he could see how beautiful Keyvan is. And how he's doing just as fine as that guy on the billboard.

"Yeah, well, things haven't changed so much. They find new drug-resistant strains every day," he said ominously. "Just wait. Pretty soon we'll all be dropping dead again."

"We're all dropping dead eventually. Who are you talking about?"

He stared at me, like he might actually answer. I waited. Finally I had to say something. "You can't keep this shit bottled up, Bobby. Look what just happened!"

"My mother's hairdresser started threatening to out me? So the fuck what?"

"No, you actually *lied* about us to some random person. Not your mom, not your dad, just someone meaninglessly connected to your mom. You never did that before."

That opened the door to a floodgate of emotion. I'd never seen Bobby cry, but now it seemed like he was making up for lost tears.

"She can't find out, Kara," he sobbed. "She just can't."

I let out a long breath.

"That fucking queen of a hairdresser is gonna be blow-drying Leila tomorrow, and he's gonna be like, 'Oh, by the way sweetie, I saw your son at a bar full of faggots last night. He was checking out all the Polaroid cocks hanging on the wall.' And she'll fucking die. I'm telling you that now. She will die."

"First of all, if the blow dryer is on, then she won't even hear what he says." I said this to get another smile from him, but it didn't work. "Second of all, your mother will not die. Your mother is resilient. She will go on, and you know it. Third of all, *that fucking queen of a hairdresser* will not tell your mother anything. He's not the bitter closet case. You are."

Bobby looked as if he'd been hit with a two-by-four. "Excuse me?"

"Shut the fuck up and drive. No, better yet, you sit here and bawl, and I'll drive. You're hysterical, so you'd probably kill us." I was startled by my own tone. But I was now on a mission.

"Where are we going?"

"If I wanted you to know that, I'd tell you where to drive."

We switched seats, and I drove toward Beverly Hills. Pa had once told me how a U.S. officer in Vietnam was quoted as saying, "We had to destroy a village to save it." Fine. Here was my chance. I would pull the Persian rug right out from under them. If my role in the Ebadi family was to hold them together, then this was the only way to truly discharge my duty. "Are you driving to my parents'?" Bobby asked. "Are you throwing a surprise coming-out party? Because we're perfectly fine the way things are."

"Absolutely," I said. "*Fine* is the first adjective that comes to mind."

Elena had said that the family had made up their mind. But she had missed one fact. *I* am a member of the family, or so they always told me. And that meant I got a vote.

"Kara, where are we going?" Bobby demanded to know, increasingly agitated by his lack of control.

"We're going someplace where you can get over the ghost of your dead brother. That's who's gonna die, not Leila."

"Leave my brother out of this. He has nothing to do with it."

"He has everything to do with it. You're afraid of disappointing your parents like he did."

"He didn't disappoint them. He died in the war. He's a hero," he said. That drove me close to rage. There was no reason for Bobby not to have told me the truth. Our relationship wasn't supposed to be based on deception. But deception was second nature to Bobby, too.

"One of these days, you're going to have to stop hiding from your parents. They're just as human as you are."

"Yeah, that's a good one. Do you know how intimidating it is to have such perfect parents?" he asked, before adding spitefully, "Of course you don't."

"Their perfection, which is hardly perfect, is just their way of escaping. Just like meaningless sex is your escape."

"You don't understand," he whined.

"Of course I don't. No one understands anyone. But I understand that you're stuck. And I understand that your parents are about as perfect as mine, just with better production values. And I understand that no matter how glamorous the closet, *it's still a fucking closet.*" I took a breath. "And I understand that your brother represents everything you're afraid of."

I pulled up to the valet of the Four Seasons. Bobby looked at me curiously. "Kara, what are we doing here?"

16

"WELL," I SAID. "AREN'T you going to invite us in?" I barged into room 2430, leaving Keyvan and Bobby at the door, staring at each other with frozen grimaces, like they'd been turned into wax figures at Madame Tussauds. I could almost see the hair on their arms stand at attention. A pair of deer caught in headlights. Or pit bulls squaring off for the lunge. Whatever they were, there was something animalistic about the Ebadi boys in that moment, a primal look of anger and fear. Bobby remained frozen in the doorway. "Well," I said. "Aren't you going to say something?" He didn't. "At least come in, Bobby." He didn't do that, either.

"Bobby?" Keyvan chortled. "What happened to Babak? You kill him, too?"

Bobby was stumped for a witty response. He just turned to me seething and said, "You had no right to do this."

I beelined for the metal box and punched in the code, which I had committed to memory. Zero-four-one-three.

"What do you think you're doing?" Keyvan demanded to know.

I pushed the stacks of currency aside and pulled out the letter I had seen when I first opened the box. The one that had caused Keyvan to quickly close it back up. The one Elena had told me about. As I suspected, the envelope, with an Iranian postmark, was addressed to Babak Ebadi, and below the address appeared a neatly-penned "Return to Sender" in what I assumed was Elena's handwriting.

"Take the letter, Bobby. Read it." I handed Bobby the letter. He held it like it might explode, and I watched him piece it all together. My first hook-up with Kyle, my suspicions, my disappearances, maybe even my tracking down the former housekeeper. The look on his face told me he was afraid of me, but also that he was impressed.

Keyvan dived for the minibar, searching for a bottle of scotch, no doubt. But he had depleted the scotch and vodka selections. He vacillated and finally chose tequila. He guzzled the tiny bottle like a shot and laughed again. "You're a piece of work," he said, though it was unclear if he was talking to Bobby or to me.

I grabbed the envelope from Bobby. "Fine," I said. "If you don't have the guts to read it, then I will." I took a breath, peeled it open as gently as I could, unfolded the letter, and began. "Dear B, I understand why you never write back. I've finally realized I can't blame you for our parents' mistakes. I started to write this in Farsi but then it hit me you can't read or write it. Which is a shame. I'm feeling such a connection to our heritage. I know you were only one when you left, but I was seven and I remember so much about it. Not that what's here matches my memory of it, but it feels good to be here. You should at least learn your language. Every letter in our alphabet looks like a piece of art on paper. And we don't write in our vowels. Could you imagine Americans having to write without vowels? They would never be able to figure anything out." I stopped and looked at my audience. Keyvan was staring out the window. Bobby was still standing at the door, as if actually entering the room was too dangerous an act. "I'm thinking of getting a tattoo of my name in Farsi," I continued. "Maman Homa has been teaching me all about the history of Iran and of our family. Did you know that our great-grandfather was a whirling dervish? Pretty cool. Maman Homa has taken me to Shiraz and Isfahan and Persepolis. School sucks here, mostly because there are no girls. But on the other hand, I'm doing really well. Much better. Maybe it's because there's less distraction. Oh another thing she told me is that on Dad's side, our grandfather's brothers were both opium addicts. One of them died of an overdose and the other one got cancer or something, but anyway I thought that was interesting too. Not that I'm looking for easy answers or ways to avoid taking responsibility for anything. It's my fault I got so messed up, and my fault I'm sick."

"Stop it," Keyvan screamed. "I don't need to relive this shit. My parents kicked me out, my brother didn't want a relationship with me. I moved on. I'm done with it."

"Then why are you here?" I asked. "And why do you carry this letter in a box?"

He was silent. I looked to Bobby, who refused to make eye contact with either of us. "I don't know how you could just turn away a letter from your brother, Bobby," I said. "I don't understand."

"I thought he was dead. I got a letter from a dead person."

"But weren't you happy he was alive?" I asked.

Keyvan, pawing around in the minibar again, blurted, "It was easier to have me dead. Persians like to take the easy way out. If your son fucks up, send him away. If your country hits a rough patch, go somewhere else. Desert the people and places that matter to you most if there's an easier path somewhere else. Isn't that right, Bobby? Isn't that the Persian way? This is why you're Persian and I'm Iranian. I actually believe in something. I'm not just some image, some façade that doesn't even really exist."

Bobby was stung by Keyvan's words; that much I could tell. But he didn't say a thing. Keyvan had been festering in this hotel room, gnawing away at what he would say if he saw Bobby or his parents again. But Bobby was unprepared. He was thrust into this room with Keyvan without warning, without a chance to script his outbursts in advance. His silence was understandable. The fact that he hadn't bolted back into the hall was enough to tell me I was getting through, enough to get me to keep reading the letter in hopes that, a decade and a half later, Bobby would finally have something to say in response.

"I hope you know I'm sorry," I read, though they may as well have been my words. "To you, not to Mommy and Daddy. It mystifies me how you handle them so well. Ever since you were little, you always knew what to say to them, how to dress to make them happy, perfect grades. On some level I was jealous. They never looked at me the way they looked at you, with any pride. But then again, all the reasons they loved you made me angrier. Grades, dressing a certain way, all these superficial things. Isn't it strange that I'm in a country that is supposed to be so closed-minded and yet here I feel loved? Not because I'm perfect, but because I'm somebody's grandson. And that should be enough. I'm somebody's brother, too. As are you. One day you will come here and you'll realize that. You'll see that we're so much more than some shitty school in Brentwood and fitting in with the rich Persian social set of Tehrangeles. Oh it's so stupid that they all call themselves Persian anyway. Let them. Iran doesn't need Persians."

I saw Keyvan smile when I read this. This letter was the beginning of

Keyvan's forming what would become his own façade. Proud, angry, nation-
alistic, opinionated, righteous.

"I want you to see all this," I continued reading. "To see your history and
know what you are, and that what you are is so much bigger and better and
more complex than the little things I know you're worried about right now.
Does being popular in Brentwood really mean anything once you realize
that a million people just died in our war with Iraq? Can you believe that?
300,000 Iranians dead they say. I know more Iraqis died but on some level, I
do care more about the Iranians. Perhaps that's wrong. I count myself lucky,
in a way, that the war just ended. Not that I would be let into the military
anyway. There's no fighting in my future, but if I could fight, I would fight
for Iran. Certainly not for the United States with their hypocrisy. Sometimes
when I'm outside Maman Homa's house, in what should have been our yard,
I imagine what life would have been like if the revolution had never happened. Of course, if the United States hadn't put the Shah in power in the
first place, there might never have been a revolution or a need for one. Think
about it. We would have grown up here. Imagine how different we could have
been. How happy. I know you would be happier here. I know it. We weren't
meant for the United States, me and you. Fate dealt us an unfair blow. Please
write back. I love you. Keyvan."

We stood in silence for an interminable minute. Finally, Bobby couldn't
stand the discomfort anymore. "I was supposed to care about some preachy
letter like that?" He waited. I looked at Keyvan, who said nothing. Bobby
went on. "Well, this was fun, but I think I'll go and let you guys fuck again.
Or whatever you've been doing."

"Don't go, Bobby. Keyvan leaves tomorrow. Say something to him."

"Jesus, what do you want me to say, Kara?" Bobby screamed. "That I forgive him? I don't. I hate him. He fucked up our lives because he was weak.
When I think of him, all I feel is ashamed." With that, Bobby stormed out of
the hotel room.

Freshman year at boarding school, during a school trip to Boston, Bobby and
I snuck away from the group and got crepes at a French bistro. It felt decadent and rebellious, and we were both high from the endorphin rush that

comes with breaking rules. Bobby said there was something he had to tell me. I hadn't heard this serious tone out of him before. The first few months of school, we focused on mocking the outfits of our classmates, deriding all the dumb jocks, and nailing down impersonations of our least-favorite teachers. I looked up at Bobby with chocolate dripping down my chin.

"I have a brother who died."

I don't remember what I said, or if I said anything. Bobby didn't elaborate much, simply stating that Keyvan had been drafted into the Iran-Iraq war while visiting Tehran. Two years later, he was killed. When Keyvan died, Bobby was thirteen, and they hadn't seen each other for two years. It had been too risky still for their parents to return to Iran.

Once I met the Ebadis, the weird, formal way that Bobby had chosen to tell me made sense. The subject was off-limits. Parents' Weekend, I made the mistake of saying Keyvan's name to Leila and Hossein as they inspected the cafeteria food they were expected to eat between chats with Bobby's teachers. I barely remember the context, but I do recall how Leila glared at Bobby, no doubt wondering why he would tell some stupid American girl about their family tragedy. They, as a family, must have felt guilty for letting their son go to Iran. And the best way to deal with guilt is to suppress it. I also recall leaving the cafeteria with the Ebadis immediately thereafter and dining at the only Persian restaurant in town. Hossein ordered plate after plate of exotic food for us to share. Leila allowed us to drink wine, knowing full well we could be expelled for it, but reasoning that she raised her kids "the French way." Bobby's dead brother didn't come up once. Instead, we discussed art, travel, and fashion. By the end of the meal, the few sips of wine going to my teenage head, I had fallen madly in love with the Ebadi family, a love affair I did not expect to last as long as it did.

Senior year, Bobby asked me to get permission for a day trip to Boston. He took me to that same French bistro, and he ordered us two crepes. I knew something was up. That's when he told me he was gay. I was the first person he told, and I felt so honored. I always kind of knew. He had changed drastically in those three years. The khakis and polos had been replaced by kitschy bell-bottoms and platform shoes, and he'd been voted best-dressed boy in the yearbook two years going on three. But having him sit across from me, being so honest, made me feel special and needed. I knew there was a reason Bobby had to take me to the bistro to tell me. I knew that in his mind, the two crepe confessions were intrinsically connected. That being gay was the same as his brother being dead: something you just never talked about, something you were embarrassed by, something you hid and repressed until it was no longer even there.

I turned to Keyvan, who had switched on the television and was watching BBC News. Something about genocide. "Are you just going to stand there, Keyvan? Go after him."

"You know why I got into news?" Keyvan asked, poking the volume on the remote. "Because every day it reminds me that there are lives more tragic and horrible than mine. It's very therapeutic, really. Soon I'll be in a war zone, surrounded by families who have lost their children to sectarian violence, soldiers who have sacrificed their lives. All of this bullshit will seem very small to me again. And you will be forgotten," he added coldly.

I tugged at Keyvan's arm, strong as a tree trunk. He turned aggressively toward me, a vein protruding from his beet-colored face, blood rushing to it from the booze and the anger. "You can go," he said.

"No," I said forcefully, grasping desperately at him, wanting him to hold me or strike me or run away from me and toward Bobby. Wanting him to *react*.

"You're twisted," Keyvan said to me. "I should have known I'd meet a psycho if I went online in this fucked-up city."

"Maybe that's why I fit in so well with the Ebadis."

"So you know my parents, too?" he asked.

"Your mother gave me this dress for my birthday," I announced.

"What, is this a game to you?"

"No. I just… I couldn't let you get on that plane. You're brothers, there has to be something to that. You spent eleven years side by side."

"Eleven years during which I was unhappy and high. I don't want to be that person anymore. I don't…" But his voice trailed off, the emotion finally getting to him. He rushed out, and I followed him. We rode down the elevator next to a family of Scandinavian tourists gossiping in their singsong language.

When the interminable ride finally brought us to the lobby, Keyvan beelined to the valet, where Bobby was waiting for his car. Keyvan approached Bobby menacingly, his body so much thicker than his younger brother's. Bobby shrunk back reflexively. Keyvan's fingers curled into a tight fist, his forearm bulging with tension. I could see him preparing to punch Bobby and yelled for him to stop. "You called Bobby and hung up so many times, Keyvan. What did you want to say to him? Say it. Don't punch him. Just talk." A small crowd of people were staring at us. Bobby pleaded politely with the guy at the valet stand to hurry up with his car. "Talk to him, Bobby. Talk to your brother. You've lived your whole life afraid of becoming him, haven't you? Afraid of disappointing your parents like him? He's the reason for all this fear and anxiety inside of you. Tell him how it feels. Tell him what it's done to you. He's a good man, Bobby. Talk to him."

Bobby looked at me as if suddenly it was all crystal clear. "Is that what this is about? You've decided after a few fucks that you love him? You meet a guy, and our fourteen years together just go in the back seat, the way they did when you met Jacques?"

"This is completely about you and me, Bobby. I'm doing this because I love *you*." He was looking away, so I turned to Keyvan. "Why did you call Bobby? Some part of you wanted to say something to him. But you hung up. What did you want to say?"

"I wanted to find out if he's really a complete asshole," Keyvan responded.

"You wanted to find out if *I am*?" Bobby spoke slowly, murderously.

Keyvan just shrugged.

And Bobby lunged at him, flailing.

Bobby's car arrived, and I quickly paid, an eye to one side, where Keyvan had Bobby in a headlock. He dragged him to the car and managed to push him into the back seat. I got in the driver's side. Keyvan stood there staring at us. "Get in," I screamed.

Keyvan got into the passenger seat, and I drove. I didn't know where I was going, but instinct was leading me northwest. "I wrote to you," Keyvan suddenly said. "I asked for your forgiveness. You answered by sending the letter back. I know I was fucked-up, but..."

"I was *a kid*," Bobby exclaimed.

"You weren't a kid. You would have been sixteen then."

"You fucked up the first part of all our lives in L.A. by being a violent, spoiled addict, and you fucked up all the time since by being this horrible, looming memory. Everything has been about you. Even after you left, you sucked up all the energy in the house."

"I'm sorry," Keyvan said flatly.

"You are not. And why the hell would I care even if you were?"

Keyvan turned around to face him, the seatbelt expanding around his torso.

"You demolished our lives," Bobby cried.

"Well, what about my life?" Keyvan rebutted. "They got rid of me as soon as I wasn't convenient."

"Oh please, Keyvan. Inconvenient. That's a wimp-out word for what you became. They sent you to every good rehab in the country. They offered you every kind of help they could."

"They offered me everything but their acceptance," Keyvan said.

"Why should they have accepted you? What would it mean for Mommy or Daddy to say, 'I accept my son the ungrateful destructive asshole'?"

"You were my little brother. I always wanted you to look up to me. But you never did. From the moment you were born, you were an arrogant, distant little fuck. Well-behaved, just like them. You masked everything, you know that? That's what our family does. And that never bothered you. You never showed real emotion. I wanted a younger brother who understood me, and instead I got you."

Bobby was sitting there with his mouth hanging open. "You think I didn't *want* to look up to you? I worshipped you when I was five. Why the fuck would I look up to you, Keyvan? When you treated yourself like such shit? You know where I learned how to treat you? From *you*. You treated yourself like such dirt my whole childhood that I figured that's what you were. Dirt. You want me to feel sorry for you? They sent you to live in a big house with a beautiful garden and a grandmother who spoiled you worse than they had. And that was horrible? You're the one who wouldn't return their calls for three years."

"You think being sent to Iran was easy? There were Koran classes full of kids half my age, run by a teacher who hit us with a strap. There were months with no friends. I was on my deathbed that first year. None of the medications were working. I had night sweats. I was scared. I was sure I was gonna die of AIDS. Iran didn't get protease inhibitors as fast as West Hollywood. The least my brother could have done was send a get-well card."

Bobby froze. Now he was all deer-in-headlights. The pit bull was gone. He looked at me, likely wondering if I knew. "Yes, Bobby," I said quietly. "I get it. And it's okay. We were safe. I don't need a pot of echinacea tea or a B-12 shot to make me feel better." I focused on the road.

"I get it now," Keyvan continued. "It was bad manners of me to become sick. It made them uncomfortable. They killed me in their tasteful fantasies. They wanted me dead on some desert battlefield, not in a hospital bed with tubes and bedpans and everything. It doesn't matter to me anymore what they did. But you made sure I stayed dead, because it was easier for you."

"How did you know?" Bobby was staring at Keyvan.

"Know what?"

"That they said you had died in the war," Bobby clarified.

"Maman Homa told me," Keyvan said. "Believe it or not, Leila's mother doesn't know how to tell a lie. I guess children really do rebel against their parents." Keyvan thought for a moment and then added, "Well, most of them, at least." Keyvan suddenly turned his attention to me and snapped, "Where are you going? You're getting farther and farther from the hotel."

"I'm going where we need to go," I said.

"Really, Kara. You're not a part of this anymore," Keyvan said. "You can stop now."

I looked to Bobby for support, but he looked at me like a stranger. "Bobby, please don't be upset with me," I pleaded.

"Upset? You think I'm *upset*? Try enraged. You were fucking my brother behind my back and lying to me about it."

"For two weeks," I countered. "You've been lying your whole life."

"To my parents, maybe. But not to you."

"You told me your brother was dead. He died in a war I knew nothing about. You manipulated my sympathy."

"I believed it when I told you," he explained. "That was freshman year. I didn't know myself until he sent me that letter two summers later."

"You never amended the story."

"You were too close to my parents at that point," he said. "I couldn't risk it."

"You pulled me into the lie when you turned me into your beard. And it's just been getting worse every year. Where was it gonna end, Bobby? Marriage? Kids? How deep into your deceit were you planning on taking me?"

Bobby turned up the radio to drown me out. Something noisy and guitar-driven assaulted our eardrums as I parked outside the Ebadi house. All the lights in the neighborhood were off. We were invading the ghost town, waking up the dead. The two brothers didn't move for an interminable minute. They simply stared at the house.

Brentwood Patrol pulled up behind us. A burly man in a mustache parked behind us and approached my window. He asked what we were doing.

"We're delivering some wonderful news to my parents," Bobby slurred. "My long-lost brother has returned from the grave!"

"Which house do they live in?" the man asked.

Bobby pointed to the house. The man informed us that he could write us a ticket for loitering. The man asked if I had been drinking. Oh, fuck, just what we needed. A DUI on top of everything. I denied the accusation, but the patrolman seemed unconvinced and demanded I get out of the car.

"Listen, officer," Keyvan said from within the car. "This is a bad time for this."

"Is there ever a good time for drunk driving?" the guy responded.

"Oh, come on," Bobby said, coming to my defense. "You haven't even tested her blood-alcohol level."

Keyvan got out. "You didn't see her driving, sir."

"Excuse me?" the man said sternly.

"She was parked on the street when you pulled up behind us."

"I heard the music. The sound was traveling."

"You're wrong," Keyvan said. "The car was parked. We were in the house hanging out, and we came in here to get a CD that was in the car. That's it. We were just retrieving a CD." Not bad, Keyvan.

"Get back in the car, sir," the man ordered.

"You're not arresting anyone," Keyvan said. "You're not even a cop. You're the fucking Brentwood Patrol. Do you know how many times you threatened to arrest me when I was a kid? In fact, I think I even recognize you. I used to do a lot worse, and you never busted me. Because you can't bust anybody."

Inside the house, a light came on. Leila's unmistakable shadow fell on the sheer white drapes of her bedroom. I looked up, and through a crack in the curtains, I saw her peering out. Her face appeared encrusted in a bright-green facemask, a surreal image, to say the least. Moments later, she emerged from the front door in a white bathrobe. When she reached us, she saw Keyvan and stopped dead. Her green mask seemed to crack. Her voice trembled as she said his name, whispered it at first, like a question, and then stated it, more firmly as she stepped toward him.

The patrolman blocked her. "Ma'am? Are these your sons, ma'am?"

Leila's face was frozen. The patrolman couldn't likely have realized she had just seen a ghost.

"Ma'am? Ma'am?" he repeated over and over again, until finally Leila's eyes registered the situation and appeared lucid once more.

"Yes. Yes, these are my sons."

"Ma'am, were they just in your home?"

"Tell them, Leila," Keyvan said. "Tell them we were just having some drinks inside and we came out for a CD."

"Is that true, ma'am?" the patrolman demanded to know.

"Well, of course it is true," she responded quickly. "My sons don't lie." She turned quickly and violently toward the rent-a-cop. Through the mask, her eyes glowed like a cat's. "Please leave before I call the real police and have them cite you for harassment."

Once he was gone, Leila took Keyvan in her arms and whispered to him in Farsi.

He whispered, "I'm good, Mommy. I'm feeling really good." Then Keyvan pulled away and looked his mother in the eye. "I don't want to be dead anymore," he said.

"We can talk about this in the morning," she whispered.

"No, Mommy," Keyvan said, too loudly. "I want to know. How could you tell people I was dead?"

"You wouldn't return our calls. You didn't answer our letters. You wouldn't come back and visit." Leila took a deep breath, searching for the right words. "I didn't know what to tell people. I couldn't tell people the truth."

"But how?" Keyvan pressed. "How does a person even come up with something so macabre?"

"I don't know. Creating martyrs is in our blood, perhaps," Leila sadly stated. "I regretted it as soon as I said it, and by then, it was too late. A lie is like a snowball. Or a snowflake. Its nature is to grow. Let's go inside."

"When did you say it?" Keyvan asked.

"It's not important."

"It is to me."

Leila quickly glanced at me, resenting my presence. "I ran into Tanaz Ma-liki in the supermarket, and she went on as usual, asking me when you were coming back and how you were doing. I was on the spot, and I didn't know what to say. And then she went off on a tangent about how awful it was that all these young Iranian men were dying in the war with Iraq, and I just said it; I said, 'Keyvan was one of them.'"

"All of this for some gossipy bitch in a Persian supermarket?"

"By the following day, she had spread the news. I either had to admit I was a liar or live with it. But no"—Leila suddenly stopped herself, and then continued—"it was more than that. It was a relief to have the world think our son had died in a war. Not that he had rejected us. I started believing it after I said it. Hossein did, too. I didn't have to wonder about whether you would ever forgive us. I accepted that you wouldn't. You had already made up your mind. You had unforgiven us, permanently." Leila seemed shaken and emo-tional, but as quickly as one recovers from a stubbed toe, she had managed to compose herself. "Now let's go inside and go to bed. Tomorrow, we'll figure out what to tell people about where you've been."

"How about the truth?" Keyvan suggested.

Leila glared at him. "That I've been lying to them for almost twenty years."

"We've all been lying," Bobby suddenly interrupted. "About everything."

"What are you talking about, Babak?" Leila asked wearily.

Bobby uttered the words I never thought he would. "I'm gay, Mommy."

There was a tense silence in the air, interrupted by the automatic sprin-klers, which rained directly onto me. "We should go inside," Leila ordered, thankful for the distraction.

"Wait," I blurted out as the sprinklers soaked me. "Let's talk about this now." Leila fixed her gaze on me, and then turned to her sons and began to speak in rapid-fire Farsi. Her words meant nothing to me, and the faster they were spoken, the more frustrated I became. "Leila," I pleaded. "Don't shut me out of this."

"I am sorry," Leila said. "There are certain conversations that just don't come naturally to me in English."

"And there are certain conversations that can't be had in Farsi. Like there's no word for *gay* in Farsi." I turned to Bobby for confirmation. "Right? Didn't you tell me that? There's no word for it…"

"We should really call the language Persian," Keyvan interrupted. "Farsi is what they call it in Iran. We don't call French *français*, and we don't call Spanish *español*, do we?"

"So you don't want to be called Persian. You want to be called Iranian. But the *language* has to be called Persian, not Farsi." This was Bobby trying to recap Keyvan's Middle Eastern political correctness.

"Exactly," Keyvan said.

"Please, can you guys talk about what really matters?" I pleaded. "And can someone turn off this damn sprinkler?"

Suddenly, we all noticed Hossein standing in the doorway, holding a remote, absorbed by the presence of his elder son. He was in plaid pajama bottoms and a white T-shirt. He held up the remote, and the spray around me finally died down and stopped. "This isn't the place to be having this conversation," Hossein said, indicating he had been standing there long enough to get the highlights. "You're all wet, Kara. You're going to catch a cold. Come inside, and we'll dry you off."

"That's an excellent idea," Leila said.

Hossein put his arm around Keyvan as we walked into the house. "You look good," he said.

As I changed into one of Leila's tracksuits in her closet, I could hear the family talking animatedly in Farsi downstairs. I couldn't understand what they were saying, but two or three times my name came up. Even if they were eviscerating me, I was a part of the discussion. I was an honorary Ebadi, after all. I stuffed my yellow dress into a dry-cleaning bag. The sprinklers had spread the Bolognese stain, turning the once-beautiful garment into a wet mess.

When I emerged down the stairs, I was shocked to find the fourEbadis battling each other. Bobby was becoming more and more hysterical as he railed in Farsi. Tears were falling from his face. I wanted to go to him and hold him, but it wasn't my love he was after. Hossein stood and announced he would drive me home. I protested. But my staying wasn't an option.

A few moments later, I was next to Hossein in his Hyundai, his headlights illuminating the dark Brentwood street. "Where are we going?" I asked.

"I don't know," he said. "We are driving."

"Okay," I said. "Sure. Just speak when you need to."

Hossein drove to Sunset, where a few cars were speeding past us. He turned west, taking us toward the beach. "In Iran," he said, "men did sleep with men. And women slept with women. But it wasn't such a big deal. Here, everybody needs to do everything in public. Everyone wants a pat on their back for their lifestyle."

"It's not a lifestyle," I said. "It's part of who Bobby is. It's not something he chooses, like what neighborhood to live in or what magazines to subscribe to."

"Why not?" Hossein wondered as he gained momentum. "In Iran, many men married women and slept with men on the side."

"That's horrible," I said. "Is that what you told him in there?"

"Of course. I told him I don't care what he does in private. Why should I? I'm not religious. He's not going to hell for sleeping with a man. But he should still get married and have children."

"Why?" I asked. "Because not doing it would humiliate you."

"Because it would humiliate him," Hossein corrected.

"Are you sure it's him you're concerned about? Why did you send Keyvan away? To save him, or to save yourself the trouble of having to tell your friends what had happened to him? You didn't want the physical evidence of his illness around, did you?"

"You are a very presumptuous and stupid girl if you think you understand what we went through with Keyvan."

"You told people he was *dead*," I blurted out.

"Which was precisely what he told us to tell people when he left," Hossein reasoned.

"Hossein. You're gonna use the words of an angry teenager to justify your actions? When are you and Leila going to stop being so stubborn and admit you made some big mistakes? Maybe I *am* presumptuous. Fine. At least I'm not cruel and delusional."

"You think the answer to every problem is telling the truth, displaying all your pain and ugliness to the world like a carcass," Hossein said with disgust. "I don't believe in wallowing. I believe in moving on."

"You have no interest in how hard Bobby's life has been, do you? Why don't you try thinking for a moment about what he went through? Think about an eleven-year-old kid burying the memory of his brother, then finding out he wasn't even dead, and then having to hide his own identity. Think about him."

"I am thinking about him. I want him to be happy. And I don't think people find happiness by deciding that their sexual behavior is their *identity*."

"Are they happier lying about it?" I asked.

"They are happier living a good life," he said confidently. "A complete life."

"And what about the poor woman he marries for your benefit?"

"You are not involved in this," he replied. "No matter how much you think you are. And we have made you anything but a poor woman."

"Anyone who becomes complicit in a lie is involved. Bobby's lie has eaten away at me for years, too. I've covered for him, and I've learned how to lie, and I don't want to be that person. I want to be honest."

"True honesty is a utopia," Hossein said. "It doesn't exist."

Sunset dumped us onto the PCH. Hossein rolled down his window and parked near the beach. The smell of the ocean invaded the car, salty and fresh.

"After the revolution, we were moving to Manhattan. But I took one look at that city and felt like I was in prison. I didn't want to raise the children surrounded by skyscrapers and drug addicts. We weren't even considering moving to Los Angeles. We only came here for a visit because Leila wanted to see Hollywood." I smiled at this. Imagining Leila as a star-struck tourist was somehow moving. "The moment we came to the ocean, I turned to Leila and said this is where we were moving. I made the decision on a whim. Without thinking. Now I think maybe it was a mistake."

"Why?"

"Who knows how Keyvan and Babak might have been different in New York?"

"You make me sad," I said.

Hossein smiled. I knew the last thing he viewed himself as was saddening. He was a self-made man, an immigrant success story; he was the American Dream. "And why is that?" he asked.

"Because," I said. "You are a man who truly deserves the respect of his sons but doesn't have it."

Hossein looked up at me, taking me seriously for the first time. "What do you mean by that?"

"You're an incredible man. You're inspiring and talented and hardworking. And wise, when you decide to communicate. Most men would be proud to have a father like you. But as it turns out, you ended up with two sons who are alienated from you." Hossein's silence informed me I was getting through to him. "Maybe if you didn't have to leave Iran, it wouldn't have been an issue. Maybe part of what drew you away from them was raising them in a culture so different from your own. Every moment in America drew them further and further away from your experience. But the thing is, even though it's not your fault you had to move here, and not your fault Keyvan had such a hard time adjusting, and not your fault Bobby is gay, how you decide to deal with all these situations is up to you."

"And what do you suggest I do?" he asked, suddenly vulnerable.

"I suggest you drive back to that house and reclaim your sons' respect."

"How?"

"Talk to them. *Reveal* yourself to them. Let them know who you are. And, as people have been telling me for a month, relax."

Hossein revved the engine and turned back east. When he drove past Brentwood, I was confused. I asked him where we were going. "I'm taking you home," he said. "You've done what you set out to do."

17

I woke at eleven a.m. in Leila's tracksuit and rushed to knock on Bobby's door. No answer, so I dialed his cell. "Hey," he answered immediately.

"What's up?" I said. "Is everything okay?"

"Sure. Mom's at the hairdresser. Dad's at golf. My brother's trying to explain to his bosses why he isn't in Baghdad." His lack of affect was betrayed by the exhaustion in his voice.

"And you?" I inquired.

"Eating Rosa Maria leftovers," Bobby said. "Nice work on my dad, by the way. I don't know what you said to him, but it took."

"We just had an honest talk."

"Well, he came back home last night and gave us this weirdly movie-of-the-weekish speech about how he loves us and all he cares about is our happiness."

"Wow," I said proudly. "So he's come around?"

"Not all the way around," Bobby said. "We all went to bed after that. Hearing him talk all sentimental like that was too much for us to handle. When we woke up this morning, it was like nothing had happened."

"What do you mean?" I asked.

"Well, my mom had Pilates and an appointment at the salon, and my dad had a golf game. We're all going to lunch. You're coming. I have some news for the whole family."

"I have something to tell you, too," I said. "I'm sorry. I'm sery, sery vorry."

"For what?"

"For lying to you, for insinuating myself into your private life, for all the harsh things I said last night."

"Honestly, Kara *djoon*," he modulated his voice, "I have no idea vat you're talking about."

"I just want to make sure you forgive me. I want to be your friend forever, even though I'm no longer your beard."

"I'll knock on your door in twenty minutes," he announced. "Get dressed."

Bobby and I pulled up and got out at La Scala. It was pretty weird to have a round table set for five after so many years of Leila's favorite square four-top in a corner.

Suddenly, there they were behind us, streaming out of Hossein's Hyundai: Hossein and Leila in front, Keyvan in back. Bobby stood up to open the door for his mother, and they streamed into the restaurant as a foursome, a reconstituted family. Just as the maitre d' approached, Bobby looked across the room. "The Cheshire Cat," he whispered.

"What's that?" Leila asked.

Bobby covertly nodded toward Tanaz, who was sipping white wine and looking even more garish than usual, her hair freshly bleached and her white blouse way too tight. "She's the Cheshire Cat," Bobby explained. At the confused look on his parents' face, Bobby elaborated, "You remember, the annoying cat in *Alice in Wonderland*. The one who shows up everywhere, when least expected, with that mischievous grin on its face."

Suddenly, Leila erupted into laughter. Not ladylike at all. No, this was something altogether different. Tension release, perhaps. The giggle fit made Tanaz look up and see Leila. She sauntered over and gave Leila, Hossein, and Bobby kisses, then asked if she'd missed the joke. "It's nothing," Leila said. "Nothing at all. Tanaz *djoon*." Then Leila said, with a nervous smile, "It's such an unexpected surprise to see you. You pop up in the most *unexpected* places." Bobby and Keyvan were stifling their laughter.

"It's not so unexpected," Tanaz replied. "You know I can't go two days without the chopped salad here."

"Are you alone?" Leila asked. "You're welcome to join us."

"No, I was just leaving." Tanaz gazed down shyly and whispered, "I was on a blind date. Tina actually set me up with one of her schoolfriend's fathers. A doctor."

"That's wonderful."

"It was boring. I can't date an American. We have nothing in common,"

Tanaz said, sighing. "And I think Tina is just trying to distract me so I stop planning her wedding." Tanaz looked up to Bobby. "You still haven't RSVPed, Babak."

"I'm so sorry," he said. "I'll be there."

Tanaz smiled, then looked at Keyvan and asked, "And who is this?" She then added snidely, "A friend of Babak's?"

"No, Babak is single," Leila said nonchalantly. "This is Keyvan. You might remember him."

"Hello, Mrs. Maliki," Keyvan said with a nod.

Tanaz looked at Leila in complete shock. "But... but I thought... I thought..."

"I know what you thought. It turns out I was mistaken," Leila responded.

For once, Tanaz was flummoxed. She stammered and finally managed, "Well, Keyvan *djoon*, now that you're alive, I mean... now that you're back, you must come to Tina's wedding. She would love you to be there. You know she's marrying a descendant of the *Qajars*."

"You don't say," Keyvan said with a smile. And then, "I'd love to be there, Mrs. Maliki."

"It will be so nice for Hossein and me to be there with both our sons and our dear friend, Kara." And with that, Leila led her family to the table.

Before Tanaz made her exit, she waved a hello my way, and we all waved back.

Lunch went on like nothing had happened. Our conversation focused first on Melanie Griffith, who was sitting in a corner booth eating a chopped tuna salad (same as me). Leila knew her plastic surgeon and couldn't understand how he could have done such a bad job. She surmised that Melanie must be cheating with another surgeon on the side. Hossein then gave us the details of his golf game, which included a birdie, a fact that seemed to thrill Leila but hold no interest for Bobby and Keyvan. Hossein asked about the Black Death project, but mostly he wondered if there was any money in it. When I explained that Bobby would be writing the script on spec and waiving his fee until we could sell the project, Hossein shrugged and said he would rather Bobby find a line of work that actually compensated him. This led to a discussion about graduate schools and MBA programs. Hossein urged both his sons to go get MBAs. Keyvan laughed at the notion, telling his father he was one of the more established field producers working in news, and getting an MBA would be career suicide. Keyvan said he had an idea for a book called *Cash*. When Hossein said he loved Johnny Cash "but isn't there enough written about him," Keyvan explained that he was writing about money, not music. A combination coffee-table book and historical analysis, he explained to his impressed father. Keyvan described his collection of currency and said he would open the box for them. He told his mother the code for the lockbox was her birthday. 0413. Of course. April thirteenth. We celebrated Leila's birthday every year on that day. A clue I had apparently missed. Another connection between the brothers: Bobby's Manhunt password was his mother's name, and Keyvan's lockbox code was his mother's birthday. It said something, perhaps about their love for Leila, or maybe it spoke to their belief that there was no way to get around her.

Over dessert, we discussed which parent Bobby and Keyvan looked like. Leila ventured that Bobby looked more like Hossein, but that Keyvan had her eyes. She was amazed at how little her sons resembled one another. Hossein felt that they both looked like Leila's side of the family. Leila, he said with a knowing smile, had the dominant genes. I contributed here and there to the conversation. My opinions floated by. No one treated me strangely; it was as if I had never shown up at their house in the middle of the night and forced a confrontation, as if I had never pretended to be their younger son's girlfriend and had a secret affair with their older son. They smiled and nodded as I told them that Melanie Griffith and Meg Ryan appear to have the same plastic surgeon because they've begun to look alike, and that Keyvan's collection of money would look gorgeous when reprinted in a glossy coffee table book. When the check came, Hossein grabbed it and immediately took care of it. He said he had a card game to get to. Leila asked us if we wanted to walk around Beverly Hills and do some shopping; Barney's was having a sale. Keyvan was the first to decline her offer. He said they could clothe themselves. Fine, then, Leila said, she would go on her own. But she said if she saw anything that would look good on them, she would buy it for them, and that was that.

Before leaving, Leila gave me a kiss on each cheek. "Pilates this week?" she asked.

"Of course," I said.

"Good. Stop by the house before. I just bought a pair of shoes that hurt my feet. Maybe they'll fit you better."

And so Leila was off, and Hossein was off. The lunch crowd had dispersed, leaving me and the brothers behind. "Well," Bobby said when I was done. "As exciting as that was, I have some fairly important news of my own."

"Yes?" I said.

"I'm going to Iran," he declared.

He said it with such finality that my first question was, "You're *moving* to Iran?"

"No, do you think I'm fucking crazy? I'm going for a visit this summer. With Keyvan. We hatched up the idea when he canceled his trip to Baghdad. The airline gave him a credit, and so he changed his first-class ticket to two business-class tickets to Tehran, via New York, Frankfurt, and Dubai."

"Wow," I said. "That's... I mean, that's great, I think. Is it safe?"

Keyvan rolled his eyes. "It's safer than Los Angeles. Less crime. No gangs."

"Just don't go online looking for sex," I said. Then I told Bobby I expected lots of pictures of him and the Ayatollah. "And you?" I asked Keyvan.

"What about me?"

"If you're leaving for Tehran from Los Angeles this summer," I said, "I take it you're staying here."

"I'll be here for a little while," he replied. "At least until I figure out if there's anything to this book idea. Then who knows? I might go back into news, but maybe I've had my share of having bombs explode all around me. It might be time to settle down."

"Meaning?" I asked.

"I thought I would die of a heroin overdose, and I didn't. Then I thought I would die of AIDS and failed at that, too. Then I figured I would definitely die in Baghdad, but even when I was hit by the IED, I managed to survive."

"Maybe you're not meant to die," Bobby said.

"Maybe I'm meant to stop tempting fate, find a nice house, get a cute dog, meet a nice girl."

"That would put you out of the running," Bobby said to me.

"Yeah?"

"If there's one thing we all know, it's that you are devious and manipulative."

"Yet lovable," I added.

Bobby and Keyvan paused and then gave each other the go-ahead to laugh. It was strange watching their new rapport. They had, in just twenty-four hours, reverted to those two kids at Disneyland.

It was as Joanne was redecorating my side of the duplex with Lindsay Lohan's hand-me-downs (a gorgeous L-shaped couch, beautiful Moroccan pillows, a set of ceramic vases, even a Persian rug) that I found a crumpled-up flyer in a drawer. It was for Antwon/Michael's breathing circle, and it was for that very day. I thought back to getting kicked out of Burke Williams. It seemed like so long ago.

"What is it?" Joanne asked.

"Nothing. It's just this thing. This breathing thing."

"I didn't know you meditated," she observed.

"I don't."

"You should," she said. "I've been meditating on my mantra every morning."

"You have a mantra?" I asked.

"I do now," she said as she hung a set of black-and-white portraits of old stars onto my wall: Brigitte Bardot, Ann-Margret, Jane Fonda, Raquel Welch. Joanne had discovered *The Secret*, and ever since, she believed in manifesting good karma. "I felt like such a bitch for giving you that T-shirt, Kara," she said as she rearranged some pillows.

"Why?"

"*Thirty and flirty?* It's so passive-aggressive. The fact is, I'm jealous of you."

"Of me?" I asked. "Why?"

"I've just always been competitive with you. Fiona is in another league, but me and you, we're just average girls trying to make our way. And the thought of you having more love, or more success, or even more friendship, scares me."

"Joanne, why are you telling me this?" I asked.

"I now believe in the theory of abundance," she announced with a smile. "There's enough happiness to go around, or at least that's what I choose to believe."

"I see," I said, worried this abundant phase of hers would be short-lived.

"Also, the reason I've been so competitive with you is because I love you so much."

"Really?" I asked, touched.

"If I didn't think so highly of you, why would I need to compete with you, right?"

"I guess you have a point." And she did. It struck me for the first time how much I loved Joanne, as well. Perhaps she cock-blocked me from time to time, but she always stuck by me, and never judged me or made me feel small.

"You don't hate me, do you?" she asked.

"Why didn't Lindsay want all this stuff?" I asked.

"She likes to shop," Joanne explained. "She had me buy four times as much stuff as we needed, and then instead of returning it, she just told me to keep it."

"She should meet Leila," I joked. "They could be compulsive shopping buddies. Anyway," I said as I surveyed my new apartment, "thanks."

Joanne unveiled a gorgeous little doggie bed and placed it in a corner of my living room. Immediately, Omar hopped into it. "That's the pièce de resistance."

"Joanne, I don't know how to thank you. And no, of course I don't hate you."

"Seriously, it's not like I'm generous or anything. I couldn't use any of the stuff. You're doing me a favor taking it off my hands."

I sat on the L-shaped couch and ran my hands along its soft fabric. Rubbing against my bare toes was the Persian rug, with its kaleidoscopic red-and-yellow design. My place, for the very first time, actually felt like a home.

In Venice, I approached Michael's run-down house with trepidation. A sign on the front door read: *If you are here for the breathing circle, please take your shoes and socks off and enter through the garden. There is some grounding oil by the entrance of the garden. Please spread some onto the soles of your feet. It will help connect you to the Earth. Please take a moment to breathe in the garden. Feel free to talk to the trees and flowers. They are there to help you.*

"*Talk* to the trees and flowers?" Keyvan cracked. "I can't believe you convinced me to come to this bullshit thing."

"You?" Bobby chimed in. "I gave up a perfectly good hook-up to attend."

"You guys said you'd be respectful."

"I only came to get a visual on the guy who tried to finger-fuck you," Keyvan said.

"He's super cute," Bobby noted.

"Should I be jealous?" Keyvan asked.

"Jesus, he's just inside. Can you two cut the commentary, please?"

I considered turning away, but just then I saw an earthy woman with curly hair walk past me. "Don't be scared," she said. I turned around and looked at her. "It's just breathing," she added. "If you're afraid of breathing, then you're afraid of life."

Keyvan, Bobby, and I followed the woman in. We took off our shoes and rubbed some of the oil on our feet. It had a smell of eucalyptus and sage. We passed into the garden. There were four people standing in silence, staring at trees. There was an avocado, an orange, and a lemon. Vines were flowing down the wall of the garden, and a patch of open space had been turned into a symphony of flowers. My earthy companion parked herself in front of the lemon tree and pondered its bark meaningfully. She looked so peaceful and introspective that I knew she was having an epiphany. What was she asking the tree? I decided to sit down on a patch of grass in front of the bed of flowers. Some white roses had bloomed to that perfect point. They weren't feeling their growing pains, and they weren't on the road to death. They were enjoying their beautiful prime. I pondered the roses. What was I supposed to ask them? Nothing came to mind. I wasn't sure I was able to communicate with nature. I looked up to Keyvan, who rolled his eyes at me as Michael emerged from the house.

"Hey, everyone. Thanks for coming. Why don't we head inside and breathe?"

Michael had us lie down on the floor. He covered us in thick blankets and gave us two rocks to hold in each hand. The rocks were to help ground us to the Earth. His house was warm and inviting. The scent of burning sage relaxed me, and the mellow beat of Indian drums from the stereo put me at ease. Michael approached me. "Is this your first time breathing, Kara?"

"You remember my name," I said, impressed. Next to me, I could tell Keyvan was taking Michael in.

"Of course I do. Is there anything specific you want to work on?" he asked.

"What do you mean?"

"It's a good idea to set an intention for your breathing. It can be anything. Any small issue or big issue you're dealing with."

"There's so much," I said. "I wouldn't know where to start."

"My intention today is going to be renewal," he stated.

"Renewal?" I echoed.

"That can mean many things. For me, it's about cleansing the areas of my life I'm unhappy about and allowing myself to start fresh without judgment."

"I turned thirty recently," I said. "That's a big renewal, isn't it?"

"More than big," he said. "It's the end of your Saturn Return."

"My what?" I asked.

"Every thirty years, Saturn orbits the sun and returns to where it was at the moment of your birth. This takes approximately twenty-nine and a half years."

"What does it mean?" I asked.

"It means you've gone through an entire cycle of life now. You've experienced one cycle of fear, joy, doubt, love, pain, confusion, loss. And now you've returned to your starting place. You have another thirty years to orbit through your cosmic consciousness."

"Her cosmic consciousness?" Bobby skeptically echoed.

"It's not as strange as it sounds. You're just beginning round two. When Saturn returns, you shed your skin, you start fresh, and you go through all those emotions with the experience and the maturity you couldn't have on your first go around the cosmos."

Michael turned to Keyvan and Bobby. "Are you two okay? You need help getting set up?"

"All good," Keyvan said.

"I've breathed before," Bobby added.

"Please be open to this," I whispered to them as we lay down on our backs.

"I traveled with whirling dervishes through the mountains of Iran. I don't need some surfer-boy masseur to give me tips on how to reach a higher state of consciousness," Keyvan answered.

"I wanna see the dervishes," Bobby said. "Can we see them this summer?"

"They're not a themed attraction, Babak."

"Please call me Bobby. I'm not eleven anymore."

"It's not like seeing the Eiffel Tower or the Sistine Chapel."

"I saw the Pope when I was in Rome," Bobby said. "He waved to me from his Popemobile."

"I'll do my best to hook you up with some dervishes in Iran... Bobby."

"Thank you, brother dearest," Bobby said.

Michael stood and glared at us. "Please be quiet and begin to focus. Two breaths in. One breath out. I'll be helping Kara for the first few minutes." Michael placed one hand on my stomach and one on my heart. "Breathe deeply into your stomach, then into your heart, then release. One. Two. Three. One. Two. Three."

I followed Michael's instructions. For the first few minutes, I felt awkward and self-conscious. But something happened after the repetition of the breath took hold. My hands started vibrating. Then my arms. Then my entire body. Memories started to come to me, like dreams. The first time I met Fiona in college. The day my parents told me they were getting a divorce. The first time I laid eyes on Jacques. Even events I wasn't there for, I could suddenly observe. I saw my father as a young man, blowing up that cop car. I could see the flames, I could smell them, and yet I couldn't do anything about the situation. I had relinquished control over my past.

The earthy woman who had ushered me into the breathing circle was now moaning loudly. A few feet away, a man was shivering and crying. I couldn't see them, but I could feel their energies drifting above me in the atmosphere of the room. In the distance, I could hear the electronic jingle of a familiar song.

"Can someone please claim the cell phone?" Michael asked with a note of unmellow irritation in his voice.

I still thought I was in a memory when I suddenly recognized that damn Britney ringtone. I bolted up and found the offending phone in the depths of my purse. "Hello," I whispered. "What? No! I'll be right there." Michael threw me the evil eye as I whispered to Bobby and Keyvan. "Janet's in labor. She's at Cedars." Awkwardly, I put on my shoes, excused myself, and rushed out the door.

As I waited for the Ebadi brothers in the garden, I stopped and put my hands on the thick body of an avocado tree.

"Interrogating the plants again?" Keyvan cracked. "You might try waterboarding them."

"Ah, the snide dickhead returns," I said.

"Every twenty-nine-and-a-half years. Approximately, I mean."

"This tree has probably been around longer than we have," I said. "Maybe it does have some answers, if we take the time to listen."

Keyvan took my hand off the tree and placed it on his chest. "A tree doesn't have a heartbeat," he said.

I laughed in his face. "Where's Bobby?"

"He's pulling the car out front," he said. "Nice job with the cell phone. I think we're gonna be excommunicated from all New Age sacraments from now on." Keyvan took a breath. "I watched you in there. You were breathing so heavily, you were so committed to the whole thing."

"You watched me?" I asked. "Isn't it bad enough the government is spying on us?"

"I couldn't help it," he responded, giving up an opportunity for a political diatribe. "I suddenly realized you were beautiful."

"That's kind of a compliment veiled as an insult. You thought I was ugly before?"

"Of course not. But I couldn't really see your beauty then," he said softly. "You hadn't revealed it to me. Not the way you have now."

"What are you saying?" I looked deep into his eyes. I knew what he was saying, but I still wanted to hear him verbalize it.

He pressed me into the tree and kissed me. I pushed him away and told him I was scared. "Of what?" he asked. I didn't have to say anything. Wasn't it obvious?

I turned back around to the tree and placed both hands on a branch, clutching it tightly. Suddenly, an image came to me: Hot Tattooed Guy.

"*L'amour est plus fort que la mort*," I whispered in my terrible accent.

"What's that?" Keyvan asked. "Still pining over the Frenchie?"

I faced Keyvan once more. "Love is stronger than death," I said.

"I have an idea," Keyvan said.

"Yes?"

"You got your chance, under the tutelage of an expert, to experiment with random, no strings-attached sex. Now, you be my coach, and we can experiment with the other kind, the kind *with* strings."

From the street ahead, Bobby was honking loudly. "Move it, bitches."

As Keyvan led me to the car, I looked back to the avocado tree. *It wasn't stupid*, I thought to myself. I brought the trees and flowers my questions, and they responded. Their answers were simple. We bloom. We grow. We survive.

ACKNOWLEDGMENTS

To Mitchell Waters, Holly Frederick, and Steve Kasdin at Curtis Brown, thank you for your guidance and enthusiasm. It means the world to me.

Jess Taylor, Scott Heim, and Greg Mortimer, thank you for helping me realize my vision for this story.

Lila Azam Zanganeh, Jessica Bendinger, Chaz Bono, Richard Kramer, Kelly Oxford, Busy Philipps, and Katherine Taylor, thank you for your support of this novel.

Rachel Jackson, Florian Klonek, and Al Nazemian, thank you for lending your images to the cover.

Patricia Shields, thank you for the author photo.

To my wonderful family, thank you for supporting and inspiring me. I couldn't have done this without you, especially my parents Lili and Jahangir, my brother Al, my cousins Dara, Maryam, Nina, Vida, Lila, Moh, Youssef, and Mandy, my aunts Shahla, Azar, and Pari Naz, and my uncles Hushang and Djahanshah. Don't forget that your family is gold.

I am eternally grateful to all who have supported and inspired me through the years, read drafts of my writing, and watched my children so I could write. Among these beloved friends are Lauren Ambrose, Mojean Aria, Jamie Babbit, Tom Dolby, David Brind, Danny Feldman, Susanna Fogel, Mark Fortin, Lauren Frances, Kristin Hanggi, Nancy Himmel, Ted Huffman, Mandy Kaplan, Ronit Kirchman, Erica Kraus, Chas Lacaillade, Erin Lanahan, Sanam Mahloudji, Ali Meghdadi, Joel Michaely, Josh Miller, Michele Mulroney, Karin Nelson, Mark Russ, Melanie Samarasinghe, Kirsten Schaffer, Micah Schraft, Sarah Shetter, Lynn Shields, Mike Shields, Jeremy Tamanini, Serena Torrey Roosevelt, and Lauren Wimmer.

Thank you to Damon Intrabartolo for inspiring me to live a creative and honest life.

Thank you to John Shields for being a partner through the ups and the downs.

Thank you to Jennifer Elia for being the sister I always wanted.

Finally, to my children Evora and Rumi, and my dog Hedy Lamarr: thank you for walking into my closet and making it a home.

ABOUT THE AUTHOR

Abdi Nazemian is the screenwriter of *The Quiet, Celeste in the City, Beautiful Girl,* and the short film *Revolution*, which he also directed. He is an alumnus of the Sundance Writer's Lab, a mentor at the Outfest Screenwriter's Lab, and has taught screenwriting at UCLA Extension. He lives in Los Angeles with his two children, and his dog Hedy Lamarr. *The Walk-In Closet* is his first novel.

You can find Abdi at www.abdaddy.com

CPSIA information can be obtained
at www.ICGtesting.com
Printed in the USA
FSHW020749101119
63940FS